CW00766983

TO THINE OWN SELF

TO THINE OWN SELF

Love leads to self discovery and sacrifice

Bradley Bernarde

Matador
5 Weir Road
Kibworth Beauchamp
Leicester LE8 0LQ, UK
Tel: (+44) 116 279 2299
Fax: (+44) 116 279 2277
Email: books@troubador.co.uk
Web: www.troubador.co.uk/matador

ISBN 978 1848765 849

British Library Cataloguing in Publication Data.
A catalogue record for this book is available from the British Library.

Typeset in 11pt Garamond by Troubador Publishing Ltd, Leicester, UK
Printed and bound in Great Britain by TJI Digital, Padstow, Cornwall

Matador is an imprint of Troubador Publishing Ltd

For my darling parents, and for my cousin Joan and her late husband Geoffrey, without whose help this book would not have been possible.

AUTHOR'S NOTE

Although no witches were ever sought or condemned in Rutland, memories of the Witchfinder General Matthew Hopkins and his dreaded scourges in East Anglia during the 1640s were still prevalent ten years later. It is from those fears and their tragic consequence, that this story evolves.

"This above all: to thine own self be true,
And it must follow, as the night the day,
Thou canst not then be false to any man"
Hamlet: Act I Scene III

CHAPTER 1

Fretson Village – Rutland
April 1657

Smiling in Church was not forbidden in the Good Lord Cromwell's England but
it was not encouraged, and if Molly Tyler had not smiled at me in Fretson
Church on that cold Spring Sunday would I now, years hence, be facing my
Creator with confidence rather than fear. A fear which has urged me to pen this
chronicle of confession which will not, I trust, when revealed to loving eyes
cause those I hold most dear to condemn me.

Molly and her elder brother Hugh, whose towering oak-like frame was no
compensation for his sadly withered mind, had been hired by Goodwife
Hargreaves, a widow of middle years whose increasing infirmity had obliged her
to find someone to cook and clean. A wealthy woman by our village standards,
her benevolence to the needy was legion, but she was also wary of idle gossip as
she did explain to my father Verger Fry, on one of his many visits from our
adjoining cottage.

"I have no wish," she said, "to live beneath a pair of prying eyes. Nor do I
wish my business talked of through the village, and the Tylers have been given
good characters by an acquaintance of mine, Mistress Slater, who hails from
their birthplace, Goodborough in Nottinghamshire. Hard working blacksmiths
the family have always been, but now there are but three remaining, the present
incumbent and these two, his cousins. The lass will suit me well. She has good
sense and has no wish to be a burden on her kin, but she will come only with her
brother and that's to the good, for the quarry will always welcome a strong pair
of shoulders, no matter the sense of their owner."

So, on that first Sunday in April after my father's drum(1) had summoned us
all to prayer and Preacher Wyman had commenced his readings from the *Puritan
Directory*(2), the Tylers entered Church. In an atmosphere already fetid from
human sweat and damp clothes from the rain, I heard for the first time our

neighbour's voice gently urging her brother into the nearest pew, opposite to mine.

Childishly aghast at their tardiness, I stared determinedly ahead as Preacher Wyman admonished them briefly with a look. But a curiosity, even stronger than my reverence for the Lord, drew my eyes in Molly's direction.

My father had told me only their names and that Molly was two years my senior at eighteen, and her brother two years more, so I looked and having done so could not avert my gaze. Molly's dark woollen gown, white collar and cuffs were no different from my own or the other village women, but there did all resemblance end, for the face above the white linen was one such as I had never before seen. Beautiful was not a word I would have used to express my thoughts, for my father had always warned me that beauty tempted the Devil, but even I, lacking as I was in worldly knowledge, knew that Molly Tyler had a quite exceptional face, and she stood tall. Indeed her height did almost equal mine own. But whereas I would bend and hunch my shoulders, Molly stood straight, displaying a dignified and calm demeanour which I, in my ignorance, thought almost wanton, and her smooth broad forehead and clear complexion contrasted strongly with the sallow skinned faces of the other girls about us.

She had seated herself and her brother immediately behind Mistress Wallace, and the dissimilarity between the two women could not have been greater. The older woman, a widow near forty years, was thin and of low stature, her well-known irascibility evident in her tightly held narrow lips and cold, calculating eyes. She was treated with wary respect by the villagers due to the official position of her kinsman lawyer Humphrey Wallace. A resident of Stamford, he was also Goodwife Hargreaves's lawyer and had, for some years, served on the Corporation where his reputation for honesty and fair judgement was somewhat marred by a tendency to be short-tempered, and arrogant.

It was when I was contemplating the dissimilarity between the two women that Molly, catching my glance, glowed with sudden pleasure and smiled. So unexpected was the occurrence that I smiled back, before clenching my wayward lips and staring down in confusion at my *Directory*, for never could I remember anyone smiling in Church. When at last I dared to raise my eyes I discovered that my fellow congregants were still listening intently to the Preacher's discourse, and no one had apparently noticed my folly.

Unlike the services of the present day when all unite in joyful praise, prayer meetings in Commonwealth England were tedious harangues of three hours or more, with Preacher and congregation locked in unhappy alliance. It was therefore past mid-day before we were released to trudge out into the mizzling rain.

Standing at the back of the pews holding out the offertory plate, the self-conscious focus of all eyes, I bid a hesitant good day to the villagers as they passed. I hated this duty, but Preacher Wyman had ordered that, as the Verger's daughter, this should be one of my Sabbath tasks and my father could not but agree.

A few of the villagers proffered their coins with apparent willingness, but most extended their palms with sullen looks which only added to my discomfort and confusion. It had not always been so. Prior to the war my father, a man of genteel speech and courteous manners, had been respected as hard working and diligent by his fellow villagers, but his decision to enlist for Parliament had profoundly shocked them all being, as they were, loyal to the King. And their hostility towards him did not abate even when his military ambitions were thwarted by a kick from a wayward mare, leaving him with a permanent limp.

On recovering from this mishap he had resumed his duties with the then minister, Master Maitland, a kind and gentle man who had attempted to reinstate my father's good name with the villagers, and did succeed with some, but in 1654 the Commonwealth's Commissioners for the Approbation of Public Teachers(3) ejected Master Maitland, and appointed Master Wyman in his stead.

Unfortunately, this circumstance not only caused the rift between my father and the less rational villagers to re-emerge, as he continued to serve his new master with the same diligence he had shown Master Maitland, it also denied him the pleasure he had enjoyed teaching the younger children in the small church school.

"Your time will be fully occupied, Master Fry," declared the new incumbent. "On Mistress Wallace's recommendation I have approached Master Flint, a young scholar newly emerged from Stamford School who is ably fitted for the task, but not in the church. The old school house was built for this purpose, and I cannot think why it was abandoned."

"Master Maitland did think the school house, placed as it is on the Stamford road, would have endangered the children should hostilities have arisen," my father had explained, only to be dismissed with acerbity as Preacher Wyman declared, "There being no such ordeal now, you will please have the building prepared for use within the next two days."

Master Flint, a thin flaccid youth with a crossed eye, arrived the following day and soon proved that not only were his academic talents sadly lacking, but that his ability to retain his pupils' attention was non-existent.

With the wisdom of years, I am now aware that the villagers' animosity towards my father was not entirely due to his beliefs and loyalties, but because they needed a quarry on which to vent their afflictions. Denied any jovial distractions from the endless toil dictated by Commonwealth laws, the previously congenial and friendly folk had deteriorated into a suspicious nervous society, which sought diversions in malicious gossip, and had no inclination to consider favourably anything or anyone, that did not benefit them personally.

Not that they could be censured for this narrowness of mind, considering their days of unremitting drudgery. Most of the men earned their bread by quarrying the stone for which Fretson was famous, and the arduous work and long hours combined with the forceful endless blows quarrying required, soon rendered shoulders and backs old before their time. Situated not far from the low-lying Fens, Fretson was damp, bleak and cold during the winter, but during the spring and summer months the countryside was vibrant with wild flowers, and well endowed fields and woodland.

Molly's second public smile was even more enthusiastic, and occurred as she walked down the aisle towards me. Unaware of how to respond I gave a nervous nod, and then directed my eyes swiftly to the floor. When I raised them I encountered those of Master Westley, the village blacksmith. A rare being in Fretson, he was a happy and contented man whose fat comfortable wife and two sons shared his disposition, and he gave me a cheerful wink as he approached.

I nodded apprehensively. My father did not altogether approve of Master Westley who had been heard to protest loudly that his regular appearances in church were due to his wife's insistence, rather than because he feared the consequences of not attending. He now smiled kindly at me, whilst Mistress Westley looked concerned.

"Ye be a mite pale today, Mistress Fry. Do ye tell the good Verger to let ye take more air."

The good woman had very modern views about young people and fresh air which my father did not share, and I nodded nervously as I saw him approaching down the aisle.

"Was that not Mistress Westley?" My father asked, looking after the retreating family. "A kindly soul but for her views on health, most ill-judged." He looked concernedly towards the church door. "Her sons are so brown with such feverish cheeks, and Master Wyman has been forced to remonstrate most severely on the matter of Sunday walks. I fear there will be a tragedy there, afore long."

I acquiesced with an obedient nod as my father turned to acknowledge Master Workman and his horde of undernourished and stunted children, all clad in an assortment of ill-fitting rags. An uncouth man and an accomplished poacher, he ruled his family with so many blows and curses it was their habit to recoil as swiftly from a kind word, as from a brutal one.

"Master Workman," my father nodded pleasantly, "and how does Mistress Workman? I pray for her swift recovery."

"Aye, though how we be feeding t'other mouth I know not," Workman glared back angrily. "Be her ninth ye know, her ninth."

"Indeed, but the Good Lord watches over all Master Workman," my father replied soothingly, his voice trailing off as Preacher Wyman approached with a piece of white linen held to his nostrils.

"Master Fry," he declared in his high-pitched voice, "is it not time the Lord's house was closed and what do these children here? Do you see to the matter." He edged his way carefully around the filthy brood and then hurried towards the porch, his handkerchief still held to his nostrils.

Workman glared angrily after him. "He do think he be so mighty, so he do. Not fit to breath same air as us common folk. And ye too Verger, ye too think so but with all ye book-learning ye've no got nowheres, have ye?"

Shocked at the taunt I glanced swiftly at my father, but his expression was tranquil as he gently ushered the Workmans towards the door. Then he blenched, as Workman defiantly cleared his nostrils and throat noisily in the church porch. Pretending not to see, I hurried up and down the centre aisle to ensure that nothing had been left behind, before joining my father outside the church.

Our rain-soaked lane, bordered at one end by the bridge crossing the Chater stream and at the other by the main Stamford Road, was a mass of congealed mud through which the villagers were now struggling, their pattens squelching noisily with each step. As we trudged towards our cottage, my father murmured suddenly, "Care not for what Master Workman said Pleasance, education is never wasted, no matter what the outcome."

I glanced up expecting to see him discomforted, but his face wore its usual calm, contemplative expression.

As the only child of my grandsire, the previous verger of Fretson Church, my father owed his education to the sponsorship of Sir Harold Berwick, the original owner of Berwick House the local manorial property. A perceptive and generous man whose own son had been a scholar at Cambridge, he had one day been astounded to discover my father, then but twelve years old, reading a copy of the 'Iliad'.

On being questioned, he had shyly explained that he had been trying to teach himself Greek. Intrigued, Sir Harold had taken him back to his extensive library, and invited him to choose any book he desired. My father's obvious joy had so touched Sir Harold that, convinced the boy had the ability to learn, he decided to sponsor his education.

At first my grandsire had demurred, implying that such an advantage would be too elevating for the son of a humble verger but Sir Harold had insisted and, within sixth months, my father had been removed from his work amidst the dust and grime of the quarry, to be enrolled at William Radcliffe's Grammar School in Stamford.

Sir Harold's convictions were soon proved correct, and as my father displayed such avid intellect the Squire removed his protege to Repton School, in Nottinghamshire. Here again the eager scholar soon fulfilled his benefactor's expectations, and on his sixteenth birthday suggestions were made that he should be sent to Cambridge. At first my grandsire, being under the impression that his son would be studying for the church had agreed, but when Sir Harold had explained it was English law in which my father had shown an interest, Master Fry withdrew his permission and demanded that his son should return to Fretson, to assist in church duties.

Disappointed, Sir Harold had recalled his protege, who then returned to the confines of his previous life, but his benefactor did not neglect him. Many times Sir Harold enlisted my father's services for journeys to Lincoln, Nottingham and Cambridge, and these distractions educated the recipient in other ways, enabling him to continue his acquaintance with people of gentility, and to meet the occasional foreigner travelling through England on business. Under Sir Harold's benign influence, my father also acquired an understanding and tolerance of other creeds which influenced him into the belief that God's word was divine to all, no matter the religion. A belief he was swift to impart to me, as soon as I was old enough to comprehend that a man's thoughts and a man's mind are utterly his own, to be ventured into only by invitation. Whether or not he ever regretted being denied the brilliant career that might have been his no one ever knew, and as he was ever the dutiful son, my grandparents noticed little change in him.

The eventual death of his benefactor, while it robbed him of a close friend provided unexpected advantages, for Sir Harold bequeathed my father a large number of his books together with a small inheritance. Now independent of his parents' control, my father could have pursued his legal studies, but within a month of Sir Harold's demise my grandmother fell heavily, incurring an injury to her hip from which she never fully recovered.

With his father occupied as an indispensable nurse, and a considerable amount of Sir Harold's legacy having been devoted to the physician's accounts, my father had no alternative but to undertake the duties of verger. Whether inspired by a sense of calling to the religious life or a desire to please his parents, he proved so dedicated a churchman that no one had questioned his right to succeed when his father died in 1637, two years after my grandmother.

Released from filial duty my father had, to everyone's surprise, married my mother Margaret Pleasance Wright, the daughter of a Stamford merchant. No one in Fretson could imagine why such a pretty, vivacious girl should want to leave her father's comfortable home and settle in a tiny cottage with their serious minded, rather dour, young verger.

Whatever her motives, as the days passed everyone had to admit that the young couple were obviously very happy, and my mother was soon a great favourite with the villagers. The five years of contentment they were permitted before the war commenced included my birth, and granted me a fleeting but everlasting remembrance of my mother.

Not that I was reflecting on the past as I trudged through the mud on that particular Sunday. The rain had now become that fine, almost invisible moisture, which penetrates garments more efficiently than a healthy torrent, and I bent low to try and obtain what protection I could from the high wall which bordered the Berwick estate.

The property, which had been sequestered from the owners by Parliamentary decree, was now the home of the Altons who had been granted the estate in 1653. Despite being rarely seen outside the park, the family were generous to their village neighbours; a largesse that was not at all appreciated by the majority of parishioners, especially since the family rarely attended church worship preferring instead to employ a private preacher for their daily prayers.

Still attempting to protect myself from the rain, I became aware of the Tylers walking amongst the small number of villagers ahead. Apparently oblivious to the weather, Molly was almost gliding her wooden pattens across the muddy ground in complete contrast to Hugh, who lumbered heavily along beside her. A feeling I recognised to my shame as envy suddenly overcame me, and I lowered my eyes from the sight of Molly's poise.

I tried to forget her for the rest of the day, and deliberately avoided looking at her during evening service but that night, alone in my tiny upper chamber, I strutted stiff and straight across the bare boards. As I did so my shadow, reflected in the tallow candle beside the bed, moved stiffly in unison across the white plastered wall. It was a caricature of my neighbour's elegant stride and mortified by my own pride, I blew out my candle and slid into bed, covering my face with the coarse hemp sheet.

My height had been an embarrassment to me from the age of twelve, when I suddenly began to grow so much taller than the other village girls. I well remember the pitying glances I received from the older women, and the way the mothers of Fretson commiserated with my father on my rapid growth. Then there was my hair, thick and red unlike the hair of any other girl in the shire. Jezebel hair the old women had called it, so I had learned at a very early age to hide it away beneath my cap.

During the days following our first encounter I saw a great deal of my new neighbour, either milking the cow behind the Goodwife's cottage, or feeding the hens. Very disturbed by the envy which I found difficult to suppress, I made another attempt to imitate her walk, only this time in the open air where there were no shadows to humiliate me. Perhaps envy was the reason why I drew my water only when Molly was absent, but the inevitable can never be avoided, and ten days later we became acquainted.

Goodwife Hargreaves having some business with my father, sent a message to our cottage by Hugh. Being alone at the time, I struggled to understand the poor lad's incoherent words and then, prompted by numerous emotions none of which I could interpret and knowing I was following a course of action both impractical and pointless, I followed him next door to see if I could assist.

Despite my father's frequent visits, I had not been inside our neighbour's home since early childhood, and the sight that met my eyes in those frugal Puritan times made me draw in a breath of amazement. Apart from the high-backed blazing fire, the long oak table was covered with plates of newly baked ham, fresh bread and farm butter, whilst suspended by a chain over the fire was an iron cooking pot, from which drifted a subtle aroma of herbs and meat. The appetising smell combined with the abundance of food represented to my narrow, repressed mind, the kind of feast I imagined was only indulged in by either the indifferent rich, or the very wicked.

The other contents of the cottage were no less opulent. There were six chairs also of oak, a low wooden chest beneath the casement, and a heavy oak dresser by the inner door. A quantity of fine brassware and pottery adorned the numerous shelves, and over the main entrance hung a great stag's head with silver mounted antlers, whilst beneath my feet the stone was strewn with dried lavender. There was also another room, built onto the cottage some years previously, but the greatest luxury were the windows. Composed of thickened glass, they were considered a miracle by those of us who still fought the elements with latticework or wooden shutters.

Transfixed in the doorway, I stared unbelievingly at the scene until Hugh gently pushed me into the room. Immediately I heard the murmur of women's voices, and tried to draw back, but he had already closed the door after giving an incoherent yell to announce our arrival, so I remained standing awkwardly by the table, silently berating myself for being so foolish as to come. Then I heard the sound of a chair being scraped across a floor, and with an assurance belying her station, Molly Tyler entered the room.

At first I scarcely recognised her, for her hair hung in thick black curls down her back and her face was flushed from some recent exertion. With shocked surprise, I saw also that her skirt had been looped high, exposing her long shapely legs and bare feet. Unaware how to respond to this exuberance, I stood silent as she greeted me warmly in a voice that was a strange mixture of a soft Nottinghamshire burr, and gentility.

The sound of Goodwife Hargreaves's voice calling interrupted the greeting, and Molly returned swiftly to the inner room. I felt most ill at ease. I did not belong in this over-furnished room with its strange almost wanton, servant girl. I turned towards the outer door but before I could reach it, Molly re-entered to explain that the Goodwife would prefer to wait until the Verger returned.

"But ye'll stay for a morsel to eat," she added with another wide smile.

Although this was the first invitation I had ever received, I was aware that to decline it without explanation would appear rude, but to remain and eat someone else's food without my father's consent was unthinkable. I tried to think of the appropriate words before stammering clumsily, "It is my father, he will be home. We eat together."

Molly smiled in apparent understanding and then, to my discomfort, taking my hand lightly in her own suggested that we should see each other again. Shaken by the unexpected physical contact and unable to understand her enthusiasm, I stuttered something incomprehensible and hurried away.

CHAPTER 2

Later that same afternoon, while attempting to patch yet another rent on my father's nightshirt, not an easy task due to the chilblains which plagued my fingers every year, I could not help contrasting the comforts of Molly's home with the frigid atmosphere of our small main room with its plain white walls, and uncovered stone floor.

The stark and chill were also emphasised by the empty grate, as my father did not consider a fire essential except during the months of November to February; and because he believed in owning nothing that was not necessary to our needs, the room contained only a wooden dresser, a deal table, two wooden chairs, and my spinning wheel and loom. His frugality extended also to our meagre fare, as indulgence in any form was a mortal sin, but it had not always been so, only after my twelfth year had these strictures prevailed.

Our only concession to luxury was a small outshut, (4) which had been added at the same time as the Goodwife's cottage had been enlarged. A compact round area, it contained a wide stone slab on which food could be prepared, a deep stone bowl in which I soaked and washed our linen, and an area for my butter churn. But I had no idea why our cottage had been so honoured, or why my father had agreed to such an extravagance.

Now, as I imagined Molly sitting before the Goodwife's high-backed fire, eating her meal of hot stew and fresh bread, I sighed. The monotony of my diet I could contend with, but the lack of a fire caused me mental as well as physical discomfort, as our cold oven obliged my father to seek assistance in the baking of our bread and meat.

With a lack of self-consciousness, often enjoyed by those who believe themselves to be in the right, he had applied to Mistress Machin wife of the village miller. An affable and sympathetic woman with a family of five children, she professed to find no inconvenience in these extra duties but as she lived in Mill Lane, some distance from our cottage, I was forced to carry my iron bowls of raw dough and meat through the streets under the derisive glances of any villagers who happened to be watching.

The mortification I experienced during these journeys was intense, but totally obedient to my father's beliefs that prudence and temperance were essential to follow the way of the Lord, I carried out these tasks with a forbearance which, I now consider, was grievously misplaced.

But the Goodwife's food and warmth had not been the only attractions. Despite Molly's impetuosity and wanton appearance she had been kind, and there had been the unexpected touch of her hand. A sensation I had not experienced since my mother's gentle caresses, and Molly had obviously wanted to talk, and talking to anyone apart from my father, had become an experience sadly lacking in my life. Despite his position in the Parish, he had never encouraged me to acquaint myself with the other village girls, preferring that I should confine myself to my studies when not occupied with domestic tasks or church duties.

Unlike the majority of his contemporaries, my father was of the view that girls should be no less erudite than boys, and as this was a view with which my mother had concurred, he commenced tutoring me when I was but three years old, adding Greek and Hebrew to my studies on my fifth birthday. Anxious to please, and too young to fully comprehend the beauty of the texts, I learned by rote and years were to pass before the depth and true understanding of all I read was to influence me.

But I realise now that these extra studies, confining me as they did to our cottage, protected me from the violence not far away because, although Fretson was spared a visit from either of the opposing armies, the soldiers had fought their way along the high ridge above the village. Not that I was untouched by those violent times for I lived my childhood through the conflict, but my privations were mainly limited to lack of freedom, especially when our livestock were housed within the cottage and I could not leave the upper storey. After Naseby the situation eased until the latter days of my mother's illness, when my father entrusted me to Goodwife Hargreaves's tender care.

My isolated way of life gave the less literate villagers yet another reason to censure my father, as they considered my application to study irrelevant and my separation from their children an affront. Most of my contemporaries were married, some with families, and the villagers criticised my father as being too particular for his own good. I was indeed mortified one Sunday evening on over-hearing two women muttering that the Verger's gawky daughter with her uppity way of speech would end her days a spinster, begging her bread from the Parish.

Despite being aware of this terrible fate, I was only too relieved that my father seemed content for me to remain unwed. I had no desire to learn the earthy secrets of the marriage bed, and found the occasional glances directed at me by the village men confusing and upsetting.

My lack of female company became a problem only when I reached pubescence. Ignorant of either the reason for the blood, or the painful cramp accompanying it, I had cowered in terror in my chamber until found by Old Mother Burrows, the village midwife, who my father employed occasionally when I was occupied in the church.

An out-spoken soul, she had berated him for his neglect of my welfare, shrieking that even if he had not wished to broach such a subject, he could have enlisted the help of his "uppity friend" in the next door cottage. My father had remained silent until the tirade ceased, then coldly refusing the offer of a tisane of Ladies' Mantle(5) potion to ease my pain, he had dismissed the old woman, forbidding her ever again to enter our cottage.

Denied even this rare contact with another being, I retreated into a secret world of day-dreams, in which a handsome gallant would ride up to our cottage door and carry me away to one of the countries so beautifully illustrated in my father's copy of James Howell's *Instructions for Forreine Travelle* (6).

But whereas it was probable that such countries would be forever beyond my grasp, my hero did have substance. He was the younger of the two Alton sons, and unlike his parents and elder brother did, on occasion, ride through the village. At nineteen years of age Robert Alton was a muscular young man with brown hair, a pleasant smiling face, and a pair of light blue eyes with which he had learned to fascinate the female population. He also favoured garments of a more colourful hue than the blacks, browns and greys worn by his contemporaries. The antithesis of every man I had ever seen, my greatest pleasure was to hide behind my chamber shutters and watch him ride his great black horse down the village street. I knew that to dream was wasteful and that my father most certainly would not have approved, but I found it impossible to control my wayward imagination, and day-dreaming seemed to overtake me at the most inappropriate moments.

As it did one morning when I was carrying out my weekly task of dusting the church, a few days after my visit to the Goodwife's cottage. In accordance with the decrees of the time, churches were kept locked Mondays to Saturdays, being accessible only to those people whose duties required them to enter. On this particular occasion, I was wielding my cloth whilst imagining Robert Alton striding purposefully down the aisle, when I heard a sound from the back of the building.

Realising with a shock that I must have forgotten to relock the door, I waited apprehensively for my father's admonishing voice. Instead, a light footstep crossed the flagstones, and to my surprise Molly Tyler walked slowly in from the porch.

For a few moments we stared at each other, before she smiled her warm generous smile and said, "'tis a shame to have no proper altar, and there must've been fine hangings here. Did the soldiers take them when they did come to the village?"

Terrified that anyone passing may have overheard I gasped, "It is sinful to say such things, and the soldiers did not come to Fretson. They did pass by on the upper road, and all was removed by my father as he was told so to do."

Molly shrugged. "So many things are sinful, 'tis sometimes hard for a body to know what to say."

I closed my eyes wishing her gone. She was disruptive and spoke dangerously. When I again looked, she was strolling up the aisle glancing sympathetically at the bare walls. "'tis the same at Goodborough, but there t'was the soldiers took everything and us village folk hid ourselves away, for fear they'd ravage our homes as well. Did the good Verger hide all that was took down so that one day it may be returned?"

"I know not, and I think we should not speak of such things," I stuttered, now really frightened of what might be overheard.

"Fret not yerself, I'll say no more," Molly gave me a reassuring look. "I'm to Royton farm. Our cow being old gives little milk, and the Goodwife is of a mind to have her slaughtered, so I came to beg yer company. The Goodwife was saying to Master Fry these past moments, that ye should have more air and he did agree that ye should come."

"My father said I was to walk with you to Royton Farm," I was astonished.

"So he did say."

My every instinct told me to remain dusting the pews. I could not believe that my father had agreed that I should forgo my duties and participate in anything so frivolous, and this second invitation would be much easier to refuse as the Church was familiar ground. So I opened my mouth to say 'no' but, instead, heard myself shyly accepting. Obviously pleased, Molly waited until I had dispensed with my apron and duster, before leading the way out of the porch into the spring sunshine.

As she descended the stone steps to the street I locked the church door, still not convinced that my father had given his approval. I suspected he may have misunderstood Molly's meaning, and was under the impression that we were going on a charitable errand. I could not imagine his reaction when he discovered the truth; and he would find out, of that I was certain. Anyone seeing me, would consider it their duty to acquaint the Verger with the news that his daughter was idling away her time, instead of applying herself to her daily tasks, and I glanced back apprehensively. But the road was empty, and only St. Luke's elegant spire glimmering in the bright sunlight seemed to gaze down admonishingly.

The silence, except for the rustling leaves and the occasional bird call, unnerved me slightly, which was foolish, for if I had been less agitated I would have remembered that most other villagers were employed in either the stone quarry or the surrounding fields.

Some yards ahead Molly waited beside the narrow wooden bridge fording the lazily rippling Chater river, but its tranquillity was deceptive, as it required only a heavy rainfall to turn the ripple into a torrent, and villagers still related stories of the floods of April 1641, when more than one family lost relatives in its depths.(7)

Very aware of Molly watching me and now feeling resentful without understanding why, I hurried towards her. As I did so I heard the sound of hammering from Master Westley's forge, then a pedlar leading a donkey covered in pots, pans, cloths and trinkets, commenced crossing the bridge from the far side. These mundane sights and sounds had a palliative affect on my nerves, and it was in a more relaxed state that I joined Molly to commence our walk.

Still preoccupied with my father's extraordinary behaviour, and absorbed by the beauty of the wild flowers which carpeted the ground, I let Molly chatter on until, feeling obliged to respond I asked, "Did you not like Goodborough?"

"'tis a pleasant enough place but 'tis not as fresh, or as pretty as here. Nottinghamshire is more wooded than Rutland, and though Goodborough be a larger village than Frestson I was glad to leave," she hesitated, her voice sounding suddenly pensive. "Folk can be unkind and without reason. Goodborough folk did mean well but they didn't understand." I waited for an explanation, but instead she asked, "Are ye unwell, ye'r a deal quiet?"

Taken aback, I stammered that I was but a little tired.

"Ye should take more air," she looked concerned. "Ye dwell too much within.

Goodwife Hargreaves did say ye should take more air and walks, and walking would straighten yer back, 'tis woefully bent." Mortified, I hurriedly straightened myself. "Woefully bent," Molly repeated. "Do you raise your head, like this," she stood in her normal posture, her head held high and her back straight.

Obediently, I raised my head and immediately felt my neck straighten and my spine unbend.

"Now we're of a height," she exclaimed. "'though ye be a mite the taller. Ye should walk thus always, for it does improve ye looks, and a woman has little else of use other than her face and body. 'tis true a high born unmarried female, orphaned at an early age, or a widow of great wealth can live as they please. but us lowly folk what else have we to offer?

"What of learning?" I ventured, timidly.

"'twould be of little use unless accompanied by highborn birth. 'twas thought, so did I learn in York, that Master Cromwell would accord to us lowly women the rights and privileges accorded to men, and many women have petitioned him so to do, but not even so a brave a soul as Mistress Chidley(8) has achieved aught for us. Why, in York I did learn that a Leveller(9)——"

"Molly we do not speak so, it is forbidden," I interrupted hastily, her revelation that she had been to York dispelled by her rash words.

"And who does forbid?" She stared curiously at me, "In York they——"

"Whatever may have been said in York," I interrupted heatedly, "is not spoken here."

Looking suddenly shamefaced, she reached out, and lightly touched my arm.

"Beg pardon Pleasance, I speak hastily, but 'tis still the truth that we women are of little importance without wealth. Even learning such as ye do have, achieves satisfaction only for ye'self for 'twill gain ye little as a woman."

I wanted to disagree and pursue the subject, but we had now reached Royton farm and I hesitated. Molly's unguarded words still disturbed me and I still doubted my father's agreement to the escapade. Seeing me stop she called from the yard, where she was now standing.

"Why d'ye no come, has the sun been too fierce? Let me draw ye a mug of water from the well."

"No," I hurriedly reassured her, "I am but a little fatigued. I will rest hereabouts while you conduct your business." I looked around for a tree stump on which to sit.

"Where will ye rest? I see naught but bare ground."

I waved a hand vaguely towards the trees as Molly made a low humming sound, but at last she shrugged and turned away. "So be it, I'll be but a moment."

With nothing solid on which to rest, I retraced my steps to a nearby tree and kneeled down beside its trunk.

"Why lass what do ye here? Why are ye no in house partaking of a mug of ale?" Master Royton's booming voice echoed through the trees. Normally a head shorter than me, he now towered above and with his bulky sweating body, thick hairy arms and broad strong shoulders he seemed to obliterate the landscape. Only his beaver hat worn jauntily over one brow denoted that he was not a tenant but a yeoman farmer, who owned both his farm and the acres of land it occupied.

"'tis unwise for a maid of so fair complexion to remain in sun's rays. Do ye come," he persisted vigorously, as two milkmaids and some labourers who had now emerged from the barn were staring curiously at us.

"I await Molly Tyler from Goodwife Hargreaves," I tried to explain, scrambling to my feet in embarrassment. "She has come for a cow, she will be but a moment."

"Lass'll be as many moments as I keep her. Now come ye lass, I'll no leave ye here and Verger Fry would ne'er forgive me if ye were to take of the sun. The house awaits as do Mistress Royton, and a mug of ale."

Mention of my father's name aroused my previous misgivings, but before I could reply Molly's clear voice echoed across the yard calling the farmer's name, "Master Royton, 'tis sorry I am to be so late, but Goodwife Hargreaves did not state an hour of the clock, and good Mistress Royton does tell me ye've business elsewhere, within the hour."

"That be not so," Master Royton shook his head, obviously perplexed.

"But 'tis so, " Molly insisted. "Mistress Royton did say ye expect grand folk from the hall." She took hold of his arm and began pulling him, protesting, towards the house.

"Lass what's the haste? Me business is but with Squire's steward, and do ye help me persuade this lass into house and Mistress Molly, if ye do pull me further ye'll have shirt off me back."

"Forgive me sir," Molly hurriedly released her grip, and bending down, whispered some words into his ear. Whatever she said impressed him because, forming a silent 'o' with his lips he gave me a kindly nod and said, "There lass fret ye not, our business'll be brief, but do ye find shelter from the sun."

Alone once more, I leaned against the cool trunk and tried to imagine how I would explain this extraordinary day to my father.

CHAPTER 3

Some fifteen minutes later, I felt even less sanguine. The purchase of one cow seemed to be taking a considerable length of time, and I glanced towards the yard buildings outside which the farm workers were now eating their mid-day meal.

After what seemed like a further eternity Molly appeared, leading a plump young cow with one hand and carrying a small mug and her basket. Reaching me, she held out the mug with a contrite expression.

"I've taken long and I'm indeed sorry. Mistress Royton did talk so, 'twas a problem for a body to leave."

My thirst having been quenched my irritation returned. From the one or two crumbs adhering to Molly's lips and the faint smell from her breath, it was obvious that she had indulged in more than social conversation. I wished to complain, but before I could speak she pointed to the basket.

"Mistress Royton has sent pasties and ale. Shall we not sit and eat our fare beside the stream, 'tis such a pleasant day?"

My immediate reaction was to declare that I could not abandon my father to an empty cottage and a bare table, but I was protesting only to my tree for Molly was already leading the swaying cow along the path. For a few seconds I remained motionless before, forgetting my dignity, I ran as swiftly as my pattens would allow to Molly's side.

"My father could not have given his permission for so long an absence?"

"He did so, for two hours didn't I say?"

Perplexed, I stared helplessly at this strange wayward girl who seemed to have no regard for the customary constraints of a woman's life, and certainly no understanding of the complexities of my existence. My father was a kind man and he had never chastised me neither with hand nor voice, nor could I recall his disposition being other than temperate, and if I had been asked why I stood in awe of him I would have been unable to say. I knew only that his presence imposed complete submission to his will, and that it was his belief that each hour of every day should be devoted to the labour of either mind or body. How then could he have agreed to idle dalliance such as doing nothing more arduous than eating a pasty?

"Ye have a deal of learning, I've no doubt?" Molly's voice broke abruptly into my thoughts.

"I know my letters," I replied briefly. The sharpness of my voice seemed to startle her, and she looked so chastened I became confused, and stammered hurriedly, "I do beg your pardon, I should not have spoken so. Why do you enquire?"

"For no reason," she replied, her face averted and her voice muffled.

I was embarrassed. I had been ungracious without reason, and now had to make amends.

Staring determinedly at her back I explained, "My father taught me all I know. He is a learned man."

We had wandered from the path into a small treeless clearing beside the mossy bank of a stream. Bushes thick with foliage and buds hemmed us in, and the sun's rays, unimpeded by overhanging branches, glowed warmly down.

Still apprehensive, I glanced at Molly and was relieved to see her smile as she explained, "I did find this place but Wednesday last, when I was searching for herbs. D'ye see, the stream bends so as to hide us from view, and no folk can walk on yonder bank, 'tis too wooded."

We were indeed completely hidden from view, and only an adventurous soul wading through the shallow waters would have been able to see us. Molly kneeled down and carefully unloaded her basket. "Come," she looked up at me, "'tis good food, do ye eat."

Still reluctant to believe my father had sanctioned this diversion, I attempted to withstand the force of this girl's will. "My father does not care for me to come so deep into the wood."

She sat back on her heels, her voice gently pleading, "'tis but a few steps from the path. The deeper wood is to the left, these be but bushes."

Wishing I could dispel my feeling of guilt, I lowered myself slowly to the thick grass and took a pasty. The taste of the meat and herbs was so exceptionally good, I felt I was transgressing by enjoying something that my father could not share. But Molly had no such doubts. She was already on her second pie, and I was scandalized to see that she had pulled off her cap allowing her thick curly hair to tumble unrestrainedly about her shoulders.

I felt the need to remonstrate, but hesitated for some moments until venturing to say, "Forgive me do, but should you release your hair in that way?"

She looked at me, in obvious surprise. "'tis of no consequence, there be no one by, unless ye object?"

"No," I felt my face glowing with embarrassment, "it is of no consequence to me, it is only if some body were to see."

"There be no body," she replied firmly, "and 'tis unnatural for women to hide their hair."

I flinched. Molly had such a loud clear voice, so I interrupted hurriedly with the first thing that came to mind, "What did you say of me, to Master Royton?"

To my surprise she flushed, and then replied hesitantly, "I did but say ye were timid, and afeared of strangers."

I frowned. It was true of course, but few people find the truth about themselves rewarding and I was no exception. A duck, accompanied by four tiny ducklings, appeared around the bend. Borne by the current the little family was soon washed up onto the bank where the fluffy chicks huddled up against their mother, as she pecked at some pasty crumbs being scattered down by Molly.

The food and ale combined with the warm atmosphere were making my limbs heavy, and I closed my eyes. My father and the chores awaiting me at home, even the church, all seemed to belong to another time.

When I awoke Molly was already tucking her hair away within her cap, and the duck and her family had launched themselves back on to the stream.

"Ah me," my new friend declared hurriedly, "'tis now too late for herb gathering, for the sun does say we must make shift. Come, hasten." She waited only to ensure that I had scrambled to my feet, before pushing back the piece of bush that formed the opening to our glade.

For a few seconds I gazed back at the tranquil scene, before following Molly to the bridge, which was now occupied by some children leading two large shire-horses into Master Westley's forge. Molly lengthened her stride, and I was running by the time we reached my cottage. Breathing heavily, I lifted the latch as she called almost pleadingly, "Thankee for ye company, and we can again meet?"

Her plea was hard to refuse, but I wanted suddenly to be within the confines of my home where decisions were not of my making, so I nodded without replying before entering our cottage to find my father sitting at the table reading. He coughed as I entered, and then looked up and smiled. "You are flushed child, but you look much refreshed. The air has benefited your health. Mayhap Mistress Westley's thoughts are not without merit. I have partaken of nourishment, so do you go about your tasks."

I waited for him to question me, but to my surprise he returned to his book, putting it aside only when it was time for prayers prior to our evening meal. We ate our cold mutton and bread in our customary silence, and after Grace I busied myself with my spinning wheel, while my father continued reading.

For a further hour nothing broke the silence but the rhythmic whirr of my rotating wheel. Spinning was a task which I enjoyed, because it enabled my imagination to travel unhindered, and on this occasion it dwelt on the afternoon's adventures and my new companion.

At last my reverie was interrupted by the encroaching gloom and my father murmuring, "The candle I think, my dear, and we will have our evening prayer."

I tried to concentrate as his precise clear voice began to read from St. Mark, but my mind kept returning to the extraordinary events of the day, and especially the fact that my father had permitted such an adventure.

The next morning, having risen at my usual hour of five o'clock and attended to the hens and milked our cow, I prepared our food for breakfast. My father was quieter than was customary, and during prayers both before and after the meal he was interrupted by a fit of coughing which only eased after a long drink of water.

Very accustomed to him departing without explanation, I bid him farewell as he left the cottage, and after drawing our day's water from the well I washed our utensils and then climbed to the upper storey to sweep out our bed-chambers. Occupied both with my thoughts and work, I was unaware that my father had re-entered the cottage, until I heard him calling my name.

Surprised that he should have returned so quickly, I entered the room to find him standing beside the empty fireplace, his hands behind his back. He motioned to me to sit down, and then seating himself on the other chair said, "I believe you misunderstood Goodwife Hargreave's intentions my child. I am, I believe, correct in this conjecture with regard to the lessons which you are to instruct the Goodwife's servant girl?" Bewildered, I could do nothing but stare at him. "The good lady did request my services," he continued, "but I did explain much as I would have wished to comply, my duties would not permit me the time to devote to such a task. So I did proffer your services child."

I frowned, as I remembered Molly's enquiry of the previous day. Now I knew why my father had not asked for an account of my activities. With his consent she had sought my company, not from a desire to befriend but because she craved a favour.

"Did Goodwife Hargreave's servant girl make a particular request to be taught her letters?" I emphasised the words "servant girl", with satisfaction.

"Indeed no, the girl made no such suggestion. I am surprised that you should ask such a question, Pleasance. It was entirely the Goodwife's request that her girl should learn. What is her name, Molly? (10) Not a name I would have given a Christian body, but no matter. The girl herself was most reluctant, and did see fit to express the doubt that your duties would not permit the time, but I did assure the Goodwife that this was not so. I believe the girl did attempt to acquaint you with the circumstance yesterday, but it would appear you misunderstood. No matter, you can commence today. She is but a poor wench, and any little we can do to bring cheer into such a life will be but an expression of God's mercy. I would recommend the horn-book, with which you did commence your letters."

He began to cough again and I rose, intending to bring him more water, but he shook his head and walked towards the staircase. As I watched him depart I wanted to refuse. Why should I, the daughter of a learned man like my father, demean myself by teaching this ignorant girl with her haughty demeanour and strange way of speaking? But I had never disobeyed my father, and did not know how to attempt such a revolt. So, instead, I tried to decide how I should instruct my pupil. Molly was so self-assured, I could not imagine being able to teach her anything.

My feelings were still unsettled when I collected the eggs, some time later. The six hens looked so comfortable in the small wooden hut bunched together on their perch, that I thought suddenly how easy life would be if I were a hen, and I laughed. Then I started, as a voice whispered, "Will it be that ye come this morning?"

Innocent though I was, I realised that Molly lacked her usual assurance and the knowledge gave me confidence as, in a clear voice, I acquiesced.

Some two hours later, I was sitting very stiff and straight backed opposite my pupil, with the much thumbed and faded horn-book lying on the table between us. Her hesitant greeting had been self-conscious, and I felt very uncomfortable. On arriving I had refused refreshment, but now wished that I had accepted. The actions of giving and receiving food would have been relaxing.

We sat thus for a few moments, and then Goodwife Hargreaves's voice called out sharply, "How do you in there?"

"Well Ma'am, we're about to commence," Molly called back, her eyes suddenly bright with laughter.

I pursed my lips. If I was to be her teacher a certain element of decorum had to be maintained, but before I could speak she leaned forward and whispered, "Ye do not mind? I'd dearly love to read."

I shook my head. It was all so strange. Here was poised and elegant Molly being taught to read by the Verger's gawky daughter who, despite her ignorance of the world, could read two languages apart from her own and write a script that her father had said was the best he had ever seen. Feeling a little more relaxed by these thoughts, I began the lesson.

I had decided to start with the alphabet so, after pointing out each letter, I pronounced it and Molly drew it on the slate. Progress was slow at first, but as she was eager to learn and I gained confidence, we soon lost our reserve, and by the time the clock had reached mid-day she had memorised a quarter of the alphabet.

"Mercy on us," she exclaimed suddenly, "'tis so fast the time has gone. Thankee indeed dear Pleasance, I've learned much and do I suit?" Her voice sounded almost pleading and I nodded, surprised at my own disappointment that I had not been invited to stay because, although I had resolved to refuse, it would have been gratifying to have been asked.

Back in our bleak cottage I washed down the outer parlour floor, and then settled down with my father's copy of *Plato's Republic*. But, for the first time, the meandering conversations of the Guardians on the education of children seemed to be irrelevant, and I put aside the book and returned to my spinning wheel.

As I worked I thought of the food Molly would be preparing for the evening meal. Some slices of ham perhaps, or a hot stew; certainly nothing like the meagre pieces of cold meat and bread which would be my fare. Sighing heavily I rose from my stool, and collected our pewter plates and mugs to prepare the table prior to my father's return. Our portions of meat looked minute beside the mental picture of Mistress Royton's pasties of the previous day, but at least we had fresh bread, and in the evenings my father permitted a spread of butter. I cut two slices from the new loaf, and placed one on each plate beside the mutton. The butter, a minute quantity in a small dish, I placed beside his plate.

There was no reason for these strictures. Our cow gave constant supplies of milk each day and my butter churn was always full, but my father always took most of the contents of each to Preacher Wyman. He had never explained why he carried out this benevolent service, and I had never asked.

I was placing the bible before his place when I was surprised by a light tap at the door, and Molly entered. "I do indeed beg ye pardon, but I did forget to give ye this," she held out a basin, from which arose a very appetising smell. "'tis pumpkin pie and the Goodwife did intend it as an offering of thanks to yerself and the good Verger, and I complete forgot. Perhaps 'twas the learning, I could think of nothing but my letters."

Overwhelmed but delighted I took the basin, and began to murmur my thanks but Molly had already departed, so I breathed in the succulent aroma. Then I gripped the bowl tightly as I realised the enormity of what I had done. I had accepted the pie without giving the slightest thought to my father's reaction. I was trying to decide whether to return it, or bury it in the yard, when he entered saying, "Why child, what have you there?" Blushing, I tried to explain and he nodded murmuring, "Such a kind thoughtful soul, she will indeed receive her just reward in Heaven."

"What am I to do with it, father?" I tried to control the longing I felt.

"Why, to be sure child we will eat a little. It would be churlish to deny such beneficence, but the main portion we will give to the Workmans. So many mouths to feed," he sighed, "the Lord's bounty is indeed munificent."

I nodded obediently, while stifling the unGodly thought that it was not the Lord's bounty that overflowed in the Workman home, but the quantity of ale consumed by its master. Then I blushed at so vulgar a thought, and carefully placed the pie dish on the table.

Never before had prayers seemed so long, nor my appetite so intense. My father seemed to intone forever but at last he finished, and unlinking his laced fingers motioned that I should serve. Trying hard not to appear eager, I placed a medium sized portion of pie on each plate. He frowned.

"It would seem you have been over generous, my child."

"Father, I am hungry," I cried out, before I could stop myself.

I remember still the expression in his eyes as they widened with shock, and for a few seconds we stared at each other before I sat down heavily on my chair, my appetite evaporating. When at last I managed to look up, it was to see my father staring concernedly at me.

"Forgive me, child," his voice had never sounded so gentle. "I forget that you are but young, and need your strength." He put a small spoonful of food into his mouth, and after swallowing murmured, "It is indeed a fine dish. Do you eat your fill."

But I ate my portion without even tasting it. Each mouthful seemed more unwieldy than the last, and when I had at last cleared my plate I pushed it away with overwhelming relief. During the meal my father enquired as to how the lessons had progressed, and I remember managing only the barest of responses.

When at last the table had been cleared I sat listening to his prayer of thanks, wishing fervently that I had been stronger and refused Molly's gift, and then we could have eaten our food and drunk our ale in our usual amicable silence. The Grace completed, my father gave a gentle smile.

"We shall keep the remainder of the pie. The mutton will suffice for the Workmans, and perhaps the remainder of the bread."

Crimson with remorse I stammered timidly, "Surely sir, it would be more fitting to take the pie."

To my relief he nodded, and with obvious pleasure declared, "Indeed, I cannot but agree, and do you rest this evening, I fear you are over-tired."

Overwhelmed, I looked up to reply, but he had already lifted up the dish and was carrying it out into the night.

CHAPTER 4

As soon as my father had departed, I went up to my chamber, and from my wooden chest, drew out two pieces of fine white linen smelling fragrantly of lavender. They had been my mother's wedding sheets, and I had always imagined that one day they would be used for my own nuptials.

I spread one of them out on the floor, and after placing on it my father's Sunday shirt, cut out an identical pattern and commenced basting the pieces together.

Thus occupied in the now speedily encroaching twilight, I heard the downstairs door opening. Thinking it was my father returning, I quickly folded everything back into the chest and hurried downstairs, to find Molly standing inside the open doorway.

She was the last person in the world I wished to see, and I felt my face stiffen as I declared coldly, "My father has taken the remainder of the pie to the Workmans. They are poor ill folk, who have nothing."

"So did the Verger say," she replied. "and if I'd but known I would've taken them the pie, but 'twas meant only as a gesture of thanks to the Verger and yerself."

"Where is my father?" Even to me, my voice sounded haughty and resentful, and she looked at me anxiously.

"He's but in the Goodwife's cottage. Have I angered ye? If such be the case, I do indeed beg pardon, but please to tell what I have done?"

Although common sense told me that it was I who should apologise, my resentment that my father had sought to confide in his neighbour and this stranger overcame me, and I cried out, "Why does my father seek to speak of such things to you and the Goodwife when I am now a woman, and full grown?"

The moment I had spoken, I gasped at my own temerity. To have questioned my father's behaviour was such a betrayal of my filial duty that my feelings overwhelmed me, and I began to cry. How long I stood sobbing I cannot recall, but I do remember two arms enfolding me and a soft voice murmuring, "Yer father seeks the Goodwife's company not mine, and only because they are of an age, and she's wise and kind. He dearly loves ye, and is proud of yer endeavours. He likens ye to Basua Makin."(11)

To be compared to such a nonpareil, and by my father, shocked into me into silence and I could only stare at Molly in astonishment. She shrugged. "I know not who she be, but 'twas with great pride he said the words."

"She is a paragon of learning," I gulped, wiping my eyes upon my apron. "At the age of but nine years, she did know five languages."

Molly laughed irreverently.

"Ah no paragon I then, 'tis only me own tongue that I do speak, and 'twill no doubt be so till I die. And now dear friend do ye light yer candle, for 'tis so dark I can barely see yer face."

I gave an inward sigh at such a lack of respect for scholarship, but the room was indeed almost devoid of light, so I lit the lamp as Molly continued, "I came but to ask ye for a walk, tomorrow forenoon."

I sank down heavily on the nearest chair. Life seemed to be moving with such speed, I was finding it difficult to concentrate. "And my father has yet again permitted such an amusement?"

"Indeed so," she asserted firmly. "He did say he feared he has overtaxed your health, and that assistance should be sought."

"Assistance?" I could not understand her meaning.

"Yes, he is to arrange for Bessie Workman to come to scrub, draw water from well and do tasks of physical endeavour."

I stared at her in bewilderment, as I tried to absorb this extraordinary announcement. After a few moments, I murmured, "Forgive me, but is it possible that you have heard amiss. It cannot be that Bessie is to come here, as a servant."

Molly frowned slightly.

"Indeed 'tis so. The Verger did instruct me to intimate to ye, that were his word intimate, that he be concerned for yer welfare and that he's to engage Bessie to assist ye, and that ye should accompany me for a walk on the morrow, and so to do each day," she finished the last sentence with an expression of almost triumphal pleasure.

I rose slowly to my feet. I had no doubt that Molly spoke the truth. A word such as 'intimate' was not in her vocabulary, but why my father could not have expressed his thoughts to me, instead of confiding in the Goodwife and a girl whom he himself had described as a "poor wench", I could not understand.

So it was next morning, after my father had departed on his duties without mentioning either Bessie or my freedom to walk the countryside, that Molly arrived to collect me as arranged. Still feeling somewhat resentful at my father's silence, I entered the front room to find her studying our bare walls as though seeing them properly for the first time. Very aware of her scrutiny, I said defensively, "My father will have no trimmings, he considers them un-Godly."

To my surprise she nodded in agreement, before asking, "Why do ye douse yer fire, and does it not make yer oven over-long to heat?"

"My father sees not the need of a fire after February," I retorted sharply, wishing she would not be so critical.

But she continued to look thoughtful, and as we walked towards the Chater murmured enquiringly, "Ye've lived always with yer father?"

"Indeed," I replied. "My mother died when I was but five years of age."

"And ye've no female kin?"

"There is but Mistress Edith Frost, my mother's cousin. She does reside with her husband and their family in London, but my father speaks rarely of them."

"London," Molly looked impressed, before continuing, "after yer mother died, who had the care of ye, such is not man's work."

"During my early years we did have Mother Burrows to cook and clean," I hesitated, choosing my words carefully. "But in later years she was intrusive and not to my father's liking, and as you are no doubt aware, during my mother's illness my father sought the Goodwife's aid, and she did care for me."

"So she did say," Molly acknowledged. "But 'tis strange the good Verger did not later seek the Goodwife's help, for there's much a girl child must know. 'tis not seemly that a man should, but forgive me, like Mother Burrows I intrude."

Once again, resentment surged through me. Who was this girl to criticise my father? I stared angrily ahead, my voice harsh. "My father has sought the Goodwife's council many times, but if he seeks not her advice it is not my place to question why." Immediately, Molly's face went very pale, and I tried to make my voice sound more conciliatory. "Mistress Hargreaves was kind to me, and I remember her ministrations well, but it was after my tenth year that she became unwell and I have seen her rarely since."

Molly was now humming softly to herself, and I was relieved to see that her cheeks had resumed their normal healthy colour. We had by now reached our secluded retreat, and she quickly pulled off her cap, crying out as she did so, "Do ye remove yer cap also Pleasance, I've never seen yer hair unbound."

I blushed. "It is not fit for showing. The village women call it Jezebel hair."

"Pah, no better than Goodborough women," Molly declared disdainfully. "Remove yer cap, please. There be no bodies here to see."

Her pleas were hard to resist, especially when her wide brown eyes begged so eloquently, so I undid the thin linen ribbons and let my hair cascade about my shoulders. She gasped, and I blushed again under her scrutiny. "Mercy on us, what a wondrous sight. Was yer mother of this shade?"

"No, her hair was of a light brown hue, but my father did once say that my mother's dead sister Martha did have this shade."

Molly shook her head. "'tis indeed a sin that the eyes of men shall never feast on this. No matter, mayhap the fashion will change when the Prince does return."

Aghast at her imprudence, I exclaimed, "Molly I pray you do not speak so. We are now alone but who knows who may be passing. There are those who listen closely to what is said."

"Think ye I am un-maidenly, to speak of the eyes of men?" Molly tapped my hand with a teasing look. "Or mayhap it is the words of him across the water that afears ye. No matter, I'll be more discreet but ye're a worried body are ye not? Forever fearful of what folk may say."

Still profoundly concerned, I replied, "There are those in the village who would do mischief if they could. Why, it was but last Michaelmas that Barnaby Crowson was soundly whipped and locked in the stocks for speaking ill of our good Lord Protector, and Mistress Close was ducked three times for much the same. You are a stranger to the ways of Fretson, I beg you do take care."

Molly's attempted to look impressed, then subsided into a merry laugh. "I'll mind me ways and curb me tongue but now do ye let me tend yer hair."

Before I could protest she had taken a comb from her skirt pocket, and I closed my eyes, for a moment lost in memory. Only one other person had held my locks as Molly did now, and I hesitated before murmuring shyly, "My mother did dress my hair so."

She stopped combing. "Ye were much blessed, mine died of me in childbed. The women said I was so wide a child the birth did kill her. But no more of sadness, there yer hair shines like the sun, and ye do indeed have a comely face Pleasance." Taken aback by the unexpected compliment I flushed, as Molly continued enthusiastically, "And indeed I think it shameful that such hair be hid away like the Hebrew women, who cut theirs off on wedlock."

"Cut off their hair?" I was astonished.

"Yes, indeed," she replied firmly, as if I had disagreed. "'tis their faith that does forbid female hair."

"But St. Paul did say in His First Epistle that women may have hair," I protested, "and that it should only be shorn if not covered."

"But those words were for Christen folk not for the Hebrews. 'tis the truth I speak for I have seen it with my own eyes."

"Seen a Hebrew woman without hair?"

"Indeed so, for when we were in York we did see the Hebrews. Dark folk with rough brown faces, from across the sea folk said, from Spain."

Molly's authoritative voice seemed to engulf me, and although I knew it was rude, I declared loudly, "The good Lord Cromwell did permit their entry, but last year(12) although there were Hebrews in Stamford until 1290(13) my father did tell me. They had a house of prayer, a school and a library, but after they were expelled all was lost, and there were Hebrews who remained in this country who many thought were of the Popish faith, and who have now abandoned their Popish ways and do live their true Hebraic lives."

I drew a deep breath. Never before had I so dominated a conversation and Molly gave me a keen look, before declaring firmly, "So I did learn for the steward knew of that, but as to his master and those Hebrews with whom he was acquainted, he did say they spoke many tongues, but the English very poorly so he spoke with them in Spanish. The folk with whom we lived while in York did know this Hebrew. A scholar he was, like yer good father, but he did have also a knowledge of medicines and herbs. I did take messages to his house and he did show me his chamber where he had many plants and bottles. Many ways to heal he did explain, and he did show me how with plants of the fields he boiled healing potions, and he did show me a fine book, *'The Complete Herbal'*(14)'twas called." She sighed, "I wished I could've read it, and the Hebrew did have many metals, gold and silver, which he put in a brazier. His servant did say he was an Alc——"

As she stammered, and I asked, "Mean you an Alchemist? But to practice so is frowned upon."

"I know not of that, but he did say that his past kin had lived in York. I do forget how long ago, but 'twas many years past."

"As I did say, before the expulsion in 1290?" I interrupted, impatient with her rambling, "but for what reason did you go to York."

She frowned. "Pleasance, please to let me tell the tale me own way. We were speaking of the Hebrew woman's hair. 'twas when I did take a message for the mistress of the house in which we lived, that I did see through an open inner door the Hebrew mistress without hair." Molly continued to illustrate the woman's appearance and I was despairing of ever hearing of her adventures in York, when she said suddenly, "'tis a long tale me time in York, and not one that I've spoken of to a body, until now. In Goodborough me kinfolk have been always smiths. Me father did have his own forge, and when he died the smithy did pass to me cousin William Radley." She glanced down at her hands suddenly, as though to avoid my eyes, before continuing, "But he could not earn our bread as well as his own, so I did seek service at the manor. 'twas while I was there that I did learn much of the ways of gentlefolk. But Hugh became restless with me not being by, so I did make shift to leave. Cousin William didn't wish us to go, but I wanted no more of Goodborough. Not that 'twas not a fine place, and the Squire a good man, but I was born and bred there and knew its ways and wanted away to travel to see the world, so Hugh and me we did go to York."

I was utterly absorbed, all thoughts of time and place forgotten. "How did you travel?"

"The Squire he did give me two gold crowns."(15)

"Two gold crowns," I repeated. I could not even imagine such a sum.

"Yes," Molly replied, rather sharply. "Such money be good for a body when ye've clothes, food and somewhere to lay yer head, but it provides little when none of that be to hand."

"But you did say you had work in York," I declared, amazed that anyone with such wealth should find it inadequate.

"So indeed I did, a Mistress Holland she was. I was to sit with her aged mother, an old lady past seventy years, but Mistress Holland wanted none of Hugh. She seemed afeared of him. So we did find lodgings in an inn. Very fine they were, two rooms with linen on the beds and water to hand, but our food we did buy and new clothes also, for I had not the time to sew and Mistress Holland did want me well clad, and bought clothes do cost much. Hugh did occupy himself with small tasks for the Inn Keeper, and it did serve until," her voice became subdued. "'twas Hugh, he did cause a trouble. He did mean no harm, but the people they didn't understand. You've seen the size of him. A horse went lame and the soldiers beat it. Hugh was afeared for its life and did fight the soldiers. They did let him go when they saw he was witless, but Mistress Holland heard of it and I was dismissed. I did go to the Hebrew to seek his help, for I did believe he'd have taken us in and given me work, but his servant told me his master was at prayer, and such was the sanctity of the holy day he could not approach him."

"And so you returned to Goodborough?"

"Aye, and there was little left of our great wealth," she sighed heavily. "Our lodgings did cost so and our clothes and travelling, and I did earn but twelve pence a day. No lass," Molly shook her head, "'tis not a deal of money with two mouths to feed, and Hugh ate much." Her face looked unexpectedly sad. "I didn't then know how much a body needs to live. We did stay with Cousin William for near five months, and then the Preacher came to say a Mistress Slater of Stamford was seeking help for her friend, and he'd recommended us."

"Would you have wished to remain in York?"

"Indeed yes, 'tis a fine city. A body can live in such a place without people knowing."

I frowned. "What is your meaning?"

Molly studied her long fingers, with their neat half moon cuticles. "I do mean that in such a city, large as it is, a body needn't tell of her life. All secrets can be kept."

Intrigued, I wanted to know more but she had already risen from her knees declaring, "Bless me, 'tis late. I did promise we'd be away but two hours, but tomorrow," she added quickly, "I'll wait upon ye at eight of the clock, so we can have a longer walk."

I scrambled to my feet, still intrigued. None of my hours of academic study could compare with the adventures Molly had experienced. To have lived in a great city and made the acquaintance of foreigners represented to me, all the excitement of which I had secretly dreamed.

Longing to hear more I tried to persuade her to continue talking, but she had already left the glade and I had to lengthen my stride to catch up, and when I did so she seemed too preoccupied to continue talking.

CHAPTER 5

May 1657

Although encouraged by Molly to view Bessie Workman's arrival as an advantage, within a few hours I was disillusioned. A sluttish child of nine, Bessie had been raised by her uncouth parents with so many blows and curses, she responded to the simplest command with such nervous apprehension, I soon realised teaching her the basic rudiments of housework was going to prove far harder than doing the tasks myself.

She also stank and was filthy, but it was when I saw the small black specks moving along her neck that I thought I would faint. Humble though our cottage was, my father had always instilled into me that cleanliness was akin to Godliness, and in a state of panic I sought Molly's advice.

"Wash her hair."

"I can not," I shuddered.

"Bless ye child, 'tis but a human head. No matter, I'll do it."

"But she is foul. Her stench pollutes the cottage, and I do believe she has no knowledge of the privy." I added the last remark in an almost inaudible whisper, having seen Bessie squatting in an ominous manner outside the hen house.

"We must teach her. Poor lass'll know nothing if she be not taught."

"I know not how," I replied helplessly.

Molly shook her head. "Fret not, I'll attend but ye be the mistress so must be by and much water must be drawn, and we'll need a tub."

I nodded, while my stomach churned at the thought of what was to follow. I felt even worse next morning when Molly appeared carrying cloths, a small mug of rosewater, and a bowl of soapwort. Having informed Bessie, somewhat incoherently, of her impending ordeal I stood as far from the tub as the narrow confines of the cottage permitted, and it was difficult to assess which of us suffered more as Bessie's garments were removed.

At first she flinched, as though to ward off her persecutor's hands, but she was soon reassured by Molly's soothing words, and as soon as the child was naked the marks of her parents' brutality were revealed. Seeing my shocked expression, Molly nodded.

"Aye, 'tis a sin how the Workmans treat their kin. Now do ye pour the water over her hair while I hold her, for she might struggle, 'tis not a pleasant sensation."

But Bessie submitted to all the indignities of being washed and cleaned with remarkable aplomb. Having apparently been convinced that she was to "look so much better", she obviously decided that she could endure whatever was to follow and the transformation was indeed remarkable. Pink cheeks and a light complexion replaced her sallow skin, while her hair proved to be luxuriant and fair.

Obviously aware of the impression she was making, she looked down and examined her own clean arm with an expression of intense satisfaction. Remembering the original reason for the bath, I stared suspiciously at her pale locks.

"Never fear," Molly laughed. "Yon lice are here, as fully dead as if drowned in Chater river." She held out the bowl for my inspection, but I shook my head trying not to shudder.

"I did not comprehend soapwort to have such strong properties."

"Bless ye child, 'tis plain ye've led a life apart from common folk. Soapwort alone'd do naught but mixed with Devil's Cherries(16), so called by Goodborough folk, it'd kill aught we wished. 'though the Hebrew he did call it Atropa belladonna."

"Belladonna," I exclaimed. "But it is most poisonous, will it not harm her?"

Molly shook her head. "Nay, mixed with care the juice from both leaf and root can be used to help the flux, or maladies of the stomach, and is most beneficial when used prudently, so did the Hebrew say. But used in abundance within the body can kill much. 'Tis not a herb I've used to cure within the flesh, but in Goodborough 'tis used frequently to destroy vermin." She appeared to consider the subject closed, for she was now concentrating on combing out the tangles in Bessie's hair, but I was not satisfied.

"From where did you find the plant?"

"It does grow in a small dell, not far from our glade."

I frowned, doubting that my father would have approved, but as always Molly's confidence subdued me. Like most country women I knew of the beneficial use of herbs, but my knowledge was confined to harmless plants such as comfrey, dandelion, parsley and mint, all of which I had used either to flavour our food, or to cure a simple malady.

Still concerned, I would have liked to know more, but Molly had already gone out to the yard to pour away the dirty water.

"tis indeed surprising how a body can change when clean," she remarked as she re-entered. "Now have ye the tinder box, for we must burn her clothes?"

I stared in askance. A serving maid, even a clean one, clad only in linen cloth could prove more of a problem than even one fully clothed, and lousy.

"Have ye no spare undershirts or petticoats?" Molly enquired, briskly. "I can supply a gown, 'tis one I wore when young, but nothing more."

"I have a chemise I wore as a child," I replied doubtfully, "and there are some woollen stockings, but they may be too large."

"No matter, all can be cut to size. Do ye fetch them while I set light to these rags."

Leaving Molly to tend the pyre of crackling garments in the yard, I took Bessie upstairs to my chamber. Clad all in white, the child had an almost angelic appearance, until she suddenly broke wind. I hurriedly threw open the casement as footsteps mounted the staircase and, thankful that rescue was yet again at hand, I called, "We are in my chamber."

Molly entered, waving a brown garment. "See, I've the gown, 'tis but a poor thing but 'tis clean and," she sniffed, "come Bessie, we'll to the privy."

Alone, I leaned on the edge of the casement. Below in the street, Master Bailey the Carter was leading his horse towards the forge, while from the opposite direction astride his black horse and elegant in dark wine breeches, doublet and cloak, rode Robert Alton.

Sliding once more into my world of dreams, with all thoughts of Bessie forgotten, I watched my Lancelot make his elegant progress. Two village women talking beside the church gate were given the privilege of a doffed plumed hat, and I closed my eyes as I imagined him stopping before our cottage door and leaning down towards me, his eyes warm and bright.

"Well 'tis done," Molly's voice invaded my imagination with the ferocity of a cannon shot. "She knows now of the privy and how 'tis used, and to wash her hands and face of a night and morning. It does seem she'd been taught only to wash in ash, hence the greyness of her skin. 'tis a strange habit but one, why what ails ye Pleasance, is aught wrong?"

"No, I am quite well," I moved away from the casement, as I tried to force my mind into the present. "She knows of the privy you say, and when to wash?"

"Yes, and I've instructed her on the cleaning of the house. Of course, I know that ye'll have done this but 'tis no matter that a body's told twice and the gown does suit, but 'tis too long. 'tis looped up, but mayhap ye could shorten it for she says she cannot sew. There's now only the bother of where she's to sleep."

I nodded, wishing Molly away so that I could observe Robert Alton returning, as I knew by custom he would, within the half hour.

"Pleasance," she looked concerned, "are ye not ailing, ye look fearful strange."

"No it is nothing, but forgive me I did not comprehend, you spoke of sleep?"

"Indeed yes, she's now beneath the table, is she not? Well, 'twill not serve. A body must be given dignity if she's to live with dignity. Can she not sleep on a pallet?"

I stared helplessly. My father had said nothing about where Bessie should sleep, and without his guidance I had left the girl to her own devices.

"Will Verger disapprove if I do offer a pallet, and a coverlet?" Overwhelmed by Molly's rush of words I attempted to gain control, but to no avail as she continued. "Then Hugh'll carry them, but when winter comes she'll want a warm shawl, or some such."

Molly's voice had acquired an authoritative ring, and I replied sharply, "If my father does agree Hugh may bring the pallet, but first his approval must be sought."

She looked surprised. "But surely, I'd not thought otherwise, when'll this be?"

"When he does return this even, or tomorrow."

Molly shook her head. "The child'll have to bed tonight. If the Verger doesn't wish it, then I'll enquire of the Goodwife."

"That will not be necessary," I surprised even myself by the anger in my voice, and quickly tried to soften my tone. "I beg pardon I was too abrupt, but Bessie is our servant and although you have done much for which I am grateful, where she should sleep is the concern of this house."

To my surprise Molly smiled, approvingly. "Well said, the child be yer concern so I'll talk no more of her needs, but if there's aught further I can do, ye've but to ask. And now I must to my duties, and we'll walk today at two of the clock." She reached out and gently squeezed my hand. "Don't be doleful dear heart, a Mistress should've always a look of happiness, 'tis good for her servants."

Her hand had a warm comforting feel, and when she withdrew it I felt strangely lost.

Bessie's personal habits having improved, teaching her domestic duties was much easier, but I could not like the girl. There was no obvious reason. She tried hard to learn, but she was too obsequious, and on two occasions I discovered her studying her reflection in a bowl of water. After a few days, I mentioned my doubts to Molly, and was discomforted at her mirth.

"Bless yer heart Pleasance, to complain of a body wishing only to please, would I'd such a one to help me."

I flushed in confusion. "I know it is unChristian to feel so, but there is something about the girl I cannot explain."

"If 'tis vanity of which ye disapprove," Molly suggested gently. "She's but a child, and'll outgrow such ways. Be patient, for ye cannot say she's not useful."

I could not but agree, and then made a silent vow to be more charitable towards my servile domestic; and with so much leisure at my disposal, I was able to devote more time to the task of completing my father's new shirt.

On one of our visits to the glade I showed it to Molly, and she was ecstatic in her praise.

"It is but a shirt," I murmured, somewhat overwhelmed.

"But so handsome, if I could but sew such a fine seam. The Verger will be mighty proud to wear such a garment."

Embarrassed, I protested, "I do not think my father will be proud to don my gift. If he says he finds it of service, that will more than suffice." To my surprise she frowned deeply, but did not reply.

The spring was now well advanced, and the late May sun glimmered on numerous honeysuckle bushes while trees dabbled their heavily endowed branches in the stream, as though seeking nourishment from the depths below. Still unaccustomed to indolence, I always applied myself to my sewing, but my friend had no such enthusiasm for industry. With her stockings removed and her skirts looped high above her knees, Molly would dangle her feet in the cool water, or sometimes paddle about in the shallows, entertaining herself meanwhile by pretending to splash me liberally with water.

It was on one such occasion, that I saw the wound upon her thigh. A gathering of her flesh, it formed a prominent small lump and was, she explained, the result of a fall from a tree when young.

So did the days progress, and I had never before been so happy anticipating with pleasure the commencement of every dawn. I particularly enjoyed our rambles across fields and meadows, and during our early acquaintance had collected bunches of wild flowers, which I had taken home to keep in my room.

At first Molly had said nothing, but one day to my surprise she exclaimed, "'tis wanton cruel, to drag them from the earth. Like pulling a body's arm from off his flesh. Do leave them be, they live in the earth let them there remain."

"But you do pick herbs, in abundance," I protested. "What can be the difference, pray?"

"Because God did give us the one for to please all eyes, and such can only be whilst the flower remains within the earth. The herbs he gave to help heal flesh, and such cannot be if they're not taken from the earth."

"And where pray, did you learn such Holy writ?" Annoyed by her admonition, my voice sounded as loud as Molly's own.

"I forget, 'twas possibly at Goodborough, within the *Book of Common Prayer.*"

"Molly, for pity's sake," I gasped. "How can you speak so? Have I not warned you that there are those in Fretson who would do mischief, for does it not say within *The Directory* that anyone who does use the *Book of Common Prayer* shall be fined or imprisoned."

For once, she looked contrite. "Forgive me I provoke ye, and I should not. But Pleasance ye truly fear too much. There's no one by, and as ye well know I couldn't have learned such things from," she dropped her voice to a whisper, "that book, for I do but now know my letters."

"Then indeed you do treat me ill, to tease me so," I declared.

"Forgive?" She extended her hands to me, pleadingly.

I sniffed. Molly's contrition did not seem to extend to her eyes.

"You do indeed make me feel foolish. Why do you so?"

She flung her arms about me, with a laugh. "Because ye be a dear, sweet soul who matters much to me, and for whom I care deeply."

Rather reluctantly, I returned the embrace for her warmth was difficult to resist, and for a few seconds we had remained with our arms about each other.

On another occasion in our glade, while I plied my needle, she asked, "Have ye no wish to travel?"

"Indeed, yes," I replied, with enthusiasm. "But travelling to me does signify seeing those countries that do lie across the sea, and all the foreign lands that comprise the globe. Not merely our native villages and towns." Then I blushed, for Molly was staring at me in surprise, and I stammered an apology. "Forgive me if I did imply that to travel from village to village, and from town to town, was not to seek adventure."

"No matter," she laughed. "A body could never compete with Mistress Fry's knowledge of the world."

Feeling thoroughly contrite, I reached for her hand. "Molly I do beg your pardon, but I have dreams and mine are to see great cities and foreign lands. My father has a book with such descriptions of France, Italy and Spain, as will make your heart race to hear of."

Understanding as always, she chuckled. "Fret not, I know ye mean no harm but I would dearly care to see the book."

"And so you shall," I declared. "I shall bring it with me for our next lesson, and if my father does permit, I shall show you his chart of the world."

Her eyes widened. "With countries that a body can see?"

"Indeed yes, my father did procure it three years past, from a Cartographer in Lincoln. He did go to Lincoln, on church matters," I added, importantly.

Molly appeared impressed, but my moment of triumph was short-lived when she enquired, "And ye did accompany him?"

"No," I replied, irritated. "It being a church matter I was not required. But I shall request the chart for our next lesson."

That evening, my father having consented, I brought down the chart and spread it out upon the table. He leaned forward from where he was sitting and pointed to the left-hand globe. "See child the Americas, the new land of hope so-called. It would please me much to travel to such a place, and spread the word of God amongst those who know not of his bounty. And here on the right-hand globe, vast expanses of land of which we know so little." He smiled as he folded the parchment carefully into its creases. "Do you show the wench what lies beyond these isles, for it is good always for a body's knowledge to be increased."

"You would have cared to visit these lands, father?" I enquired, timidly.

"Aye, but it was not to be. My life is here, within the confines of this village, but perhaps one day, Pleasance, you may be granted the privilege of seeing such things as 'dreams are made of'."

To my surprise he laughed suddenly, but my father rarely expressed true mirth and he now quickly subdued his exuberance with a gentle smile. "That is a quotation child, from a theatre play that one day you may read. Your dear mother knew much of such reading, and poetry."

I was astonished. For my father to have mentioned his secret longings, and quoted so light-heartedly from such frivolous literature as a play, was astounding. I longed to hear more, especially about my mother, but the sudden arrival of Bessie from the outer parlour interrupted our reverie and my father rose, saying that he had to see the Preacher on church matters.

CHAPTER 6

May 1657 – June 1657

I was still reflecting on my father's confidences when, later that same morning, I opened out the chart on Goodwife Hargreave's table. Molly stared down at the parchment with wide eyes.

"What a sight for a body to see, and these folk who be they?" She pointed to the four explorers in their oval frames, one each corner of the two globes.

"Sir Francis Drake, Ferdinand Magellan, Oliver van der Noort and Thomas Candith. They were the men who did explore, and did discover many of these lands."

"But for sure the spelling of that name is M.A.G.E.L.L.A.N.U.S.," she exclaimed, pointing out the intricate script with a slender forefinger. "As is this man's name O.L.I.V.E.R.U.S. Whyfore then are they spoken of as Magellan and Oliver?"

"Because that is the Latin spelling, but we do call them the English way."

"But if a body's name be spelled one way, whyfore should we call him another? I'm Molly, and I'd be much affronted to be spelled aught else."

I tried to hide my exasperation. Her desire to know something I could not explain was annoying. "I know not why the names are pronounced so, I know only that they are. Let us now see where the different countries lie, and what they are called."

"What's there?" She pointed to an empty space, below the Indian Sea.

"The Southerne Unknowne Land," I replied, reading from the chart. "It does say that there is a land, not yet known and so uncharted. It has yet to be discovered."

"How do they know this, if they have yet to discover it?"

I was beginning to feel inadequate, and said in some exasperation, "Do you now wish to know of the lands with which I am acquainted? You will learn little, if you do not ask me questions of which I know the answer."

"I beg pardon," she murmured. "But certainly I wish only to learn of what ye know."

I glanced at her sharply, but a very demure pair of brown eyes stared back at me, and the lesson continued without further interruption until we commenced studying the two astrological globes, when Molly declared, "They be the magic circles, the Hebrew in York he did tell me of those. They do plan a body's life from birth to grave."

Magic circles were not something spoken of in a Christian house, and I tightened my lips as I replied firmly, "They are the Cartographer's indication of the stars, and their place in the heavens, so did my father say."

"Nay, 'tis not so," Molly insisted. "The Hebrew drew a chart, his own. 'twas a mighty thing with symbols, and did say he'd travelled much."

Frustrated by her obtuseness, I retorted angrily, "These symbols mean no such thing, and I do not think it wise to talk so of magic."

Obviously startled, she exclaimed with a contrite look, "I do beg pardon my foolish tongue again, forgive me please."

My anger receded immediately, and feeling ashamed I muttered, "I fear only that someone is by."

"I care not for who is by, I care only not to fret ye," she repeated, her eyes moist.

I stared back helplessly and, obviously encouraged by my expression she reached out, and taking my hand squeezed it gently, as she said pleadingly, "Dearest Pleasance, I would not for my life, distress ye, and may we now return to the lesson and travel across the world, for 'tis travel that does make a body wise. It does teach one as to who are good folks, and who bad." She gave me a wary glance. "Master Wyman now, I know I should not speak so but he does give himself airs, and smiles only at folk who he knows do have position. He grovels much when young Squire rides down yonder street and never at us humble folk. He never looks at Hugh, and Hugh would so like to be addressed by the Preacher. And him unwed, 'tis not natural that a Preacher should have no wife, and the travelling to Stamford for no reason as I know of, for all he does need is in the village, and I do pity that poor Mistress Burridge who has care of him, sourpuss though she be, for he's so particular she does spend a quarter of each day a washing of his linen."

I listened helplessly to this strange confusing woman, who had turned a lesson on the world into a diatribe against the Preacher, and I knew not how to respond. My father revered Master Wyman and I knew expected me to do the

41

same. I slowly closed the book without replying, and our differences forgotten, the lesson ended with pasties, laughter, and a jug of ale.

But from that day forward I watched Master Wyman closely, and was disquieted to see that on the few occasions I was able to observe him and Hugh together, how assiduously the Preacher did ignore the lad, in much the same way that he assiduously avoided the Workman family, or any other of his less immaculate parishioners. But Hugh was not offensive. He washed every day after working in the quarry, and on Sundays was always clad in a clean white shirt and well brushed leather jerkin and breeches.

In my innocence, I assumed Master Wyman found him difficult to understand, for the youth's loud raucous voice could sound incoherent; then I noted how the Preacher attempted to impress the more prosperous of our villagers, such as the Machins and Mistress Wallace, and realised reluctantly that Molly was correct. Master Wyman was indeed an obsequious, greedy man interested only in his own welfare, who left my father to visit the sick and bury the dead, while he himself was either absent on one of his journeys to Stamford, or visiting noble folk outside the Parish.

I was also concerned to see that these absences had become more frequent of late, forcing my father to undertake even more duties, than previously. Indeed, I became so worried I consulted Molly as to what I should do.

"Naught," she replied briefly. I was aghast at her lack of understanding, and obviously concerned by my expression, she slid her arm gently about my shoulders. "Think me not harsh, Pleasance, but there be naught ye can do. Master Fry knows his business best. 'tis hard for me to say, but I think he'd not take it kindly if ye were to protest. 'tis his way. Is it not that he's never sought yer advice?"

I acquiesced dejectedly, and Molly pressed her cheek to mine, murmuring gently, "If a body must seek another's mind on how to address her father, then 'tis better that body does naught. But," she added quickly. "'tis flattered I am that ye should ask, and Pleasance, how ye've changed. When would ye, but three months gone, have thought of addressing yer father on any matter. 'tis good, indeed 'tis."

On the occasion of this conversation we were walking towards Chater Bridge, when the sound of an approaching horse drew our attention. We both walked quickly off the path to allow the rider to pass, but instead of galloping by the animal reared suddenly, throwing its rider Thomas Whyte, the Post Boy, to the ground. The youth's cry as he fell was loud enough to alert Master

Westley, who emerged immediately from his forge closely followed by his wife and two women, whom I recognised as a Mistress Bell and her kinswoman Mistress Withers, well-known village gossips.

Molly despatched me immediately to the stream to soak her kerchief, and by the time the others arrived she was kneeling beside the unconscious boy, gently feeling his body for broken bones. As I returned, Mistress Westley was instructing her husband to carry the boy to their cottage.

"And quickly mind, the sooner he be within doors the better."

"If ye please ma'am," Molly interrupted hurriedly. "I do not think it wise to move him. With an injury to the head, 'tis better to let consciousness return 'afore moving the body. It does avoid the fever."

"Well I never," Mistress Westley exclaimed, as she lowered her heavy frame clumsily to her knees. "'twould seem to be the reason, would it not husband, that our Adam did have fever after a fall last early winter upon some ice. His head did crack with a fearful bang, and then such a fever he had, a sweating and a crying out, but there, I take on. 'tis this lad to whom we must now attend. Now husband, and ye Adam and Simon, do ye bring some planks that they may carry Thomas, as soon as he be able."

"And that will be soon ma'am, for he does stir a little," Molly pointed to Thomas's foot which had begun to wriggle slightly.

"Indeed yes, what a good nurse do ye make, Mistress Molly," Mistress Westley smiled kindly, while the other two women exchanged glances.

They were spinster cousins who lived together on a small legacy from a Stamford relative, and were notorious, not only for their tale bearing but for their parsimony and greed. Critical of anyone who did not conform to their austere opinions, they were also friends of Mistress Wallace, and the three women always ensured that they kept each other acquainted with all the village gossip, no matter how trivial.

They were now standing a few feet away listening, as Mistress Westley continued, "Ah me, how his mother will fret. Mistress Bell and Mistress Withers, be ye so kind as to take these kerchiefs and soak them in the stream."

Ignoring the proffered cloths, the two women replied agitatedly, almost in unison, "Indeed Mistress Westley, do remember your bad leg, kneeling there. Did you not last March complain that it pained you so you knew hardly how to stand."

"Stuff and fiddlesticks," Mistress Westley exclaimed furiously, "yon boy be ill, do ye both go and soak these cloths."

Neither women moved, so I took both kerchiefs, and by the time I returned the cousins were hurrying across the bridge, and Thomas was opening his eyes.

"Hush now, do ye take yer time," Molly said gently, adding softly to Mistress Westley, "see ma'am, he tries to speak so 'twill be safe to carry him to his cottage, and Mistress Fry, would ye be so kind as to hasten to his mother to reassure her that he will be well."

Amused by her formality, but flattered that she should so address me before other villagers, I turned to go but as I did so, Mistress Westley struggled to her feet declaring, "And I'll accompany thee, Mistress Fry, for we must reach her afore those two scolds, as they'll no doubt fret her badly. And her having had so much to bear this past two year, with her husband dying so sudden, and then her own health so bad. But set her mind at rest we must, that her lad be mending."

But despite our determination we did not succeed, for the good woman's leg would not allow haste, and by the time Master Westley and his sons had reached the cottage with Thomas, the two women had created enough havoc to cause a small crowd to gather. They had apparently also succeeded in convincing Mistress Whyte that her son had either broken his neck, or been crushed to death by his horse, as we arrived to find her clinging agitatedly to the cottage door.

So distracted was she, that it took Molly some minutes to reassure her that Thomas, although bruised and shaken, would soon recover with careful nursing by which time the crowd, having nothing fatal at which to gawp, quickly dispersed.

The invalid having been carried upstairs the Westleys departed and, having ensured Thomas was comfortable, Molly hurried away to collect some physic, leaving me to remain in case Mistress Whyte should seek my services.

Absorbed in examining the stark but spotless parlour which lacked everything but the most basic essentials for living, making me consider my own home a place of luxury by comparison, I was so engrossed, I did not hear the sound of horse's hooves, until a voice said, "Mistress Fry, good day ma'am, I did hear our Post Boy has taken a tumble. Does he now thrive?"

Startled, I stared up into Robert Alton's laughing eyes and then, remembering my manners, made a wobbly curtsey before stuttering, "Indeed sir yes good day, he did fall, Molly, Mistress Tyler does tend him."

"Ah, yes, our admirable Mistress Tyler, she is within?" Too overcome to reply, I could only manage a nod and Robert, with a broad smile, doffed his elegant brown velvet cap and continued on his way.

Almost paralysed with emotion, I was unaware that Molly had returned and was now descending the stairway announcing cheerfully, "Mistress Whyte does send her best, and Thomas is much improved, and with sleep will soon be fully recovered," she dropped her voice. "The poor bodies are much impoverished. She did say if Thomas ceased his work, they would starve. Goodwife Hargreaves and yer father do give bounty this I know but, poor souls, how did they make shift afore he was Post Boy?"

"Mistress Whyte did launder for anyone who cared to give her their linen," I gasped, as I desperately tried to make my voice sound normal. Molly looked at me with obvious curiosity.

"What ails ye Pleasance, ye are much flushed and yer voice does make strange sounds?"

I fanned myself energetically. "It is the heat, nought but the heat."

"Indeed," Molly did not sound convinced, and she glanced up and down the road. "Did some body pass? I did hear a horse."

"I think a tinker with some wares, I did not notice."

"It did sound more like a mounted horse, but no matter. Now that Thomas is attended I must to his mother, for she does have such a cough. I am to take a potion of Coltsfoot(17) to ease her. 'tis a goodly remedy for the chest."

Having recovered somewhat, I remembered suddenly my father's cough.

"The potion of which you speak," I asked hesitantly. "Do you have a considerable quantity, or enough only for Mistress Whyte?"

"Why bless ye more than enough," Molly gave me a sharp look. "'tis for Master Fry that ye ask?"

"Yes, and I worry greatly Molly but he must not know," I added, agitatedly.

"Hush lass," she pressed my arm gently. "Of course I'll no speak, and ye may have some and I'll tell ye how 'tis made. Then 'twill suffice, if ye do say to the good Verger that ye gathered the dried flower-heads on our walks, and have heard how to mix them to a potion." Grateful for her understanding, I asked what manner of medicine she had administered to Thomas.

"The ointment was arnica, and the potion a liquid of my own making, a mixture of a sleeping herb."

"Not belladonna?" I enquired, nervously.

"No lass, valerian(17)," Molly replied soothingly. "'tis a goodly herb, wisely used."

I frowned. "But it has strong properties, has it not? I did hear of a man in Stamford who slept for over seven days."

She laughed. "I fear 'tis the wise old women's tales ye hear, valerian has no such properties. 'tis more a herb for giving calm happiness, than deep sleep."

"Calm happiness? Surely did you not say that Thomas has to sleep, I do not relate calm happiness with sleep."

Molly lowered her eyes, and I was surprised to see a look of confusion on her face. "I did say that wisely used, 'tis a goodly herb," she replied hurriedly. "I'll away now to bring the Coltsfoot." She returned within minutes carrying the potion, but before I could thank her she had turned abruptly into her cottage and closed the door.

Later that same evening, I attempted to broach with my father the subject of his health, but he seemed very weary, and retired early. That night he coughed almost continually and after lying awake listening to the racking sound for what seemed like hours, I knocked on his door and enquired if he would care for something to drink.

"No, do not enter," he cried out harshly, and I could do nothing but return to my bed, where I pulled the rough sheet over my head to shut out the sound.

The following morning I again knocked on his door, and this time he called out that all was well, but he did not descend until after Bessie had departed to feed the hens. As soon as he appeared I told him, somewhat apprehensively, of the potion. To my delight he accepted the physic without demur, and agreed to partake of a dose three times daily. Within two days I was relieved to see that his health seemed to have improved, and I decided to request Molly for some more of the draught. Unfortunately, before I could so ask, He who decrees all our fates had decided my friend's attentions should be directed elsewhere, for at mid-day three days later, Goodwife Hargreaves died.

CHAPTER 7

June 1657

The Goodwife's death came as a profound shock to the parish, and greatly was she mourned by those villagers who would not have survived but for her bounty. Within hours of the bereavement, small groups of folk from both Fretson and the surrounding villages gathered outside her cottage, while in my chamber I sat on my bed listening to the murmurings in the road below. Hugh had brought the news to us in an incoherent wail, and immediately my father, with an ashen face, had accompanied the sobbing youth next door.

Two hours later, awaiting my father's return, I could think only of how empty life would be without Molly's companionship, for she would be obliged to return to Goodborough to earn her bread. The only work for hire in Fretson was either in the quarry or farm labouring, and although there might be employment for Molly possibly in Stamford, no one would want the added responsibility of accommodating Hugh.

The sound of approaching footsteps had me running down the staircase, to find my father standing before the empty fireplace, his hands gripped tightly behind his back. "It was a peaceful end, and such a charitable soul deserves no less. Ah me, a sad loss. It will be much felt by the Parish, and I shall miss her greatly," he sighed deeply. "She was a good, dear friend to me."

I nodded, not knowing how to reply, for I had never before seen him so emotional. His friendship with the Goodwife had always been a mystery to me, mainly because Mistress Hargreaves's way of living was so at variance with our own determined frugality and thrift. Watching him now, as he stared into the empty fireplace, I realised suddenly how he had aged and how much thinner he was since the beginning of the year. He was now two and forty years old, but when my mother died he had been but two and thirty, a man in the prime of his life. I wondered suddenly why he had never remarried. He must have experienced intense loneliness as a widower for so many years, with only a child for company. I dropped my eyes ashamed of such intrusive thoughts, but once released my mind would not be stilled, and I remembered his sudden burst of laughter two weeks previously, and the way he had so abruptly recited the poetry.

Apart from his greying hair and rather gaunt cheeks, he was still tall and straight with a muscular body supported by two strong shapely legs. Despite my endeavours to control them my unfettered thoughts rushed on as I realised that, if my mother had lived, there would no doubt have been brothers and sisters to fill the cottage.

"So much to be done." His voice returned me abruptly to the present. He was smiling gently at me, and reaching out lightly placed his hand upon my head.

"Why do you not pay your last respects, my child. The girl Molly has done all that is needed, but as my daughter you should make a final visit."

I nodded my head dutifully, as my father lowered himself heavily onto the nearest chair. Sad though I was to see him so despondent, I had no desire to comply with his wishes as I had never witnessed death but, forever obedient, I collected my shawl and opened our cottage door. As I emerged I saw a few villagers still huddled beneath trees on the far side of the road, murmuring quietly.

Molly's door opened almost immediately in response to my knock, and my friend drew me in swiftly, with a warm embrace. "I did know ye'd come dearest Pleasance, and pleased I am to see ye."

Surprised at her lack of sorrow, I saw that the parlour looked as welcoming as ever, and that the only sign of sadness to be seen was Hugh's dejected expression.

"He does think we're for Goodborough, and does fear to return there," she explained. "She did have a peaceful end," she added. "The good soul did slip as easily from this life, as she'd have wished. Ye did come to see her?"

I blenched. My mother's lifeless form had been displayed for all to witness, except myself. Ever observant, Molly smiled kindly. "She looks but asleep and 'tis perhaps to yer common good that ye should see her. A gentle death such as hers is an easy one to witness, if ye've never afore seen such. Come, pay yer respects I'll be by and there's naught fearful in death, only sorrow."

She held out her hand, and gripping the strong capable palm very tightly, I braced myself for the sight of an old gnarled body and a withered face, but the tranquil corpse that greeted me was that of a woman not yet old, with a skin that still retained the smoothness of youth.

Relieved, I glanced curiously around the room which was full of furniture. Apart from the bed, there was a tall cedar wood mule chest, an oak cabinet decorated with carved flowers, a number of covered chairs, two low wooden stools and what appeared to be a small wall mirror in an ornate metal frame, hanging by a chain beside the bed.

"'tis so," Molly whispered. "She'd look at herself many times a day."

I looked at the mirror, and tried to imagine what my father would have said if he had known of its existence, then Molly took my hand and drew me gently towards the door.

"We'll now leave her, but Pleasance ye did look upon her as if for the first time. Do ye no remember her from the past?"

I shook my head. "I was with her but a short time, and I remember only that she was kind and held me close, as my mother used to do." My voice must have sounded wistful, for Molly slid her arms about me and gave me a hug, then we gave the peaceful corpse one last look, and returned to the parlour.

Remembering what I had heard from Old Mother Burrows, and the other village women, I asked, "Were the Goodwife's limbs much malformed?"

"Malformed, why bless ye should the poor soul be malformed ?"

"For sure, was she not a cripple these last few years?"

"Nay lass, she was no cripple. She did have a malady, but 'twas not a crippling one."

"But I did think," I began, but Molly interrupted me before I could continue, "There are many still to pay their respects, some as she would've not given house room to but no matter, come they must. The burial is to be Thursday noon."

I hesitated, before asking the question, the answer to which I dreaded, "And when will you return to Goodborough, now that you no longer have a place here."

There was so long a silence I was about to repeat the question, believing I had not been heard, when Molly replied in a voice, unexpectedly abrupt, "'tis for the good Lord to decide what'll become of us."

Before I could respond there was a knock on the door, and Mistress Machin entered accompanied by her eldest daughter, Bridget. Molly rose immediately to greet them and, as she did so, Hugh stumbled in to announce loudly that two hens had escaped from the coop. In the little confusion that followed, I slipped away.

Everyone in the village attended the burial, including Sir Oliver and Lady

Alton with their sons. My profound shock on seeing Master Robert without the benefit of his mount, makes me now smile. I could not believe that this extremely short youth was the Adonis I had for so long admired, and I thought at first I had confused him with his brother. But John Alton was not only taller, he had stronger more composed features, and although he lacked Robert's panache he exhibited a gentility lacking in his younger brother.

Momentarily ignoring Preacher Wyman's admonitions to everyone to remember their Christian duty and prepare for the end, I was examining John Alton through half closed lashes, and trying to imagine what he might look like astride Robert's black horse when I realised that his eyes were fixed on Molly, who was standing beside Hugh at the open grave.

The admiration in the young man's expression was quite blatant, and I could see that Molly was very much aware of her admirer's gaze. Quelling a sudden surge of jealousy, I tried to concentrate on the men shovelling earth down into the grave. Most of the villagers were crying, especially Hugh, but to my surprise my father stood impassive, and dry eyed.

Within hours of the burial Master Humphrey Wallace summoned the more eminent residents, including my father, to a meeting at the Goodwife's cottage where he announced that she had willed the property, its contents, and all her wealth to the Tylers. As soon as the news was public there was an indignant outcry. Everyone agreed that two impoverished strangers to the village should not be allowed to inherit, and Mistress Wallace insisted that her brother bring the matter to the notice of Sir Oliver. Only my father demurred, saying that a dead person's Will should be honoured, regardless of the beneficiaries.

His opinion was ignored, and there was a brief investigation held at the Hall, during which Molly was closely questioned by Master Wallace and two lawyers, brought especially from Lincoln. No irregularities having been discovered, they instructed Sir Oliver's Steward to confirm, with his master's authority, that the Tylers were indeed the rightful heirs, and that they were to be allowed to remain in the village, if they so desired. At first there were a few grumbles, particularly from Mistress Wallace and her friends, but as no one dared oppose Sir Oliver's authority, Molly and Hugh were left to continue their now very comfortable existence.

Although I was delighted to learn that I was not to lose my friend, I found Molly's sudden acquisition of wealth unsettling, and I was also distressed that my father had not been mentioned in the Will. I knew with his practice of frugality, he would most probably not have accepted a benefice, but I resented the fact that he had not been given the opportunity to choose.

I also realised, that the unsettling emotions I was now experiencing were as a consequence of Molly's brilliant future, for brilliant it would be. As a single woman with her own home and income, she would have all the independence she used to complain was denied to women of her rank.

Somewhat overawed by her new status, I was reluctant to intrude without an invitation, and there was also another reason for my reticence. News of Molly's success in administering to Thomas Whyte had spread into the county generally, and people were coming from surrounding villages as far afield as North Luffenham, Barrowden and Empingham, to enquire whether she had a cure for their own ailments.

Her fame even reached the ears of an eminent surgeon in Stamford, who paid her the honour of a visit to examine the ointments and potions, and his arrival caused a great stir in the neighbourhood, especially as he was accompanied by two liveried servants.

The less generous villagers, including the Mistresses Burridge, Wallace, Bell and Withers, expressed the view that Molly's success was due to the fact that she never charged anyone for her physic, but this vindictive gossip was attributed by others to jealousy, and my father especially, extolled Molly's virtues at every meal.

"A most benevolent and virtuous young woman, worthy of grace. To give so much and wish for nothing in return, her soul will be most blessed. It was indeed a most propitious circumstance that sent her to our village."

I listened to him obediently, but feelings of jealousy and resentment which I could not subdue persuaded me not to seek Molly's company. So I remained solitary until one morning, ten days after the burial, when there was a loud knock on the cottage door. Hesitantly, since I anticipated Molly on the step, I opened it to discover Hugh, very spruce in new gaiters, boots and shirt, and with his eyes almost obliterated by an enormous smile.

In his customary incoherent manner, he announced that Molly would be very pleased to see me, if I had a moment to call. Feeling reluctant and intrigued by turns, I followed him into the next-door parlour, which I was surprised to find exactly as it had been on my previous visits, but the same could not be said for its mistress.

As she came towards me, her arms spread wide in welcome, my friend exhibited all the signs of a young lady of means. Her customary drab black gown had been replaced by a new one of light brown wool, and her plain white linen mob cap, collar and cuffs had been changed for dazzling white concoctions edged with lace. But despite her change of garb, I soon discovered that the wearer remained as I had always known her, for she flung her arms about me with a glad cry of welcome, and then ushered me to the table on which lay three large, tasty looking pasties.

"I'm indeed glad to see ye, but why've ye stayed away so long? And so distant were ye with me in church. I did think I'd offended ye, and then believed ye may be ill, so I did send Hugh and here ye are."

Rather self-consciously, I returned the embrace and, as I did so, all my resentment evaporated and we were soon sitting at the table chewing contentedly, while Molly told of her surprise on hearing of the legacy, and the interview with the two lawyers from Lincoln.

"I was indeed afeared, but Sir Oliver and his son John, they were most kind and told me I'd only the truth to speak, and answer questions with what I knew. And so I did, and the gentlemen and Master Wallace, they did seem satisfied. And Berwick House is a fine place, with hangings and great chairs that a body could almost sleep in, but 'twas a great shock, for she said naught about the Will, and I did think it more fitting for yer father to inherit, being as he was so close a friend."

"My father would never have accepted anything," I replied defensively, imagining Molly at the great house in conversation with John Alton.

"Indeed no," she replied soothingly, "I know he'd not. But 'tis a mite strange. No matter," she smiled her warm generous smile. "We'll have such times, us three. I'm to Stamford Friday week to market, and to visit on the surgeon who did call. So surprised was I to see so great a man. Doctor Percival, he's named, and he did ask me many questions and did look most closely at my potions and how I'd mix them together. I did take him to the poor dear Goodwife's room, wherein I now keep my herbs and mix my physic. 'tis such a busy time I've had Pleasance, but help these poor folk I must. I've now so much and they've so little. As the good Lord does lead, so must I follow, and Doctor Percival do wish to show me how to mend a bone when broken, and so I will call, and I've received notice also to attend on Master Wallace. So we're to Stamford town Pleasance, for ye will accompany me. Indeed I have such plans for us Pleasance, such plans as ye cannot think of."

"To Stamford, but Molly my father," I stammered, completely overcome.

"Do ye but leave such matters to me. Verger Fry has helped us much, and said he was glad we were acquainted. He'll have no objections, I'm sure."

"He helped you, how pray?" I tried to comprehend her meaning.

"By attending us near every day. There was much to do, the Goodwife's clothes to give away and other matters in which the good Verger helped. I would've not known how to make shift without his wise counsel."

As Molly re-filled our mugs, I could think only of my father visiting that same comfortable room, while I remained next door with only Bessie for company. Why had he not told me, and why had I not been invited to accompany him?

Resentment surged back into me and I stared morosely at Molly, but she appeared not to notice, for she continued chatting about our Stamford visit in her customary, warm manner. Having reluctantly accepted a mushroom pie, I returned to our cottage and climbed swiftly to my chamber. Once there, I raised the lid of my wooden box and knelt beside it, looking for some time at the exquisitely sewn linen of my father's new shirt.

Later that same night his coughing once again awakened me, and I hurried to his door. Knocking softly, I would have entered but for his agitated cry, "All is well, I have merely a little breathlessness. I require nothing, return to your chamber."

Frightened by his vehemence, I sped trembling back to my own room and, for the first time since her death, longed for my mother's presence. Then the moon, as if in answer to my woes glided from behind a cloud, and I was bathed in a shimmering reassuring glow. But it did not dispel my grief, and still feeling abandoned, I crawled back between my covers, and cried myself to sleep.

CHAPTER 8

June 1657

Next morning my father made no reference to his cough, but to my relief he swallowed more of Molly's potion saying, as he did so, "Yon lass has a wise head, and as she did devote herself to my dear friend, so does she does continue to devote herself to others, services for which she will be much blessed in Heaven. She does now tell me a visit to Stamford is being planned?"

"So did Molly say father, but only if you so wish."

"I have no objection. It is now surely time you did see more of the country. I would my duties allowed me to widen your knowledge, but since that is not to be you must take advantage of the opportunity that is offered." He smiled. "And if I recollect correctly, the date chosen is most auspicious, for is not the twelfth your birth date?"

Never before had my father drawn attention to my date of birth, and I tried to hide my surprise as he stared reflectively at me, the long fingers of his right hand beating a light tattoo on the table-top.

"Ten and seven, indeed a woman grown 'though such has been the case these past two years. I fear I have neglected you in many ways, my child. The years do swiftly pass and what is before us to clearly see, is not always what our eyes perceive. You have grown well. You have a calmness of temperament and demeanour which is to your good, and I have noted of recent times a lively colour in your cheeks. It is becoming." He pushed his chair back abruptly from the table. "May the Good Lord grant you a day of contentment, and I do anticipate a full account of the proceedings."

Almost convinced that I had misheard, I was still reflecting on his words with pleasure when Molly arrived, to announce excitedly, "'tis all arranged. Thomas has hired for us Master Bailey's wagon and we ride in grand style. Now do I wish to tell ye of my cousin William Radley," her voice rushed on enthusiastically. "I did speak of him some months since, when talking of Goodborough, and he's a fine man is Will."

"I do now recollect him being spoken of," I replied briefly, more interested in our visit to Stamford than Master Radley and his profession, but Molly seemed not to hear for she continued, "And all folk want blacksmiths, there'll always be horses to be shod, and he's many good qualities and'll make a fine husband, with a trade and all. And he's tall and straight like me, 'though he's the taller and has a fine black beard."

"Indeed," I replied, without enthusiasm. Beards were not considered an attribute in Commonwealth England, and I had never seen one.

"And with his forge there's a house, not large but with all the rooms a body could want. And he's built," Molly dropped her voice, "a privy as near to the house as I'm to ye. And a great wide bed he has which'll last for as long as he lives. I would you could meet him."

I frowned. "For why should I wish to meet your cousin?"

"He's a good man," she replied, looking so mysterious I said irritably, "If he is so very good and honest and just, and so capable in his profession, whyfore do you not wed him."

"'tis no good for cousins to wed," she replied sharply, "and Will'd not care for me for wife. He's bookish, for our Squire he did have Will taught his letters, and he likes to read of a night. He has many books, and reads his bible a plenty. I'm of the wish to see him, and if ye please would beg yer help. 'tis the writing," she added hurriedly, before I could reply. "I wish to send a letter and writing 'tis still a chore."

Suddenly realising the intent behind her words, I replied hurriedly, "My father does not care to meet strangers."

"'tis not for to meet yer father that I wish Will to come," Molly replied with a laugh, and she took some writing materials from her basket and placed them on the table

With my fingers tightly interlaced, I blushed violently and asked, "What pray is it that you desire to say, to your cousin."

"Why indeed to wish him well, send mine and Hugh's good wishes, and ask him to Fretson for as long as he is able."

"And where will he reside, pray?"

"In my cottage, where else should he be?"

I was shocked. "Do you think it seemly?"

Molly laughed. "And why for should it not be seemly? He's my blood kin. We dwelt together for many a month in Goodborough." She stared expectantly at me and, reluctantly, I made a few suggestions as to the letter's content.

Apparently satisfied, she sat down and began to write. As soon as the letter was finished, my disconcerting thoughts of Master Radley were banished by Molly's announcement that she had made a new bodice and skirt for our visit to Stamford.

I listened in consternation, for although it was immoral for me to be concerned with my apparel there was, nevertheless, a problem. For a few days, I considered wearing my Sunday gown, then years devoted to prayer and tradition guided me back to my senses. Such a garment was for praying in, not for enjoyment, so instead I sewed a new collar and two new cuffs onto my day gown, and made myself a new white cap.

My enthusiasm for our forthcoming visit must have been infectious, for my father talked incessantly of the day, and on the evening before gave me a silver fourpence(18)to spend. Never before had I handled money, and I stared down at the coin in astonishment, until he laughed softly.

"It is but a coin child, would that it were more but if it gives you pleasure on the day, then it has served its purpose."

It was some time later that I heard a horse stopping outside Molly's cottage, and within seconds she had scampered up the stairs, and burst into my chamber triumphantly waving an opened letter.

"A speedy reply I've had. He's to come and before next full moon and all," she looked quickly at the paper and then thrust it forward. "But do ye look for yerself, I've read only the first three lines, 'tis not easy for a body to read such script. Do ye tell me what he says, please."

With my heart beating unnaturally fast, I took the paper. William Radley's script was clear and well formed, and his reply brief and concise. He thanked his cousin for her good wishes, which he heartily reciprocated, said he would like very much to see her, and suggested next Wednesday week for a stay of thirty days or more. He added, that as his apprentice was a capable lad and well able to look after the forge, the summer would be a good time to come while the weather was fair, as rain and mud made travelling difficult.

"Is it not good, and the end, how does he write the end?"

"With all his best to you and Hugh," I replied, ignoring the postscript.

"But the writing below, what of that?" Molly pointed a finger at the lines written beneath the farewell greeting.

"It is a postscript," I replied, as I felt the blood rush into my face, but since the inevitable could no longer be avoided I said, with increasing discomposure, "It says to give me his sincere respect, and that he does anticipate our meeting with pleasure." Almost in tears, I thrust the letter back into her hand. "Molly why did you mention me? It is not seemly. indeed it is not, to send any message from myself that I did not permit."

"Why lass, pray do not fret," Molly shook her head in apparent surprise. "I did mean no harm. I did add the words when ye had left, and 'twas but a friendly greeting I did send."

I clenched my lips, in an attempt to control their trembling. "My father would be most displeased, were he to learn of this; and I will not see your cousin, I will not."

"Hush there," her voice now sounded anxious. "I'd not cause ye pain for aught, and if ye so wish ye shall not meet him. I'll say ye are indisposed."

"Say nothing but that I have no wish to make his acquaintance," I cried. I turned away to hide the tears of vexation, which were now forcing themselves through my lids. The silence that followed seemed almost noisy, until Molly's footsteps indicated that she was leaving the room.

Alone in my chamber I sat for some time on the bed, staring unseeingly at the plain white walls. Tomorrow we were to have gone to Stamford, but having quarrelled how could this be? Molly would now go with only Hugh for company, and my father would have to be told. I trembled at the thought of having to explain. Suddenly heavy footsteps sounded in the street below, and someone entered the cottage. There was a pause, then my father's voice called, "Pleasance, you do have a message."

Slowly I descended to the front parlour. My father was seated at the table, reading. He looked up with a gentle smile, and pointed to a piece of folded parchment.

"I know not who left yon piece of paper, but it was lying on the table when I entered."

Trying to appear unconcerned, I opened the missive. Molly's apology, written in very uneven script, stared up at me.

"Father, pray excuse me there is a matter I must discuss with Molly."

"Of course, child, go your way."

She was sitting dejectedly on a stool before the fire, her face wet with tears. Hurrying across the floor I sank to my knees, and enveloped her in a great hug. She gave a gasping sob. "I didn't think." She shuddered slightly, and I tightened my grip. "I meant no harm, and did not intend to offend indeed I didn't."

"You did not offend," I gabbled desperately, "and there was no harm. I, too, must beg forgiveness for I acted foolishly. If you wish for me to meet your cousin, then of course I will."

"There's no need. Oh Pleasance, yer me only friend, and I do love ye dearly, 'twould break my heart, if ye'd no wish to see me more."

"Indeed we are friends, and shall remain so, on that I give my word," I replied quickly, and we clung together for some moments until interrupted by Hugh, entering from Molly's medicine chamber. The shrewdness of his glance surprised me. I had never seen him look so intelligent, and for the first time I wondered how much he understood.

Having recovered her composure, Molly offered mugs of ale and we sat talking of the following day's journey. But the atmosphere was subdued, and it was in deep thought that I returned home. Molly's reaction had been unexpected, as had the knowledge that I had so great a power over her and that, for all her self-possession and awareness, she was the weaker. But why she was the weaker, I had yet to learn.

CHAPTER 9

I awoke next day to a clear blue sky, and by the time Master Bailey's cart had commenced its jolting way through the ruts of the main highway, the sun had begun to glow with a radiance that could only signify a glorious day.

Snuggling into the shawls which Molly had provided to line the hard wooden sides and floor of the cart, I sighed with contentment. She laughed.

"'tis good, is it not?"

I nodded happily, and as we swayed along the tree-lined road, with Thomas as outrider and Hugh perched on the ledge of the forehead, we were hailed with friendly waves from men trudging their way to work in the quarry. Further along the road we caught up with Mistress Workman, and her sister Mistress Brewster, accompanied by a number of unruly children, and remembering how my father wished me always to acknowledge all the villagers, I waved a hesitant greeting. In response, some of the children gave jovial yells, but to my mortification both women responded with resentful stares.

Molly shrugged. "In faith, 'tis strange how some folk do behave, but fret not, 'tis of no consequence to bodies such as us out on our great venture." She gave me a saucy grin, and to my embarrassment, stuck out her pink tongue in the direction of the two women.

I sighed inwardly, imagining how they would enjoy relating the tale to such as Mistresses Bell and Withers. But I could not be distracted from the joys of our day for long, and accustomed as I was only to the occasional visiting tinker or pedlar, I was soon engrossed studying the other travellers on the road. First two coaches trundled past, both with liveried outriders, then a gentleman on horseback, accompanied by a servant with a pistol in his belt.

Molly appeared unimpressed by these sights, and seemed to find amusement in my fascination, but I did not care. For the first time I was experiencing a life outside of the confines of my own, and I wanted to continue quietly contemplating these new circumstances, but Thomas, having become bored with riding alone ahead of the cart had reigned in alongside, and was holding forth on his experiences as a post-boy.

An intelligent and conscientious lad, he was proud of his position, but as there were only three deliveries of post a week a great deal of his time was spent loitering outside The George Inn at Stamford.

"And 'tis the law mistress, that all mail must travel through our great capital, afore they be delivered. So letters do they go from here to there, afore they come back here from Swan Inn in Holborn, and Friday being mail day I'll be there to collect, so I will."

"Pleasance look yonder, flying swans."

Obviously offended by Molly's interruption Thomas pouted, before reluctantly trotting off to return to his out-riding position.

"Poor lad," she looked contrite. "I fear I have done him ill, but he does go on so, and 'tis not as if 'tis news. Think ye Pleasance, he has taken affront?"

I shook my head. On such a day no one could take affront, and she looked relieved before adding, "We are to Master Percival's at noon, where 'tis possible we shall be served a jug of ale. Oh, Pleasance, life indeed be good."

We were entering Tinwell, where the villagers were busy going about their day and gave us but a cursory glance, when Thomas reined in his horse to announce, "I said to Master Bailey so I did, when I was asking of him to let yon Hugh sit aside him, should a highwayman challenge us, yon Hugh could smite him down so he could."

I sat up quickly, and stared up and down the road. "Mercy on us, is it possible?"

Molly laughed. "Nay, 'tis naughty lad's revenge on me for the swans and for sure, 'twould be a foolhardy highwayman who'd risk his all, to rob two poor girls in a wooden cart." She shook her finger at Thomas, her eyes bright with laughter. "Shame on ye afearing us so, 'tis my broom I will take to ye, should ye not take care."

He responded with a cheeky grin, and then his expression changed as he gasped nervously, "Yonder, Master Bailey, yonder come soldiers."

The carter, notorious in Fretson for his bad humour, growled angrily, "I do seem 'em I'm not blind, yon lass has wished 'em on us."

As he pulled his horse into the side of the road, I peered through the space between him and Hugh. I had seen soldiers only once before, when a small number had come to sequestrate Berwick House, and then I had been but a little child peeping at them through the lattice.

Staring apprehensively at the approaching cloud of dust, I remembered that although my father had always instructed me to treat the military with politeness, he had also emphasised that conversing with them was unwise. I was dismayed, therefore, to see Molly pull herself up the side of the cart, and stare eagerly down the road at the approaching cavalry.

Trotting swiftly, the twenty-one fully armed men were almost abreast of the stationary cart when the leading rider, a heavy looking man clad, like his platoon, in a lobster-tail helmet, metal breast plate and polished leather strappings, ordered his Company to pull in their horses to permit our cart to continue.

Master Bailey immediately whipped his animal into a canter, and closely followed by Thomas, rumbled passed the soldiers so violently that we were thrown into a heap on the floor. As I fell, I was aware of a number of amused glances from the soldiers, and an overwhelming smell of horses, human sweat and leather. Only too relieved that the incident had passed without difficulty, I was disconcerted when Molly, having struggled upright, began to berate Master Bailey for his rudeness.

"They did mean us no harm, and ye did act right badly, Master Bailey, with not a thankee, nor a nod of greeting, and we could've met injury from the way ye did urge yer horse."

"Mistress 'tis better as 'tis, ye shouldn'a meddle with soldiers, leave well alone my mother do say," Thomas exclaimed, while Master Bailey muttered something about folk not being grateful, a remark which only seemed to increase Molly's anger.

"'tis not gratitude that's wanting," she retorted, "but plain courtesy."

The carter grunted again but this time without responding, and Molly had to satisfy herself by pulling a face at his broad back.

"Yer good father, he did not fight?" She asked me suddenly. "'twas an injury of the foot, so the Goodwife did tell me?"

"Yes, he did step upon a scythe. I was but a child and remember little, but he was abed for many days and when he arose he had the limp with which he now walks, and could not therefore join the soldiers."

Molly nodded sympathetically, but the carter gave a sudden guffaw. "Aye, 'twas very sad so 'twas not to join the soldiers. And which soldiers, little mistress, would ye fine father have favoured, tell me that?"

I flushed at the implication, and Molly's eyes narrowed. "Shame on ye Master Bailey, to ask such a question when we do all know the answer, and has yer family not benefited from the Verger's kindness?"

Very embarrassed, I awaited the carter's answer, but he only growled indistinctly while Molly glowered at his back. Then she gave a sudden cry, "Look Pleasance, here do come more travellers and a fine coach."

Master Bailey's taunts forgotten, I twisted around to see a great coach approaching, accompanied by four outriders. Much larger than the two we had seen previously, it was drawn by four fine bays, and as it drew near I saw it had a crest painted on the door, and glimpsed and the one occupant, partially concealed behind a curtain.

"Now who might that be, that he wishes so much to remain unknown?" Molly exclaimed.

Master Bailey gave his customary grunt, "'tis not for us humble folk to question the gentry, as ye well know."

She frowned, but contented herself with yet another grimace at the carter's back, before carefully counting out some coins into her lap.

Market day was at its busiest as we drove towards St. Peter's Gate, beyond which lay St. Peter's Hill, one of Stamford's main streets. A number of carts and wagons were moving steadily ahead, but the traffic was making slow progress, even for market day. Suddenly, a commotion at the gate entrance brought everything to a halt.

"What's amiss?" Molly demanded, struggling to her feet to obtain a better view.

"I'll to enquire," Thomas replied and, leaping from his horse, pushed his way into the crowds. For a brief time he was lost in their midst, and when at last he managed to struggle back to us, his eyes were wide with excitement. "'tis a witch, and she's to be tried at Oakham. They do leave by this gate, for there's been a fall of earth at St. Clement's, that's why so many folk are gathered, and Master Purvis the Prosecutor, he's been to Stamford and..."

"Do ye quit yer squalling lad, can ye no see my horse is afright," Master Bailey cried, pulling hard on the reins in an effort to calm the agitated animal.

Chastened, Thomas fell silent, whilst all about us people pushed forward in an effort to see.

Not wishing to witness anything I cowered down, but Molly leaned dangerously over the side of the cart, exclaiming, "They clear a way, she comes now."

As she finished speaking curiosity overcame apprehension, and I scrambled to a standing position in time to see two soldiers, accompanied by two mounted men. All four were attempting to force a way through the crowd milling around the city gate. The civilians were rough looking and shabbily dressed, but it was not until they were almost abreast of our cart that I saw the woman following behind.

Her hands were tied behind her back and she looked but young, with a plump figure and long brown, unkempt hair. Encircling her waist was a thick hemp rope, the end of which was tied to the saddle of the second man. As she came nearer I saw her scratched and blood stained feet, her filthy face and hands and badly stained torn gown.

"Merciful Lord protect her," Molly muttered, her face ashen, and I slid quickly down to the floor of the cart, my stomach churning. I knew witches existed, for Old Mother Burrows had told me of Matthew Hopkins and his great witch hunts of the sixteen forties, but this was my first sight of such a phenomenon.

I closed my eyes, and began reciting the twenty-third psalm. I had reached verse 4, when Molly cried, "Her feet, do see the poor soul's feet."

"And do ye hush yer voice girl, 'lest you do wish us to walk to Rutland Assizes along with yon hag," Master Bailey's voice hissed furiously, and I opened my eyes to see that some of the people surrounding the cart were looking curiously at Molly.

"Yes, Mistress," Thomas agreed, urgently. "Do ye be silent for Master Oswald the Witchfinder be within the town and see, he do come now."

I could hear the crowd muttering excitedly, and as the murmurs increased the sound of trotting horses grew louder. I closed my eyes again until I heard the riders pass, but as the noise subsided, I looked up just in time to see the backs of two mounted men, both dressed in dark cloaks and tall felt hats, trotting after the running girl.

CHAPTER 10

Master Bailey was still grumbling at Molly, as he pulled his horse in beside St. Peter's Church.

"She want to mind herself, that she do."

But my friend was too occupied trying to calm an agitated Thomas, who was still exclaiming excitedly, "Did ye know mistress, that Master Oswald did attend the trial of Anne Bodenham(19) for 'tis said he did know Master Hopkins, and folk do say yon witch was floated."

"Indeed," Molly interrupted sharply. "Now Thomas calm yerself for Mistress Fry and I are to Doctor Percival at noon, and 'tis in Barn Hill. Know ye the place?"

"Barn Hill be near to the Church of All Saints, Mistress, but I know not the house of Doctor Percival."

"No matter, there'll no doubt be many folk to guide us."

"Do ye ask for Master Wolph mistress, his house be close by," Master Bailey suggested, with a sly wink at Thomas, who grinned back and then trotted away towards The George Inn.

Molly frowned and, to my consternation, remarked in her customary clear voice, "I know not of Master Wolph, who be he?"

"Molly I pray you, let us depart," I whispered in an effort to silence her, as some passing townsfolk stared at us in surprise. She looked annoyed, but before she could speak again, I explained hurriedly, "I will reveal all to you later."

She sighed. "'tis yet another matter of which I must not speak. A body has much to learn these troubled days, and I shall demand to know of this great secret Pleasance, as soon as we are able, but now to market. Good day to ye sir, and we'll see ye at two of the clock, near to the Old Mill stream."

Without waiting for Master Bailey's reply, she led the way determinedly along the crowded street, with Hugh clinging tightly to her hand. Still shaken by my encounter with the witch, I followed as closely as I was able through the throng. I had never seen so many people in one place before. Soberly clad townsfolk mingled with tinkers and traders whilst farmers, with livestock and produce to sell, attempted to drive their wagons towards the market square; and how swiftly they all moved, as if each one had a place of appointment to reach within a given time.

Pushing my way with difficulty, I could not help overhearing raised voices everywhere, excitedly discussing the witch.

"They do be hanging her," exclaimed a young worthy, with an enormous drink sodden nose and stained breeches.

"Damn her eyes, 'tis fenlands that does fret me," retorted his shabby companion. "With them taken for planting, we do lose fishing and fowling rights and the money as goes with 'em."

Despite Stamford's close proximity to Fretson, this was only my third visit to the town. In 1648 I had accompanied my father to a thanksgiving service to celebrate the birth of Lord Burghley's eldest son John, but I remembered little of that occasion. My second visit five years later I vividly recalled, for we had attended St. Martin's Church in December to pray for the life of Master Cromwell, on his appointment as Protector. The journey on that occasion had been bitterly cold and hazardous, and sheltered within my father's cloak I had not seen the armed soldiers who, he told me, patrolled the road.

I could not now but help compare that time, when we had encountered a sombre atmosphere and muted murmurings from morose and servile townsfolk, with the present day. There were now no soldiers to be seen, and everyone appeared determined to enjoy themselves. As for me, today I was now a responsible woman of seventeen accompanying my friends to town, with money of my own to spend on whatever goods I cared to purchase.

"Do ye take care," Molly pointed to the filth that littered the ground, and I hurriedly lifted my gown to avoid a heap of rubbish. "And now I do beg to know the secret," she dropped her voice conspiratorially.

"It was said Master Wolph(20) did shelter the royal traitor," I whispered reluctantly.

Her eyes narrowed, and to my consternation, she declared, "Royal traitor, Nottingham would not have it so, but no matter we'll not be torn as were many of this land. And what of his fate, he of Barn Hill?"

"I know not," I whispered desperately. "We do not speak of such matters."

She shrugged. "I'll not fret ye further, and 'twas no doubt some foolish speech that caused yon poor woman's fate. Was that not the Lord's Prayer I did hear you saying?"

I nodded, as I tried to think of something to channel her into safer waters. "Are we not now near the market square?"

"It would seem so, from yonder clamour," she leaned closer. "Pleasance, think not that yon poor woman was in some way evil, and could do mischief. Witchcraft is but the cant of fools. 'tis possible she displeased a body, so that body did take vengeance, and if the poor soul could swim, floating would have condemned her, afore a trial," she sighed. "No matter, I know ye think me foolish to speak so and are afeared we'll be overheard, so I'll speak no more, and we'll to market, come now."

I did not agree with Molly. Witches were ministers of the devil, and had marks to prove it. Had not Old Mother Burrows told me of the women in Essex, on whom Witchfinders had found special teats which were used to suckle imps, and familiars? And yet the witch outside St. Peter's Gate had seemed so ordinary, just a poor girl who had looked no different from anyone I knew in Fretson.

The noise and commotion increased as we approached Browne's Hospital, from where it was but a short step into the large square which fronted the building. The mass of humanity and their uproar was now intense, as men and women vied with each other to gain access to the stalls, while children scrambled around excitedly, either pushing between peoples' legs or crawling about on the ground.

Added to this clamour were the cries of rat-catchers, knife-grinders and pedlars, all of whom shouted loudly to advertise their services, while most of the surrounding houses had been turned into open fronted shops, where bakers, clockmakers, saddlers, cobblers and tailors, were busily occupied at their tasks.

Amidst this mixture of humanity I was surprised to see a number of elegantly clad ladies and gentlemen, preceded by manservants, edging their way through the crowds, apparently as intent as everyone else on making a good purchase.

I could not but admire their garments, especially the women's hats with their wide brims and tall crowns, and I noticed some identical ones for sale on a nearby stall. For an impulsive moment I thought of purchasing one, but then dismissed the idea as foolish, for my father would certainly not have approved of such frippery.

Despite the noise and proximity of so many people, I was enjoying myself. Even the unpleasant smells that permeated from the crowd, and the rubbish with which the ground was littered, were bearable. There was so much to see, and the experience was so new I found it exhilarating. I had decided to purchase a new belt for my father, since his present one was extremely worn, and a new candlestick for Bessie, since she had complained that she found her present one too large and unwieldy. As I explained my requirements to Molly, she frowned.

"A belt and a candlestick, will ye not buy something for yerself? Perhaps some lace, or some ribbon or linen cuffs or mayhap new falling bands(21), and did I not see ye looking at yonder hats?"

"No indeed," I declared, annoyed that perceptive as ever she had seen my glance. "When would I wear such a hat? And as to cuffs and falling bands, I sew my own, and I would never wear lace or ribbon."

I had not intended to sound so abrupt and glanced warily at her, but she appeared unconcerned for she merely shrugged, and replied, "So be it if yer so decided, and do ye seek yer belt at yonder leather shop, for his workmanship is much the best we've seen, and do ye take Hugh," she added. "For I fear we'll lose ye, should ye venture alone."

I left her to examine some fine linens and laces and, closely followed by Hugh, eased my way through the almost solid mass of folk to the leather stall. Having made my purchase, I was about to return to Molly when suddenly Hugh growled, and pointed towards a young man locked in the town stocks. Although I could see from his exhausted state, and the dung and filth that had by now dried onto his clothes, that he must have been sentenced many hours previously, a gleeful crowd was still pelting him with rubbish.

Remembering Hugh's exploits in York I gripped his coat, and tried to pull him away. At first he resisted but I pulled harder until, to my relief, he followed me back to Molly still grumbling.

"I did fear Hugh would attack those folk," I explained as soon as we reached her.

"Aye so he would," she replied briefly, before adding in a warmer voice. "And be that the belt, 'tis very fine? Master Fry should be well pleased."

"I will present it to him, with the shirt," I replied.

She looked surprised. "Ye've not yet presented it, but was it not completed some weeks past?"

"Yes," I replied reluctantly, "but the opportunity did not arise."

She gave me a puzzled look, then said, "For sure it's no easy matter to choose a time, but in Goodborough 'twas the fashion to exchange gifts on our birth date," she smiled. "I fear I've now much time to await for me next great day for I'm February born. When did yer mother have her day of great travail?"

I flushed self-consciously, "It is today ten and seven years ago."

"How secretive a soul ye are, Pleasance. For why did ye not tell me? No matter, now to the cobblers for 'tis fitting that Hugh and I should have new boots, and then we'll to Barn Hill, to Doctor Percival."

"Does Hugh not already have new boots?" I asked in surprise, glancing down at the young man's sturdy new footwear.

"Yes so he does, but they are for all weathers, 'tis for better wear we go."

I frowned. I knew of no villager in Fretson who owned two pairs of boots, and could not imagine to what "better wear," Molly was referring.

The shoemaker, a pleasant faced young man considerably shorter than any of us, displayed sheets of leather for Molly's inspection. After some consultation, a highly priced brown leather was chosen for Hugh, while Molly selected a piece of equal quality, which she asked to be dyed dark red, and fashioned into mules with applied silk braid. The shoemaker was obviously delighted that he had been requested to make something different from pattens and working boots, and he measured Molly's feet with great care, telling her the combined cost for her wares would be a crown.(22)

I was astounded. So much money would have succoured many a Fretson family for weeks, and it was to be squandered on mere boots and shoes. And where would Molly wear such mules? Certainly not collecting her eggs, and walking to Chater Farm, and Hugh's fine leather boots would be far too good for Fretson's muddy streets.

I wanted to remonstrate but hesitated, nervous that my reaction might be misunderstood. Then commonsense told me I must protest, so I said timidly, "Do you not think it would be wiser to purchase stronger, more hearty boots and shoes?"

"Hearty boots and shoes," Molly laughed. "Bless ye, 'tis something of refinement that I crave. I have always on my feet such heavy boots, 'tis the reason I walk unshod within the house. Goodwife Hargreaves she did say that I should buy such shoes as I did wish, and so I would have done had she not been so ill and me not able to leave the house. No Pleasance, 'tis not hearty boots and shoes I have come to purchase in Stamford town."

The shoes having been paid for, Molly enquired of the cobbler the way to Barn Hill. From the young man's reaction it was obvious that Doctor Percival was a citizen of consequence, and we were ushered on our way with many bows, and good wishes.

Barn Hill was not far from the market square, lying as it did to the north of the Church of All Saints, and we were soon standing before an imposing looking house with overhanging gables, glazed casement windows and a stout oak door. A large ornamental knocker hung on the left side of the door, and Molly stretched out her hand towards it. The noise of it's crashing had resounded up and down the street, by the time the door was opened by an elderly man dressed in brown coat and breeches. Assuming him to be the doctor, I was relieved to see he had a pleasant, gentle face, and that he smiled kindly at us, as he enquired our business.

Returning his greeting, Molly announced, "We are for Doctor Percival, he did say we were to call when he visited my house. I be Mistress Molly Tyler of Fretson, with whom the good doctor is already acquainted, and this lady be my neighbour, Mistress Fry, and yonder be my brother Hugh."

"Mistress Tyler of Fretson?" The man hesitated for a moment, before adding, "Would you please to enter ma'am, I will tell my master you are here. Please to leave your pattens by the door."

We followed the man into the oak panelled hallway, with its high ceiling and carved panelling, and waited as he knocked on a nearby door. There was a short pause, before he entered in answer to a summons from within. As soon as he had closed the door, Molly whispered loudly, "Yon man is the doctor's steward. He did tell me he had a steward, and four servants in all. This is indeed a fine house, is it not Pleasance. It does remind me of Goodborough Hall."

I glanced at the heavy oak furniture upholstered in brown and yellow brocade, and murmured uneasily, "I do not think that we should be here, the servant did not know you."

Molly frowned, but before she could reply, the steward reappeared, looking concerned.

"My master requests that if you have aught for him to give it to me, for he says you did say you would bring a recipe for him to study, and he does enquire whether Mistress Fry is, by chance, acquainted with Master Adam Fry, the Verger of St. Luke's Church in Fretson?"

"Yes sir, I am his daughter" I replied, and then I turned in surprise as a voice behind me cried out, "As I did think, a most respected member of our community. I am indeed most honoured to make your acquaintance, ma'am."

I stared in bewilderment as the extremely fat man before me, dressed in what appeared to be numerous garments of dark red velvet, made an exaggerated bow. Before I could respond, he approached nearer and, taking up my right hand, swept his damp lips across it.

Astonished, I stood motionless as Molly bobbed a courtesy and exclaimed, "Indeed sir yer most kind, but I fear I do not have with me any recipe. If I do remember ye did say I was to call, for ye to show me the setting of a bone and yer room of medicine."

"Of course, of course," Doctor Percival waved a dismissive hand. "And how does the good Verger? I did find myself much disappointed when I did call upon Mistress Tyler here, to learn that the Verger was away on church matters. I had hoped, indeed I had, to renew our acquaintance. So do you give him, my dear young lady, of my very best, my very very best," he gushed as he ushered us towards a low door, at the back of the staircase.

"I thank you sir," I replied, trying to imagine how this extraordinary man could ever have been acquainted with my father. The back of my hand was still damp from his wet lips, and I wiped it surreptitiously down the side of my skirt.

"Now do you take care, the steps are steep, and inclined to damp. Edward, do you bring the candelabrum, hurry now."

Without waiting for his servant to comply, Doctor Percival took up a single lighted candle from a nearby table and followed by Molly, began descending a narrow flight of stone steps. I looked back to where Edward was lighting four large candles and, as he smiled reassuringly, I followed him down. On reaching the bottom, he placed the candelabrum on the only table in the room, and looked expectantly at his master.

The doctor gave him a brief nod. "Do you tell Mistress Percival, I will be but a short while."

As the steward hurriedly withdrew I examined the chamber which exuded a pungent smell, and appeared to be built entirely of stone. There were no windows or visible outlets, and the damp walls were lined with shelves on which were large bottles, full of objects floating in a dark green liquid. There were no chairs so I remained standing beside Hugh, who kept shuffling his feet and glancing in an agitated manner at the stone stairway.

On the other side of the room, talking rapidly while glancing constantly in my direction, Doctor Perival held out some dishes for Molly's inspection.

I felt very uncomfortable. It was obvious that Doctor Percival was determined to impress me, and I found his attentions embarrassing. From what he had said, I now realised that his journey to Fretson, ostensibly to see Molly, had been an excuse to reacquaint himself with my father, though for what reason I could not imagine.

I watched as he condescendingly patted Molly's arm, as if she were a child.

Then, as she attempted to ask a question, he said, "And your dear father Mistress Fry, how does his ailment?"

I frowned. "His ailment, I fear I do not comprehend sir."

"No matter, my very best to him I pray, my very best, and you are always welcome ma'am. Now I fear I must withdraw, most reluctantly, from your presence," he made a sweeping bow and afterwards, in a sharper tone, addressed Molly. "Should you return to town Mistress Tyler you must indeed call, but first perhaps forewarn me of your visit."

Still distracted by his mention of my father's health, I listened to the sound of his footsteps receding up the stairway and then glanced at Molly, but she seemed unaware of anything except her surroundings, and stood staring about the room, her eyes wide with admiration.

"Such a chamber Pleasance, would I had such a place. All these bottles full of physic that the good doctor does administer. He do say he has potions for all manner of ailments, and be renowned here about for his cures."

I glanced at the bottles, and pulled a face. "The liquid seems much clouded, and what pray, floats within? And was he not to show you how to set a bone?"

"They be exotic herbs from foreign lands, as to the bone, I'm to call another time for he's much occupied at present."

I examined a bottle of murky liquid more closely. The object within appeared oval and dimpled, and bore no resemblance to a plant. As I stared, Hugh began to mumble and Molly smiled sympathetically.

"We must away for poor lad's fair clemmed, and we've yet to call upon Master Wallace." She ushered us towards the stairway. "So kind of the good doctor to show us his treasures, but we must away."

On emerging into the hallway I was surprised to find it deserted, and whispered, "We cannot leave without paying our respects, shall we knock upon yonder door?"

"No," Molly replied, leading us towards the front door. "Grand folk do often treat visitors so, and the good doctor has much to do, as he did say."

I silently disagreed. Even in the most humble of Fretson's cottages, villagers never left their guests unattended, but I was glad to be once more in the street. Stamford's air was not as fresh as that of Fretson, but it was preferable to the fetid atmosphere of Doctor Percival's strange chamber.

Molly continued to praise the doctor, until we reached Master Wallace's house in Castle Street, where our knock was answered by the lawyer himself. Clad in his customary severe Puritan garb, he was a thin, undernourished looking man, and although his welcome was polite, his expression was cold as he suggested Hugh and I should await Molly in the small square hallway, while their business was conducted.

It was not a pleasant wait. The hallway was dank and gloomy, and Hugh was restless. He seemed nervous and I was wondering how to distract him, when a door opened and Master Wallace emerged, followed by Molly carrying a large leather purse.

"So you will Mistress Tyler, please to keep me informed," the lawyer's thin lips were very taut, and his voice was sharp and rasping.

"But of course sir, that I'll do and kind ye've been, and when'll ye wish me again to call?"

"I see no reason for a further visit, prior to Lady Day(23)," Master Wallace opened the front door, and made me a rather stiff bow. "Good day Mistress Fry, my best to your father."

Before I had a chance to respond the door closed, and were once more standing in the street. Molly gave me a satisfied smile, and thrust the leather purse deep into the pocket of her skirt.

"I'm pleased that I am, to have such wise counsel. Good Master Wallace did say much that was of help. The river bank, I do think should be the place to eat, for the Welland be a pretty sight from there."

Surprised by her praise, I asked, "Is not Master Wallace a most severe man, for so he is thought of in Fretson?"

"Bless ye, so are all men of such matters. Goodwife Hargreaves did think him a man of honour, and so he has proved to be with me. For why do ye ask?"

Remembering my father speak once of the lawyer's many visits to our late neighbour, I enquired, "Why did he not call upon you, as he did the Goodwife? I do never recall my father saying that she did ever travel to Stamford to conduct her business."

Molly shook her head. "Why bless ye child, the poor soul could no longer call on any one. 'twas rare she ever rose from her bed, 'tis fitting that I should call on so great a man."

Still dubious, I persisted, "Master Westley does bring my father a horse when one is so required. My father is not expected to collect it from the forge."

Molly stared at me in apparent surprise. "Of what import is that, pray? As I did say, on so great a man it be fitting that I should call."

Obviously convinced that I knew nothing of such matters she gave me a quick hug, and then guided us to the Welland. I refrained from pursuing the matter further, but I knew she was wrong. Goodwife Hargreaves had never been known to visit her lawyer, even before her illness Master Wallace had always visited her cottage, had there been any business to conduct.

I glanced at Molly's animated features, and thought how strange it was that someone so astute, could be so easily deluded by men such as Master Wallace and Doctor Percival. Thoughts of the doctor, reminded me of his remarks regarding my father and I said, "I could not comprehend as to what ailment Doctor Percival referred, when he did speak of my father."

Molly gave one of her shrugs. "'twas possibly yer father's cough."

"His cough?" I gave Molly a sharp glance. "Did you speak of it to the doctor, when he did visit you?"

"'tis possible I talked of it, in passing," Molly cheeks reddened. "The physic I did give ye the doctor did remark on and asked to whom 'twas administered. He was much impressed, as I remember." She flushed even deeper, and gave me a wary glance. "Are ye displeased? I meant no harm."

Quelling my irritation, I replied, "I am not displeased, but I did say to you most clearly Molly, that I did not wish my father's cough to be spoken of. He does not wish to talk of it. But no matter," I added hurriedly, seeing her worried expression. "No harm has been done, but I am much bewildered by his inference that he does know my father. How, I wonder, can they have become acquainted."

"Perhaps it's an acquaintance of long standing," she suggested. "Mayhap the doctor did attend yer mother's lying-in."

"My birth, Molly you do indeed speak in a most singular manner."

She laughed. "Not so, we're all born and a body must be by to tend us. Why not the good doctor?"

"It is not seemly to speak so, especially before your brother."

She smiled gently. "The poor lad'll not comprehend, and if he does, 'tis not likely 'twill stay within his brain more than a mere moment," she looked away for a second, then laughed. "Now must we find ourselves a place to sit."

Having settled on the high grassy bank of Castle Meadow, we had an excellent view of the George Inn, and as we ate could watch the departure and arrival of coaches, riders and great carts, as they traversed the road from north to south.

"Would it not be splendid to be travelling down yonder road, to the great city?" Molly exclaimed, as a brilliantly painted coach drove away from the Inn.

I nodded, thinking of the seas and lands beyond the great capital, and she laughed. "And now I have set ye dreaming, and what fine land do ye see?"

I sighed. "I fear I dream too much, it is a bad trait."

"Not so," she replied. "We must all dream, or life would indeed be hard. Why, here does come our brave knight," she added, as Thomas came cantering towards us along the river-bank, enthusiastically waving his hat.

"'tis time mistress, Master Bailey does await ye at yonder gate, if ye please that is."

I was apprehensive that the carter might still be in a bad mood, but he had obviously eaten and drunk well, for he gave us a hearty wave as we approached. His joviality increased as the journey progressed, and he was regaling us loudly with more ominous stories of highwaymen when Molly cried out, "Master Bailey, do ye kindly stop the cart. Pleasance, see ye the poor creature in yonder field?"

Before any of us could reply she had jumped down from the cart, and was running towards three boys who appeared to be throwing stones at something on the ground. Thomas, who had been trotting ahead, turned his horse and swiftly followed Molly, who was now chasing the fleeing boys.

"What in the Good Lord's name?" Master Bailey exclaimed, putting a restraining hand on Hugh, who was attempting to jump down from the cart. "Nay lad, do you be still. What's to do, Thomas?" He called out to the Post Boy, who was now cantering back towards us.

"Some lads throwing stones at yon cat. Half dead 'tis, but mistress she says she can cure it. It be very small," he added, as Molly reached the cart calling to her brother, "Hugh, do you jump down and assist me, and Pleasance do ye take this poor creature."

I hesitated. The cat was bleeding profusely from a number of small gashes on it's flanks, and I was reluctant to soil my gown. Then pity overcame my distaste, and I put out my arms as Hugh jumped down to assist his sister. As he did so he glanced sharply up at me, and I wondered, yet again, how much he understood.

The cat and Molly having been ensconced comfortably in the cart, and Hugh having closed the backboard, Master Bailey gave him a friendly slap on the back.

"'tis a good head ye have on yon shoulders lad, no matter what folks say." He twisted round in his seat and stared down at the animal, now resting contentedly in Molly's lap. "And what'll ye do with yon creature? 'tis more dead than alive, so 'tis."

"I shall succour it and 'twill survive, Master Bailey, ye'll see," she replied firmly, before adding indignantly, "Did ye see the cruelty of those lads, Pleasance? The poor creature had done them no hard, why 'tis no more than a kitten. How cruel are some folk, how very cruel."

I gave a reluctant nod. The only animals I was acquainted with either worked for their keep, or were kept to be consumed, and the few dogs in Fretson were used for hunting. As to cats, there were none I knew of in the village, and I remembered Old Mother Burrows' tales of a time, before the war, when village folk kept animals for pleasure and companionship but that was before the witch-hunts and the revelation that such animals could be familiars. I wanted to tell Molly of my concern, but knowing that she would only laugh I said nothing, and remained watching as she continued to stroke the animal's soft fur.

CHAPTER 11

Immediately upon my return, my father questioned me with great interest about our day, and after accepting the belt with gratifying pleasure, he looked most thoughtful when I spoke of the soldiers we had encountered.

"A company riding south, most singular, perhaps the rumours of a great happening in London town has substance, though I know not of what it is(24). But none of this is of any consequence to us child; now, what of the physician and Master Wallace?"

"He was most civil father and did send his best to you, but Doctor Percival did say you were acquainted."

He gave a deep laugh. "I did know him well, but our ways have not crossed for nigh on one score years. A good man, but he has strayed I fear. Mammon has touched him with her tawdry hand, and he has forgot that the brain the Good Lord gave him is for the many, not the few. But I will not speak ill of him for he does help those who seek his aid, and has gained some note in his profession with his discussions of Master Harvey's study of man's blood.(25) How very singular that you should have met, and I see from your look of disbelief child, that you cannot conceive how such as he and I could have been acquainted. But you are now old enough to comprehend my little tale. Our acquaintance did commence when I first visited your dear mother. I was one of many suitors for her hand and Master Horace, for that is his given name, were friends and rivals too. He had much to offer, but she did have a preference for me, and my life here. Horace was much discomposed, and unable to comprehend why your dear mother chose to deny herself the life of ease she would have enjoyed, had she married him."

As he spoke, an expression of tranquillity settled on his features and I hesitated to intrude, but my curiosity overcame me. "I saw no children, does he not have family?"

"No, he and Mistress Percival were never so blessed. It is the greatest sorrow of his life, but she being a sickly lady mayhap it is for the best. Now, the hour is late, and you are weary, you must to bed."

I rose obediently, but there was one more matter I had to report to ensure a restful night. "We did see a witch father, taken to the Assizes at Oakham town."

"A witch?" He looked concerned. "I had not heard of such a matter. What was her sin?"

"I know not, I saw only a woman roped to a horse and soldiers, and they did make her run and her feet bled and I did recite the Lord's Prayer, and downcast my eyes for fear."

Despite my efforts to retain my composure my voice began to rise, and my father leaned forward and taking my hand, said gently, "Hush child, do not distress yourself. Many painful sights are seen these troubled times. Here in this quiet village we know little of the outside world, but it is only right that you should learn of what occurs." He released my hand with a gentle pat. "A passing matter of no concern to you; now to your bed, and I will call Bessie from the outer parlour to her pallet, and thank you again my child for the gift."

It was not until I had said my prayers, and was almost asleep, that I remembered that I had forgotten to give him the shirt, or tell him about Molly's new cat. But these problems were soon forgotten a few days later when, to my discomfort, my father announced, "It is I believe on Wednesday that we may expect Master Radley's visit, is it not child?"

"So I understand father," I replied, working my wheel energetically, perhaps too much so for, from the corner of my eye, I saw him give me a puzzled look. I had deliberately kept myself well employed since the visit to Stamford, but my attempts at concealment were to prove unnecessary, for Master Radley chose to arrive at his cousin's cottage during the early hours of the morning.

Awakened by the sound of a horse's hooves I scrambled from my bed, only to reach my shutters in time to hear Molly's cry of welcome, before her cottage door closed. Later that same morning, after my father had departed to his work, I retired to my chamber to seek distraction with *Homer,* and attempted to concentrate on the burial of Patroclus. But Achilles's rallying call to the Myrmidons seemed to lack a certain element of substance, when compared with the sounds of male laughter I could hear emanating from next door. After an hour, during which I was able to translate only four lines of a stanza I knew by heart, I decided that possibly a little spinning might prove more absorbing.

It was as I was returning The Iliad to its place on my father's chamber floor, that I noticed the cloths. Neatly folded on his bed, they must originally have been white, but were now stained a pale pink hue, and appeared to be well worn. Assuming them to be some part of a man's undergarments, but without remembering having ever washed such articles, I turned away, not wishing to intrude on my father's privacy. He returned a little later to announce that he had now met the visitor, and considered him to be an articulate, well read young man, of sense and pleasing aspect.

"I must confess I did not expect such a man of education. He did make a fine account of himself, and all that he wishes to achieve. I was impressed. He talks of opening a further forge at the next village, and is to take two more apprentices at his forge in Goodborough, where he has already another man."

I tried to look impressed, as my father cleared his throat with apparent difficulty, before continuing, "I fear I am to Duddington before sunrise tomorrow morn, child. Preacher Wyman does have the colic and cannot go. It will be a visit of no more than two days. I have hired Master Bailey's roan mare. She is a quiet beast, and should give no bother." He tried to clear his throat again, but only succeeded in coughing heavily, and I rose swiftly to offer a cup of water, but he waved a dismissive hand and gasping, "Excuse me child," hurried towards the stairway with his kerchief to his mouth.

The next day I awoke to discover he had already gone, and the rain pouring heavily. Apart from my concern for his welfare, I was only too relieved to be confined indoors where, once again, I spun energetically while Bessie kneaded her dough. After eating, I despatched Bessie to Mistress Machin and was once again attempting to concentrate on Homer, when I realised that Bessie had been absent for longer than was customary. Concerned, but reluctant to leave the safety of my retreat, I was about to prepare the evening meal when she reappeared, very dishevelled and gabbling, "Mistress Machin did keep me, mistress, and I did fear ye'd be angered if I was too wet so I did shelter as best I could."

Her explanation seemed strange. Mistress Machin was a somewhat haughty matron, and I could not imagine her finding anything to discuss with a girl such as Bessie Workman, so I asked, "And where did you take shelter?"

"''twas here and there, mistress; here and there," she gulped. "For sure sorry, that I be."

Seeing her distress, I said reassuringly, "No matter, it is of no consequence. But do you next time explain to Mistress Machin, politely mind, that you have duties and cannot stay."

The rain was still pouring when I was aroused next morning by the sounds of cartwheels and horses struggling through the mud. Without Molly's lively company the hours stretched monotonously ahead, but they were a panacea compared to the terror with which I anticipated the Lord's Day, when I would be forced to meet her kinsman.

My father returned home late on Saturday evening looking pale and tired, and coughing heavily. The journey had been difficult, due to the muddy roads and his horse having cast a shoe. I wanted to offer him a hot drink but we had only cold milk and water, both of which he declined. I thought how, but for the intruder next door, I could have warmed the milk and made some gruel on Molly's fire, or begged a portion of the stew which was probably heating in the large iron pot.

Contrary to my hopes, since I foolishly believed that poor weather might have persuaded the visitor to forego Sunday worship, the dreaded day dawned fine, with a strong June sun pouring her glow into my chamber. Having spent an almost sleepless night, I accompanied my father and Bessie to church with my eyes directed to the ground. As was the custom we were the first arrivals, and while he was occupied with his drum, I followed Bessie to our usual seats with a trembling stomach.

The first congregants to arrive were the Westleys, followed quickly by the Machins, and Master Bailey and his family. Mistress Burridge arrived next, and then the church began to fill rapidly. Very aware that Molly and her party were still absent, my stomach continued to churn and the sensation increased when, suddenly, I heard an unfamiliar male voice.

I gripped my Puritan Directory tightly, while trying to concentrate on words that had suddenly become very blurred, as Bessie squeaked, "'tis Mistress Wallace's son, be he not handsome?" She pulled excitedly at my sleeve as a young cavalry officer walked past, preceded by Mistress Wallace. The task of quietening Bessie calmed me, and relief seemed to encompass my entire body, until I heard Molly's voice urging Hugh into his place.

Never had Preacher Wyman's address seemed so long, but the boredom did at least calm me to the extent that my hands stopped sweating, and my stomach regained some form of equilibrium.

The meeting having ended, some people began moving into the aisle, while others congregated around the Wallaces. Ignoring Bessie's urgings that I should take my customary place at the back of the church I remained sitting rigidly in my seat, as I heard Master Westley's voice boom out in response to Molly's introduction, "I'm indeed pleased to make yer acquaintance, Master Radley. Ye must come to me forge. I would fain know what ye think of me ways, and I indeed wish to hear of yer cure for greasy leg which, Mistress Tyler tells me you do practice in Goodborough."

"Indeed sir, it will be my pleasure." The calm and confident reply was expressed in a gentleman's voice, with the deference a well-bred younger man adopts when conversing with his elders.

"Mistress?" Bessie was obviously impatient to move, but I remained seated as my father approached from down the aisle.

"Pleasance, you have not taken your customary place, ah, Mistress Wallace." He turned hurriedly, as my unexpected saviour approached with her son, followed closely by Preacher Wyman.

There was a flurry of greetings, and I glanced up to see Daniel Wallace smiling at me. I remembered him as a thin pale youth, forever subservient to his mother's slightest wish, but the years of military service had changed him into a muscular, strong-faced man, with a pleasant expression and easy manner. He bowed, and good manners forced me to rise in acknowledgement. As I did so, I heard my father present William Radley to the assembled company, which then moved slowly in a body down the aisle.

Protected by my father's form, I glanced surreptitiously at the visitor. Contrary to Molly's description he was clean-shaven, and taller by a head than Daniel Wallace. His back and shoulders were also wider, and what I could see of his face appeared refined, rather than handsome.

Outside the church, Mistress Wallace made much show of presenting her son to those folk still gathered in the roadway, while Molly and her little family commenced walking towards their cottage. Watching them, I wished suddenly I had the courage to follow.

"Mistress Wallace does tell me her son has been unwell, and has been returned home to recover," my father announced later, as we ate our meal. "A malady of the shoulder, resulting from a fall from his horse at Plymouth. These mishaps when riding do seem rife, do they not, when one does think of poor Thomas, thrown not so long since? And what think you of her other news, that our Lord Cromwell has now been proclaimed Lord Protector? Those soldiers you saw child on the road to Stamford were no doubt summoned for the ceremony. But what of our new neighbour," he added abruptly. "Did you not think I was correct in my judgement?"

I swallowed the suddenly unwieldy food with difficulty, before replying, "I did not speak with him father, but he was indeed polite and seemly. But the Lord Cromwell," I added, hoping to divert him, "is it not a great honour?"

He gave me a rather intense look, before murmuring, "It is rare to meet a young man who can combine scholarship, with labour and endeavour. As to our Lord Cromwell's elevation, I doubt it will touch humble folk the likes of us."

There was a brief pause, during which I occupied myself gathering our used plates, very aware of my father's reflective glance, but to my relief Master Radley's name was not mentioned again, and the evening service passed very much as the morning had, with Molly and her companions leaving without further introductions being made.

The next day being Monday, it was one of Bessie's duties to scrub and wash down the stone flags and the entrance. She hated the work, and I was always forced to be present to ensure she performed to my satisfaction. On this particular occasion I decided to leave her to her own devices, rather than expose myself to the possibility of encountering William Radley. So I retired to my chamber where, leaning on my casement, I watched the road below.

There was not much of interest to observe, there being only three villagers and two horsemen passing within a half hour and I sighed, thinking how I would have been occupied in Molly's cottage, had there been no intruder present. I was thus absorbed when from below, Bessie screamed, "Mistress, 'tis the master, please to come."

Shocked, I rushed down the stairs in time to see my father, white faced and his garments splattered with tiny drops of blood, stagger heavily to the floor. Shocked, I sank to my knees to try and assist him, only to discover that he was unconscious. Realising my helplessness, I cried out, "Go bring Mistress Tyler."

As Bessie fled, I attempted again to raise him, and this time succeeded in pulling his shoulders onto my lap. Assuming he must have fallen and hit his head, I searched for a bruise, but the only sign of injury seemed to be his bleeding nose. I was dabbing at the blood, when Molly rushed in, closely followed by her cousin and Daniel Wallace.

"Dear Heaven," she exclaimed. "William and Master Wallace, do ye carry Master Fry to his chamber. 'tis the one atop of the stair, is it not Pleasance?"

I nodded, and struggled to my feet as the two men lifted my father and began carrying him up the stairway. In his chamber they laid him gently down on the bed, and Molly loosened his bands while I stood helpless, staring down at the inert form. Preoccupied thus, I only realised Molly was no longer with us, when William said softly, "My cousin has gone for her physic. Is there aught else I can do?"

"I fear I know not," I whispered, trying to control my shaking limbs.

Then I saw that, though still unconscious, my father's face seemed to be regaining its normal colour and his breathing appeared easier.

"Has Master Fry before been taken thus?" Daniel asked, his voice curious.

"No, I have never known him to be ill, or to fall," I gasped as a great sob shook me, and I covered my face with my hands as Molly bustled in.

"There now, 'tis sorry I am to take so long, but all will soon be put to rights." She was carrying a small basket and some pieces of clean linen, and was followed by Bessie carrying a bowl of water.

"Now William, do ye go to my parlour and bring a little of the heated wine. Hurry now, and Pleasance," she added, pouring some liquid into a cup, and handing to me, "do ye take a little of this potion, 'twill calm ye, and Bessie do ye bring all the pillows in the house, while Master Wallace does help me remove Master Fry's soiled coat."

Sipping the thick, sweet liquid, I watched as my father was administered to until, feeling the need to break the silence, I said, "I cannot think how he could have fallen, never before have I know it to happen."

Molly gave me a worried look and appeared about to speak, when William entered carrying a tray on which rested a steaming bowl. "Is aught else required cousin, perhaps a fire below to heat the house?"

Before I could protest at his suggestion, Molly replied hurriedly, "No, only a warm coverlet from my chamber. Do ye go again cousin and fetch one."

By now Bessie had arrived with the pillows, and as soon as they were placed beneath my father's head his breathing became easier, and his eyes flickered open. Encouraged, I took his hand, only to flinch at the strength with which he gripped my palm. As he did so Molly raised his head, and held a cup of wine to his lips. He drank deeply, and then smiled at us.

"Pray forgive me for causing such a tumult, Pleasance. What did happen?"

"Ye did fall sir," Molly replied briskly before I could answer. "And now does come my cousin with a warm coverlet."

She spread the woollen sheet across my father's chest, and almost immediately he appeared to fall asleep. Considerably calmer and more aware of myself, I noticed that Daniel Wallace was glancing with obvious curiosity about the room.

"'tis a sparse chamber, Mistress Fry," he began, only to be interrupted quickly by William saying, "A scholar's chamber, I do envy your father his fine collection of books, Mistress Fry." He squatted down on his haunches, beside the neat heap of volumes. "The Verger does favour Master Donne and, I declare, a copy of Master Wilkins's '*A Discourse Concerning a New Planet*' and here we have that good scholar's '*Ecclesiastes*'. Molly lass, should you wish to bestow on me a gift, a copy of John Wilkins is my choice."

"John Wilkins, and who be John Wilkins?" Molly whispered, arching her eyebrows, and while Daniel laughed, I hurriedly explained, "He is a scholar of the sciences. My father does admire his work greatly."

"Master Wallace, sir," William Radley's murmur sounded vexed, "not so loud, your laughter is too robust for this chamber, and please forgive me ma'am, I did not mean to pry, but so many books, "tis a great temptation for a man who reads." He replaced the volumes carefully on their respective heaps, and stood up.

"Pleasance, child," my father's voice made us all turn to look at the bed, where he now lay with his eyes wide open. "It is strange that I should remember nothing that took place. But these kind friends, they have assisted you? I am most grateful and now child, I think I shall rest as I feel very weary."

"And we'll leave ye in peace, Master Fry," Molly replied gently. "But should ye have a thirst a little of the wine will revive you." She gave him a radiant smile, while murmuring to me. "Do ye have some linen to staunch the bleeding, should his nose again erupt."

Reluctant to say anything my father could not hear, I pointed to the linen chest. With an understanding nod, she raised the lid slightly and withdrew one of the clean, but stained pieces, and after giving it a cursory glance, tucked it neatly beneath my father's chin.

"There, could a body wish for more," she stepped back, surveying her handiwork with obvious satisfaction. "Now we must leave to let good Master Fry rest. Bessie, ye'll sit by yer master, and should he require drink do ye give him some of the wine on yonder chest. Mistress Fry will join us for some victuals. Should his nose once more bleed, do ye call me at once, at once d'ye mind."

"But I be hungry too," wailed my contrary little maid.

"Cease yer squawking, child," Molly admonished, but not unkindly. "Master Radley'll bring ye food, a fine pasty, and some bacon and beef pie." Bessie's subsequent smile stretched with an elasticity rarely seen in a human face, as Molly continued, "Now do we all depart. Master Fry will sleep for mayhap two hours. Come Pleasance to a warm meal, 'twill improve yer strength,"

"I do not think I should leave," I began, but Molly took my hand and ushered me to the stairway.

Before I was fully aware of what was happening, I had entered the friendly warmth of her cottage, to be greeted by the sight of the little black cat curled into a sleeping curve beside the fire.

Crouched on a low stool before the blaze, I sipped a mug of mulled wine and watched in silence, as she first despatched William with Bessie's pasty and beef pie, and then gently chided Hugh for spilling some ale down his shirt. It all seemed so friendly and familiar, and no one could harm me while I was with Molly, no one at all.

Lulled by her comforting attentions, I recall that I took my place beside William without any of the apprehension I had felt previously for, as so often is the case, the unknown had revealed itself to be but a terror of my imagination. Albeit our conversation was but trivial, and on my side barely audible, but any lack of response on my part was due to weariness, not fear.

But William's natural good nature and humour could not be subdued, and expressed itself many times, especially with regard to Bessie, of whom he asked with some hilarity, "How do you fare with yonder little maid, Mistress Fry? She is indeed open in her speech."

"I try," I commenced, only to be interrupted by Daniel, who announced with some disdain, "She is the oldest Workman, is she not? A flighty family, my mother would have them gone from the village."

Disconcerted, I glanced at Molly for support, but to my surprise she made no effort to defend the Workmans, concentrating instead on the cat which had jumped into her lap, and was now mewing loudly. Daniel rubbed its ears and grinned.

"I would judge that beast to be a wench. Only a female would rouse such clatter."

"Aye so she be," Molly retorted, gently stroking the soft fur. "But 'tis no clatter, it be but a mere wish to partake of our company."

"And our victuals, cousin," William interrupted laughing. "I fear Tannakin would fain partake of what we consume, than our company."

"Tannakin?" Daniel looked puzzled.

"Aye, so has my cousin named her," William explained. "But the explanation I cannot give, for 'tis more of a maze than any we could tread."

"Not so," Molly replied with some asperity. "'tis simple. 'Akin', because in truth so she be now to me, and Tann for 'twas the name given to the Hebrew's horse, and does remind me of my days in York."

Daniel frowned. "You must tell me of your time in York, mistress, for I did not find it such a goodly place. Scowls aplenty we did rouse, and a body would have thought Marston Moor(26) but a day distant, for all the welcome we did receive."

"'tis shameful," Molly protested, "that folk should be so treated, when they be innocent an' all."

"Innocence I fear cousin," William replied, "is of no avail, memories do not die and 'twas a fearful slaughter."

I watched uneasily as Daniel and Molly nodded agreement. My father would not have sympathised with the Royalists at Marston Moor, no matter what the slaughter. Possibly because of my expression, Molly commenced a considerable fuss whilst removing a steaming apple and cinnamon pudding from the oven. As it was sliced into generous portions, I was aware suddenly that I had consumed all put before me without one thought of frugality or moderation. Suddenly ashamed, I rose hesitantly, murmuring as I did so, "I will take Bessie's portion to her, for I would see how my father does."

"That ye will not," Molly retorted quickly. "The good Verger'll sleep sound for a many a time as yet, and William'll take Bessie her pie. Go lad, do as you are bid."

Thwarted, but too tired to argue, I sank back onto my seat as William obediently collected the dish. He had been gone but minutes, when there was a knock on the cottage door. Immediately Molly arose, and crossed swiftly to the entrance.

"Do not fret yerselves, 'tis some folk come no doubt for physic."

Although she attempted to fill the opening with her body, I glimpsed through the space that remained that the caller was Master Royton's daughter, Esther. A brief conversation in lowered tones followed, after which Molly closed the door.

"Another of your poor souls, come to seek your expert counsel Mistress Tyler?" Daniel grinned, flippantly so I thought.

Molly frowned, and her voiced sounded unexpectedly sharp, "No, she did come to enquire of a milking cow."

"A milking cow," Daniel laughed. "Why, mistress, do you now extend your physic ways to curing animals?"

Obviously distracted, Molly gave a weak smile, and then busied herself heating some more wine.

Apparently oblivious to her lack of response, Daniel gave another hearty laugh, and then remarked, "I wonder how does Master William fare. Think you yon little Workman will devour him with her pudding? You have a goodly bridle on him, mistress. Do you train all your men-folk to your ways?"

I considered Daniel's speech and manner to be impertinent but Molly responded in a roguish manner, saying archly, "Indeed sir, ye take liberties. My menfolk, as you so call them, are but Hugh and one cousin."

Daniel grinned, and I began to feel uncomfortable. There was a strange humour between Molly and this man that I could not discern, and I was relieved when William returned. Despite having consumed double the quantity of everyone else present, he made none of the digestive sounds customary on such occasions, and I noted how delicately he ate and how, like my father, he chewed with his mouth closed and wiped the grease from his fingers onto a kerchief spread across his knees, and did not brush his hands down his breeches, as did Daniel.

Taking advantage of his attention being diverted elsewhere, I examined him through half-closed lids. Like Molly, he had the same long slender nose and wide generous lips, but William's hair was a deep chestnut, and the eyes that suddenly raised themselves to mine were a dark clear grey. Caught unawares I felt myself grow hot, but he merely smiled gently at me, as he asked Molly for more pudding.

"In faith Will, you do consume much food," Daniel exclaimed. "'tis no wonder you are such a size."

"'tis work he does, not sit upon a horse and wave a sword such as the likes of ye," Molly retorted, and the two men laughed but Hugh, who had until then been silent, suddenly began muttering and staring angrily at Daniel. William quickly gripped Hugh's left hand tightly in his own.

"There my lad, not to take on so, 'twas no harm meant, 'twas mere funning."

"He did think I was angered," Molly smiled affectionately. "He can't abide when I'm distressed."

"Nay lad, I did mean no harm," Daniel sounded reassuring. "'twas as your cousin does say, naught but mere sport."

Apparently reassured, Hugh subsided into silence as William asked, "Mistress Fry, I have much interest in the limestone quarries hereabouts. I would visit them."

Taken unawares, I hesitated, then with growing confidence replied, "Indeed sir, I am sure someone will take you. Most men hereabouts who do not work the land are so engaged. Walter Osborne and his two sons do work a number, and

Master Pridmore and his eldest son and the Naylors and, of course, Hugh and many more, but it is hard, so my father tells me and not work that is good for health."

"William does collect stone," Molly explained. "Old stone of past days."

"Old stone," I repeated eagerly. "Why sir, my father has told me of such an interest. It did begin in Italy two centuries gone, with the finding of ancient Greek sculptures."

"Yes, indeed," William replied with equal enthusiasm. "'tis said there is much more to be made known, if men could dig thereabouts for, from these ancient stones much of past history of this world can be found. Know you of one William Camden? A true scholar, he did learn both the Anglo-Saxon and Welsh tongues, so that he could study the place names of his interest. He did write a fine book, by name 'Britannia' . Did I not see this manual amidst the others of the good Verger's library."

"Yes, my father does indeed have such a book," I hesitated before murmuring impulsively, "if you would care to read it, sir, I am sure he would not object."

"I would most certainly, Mistress Fry, but I would not wish to intrude upon the Verger's privacy. I did take liberties but a while since, when in his chamber."

Suddenly aware that Molly and Daniel were no longer in the room I flushed, and muttered, "I think I must now to my father."

"Of course," William stood up. "Cousin, Mistress Fry must leave. Did you not say you wished to accompany her?"

"Indeed 'tis so," Molly emerged alone from the back parlour. "'tis possible the Verger be sleeping still, but we'll see."

"For the time being, Mistress Fry, thank you for your company," William gave me a quick bow and a smile and I nodded in return, before following Molly from the cottage.

Back in my own front parlour, with its dank cold atmosphere, I began immediately to shiver violently, and Molly regarded me with concern. "Please, I do declare ye should let us set a fire. 'tis a cold day, despite the month and with yer father ill, and all."

"I will ask him," I replied hurriedly, feeling suddenly overwhelmed by her presence. "Please let us go and see how he does fare."

"He'll be sleeping and will not wake till morn'."

"Morning, but Molly that is hours hence."

"So do I know, but 'twas of consequence that he did sleep. His malady will demand much rest."

"Malady?" I felt again the fear of earlier returning. "You speak again of malady?"

"Come let us sit," she guided me to a chair before continuing. "Ye've spoken to me of yer father's cough."

"Yes you know full well I have."

"And ye did see the stained linen in his chamber?"

I nodded, and my stomach contracted sharly.

"Well, "tis a malady of the chest, which causes blood to flow when ere he coughs."

"Why did he not tell me?" I clenched my fists, overcome with resentment. "When did he tell you, and why have you not disclosed such to me before?"

"Master Fry did not tell me, and I did not know prior." Molly's voice so calm and measured only incensed me more, and I wanted to hit out at her soft mouth and gentle eyes as she continued, "'twas only when I saw the blood did I comprehend the case. 'tis due to his wish no doubt, that ye should not be distressed, that he did withhold the truth from ye."

"And for how long, pray, does the malady last?" I asked, almost fearful of her reply.

"It can last many months, but with physic and warmth the pain can be eased and the flux lessened."

"Pain," I gasped from a mouth that had gone suddenly very dry.

"Aye, there be pain as the malady does spread."

"The malady spreads, does it not lessen? Is he going to die?" Her brow creased as she nodded, and I asked agitatedly. "How can you say thus? How do you know of this malady?"

"'tis a bloody flux of the chest." Her voice had dropped to a whisper. "I've seen much of it in Goodborough and in York. The Hebrew did have a servant so struck down, and I did learn much of its nursing. We'll help him Pleasance, we'll give him physic and I'll be but a few steps distant. Now do ye let me send for Hugh to lay a fire, for 'tis necessary that there be warmth. We have the wood and 'twill take but a moment. Then I'll send in hot porridge with which yer father can break his fast."

"He will not permit a fire." My voice rose as hysteria overcame me. "And my father is a good man. Always he has prayed to the Good Lord for help, and so shall I. He will not desert us, I know he will not." My words ended in a convulsive sob, and I began to cry. After that I remember only the sound of footsteps and movements before our grate, then the gradual feel of warmth as the newly laid fire began to radiate its heat about the room. Someone, it must have been Molly, urged me to my chamber where gentle hands disrobed me, and helped me to slip beneath the covers.

My last memory of that strange, and terrible day, was the thick sweet liquid which she bade me drink, before comforting arms entwined themselves about me, and I fell into a deep, dreamless sleep.

CHAPTER 12

July/August 1657

The liquid Molly administered caused me to awaken refreshed and calm, until I remembered my father's illness. I hurried to his chamber. The room was empty, and the bedcovers smooth. There was nothing to indicate that it had been the chamber of an ailing man. Bewildered, I ran down the stairway to discover him sitting in his usual chair, with his legs propped on the fender before a high-backed fire, reading his bible.

A surge of relief engulfed me like a palliative, only to be followed immediately by anger. How wicked of Molly to frighten me, when my father was so obviously not ill. He certainly had a cough, but many people were so afflicted, especially during summer. I stepped forward, and he looked up.

"Child, you will take chill. Do you return to your chamber, and dress?"

"I came only to see how you did, sir"

"I do well Pleasance, go now and dress yourself."

He frowned, but never had a rebuke been so gladly received. As I hesitated, Bessie entered from the back parlour.

"Mistress you so clad and Master Radley coming in an' all." As she finished speaking, I heard the sound of footsteps on the path, followed by a knock on the door, which sent me fleeing back upstairs.

In my chamber, I gave way to my joy by wrapping my arms about my body, and giving myself a tight hug. As I stood thus Bessie entered, carrying a jug of steaming water. "The master did say I were to bring this, and 'tis fine we are now with hot water, and I did wash myself all over this morning so I did, and master did have hot porridge and hot drink."

As I took the jug, she retrieved my chamber pot from a corner of the room. Remembering William was below, I said hurriedly, "You may leave that until later."

"Master Radley be gone now," she gave me a sly glance. "He stayed no more'an a minute."

I ignored her. There were times when Bessie could be irritatingly astute.

When she had gone, I washed slowly, bathing first my arms and then my breasts, enjoying the feel of warmth against my skin. Then I remembered with a shock that I had promised to lend William my father's *'Britannia'*, without first obtaining permission. Concerned as to what I should tell William if my father refused, I finished dressing and then hurried apprehensively downstairs. As I entered he looked up, and pointed to the fire.

"It is an extravagance, but one in which we should indulge. I fear it is possible we have been too frugal in our endeavours to follow the Good Lord's way. Why did you not tell me child, that you did have pained hands each winter? And we must in future retain a little more of our milk and cream. Now do you eat, Bessie has laid your bowl upon the table but a few seconds past."

Any resentment I felt that these luxuries were due to Molly's intervention, were quickly dispelled by the sight of the steaming porridge and jug of cream. Almost afraid that the delicacies would vanish before I could consume them, I mumbled Grace with a speed that I now reflect on with shame. As I ate, I was trying to decide how to broach the subject of *'Britannia,'* when my father said:

"Why child I near forgot, Master Radley did say Mistress Molly requests your company this morning, and I did accept on your behalf, that is so, is it not?"

"Yes, father," I replied, before adding apprehensively, "I do beg forgiveness for so doing, prior to requesting your assent, but I did say Master Radley may have a sight of *'Britannia'*, for he has an interest in ancient works."

"William Camden's instructive tome, certainly child you may take him the book. It is a goodly manual, and one he will find edifying. I would John Leland's works of a similar nature had been published, but I fear that was not to be.(27) He was Keeper of King Henry VIII's Library and made a great study of ancient structures, but was fearful of arousing his royal master's displeasure, were he to prove himself more academically accomplished. This is but hearsay, and I have no facts on which to base such a pronouncement. Mayhap Master Radley has more extensive knowledge, and could enlighten you. He is a goodly lad, I like him." He smiled gently, before continuing, "Now I fear I must bid you good day, child. For work calls me away."

My meal having been completed, and my father's copy of *'Britannia'* having been procured, I proceeded next door. Walking past Molly's parlour window, I saw myself reflected in the glass, and blushed. I looked as if I was bouncing instead of walking, and the smile, which somehow I could not subdue, seemed to raise my cheekbones almost to my eyes.

William opened the door, and overcome with sudden embarrassment, I thrust the book at him. "I thank you, Mistress Fry that is most kind. Please to enter, cousin Molly will be but a moment. She is administering physic to young Jacob Pridmore, your good tanner's youngest son"

"Pleasance, dearest friend I did not hear yer knock."Molly bustled in from the back parlour ushering out Mistress Pridmore, and Jacob, a child of five who looked very weak and flushed. She put an arm about the older woman's shoulders.

"Now do ye give Jacob the potion and do ye spread the liniment on his skin, and within a few days all will be cured."

Having urged the grateful mother out of the cottage, Molly closed the door. "The poor woman's so distressed, but 'twas a mere boil that needed lancing."

"But would that not cause great pain," I exclaimed. "I did not hear him cry."

"Molly does have many ways, her cures to perform, Mistress Fry." William grinned. "Did you not know she weaves especial spells?"

"Hush yerself," Molly interrupted quickly, "such foolish talk is not for polite company. Come now Hugh, whyfore do ye not greet our guest? That be better, a smile's always a welcome sight. We are to Royton Farm Pleasance, for I've some medicines for a milk-maid with the quinsy."

"And what of Master Royton's cow?" I asked, remembering Esther's visit of the previous day.

Molly frowned, then replied, "Nay lass, that was but jesting. Poor Esther had but mild colic. She did return this early morn, and I did tend her."

William looked at his cousin in surprise. "I heard nothing at what hour did she call?"

"I forget. Ye were at Master Westley's forge, but it be of no consequence. If I did tell ye of every soul who does visit me for physic, we'd remain within for the day. Come now Will do ye move, for with your great size before yon door, us poor souls can't see light of day."

The cousins continued to tease each other as we walked towards the bridge, and as we passed Master Westley's forge the farrier gave us a cry of greeting, which William acknowledged with a wave.

"Did you find aught at the forge of interest that you do not have at Goodborough?" I enquired.

He nodded enthusiastically. "It is a fine place he has, but understand I cannot why he does not have an apprentice on hire. It would be good for a lad, to be taught by so fine a master."

"William do believe that knowledge should be passed to all, as do ye to me," Molly explained.

William smiled. "I must thank you Mistress Fry for teaching my cousin her letters. Such a feat I did try many times, but to no avail."

"Did try many times," Molly exclaimed. "Why 'twas but once, and a shabby struggle 'twas too."

"But you did not stay beyond a ten minute," William protested. "My cousin, Mistress Fry, did wish to stay within the big house, rather than visit my humble home and though, in good faith, I did try to teach her, she did not linger to read a single word."

We had now reached the outskirts of Master Royton's apple orchard, where village women and girls were busy collecting the first apples of the season. At the sight of William, a few of the women called out saucily, inviting him to join them. Embarrassed by their ribaldry I looked away, but William returned their laughter, and having begged four apples from one of the older women handed them out to us with an air of triumph.

Molly laughed. "Ye could coax ducks off a pond, so ye could Will."

"Ducks are not of interest," he replied with a grin. "But the comfort of ladies is, and I would suggest we rest to eat our booty." So saying he took off his coat and spread it over some dry grass. Immediately, Hugh removed his own coat, and imitating his cousin spread his garment alongside. With a big sigh Molly sank down onto the coats, pulling me down with her, and we sprawled helplessly across each other, our arms entwined.

William laughed. "Well now, here be a pretty sight."

From where I lay looking upwards, he seemed gigantic, bestriding the ground as I imagined had the Colossus of Rhodes. Aware suddenly of his eyes upon me, I felt my face begin to glow and struggled to a sitting position, as Molly hit out playfully at William's legs. He grinned, and then sitting down cross-legged before us, he held an arm out to Hugh. "Come lad, do you sit as well."

With an enormous smile, Hugh squatted down on his haunches as William said, "Molly does tell me, Mistress Fry, that you did show her a fine map of the world."

Remembering my father's words that morning, I replied with enthusiasm, "Would you care to have a sight, Master Radley?"

"Indeed I would, if the good Verger does not object to yet another of his books being so used? Is it not strange that men did think the world to be flat, and that a fine scientist who proved otherwise, should have suffered so?"

Molly frowned. "Of whom do ye speak?"

"Galileo Galilei," I explained. "He was a most learned Italian who did teach in Pisa and Padua, two towns of that country. He did write that the heavenly bodies do move around the sun, not otherwise as had been believed. But the Inquisition did believe this thought unGodly, and he did renounce his teachings."

"For why?" Molly frowned.

"I do believe they did threaten him, with death," I replied.

"And these were great teachings?"

"The work of his life."

"And he did deny them?"

"Yes."

"Then he deserved not such a mind, to cast off all in which he did believe," Molly spread her hands in disgust.

"But they did threaten him with death," I protested.

"I would I'd such a brain," Molly replied firmly. "For I could be threatened with two horses to tear me asunder, afore I'd deny what I know to be true."

"But.." I began again, before William interrupted, smiling, "In faith Mistress Fry, I fear you will not persuade my cousin to another way. Not when she is in such a thinking manner. You will have read of Nicolas Copernicus(28), for his were the writings that 'tis said did influence Galileo."

I nodded, as Molly declared, "And Nicholas Whatever, did he too deny himself, and cast off the work of his life?"

"Nay, he did die in his bed, a much revered scholar," William replied, with a laugh.

Molly sighed. "I fear my letters and my reading will ne'er reach a whit of you, or Pleasance."

"Fear not cousin, you have qualities neither of us can boast, is that not so, Mistress Fry?"

I nodded eagerly, and then flushed as William raised Molly's right hand to his lips, and gently kissed it. She pulled her hand away, and tapped him lightly on the cheek. "Away with you, villain, "tis my venison pie, and my apple pudding that does move ye so. He does know that both do lie within this basket Pleasance, and does know how to please, when he has wishes of his own. Trust him not, for he is such a man, I fear."

She gave her cousin a playful glance and he sprang to his feet, to assist us both to rise. As his hands took mine they felt warm and dry, and for a reason I could not comprehend, the sensation made me feel safe, and protected. We continued strolling in friendly silence, until I enquired of William when he intended to visit the quarry.

"Master Westley is to arrange for Gideon Osborne, the eldest of Master Osborne's sons to take me today week."

We had now reached Master Royton's farm where we were greeted by the jovial farmer, and after he had ushered us into his wife's huge friendly kitchen, Molly hurried away to administer to the dairy-maid. The table was covered in platters of freshly baked pasties, but before Mistress Royton had a chance to offer us anything, Molly returned saying we had another call to make, and bustled us out into the yard.

"Do you not wish to see how Esther does?" I asked.

"Nay, the lass did say her mother over frets, and 'twas naught but colic, as I did say. Now shall we to our glade and take some food. I've told Will of our secret place and he's eager to see it. Come quickly now, for 'tis near midday."

Puzzled by her abrupt manner, when there was no need for speed and certainly no other call to make, I followed Molly into the glade where William immediately began comparing the area, with a similar glade near Goodborough. "Do you not remember cousin, when you did return from York?"

"Yes, indeed," Molly interrupted, rather too hurriedly, I thought. "Now do ye sit and let us eat."

The food having been distributed, we sat eating contentedly until the sun sent beams glinting through the overhanging branches, and a swan appeared gliding elegantly across the water.

Molly stared admiringly. "There be a fine sight. 'tis the first time be it not Pleasance, that we've seen such a bird. Are swans common, hereabouts?"

"It is the first one I have seen on Chater stream," I replied. "At Berwick House I do believe, they have many. Mayhap, the swan did fly from Berwick lake."

"No matter from where it comes, it is a majestic sight," William nodded reflectively. "But 'tis not common to see one swan alone. Like us folk, they unite for life, and should they lose their spouse they do pine until they die. Did someone not write,

The silver swan who living had no note,

95

When death approached unlocked her silent throat,

Leaning her breast against the reedy shore,

Thus sung her first and last and sung no more."(29)

"That's right fair, Will," Molly exclaimed. "Is it not fine, Pleasance?"

Very aware of William's eyes staring at me I nodded, as he said, "Fine it maybe lass, but also sad, for swans do but sing when they die."

There was a short pause, during which William gazed reflectively at the stream, until I asked shyly, "From whence did come that poem, Master Radley?"

"I know not the author's name, but "twas in a book I did once see in Nottingham town. Are you a reader of poetry, Mistress Fry?"(29)

"No, that is, my father does not have such books. I did think they were forbidden," I finished lamely, cross with myself for sounding so confused.

He looked at me quizzically. "So 'tis said, but I do believe that our good Lord Cromwell does indulge himself in verse."

At first I could not believe what I was hearing, and Molly looked most impressed, then I saw William's expression and laughed. "Forgive me but I think you jest, Master Radley."

"Indeed he does," Molly replied quickly, as if to hide her mistake. "Didn't I say he was such a man."

"But cousin, from your expression you did think I was speaking of what I knew," William teased. "While Mistress Fry, now she has the wit to know I did but jest."

"Yer indeed a scoundrel, and not worthy of my affection. Away with ye I love ye not."

While the cousins continued to tease each other, I watched the swan, which was now treading water near the bank. It was all so tranquil and friendly, and to my joy, I was part of this happiness. When at last it was time to return home, Molly insisted on walking ahead with Hugh who, she said, wished to speak with her, leaving William and myself to stroll along behind.

Apart from my father, there was no man of my acquaintance taller than myself, and it was most pleasant to walk beside someone whose height and breadth, made me feel small.

For some reason Molly and Hugh appeared to walk more swiftly than William and myself, and we were soon some yards behind, when he said, "As I recollect Mistress Fry, you said you do not read poetry?"

"My father does prefer me to learn the history of past centuries, and of the world, and of course the bible."

"Yes indeed, the Holy Tome," he replied, somewhat flippantly I thought. "But what do you read, yourself? What are your choices of literature?"

Taken aback, I murmured, "I read as my father bids me. He does prefer me to read such books, as will widen my knowledge of the world."

William pulled a small branch from an overhanging tree, and waved it energetically, as though for emphasis. "But a surfeit of worldly knowledge can impair the brain, with as harmful a result as if we were to indulge ourselves to excess on my cousin's tasty fare. 'tis only by reading all manner of literature, and acquiring the thoughts that such literature arouses, that we do truly grow. Life, as you must know Mistress Fry, is not all seriousness and cloud. Laughter, sunshine, and bright stars too, have their place in our human firmament."

"But I read Homer and Euripides," I declared defensively, "for I have the Greek. And my father does have Master Donne's works, as you have seen."

"Aye, and most commendable they are too. But the poets of our times, they too have much to say. I do know 'tis preached that we should not read overmuch the literature of the mind, since we Puritans are suspicious folk and not inclined to trust what is not proven truth, but there is much written which can be read for its own sake. With written verse 'tis possible to ford great seas, and travel distant lands. With poetry, Mistress Fry, your cottage could become a palace built on foreign soil for, *'stone walls do not a prison make, nor iron bars a cage.'*"

Remembering the verse my father had recently quoted, and also his words that perhaps one day I may so indulge myself, I wanted to confide this fact to William, but he was a stranger whose trust had yet to be tested so, instead, I said, "I do indeed travel sir, with my books of the world, and I study my father's chart, and can imagine myself anywhere I wish."

He laughed. "I beg forgiveness, Mistress Fry. I did but wish to say that reading should encompass all literature, so that we may consider the words and construct from them ideas of our own. As to those lines of verse, I quoted them merely to enhance my meaning. They were written by Sir Richard Lovelace."

He pronounced the name as easily as if speaking of a village friend and not wishing to pursue such a subject, I merely nodded and looked away. Lovelace had been a Royalist whose loyalty for the late King had gained him notoriety, and a prison sentence. It was difficult for me to believe that William, a professed Puritan, could be an admirer of so infamous a Cavalier.

As though reading my thoughts, he said slowly, "He was indeed a King's man, but whatever his politics, they should not obstruct one's mind to a man's ability to create beauty with his pen."

Unable to argue with the sense of this remark, I tried to think of something safer to discuss. But it seemed that William had tired of Sir Richard and his scholarship, for he commenced describing Goodborough, and how the village compared with Fretston, and continued in this vein until we concluded our walk.

With his easy disposition and courteous manners, he proved a popular addition to village life, and many invitations were extended from villagers eager to make his acquaintance. He paid his promised visit to the nearby quarry, from where he returned covered in white dust and carrying, with great care four pieces of stone which, he assured his amused cousin, could possibly be rare.

Molly's insistence that I should be included in all the invitations, resulted in my every day being occupied and the visits benefited me socially, for I had to make conversation and discuss topics on which I had only ever listened.

Every morning I would dress full of anticipation for the day ahead, while every action and every thought seemed to have acquired a new significance, and I became very concerned regarding unimportant things. Never before had I spent so much time ensuring that my collar and cuffs were neat and spotless, and my gown well brushed; also in William's company my confidence increased, and there was nothing I enjoyed more than defending my opinions, when they opposed his.

One of our many such discussions occurred when we were sitting at Molly's table, examining my father's chart. I had been describing the foreign countries in which I was interested, and one of these being Italy, our conversation had turned to the Medici patronage of Florence and two of the men with whom they had been associated, Niccolo Machiavelli(30) and Girolamo Savonarola.(31)

My opinion of the latter met with William's approval, but when I criticised Machiavelli, he shook his head. "I cannot agree, Mistress Fry. Although "tis true that in times past he was considered base and was identified with Satan himself, these opinions are the babble of untutored minds. He was a man of vision, concerned not with selfish ideals, but with establishing sound, durable government."

"But sir," I protested. "What of his manual, wherein he does state that his personification of goodness is a calculating personage, of vicious and low temperament?"

"You have read this manual?"

"No, but such was my father's teaching from a book of historical reading, and I do believe they are words not now welcome in this country. "

William shrugged.

"So 'tis said, but my preference is for readings of the present day, and how we did arrive in so parlous a state."

I frowned, and looking at me keenly, he said, "Was it not the intention of those who created such upheaval in this land that the consequences should benefit those of our population who are poor, and needful? But 'tis not now so, for all has been to the advantage of the gentry and merchants, and poor folk remain poorer still. In my journeys to Nottingham town I have heard much of Diggers, Levellers, (32) and many such besides. All of whom protest they have a vision of what this land and its people should become, but though in their own minds the method and execution of their plans may seem just, the resultant disturbance causes naught but suffering to common folk, who must harvest from land laid waste with fire, and draw water from wells tainted by dead men's blood. Better that Master Winstanley and Master Lilburne had looked to the welfare of their families, and left the laws and ruling of this land to folk fitted for the task. Do you not Mistress Fry, in all truth believe this to be so?"

He stared at me expectantly, and despite the sense in his words I was uncertain how to reply. My father had explained the reasons for the Civil War, and described the administration of Parliamentary Government, but only academically. I had never been expected to proffer an opinion, and the subject now being discussed was, I feared, too dangerous a one in which to become involved.

My hesitancy proved too much for William, for he frowned and said, "Come Mistress Fry, I cannot believe you wish to remain silent. Did I not express myself clearly?"

I struggled to find the words which would placate him and yet enforce my own opinion, so I replied slowly, "My father has told me much of Master Winstanley's desire to educate both men and women, and of Master Lilburne's pamphlet 'The Freemans Fredome Vindicated' in which he did say that men and women were by nature equal and alike in power, dignity and authority. Do you not agree, sir, to these assertions? My father does believe that the education of women should be given much thought."

"Aye, the good Verger speaks sound sense. I would not deny that women should be taught to read and write, or indeed be denied any learning that they so desire, but until those that govern us do take head and act, all preaching of a like sort remains mere cant. Indeed, poor Mistress Lilburne(33) cannot, I fear, be judged the most fortunate recipient of her husband's concern for the weaker vessel." He laughed. "Nay, if we must champion one of these fine gentlemen then I would stand by Master Winstanely. For did he not say that every man and woman should marry where their hearts did lead?"

I dropped my eyes hurriedly, and to my annoyance felt myself grow hot. I had no idea of what William referred to in respect of Elizabeth Lilburne, but there was no mistaking the inference of his words concerning Gerard Winstanley.

Fortunately, at that moment Molly chose to return from where she had been occupied in her room of physic to ask, "And where pray would a body procure the manual of which ye spoke?"

"Pray forgive me cousin, but to what manual do you refer?"

"Yon Mach... ah me, the strangeness of these names," she pulled a face, and he nodded understandingly.

"You refer to Machiavelli, but I fear you are too late cousin, he has now been replaced by more recent men of note." He laughed. "And as to his manual, I fear such reading matter is not to be found hereabouts nor, indeed, in your fine town of Stamford."

She shrugged. "I did but ask for, when I was in York, I did go for the Hebrew to a man who had many such new manuals. Great ones some were, with drawn pictures and of much weight and none, so his servant did tell me, had been opened or read."

"How wonderful it would be," I murmured, "to hold in one's hands a newly printed unread book."

William smiled. "It would give you so much pleasure, Mistress Fry, to own such a book?"

"Yes, indeed, sir," I enthused. "For I have never...." Suddenly aware that I was the centre of attention I hesitated, before adding in a quieter tone, "But it must, of course, be a book of merit. To own a book lacking distinction and scholarship, would be of little worth to the reader."

"Well said," William exclaimed enthusiastically. "So does speak a mind of true regard."

I tried to appear calm, but knew that my hot face exhibited embarrassment, while Molly beamed at us both and then, laughing, said, "'tis good not all bodies do wish to talk of ponderous matters, else how'd our food be cooked? But do ye talk, for a body can learn much from your words."

William grinned. "Well, Mistress Fry, we have indeed received our orders, so do you choose a subject to discuss."

His expression was so quizzical, I laughed. "Is it not possible that Molly can instruct us on the subject?"

"Yes, indeed," she replied. "You spake of men all of whom achieved greatness but suffered. Was there not a man who achieved much and was not made to smart for his endeavours?"

"Michelangelo Buonarroti(34) was such a man," William replied with a smile. "He was a sculptor of great statues who was held in high repute for his craft."

"Statues?" Molly appeared unimpressed. "And what were these statues?"

"Mighty marble edifices of men and women, mostly of a religious bent," William replied. "But another of his crafts was painting, for he did cover a great ceiling with his art, and poetry too was another of his talents."

"Poetry?" I questioned in surprise, for although my father had spoken of the Florentine's craft, he had never mentioned that he was a man of literature.

"Yes, indeed," William said. "And Mistress Fry, by chance, when last in Nottingham town I did purchase a slender volume of his verse. 'tis an old copy but if your father does approve, would you give me the pleasure of accepting them? They are harmless words without inclination towards politics or sophistry or, if you do not wish to accept the volume, I can copy the verses and send them to you, if you would so permit."

I felt myself growing warm again, but was saved the problem of replying by Molly declaring, "And t'other man, this Savonarola, did he forsake or stand strong on his thoughts?"

William laughed. "How flies your mind, cousin. "'T'other man' as you so call him, did stand very strong but in the face of death, not prior, for he was tortured. And although 'twas said by some that he did recant, others denied this and did affirm that he withstood the pain, and that the torture was but the commencement of a plan to deny him life, no matter what the outcome."

"So he did die, and how?"

"He did burn," I replied, with a shiver.

"Nay," William said quickly. "Folk present declared he was first put to death, and then his body burned."

"No matter," Molly replied firmly, as she placed eating utensils on the table. "He did die for that in which he believed. Such a man can I admire, and does it not put yon man Gallileo to shame."

I wanted to protest that there were far more suitable men of history for Molly to admire, but Hugh entered noisily with more wood for the fire, so I lapsed into silence.

So passed those halcyon summer days, and all was bliss for me. My father consumed without demur the physic and food Molly administered, and although I did occasionally hear him coughing in the night, the bouts were very brief and appeared to cause him little discomfort.

I was also relieved to see that Molly's preoccupation with William appeared to have terminated her friendship with Daniel Wallace. He had not visited the cottage since the night of my father's illness, and Molly's manner towards him in Church was so distant, I could only assume she no longer cared for his company. This I felt was to the good, as I knew from Bessie's gossip that Mistress Wallace and her friends strongly disapproved of Molly's medical administrations, considering them intrusive and unethical.

It was on the morning of William's departure that I was surprised to see him outside Molly's cottage, in apparent intense conversation with my father. Hidden by my shutter, I watched until, their business apparently completed, William bowed and continued on his way to Master Westley's forge.

Puzzled, since I could not imagine on what matter they had been so intent, I descended to the parlour where Bessie stood muttering to herself, "Yon master, his skin so pale and paler every day he gets, and me ma do say…"

Although I knew she spoke the truth, for my father's pallor had increased of late, I turned on her and retorted angrily, "What nonsense you do speak. My father looks as well as any man, and when pray did you speak with your mother? You know it is forbidden."

She mumbled incoherently, but I was too concerned with William's departure to pursue the matter, and opened the cottage door in time to see him astride his horse, trotting towards me from the forge.

"I fear my father is occupied elsewhere, sir," I explained.

He smiled. "It is of no consequence, mistress. We have already made our farewells."

He dismounted as Molly and Hugh emerged from their cottage, and embraced and kissed them both warmly. Then, after making me a formal bow, he re-mounted and was gone.

Our farewell was so swift I was left shocked, and speechless. I could not believe that he would not turn his horse, and retrace his steps to Molly's door.

But the broad back progressed towards the Stamford road, and when he did turn and wave I was so distressed I could not respond.

But these feelings were soon subdued on witnessing Molly's bitter sobs. Distressed by her obvious grief, and the agitated murmurings of Hugh as he stood stroking her hair, I embraced my friend before leading her gently back into the cottage.

CHAPTER 13

August/September 1657

For some time Molly sat beside the fireplace, staring wistfully into the flames, until with a sigh she said, "I love him so, and so much have we suffered together. Now he's gone, and 'tis possible years'll pass afore we again meet."

I hesitated before gently removing my arms, and saying the words that caused me an almost physical pain. "If you do care so much for him, why do you not return to Goodborough, and is it not possible that one day?"

I could not finish the question, but there was no need. Molly was untutored but she was not a fool, and with a gentle smile she said, "We could not wed, Pleasance, for though we love each other dearly, 'tis the love of a brother for a sister, for so we are." The wave of relief I experienced at her words, seemed to encompass my whole being as she continued, "'tis a strange tale I tell, but William has said I must, for ye be me dearest, kindest friend, but if I do tell 'twill not lower me in yer eyes?"

I could not imagine what she meant, but shook my head as she commenced, "Me known father, he who was the farrier of Goodborough, did marry me mother when he was much in age, full five and forty years and she but fifteen, the younger of two sisters. She did not wish the match but Master Tyler was a man of wealth, and did pay me grandsire a goodly sum for his wife. But 'twas an ill-matched mating and he did beat her, and me mother fled to her sister, who took her to the squire. When 'twas found she was with child the squire gave her shelter but the beatings had told, and when Hugh was born, he was as you now know him. Me mother stayed then at the hall, and the squire being without a wife took her in and I was their issue, but I was a child of width and the birth was fearful hard. Ye are indeed blessed Pleasance, that ye did know yer mother, even for so short a time. I would I'd known mine. Because he was afeared of gossip the squire did pay Master Tyler to say he were me sire, but as he had no wife I lived at the Hall. The squire was always kind but he would not permit me to learn my letters for he did say that 'twould stand me in better stead to learn to cook, sew, weave and spin, and these were the skills I did learn. But I'd fain have learned me letters, and the ways of speech that ye do use."

"And the elder sister, your kinswoman, she was William's mother?" I ventured hesitantly.

"Aye, she were a woman of much beauty. When the squire saw her he did take her to the Hall, where she did live until with child at which time he did marry her to his steward, Nathaniel Radley, who did treat her well and acknowledged William as his own. But because the squire was proud of William and loved him dearly, he had a man to teach him many things a gentleman would know, like how to talk the way you do, and many graces that are practiced by the gentry. When Master Tyler was dying, the squire did make him sign the forge to William, for although he could not acknowledge him as his own, he wanted him to have a trade by which to support himself. Not long after that William's mother and the steward did fall ill, a sickness of the stomach, from which they both did die."

She looked so sad, I rose swiftly from my stool, and putting my arms around her shoulders, murmured gently, "At what time did you discover that William was your kin?"

"When Master Tyler died the squire did tell us. 'twas a great shock, for I did think I was true born, but William seemed not overmuch concerned. He had been well tutored, and had all the skills denied me, for the Squire did wish him to be a man of knowledge, and sent him to a place of learning in Nottingham but," she added quickly, "to both of us he showed much kindness, and gave much money. He became ailing after falling from his horse, while hunting. A crushing of the chest brought on a fever, and he lived but two days thereafter. Never having wed he had no heir, so the Hall and all else was passed to distant kin, but he did remember us with great kindness, for to Will he did leave a fine clock and twenty Double Ryals,(35) making him a man of wealth, and to me those coins of which you already know."

I thought of the considerable discrepancy between the amounts, and how deluded Molly was to believe her father had been kind, while denying her the education she had obviously craved; but it was not my place to comment so, instead, I asked, "And no one knows of this"

"Naught but for William, meself and ye, and I am indeed glad I have told ye Pleasance, for 'tis a fearful great secret to carry all alone. But 'tis a shame the

Squire died when he did, for he cared much for us and would've acknowledged us, had the world been a kinder place."

I made no comment. Worldly experience I may have lacked, but even I, within the confines of my narrow existence knew that the nobility rarely, if ever, acknowledged their bastards to the world.

Molly must have been concerned by my silence, for she put a tentative hand on mine, and said in an anxious voice, "Ye think not bad of me, Pleasance, yer still my friend and will keep this secret close into yer heart?"

"For sure I am and will forever be your friend," I reassured her impulsively. "And I swear no mention of our talk, will ever pass my lips." Remembering this promise, made so long ago, I can with relief assert that in this circumstance at least, I did not betray her.

We remained with our arms entwined around each other until she released me, and murmured that she was tired, and wished to rest. As I helped her rise, she murmured, "If you had denied me, Pleasance, I would have had no wish to live, for without your love and friendship I have no life."

The passion of her words embarrassed me, and I stood in silence as she walked slowly towards the stairway. When she had ascended I returned home, and collecting the church key sought the buildings cool embrace, to consider the past hour. Molly's declaration of friendship had shaken me greatly. I cared for her, but raised as I had been to control my feelings, such violent declarations of passion were beyond me to return. It was most puzzling, because I also knew that if she were to leave the village I would be bereft, and what of my acute distress when I sought her answer as to whether she would wed William, and my relief when she divulged the truth?

For some time I sat within that holy place, reasoning to myself that if I truly cared for her, surely I would wish her well regardless of how I fared, and it was not until I rose and commenced carrying out my customary tasks, that the calm atmosphere and order of my surroundings restored me to my natural demeanour.

My work completed, I was about to leave when thoughts of the morning once again overwhelmed me, and I knelt down in a pew. I wanted to pray for Molly and ask God to give her peace, but I found myself thanking Him for sparing me the torment and anguish that she had experienced, and for bestowing upon me such a good, kind, and caring father.

The day following William's departure, my father recommenced coughing heavily and Daniel Wallace visited Molly. I saw him entering her cottage just as I was about to visit myself, and reluctant to intrude I occupied myself spinning until I heard him depart.

Annoyed that I should have been denied her company for so long, I entered the cottage with some abruptness to find Molly standing beside the parlour table, her face glowing with a radiance that increased when she saw me. "Please to come, dear friend," she held out both her arms, in a warm embrace. "Esther Royton is to come for bed and board, so that she may learn to sew a fine seam."

"But I did think you did not care for sewing?" I exclaimed.

"Bless ye 'twas once so," she replied, most casually I thought. "But I've sewn much recently, and have grown accustomed to the art. And I do now sew a fine seam, and 'tis a fine seam Esther wishes to learn for her wedding clothes."

"Wedding clothes? I did not know she was to wed."

"She's not as yet, but 'tis for the day."

"And Master and Mistress Royton, they do approve?" I asked, for it seemed a most unusual occurrence.

"For why should they not, 'tis fair exchange? They do sell me produce, and in turn I do instruct their daughter." Molly began humming quietly to herself, as if I were no longer present.

Subduing a sudden feeling of resentment, which I could not comprehend, I murmured my farewells and returned home to resume my spinning, with an energy that was more damaging than productive.

The next day being Sunday we met in church as usual, and after the service Molly and Hugh joined us for the return walk home. As we stood waiting for my father, Daniel walked past accompanied by Mistress Wallace. They both acknowledged me with a polite nod, but neither of them looked at the Tylers. Shocked by such blatant rudeness, I stared wide-eyed at Molly but she avoided my glance and looked away. No further mention of the Wallaces was made, and we returned to our respective homes.

Some time later, as I was helping Bessie prepare our meal the girl gave a sudden snigger. "Did see mistress, did see what he did, her soldier? He did make as she were nothing, ow."

Bessie's scream was due to my sharp slap, which also scattered spoon, pewter bowl and broth, across the parlour floor.

"Never again," I gasped. "Never again do you speak of Mistress Tyler in such a manner."

Shaking, as much from the reaction of having chastised a body for the first time in my life, as from the anger I felt at Bessie's insolence, I towered over the grovelling child. Then I heard my father descending, and reaching quickly dragged the terrified maid back to her feet.

"Do you bring cloth and water, and clear the floor, I snapped. "I will serve the food."

Still gulping noisily, Bessie scuttled away as my father entered.

"I did hear, ah a slight mishap I see, of no importance, my dear. I trust you did not over-scold Bessie, to err is human, is it not?"

Later that same evening, as I sat in church beside a very subdued Bessie I watched Daniel Wallace closely. On entering the church he again ignored Molly and behaved the same way on leaving, but what was even more puzzling was the fact that she, in turn, had acted in the same manner towards him. Bewildered, and experiencing a sense of foreboding without knowing why, I decided to ask her for an explanation.

But next morning I emerged in time to see Daniel Wallace entering Molly's cottage, this time without knocking, closely followed by Mistress Whyte carrying a large basket of linen. I closed my cottage door with a feeling of helplessness. How could Molly permit Daniel to enter her cottage, after he had ignored her only the previous day, and the sight of the washer-woman reminded me of another matter.

In Fretson only the Altons and Mistress Burridge sought Mistress Whyte's services, and although I guessed the only reason Molly was doing likewise was to assist the poor woman in her struggle to make a living, the village gossips were already declaring that my friend was now too proud to cleanse her own dirt.

Three hours later, while still trying to decide how to explain to Molly the rashness of her ways, I heard the sound of a horse's hooves receding along the road. Immediately I hurried next door, only to find the entrance locked. Puzzled I knocked, but despite my persistence no one answered, and I returned home feeling dissatisfied, and cross.

The following morning Esther Royton arrived, and when I visited that afternoon the visitor was busy spinning beside the fireplace, with Tannakin curled contentedly on her lap. Unable to speak openly in Esther's presence, I had to satisfy myself with a few pleasantries, and three sweet cakes. The next day Molly sent me a message by Hugh to say that she had a sneezing fit, and advised me not to visit until she had recovered. Frustrated but obedient, I passed the time accompanying my father on his calls around the village.

It was as we were sitting with Mistress Machin in the latter's parlour, that I was surprised to hear her remark, "I do indeed miss the visits of your little maid,

Mistress Fry, now that you do bake your own bread. So very droll the child was, scarce staying long enough to let me take the dough."

"But did she not talk," I began, only to be interrupted by Mistress Machin with a laugh, "Talk, bless you child, she said never a word. 'twas in and out of the cottage, afore I could open my mouth."

I forced a smile in reply, while remembering the many times Bessie had complained of how she had been made to tarry, especially on the night of the heavy rain. It was quite clear to me now, that despite having been forbidden their house, Bessie must have been visiting her parents, since there was no other dwelling to which she had entrance.

I sighed inwardly. How to punish the child was the problem. A beating was unthinkable. The experience had proved too degrading for a repetition, and curtailing Bessie's freedom for a week or two would cause the maid far more distress, than a few strokes of the birch. I was still deep in contemplation on returning home, when my father's voice said sharply, "Child what ails you, I have spoken twice, and you have not answered, are you unwell?"

"I beg your pardon Sir, I was thinking of Bessie."

"Why, what has the wench done to displease you? But no matter, I was speaking of what Master Machin did impart. We live so away from the world, we know not of what occurs. It is said, or so the news from Peterborough does imply, that our Lord Protector was in March offered the crown, but he did refuse as the Good Lord would have him do. But it does seem that much has changed in London town. The Lord Cromwell does now live in Whitehall Palace, and travels in a great carriage. His power is absolute and with his enhancement as Protector for the second time, none can say him nay. Even his wife and daughters wear satin and lace and, Master Machin tells me, indulge in dance, though this I cannot believe." He sighed heavily. "If life is to return to what it was, why did men die, and what did they achieve?"

I listened in awe. For my father to have spoken so critically of a man he had always revered as a Saviour, and to me, was astonishing. He was now looking at me, and smiling gently said, "Do you ever think child of what your life may be, five or ten years hence?"

Confused at so unexpected a question I stammered, "I cannot recall having had such thoughts father, but will not the Good Lord provide?"

"Aye, so we have been taught, but the Lord does also give us a mind with which to act. Should you be given at some time hence, a moment in which to take up your life, do you think well and hard before denying what may give you happiness. Do you mark me, child?" His voice had become forceful, and although I had no idea as to what he alluded I was too bewildered to do other than agree. To my relief he appeared satisfied for he smiled and we continued our walk in silence.

The following morning, having challenged Bessie and refused to believe her stuttering explanation that she often lost her way, I confined her to the cottage for two weeks, and settled down before my loom. But I had worked only a short while, before I was interrupted by the arrival of Thomas Whyte with a package. The post-boy had barely walked from the cottage before my father entered the room, from the stairway.

"A visit from young Thomas I see, with a plump package. Now, who do you suppose child, has sent such a missive?"

I had no idea, so for want of a reply answered, "From a church matter, father?"

To my surprise, he gave me a disappointed look. "I think not. It is from young Radley and we have two letters, one for me and this other I do see Pleasance, is for you."

He coughed suddenly, and quickly put his kerchief to his mouth. The bout was soon over, and he wiped his mouth carefully, before thrusting the kerchief deep into his jacket pocket. I stared down at the first letter I had ever received, and flushed in embarrassment. My father smiled.

"Do you enjoy your missive, child. I have no wish to know the contents nor your reply. I am now to Preacher Wyman."

Alone with my letter, I opened it to reveal William's neat writing, and began to read. His greetings were brief. He wished me well and wished me also better weather than he was experiencing in Goodborough. He then described how, due to impassable roads a number of horses had fallen on slippery mud, and had to be destroyed. This news took up one side of the paper, while on the reverse he stated that he had now penned the first of Michelangelo's verses, as promised, that the remainder would follow, and that he trusted that I would find them of interest.

Too much good luck no less than misery
May kill a man condemned to mortal pain.
If, lost to hope and chilled in every vein
A sudden pardon comes to set him free
Beauteous art, brought with us from heaven,

110

will conquer nature; so divine a power
belongs to him who strives with every nerve.
If I was made for art, from childhood given
a prey for burning beauty to devour,
I blame the mistress I was born to serve.'

Never having read poetry, my untutored brain absorbed the words with a sense of disappointment, though why this should be I could not comprehend, and he had presented me with yet another problem. Not to respond would be churlish and, having made my decision for reasons of politeness, I sighed. Friendship, it seemed, carried weighty responsibilities.

Molly had now been ill with the "sneezes" for five days. On day four I saw Esther Royton leave, but instead of the invitation I expected, Hugh delivered a message to say that Molly was still unwell.

Again confined to my cottage, I occupied the time with domestic tasks which were not enough however, to distract me from the annoyance I felt at my friend's neglect. And they were not so absorbing late one afternoon, to obliterate the sounds of Daniel Wallace's spurred footsteps departing from her cottage. I was shocked. It was almost dusk, surely Molly must be aware of how indecorous it was, to permit Daniel to remain so late, even if she did have Hugh for company?

She was my friend, and I had no right to sit in judgement, but there had been an increase in the number of ill people visiting the cottage, and Mistress Whyte continued to make her weekly visits, to collect and return the Tylers' linen. If Molly were so unwell, would it not have been wiser to postpone such visitors, until whatever ailed her had ceased? And if so many people were permitted her presence, could she not have sent at least one message to her friend next door?

However, any concern I may have felt for Molly was soon dispelled by greater concern for my father, who returned home that evening coughing violently, before retiring wearily to his chamber. Preoccupied as I was, I had forgotten Bessie's misdemeanours until later the following day, when she asked permission to take a walk.

All my pent up anger at Molly spewed forth and I ranted at the helpless child. "Take a walk, fie on you miss. Have I not told you to stay within the cottage for ten days, some four more of which remain? And it is no walk, you wish to take, but some prattle to your mother, is it not?"

111

Bessie cowed against the wall, and began to cry. "'tis me mother. She do say she'll beat me, if I tell not all."

"Tell all? To what all do you refer?"

"Her doings, spells and such."

"Spells." Shock replaced my anger. "Mistress Tyler makes no use of spells. She is a physician, and does give naught but the purest of herbs to ailing folk, and that is an end of the matter. Should I be accosted by your mother, I will explain," I declared, trying to recover some semblance of calm, as I realised that to remonstrate too strongly would make much of an issue, which could only be subdued by being treated lightly. In a much more modulated voice, I continued, "And you will remain within the cottage for the further four days, and not venture out. I shall carry out all messages, and make whatever purchases we require."

At the same time as Bessie departed muttering to the outer scullery, my father entered the room looking pale. I looked at him anxiously.

"'tis nothing child, but a little breathlessness. Yon lass's physic does me very well. Now, did I not hear you admonishing our little maid?"

I hesitated. I wanted to confide in him everything that had taken place, including Daniel's visits, but caution overcame me, and I told him only of the spells. He looked concerned.

"That is indeed, most grave. I must speak with the Workmans. Such idle gossip is most unwise. That such depravity should be implied against someone so very virtuous as Mistress Tyler, is disquieting. Do you leave the matter with me, my dear. I will attend to it." He smiled. "Do you now bring me my Bible, Pleasance, and then we will eat."

My father's approachable manner, made me suddenly bold. "There is father, another matter of which, if you so please, I would speak." He nodded, expectantly.

"It is Master Wallace."

"Such a very fine young man, and so devoted a son. He has I believe, almost now recovered from his wound to which Mistress Molly has been administering. You recollect child, that he was wounded at a rising in Plymouth?"

"Yes, of course," I stammered.

There being nothing further I could say, I handed him his Bible. To contradict my father and explain my fears required a courage I did not possess.

Molly's illness lasted one more day, during which Daniel made another visit, and then a tap on our cottage door revealed my friend, looking exceptionally radiant and healthy. She smiled and gave me a big hug, which I returned with some reserve.

"'tis sad I am to have deserted ye so. But the sneezes were so bad, and the sewing, ah me a pretty lass she may be, but so long to learn a seam. Now do ye wrap yerself in that thick shawl, and we'll take the air, but first," she took a large packet from beneath her cloak. "See you these, the carrier did leave them. I know not why but he did say they were for Mistress Fry."

"For me, but I expect no package. Mayhap you misunderstood, and it should be directed elsewhere."

"No," she replied firmly. "Fry he said, and there be no other body hereabouts with such a name. Do you open it, perhaps there be a letter or some such."

Very slowly, I cut the ribbon, and spread back the pieces of linen cloth. Inside was a lace collar, a lady's high crown leather hat, and a pair of white linen cuffs embroidered around the edge.

"Oh, Molly," I stared in amazement, as my resentment at being neglected seemed to melt away. "They are beautiful, but I cannot accept them."

"For why?" She stared at me, wide-eyed.

I could think of a dozen reasons, but the only one that mattered was, "My father would not approve."

She shook her head. "I think not the Verger would be displeased. For why pray, does he not approve of our friendship, and did he not welcome William? I do believe Master Fry'll look kindly upon his daughter's finery, for 'tis no more than that in which the Puritan merchants do clad their wives."

I quenched an inner sigh. Yet again I could not think of the words to explain to this generous, impulsive girl, that there was a limit to my father's liberality, and what other people did concerned him not, because he lived within a rigid set of rules from which he rarely strayed. Just because Molly had persuaded him to have a fire, and he now allowed me more freedom, did not mean that he had relaxed in any way his attitude towards life. He did have a high opinion of her, but that would not blind him to the fact that she was but human, and in common with other folk, had her faults.

Only the previous morning he had concerned me by expressing doubts about her cat. He had seen the animal scratching amongst our chickens and, with obvious surprise, enquired as to its origins. On being told he had frowned.

"How unwise of Mistress Molly, did you not advise her against keeping the animal, child? I fear Preacher Wyman would not approve. And to name the beast as if it were a kindred of the blood is, I fear, most unwise especially with regard to the remarks which yon Workmans made. I have spoken with them, but

I think a guiding word with Mistress Molly would not go amiss. There is no necessity to speak aught of the gossip."

I had intended to speak to Molly as soon as she appeared but now, holding her gifts in my hands, I stared at her helplessly. Then as gently as possible I murmured, "I do not believe my father would approve. Not because the collar and cuffs are made of lace, but because I have already garments which I wear, and such extra clothes as these are vanity, and vanity is a sin."

"But I do wear such a collar and such cuffs. Does the good Verger complain that I am vain?"

"No, Molly, his regard for you is most high."

"Then I do not comprehend." Molly spread her hands wide.

There was nothing further I could say, so I folded the collar and cuffs and placed them neatly inside the hat. Then I kissed her on the cheek, and followed her from the cottage to commence our walk.

We were approaching Master Westley's forge, when I remembered that my father's concern for Molly's cat had not been discussed. I gave her a wary look before murmuring hesitantly, "My father did remark upon seeing Tannakin in our yard, as to how you came by the animal."

"The good Verger ever observant, and did ye tell him of poor Tannakin's ordeal?"

"Yes, but," I began, only to be interrupted by her cry, "Pleasance, do ye see, flying geese. Are they not a fine sight?"

I glanced upwards at the great white birds, flying low over the trees. Molly seemed entranced, but I was determined to pursue my difficult subject and continued, "My father did not think it wise for you to have…"

But once again my companion seemed distracted, as she called out to the farrier's wife as she emerged from her cottage, "Mistress Westley, how goes it with ye today?"

"Well, Mistress Molly, well I thank ye, and is it note a fine day? And pleased I am to see that ye have now recovered from your ailment."

"I thank ye, ma'am, we're about to take the air."

"And a pretty sight ye both make, indeed ye do," Mistress Westley nodded with a kindly smile before adding, "Why, Mistress Burridge, do ye too walk this fine day?" And she beamed at Preacher Wyman's housekeeper who was now approaching down her cottage path.

"Indeed I do, Mistress Westley, the day being so fine. And how goes it with you Mistress Fry?"

"Well, I thank you ma'am," I replied, resignedly. The cat would have to wait, as it would seem, for now, that the Good Lord was smiling down on Molly.

"And Verger Fry how goes his cough?" Mistress Burridge's small eyes seemed to narrow enthusiastically. "So troublesome it was last Sunday. Behind a tombstone I did find him, coughing so heavily he was, and so much mucus and so strange a colour."

I stared aghast as Molly cried out, quickly, "'tis a good sign the mucus. Does mean the cough is on the wane, 'tis the mucus that does cause the retching."

I saw the two women exchange glances, and Mistress Burridge frowned. "I have not heard 'tis so."

"Yes indeed, so 'tis," Molly insisted. "Mistress Westley, is that not Simon calling ye ma'am, from the forge?"

"My goodness, so it be," Mistress Westley declared. "I must to my duties. Do ye have a pleasant walk my dears, young people must enjoy themselves while they can, is that no so Mistress Burridge?"

The housekeeper nodded without replying, and she gave us only a brief nod of farewell, her expression towards Molly cold and distant.

Preoccupied with Mistress Burridge's revelations about my father, I could only think of the fact that, yet again, he had not confided in me.

Distressed, I was about to speak when Molly said, "What ails ye Pleasance, there's much concern about your features, is it of yer father's mucus that ye think. If so there's naught to fear. It is part of the illness and will pass. Trust me dearest Pleasance, for I know that 'tis true. Now is there aught else I should know?"

Taking advantage of the question, I ventured, "My father did say that perhaps it is unwise to have Tannakin."

"The good Verger did advise against Tannakin, but for why pray?"

"Animals are not welcome, hereabouts," I replied, wishing she did not look so fierce.

"Animals not welcome, but how can that be? What of the cows, pigs, hens, goats and horses pray? What are they if they are not welcome?"

"He referred not to farm animals," I explained, desperately. "But of animals that do not serve a working purpose, such as cats."

"Animals that do not serve a working purpose? I know not what ye mean." Her eyes flashed and I tried desperately to extricate myself.

"Molly, it is not I that have made the comment, it is my father. He is a wise man who knows much of the world. Please to heed him, I beg."

"I'll speak to him," she almost snapped. "I'll ask him his meaning. Now I wish to return. It is cold and I am tired."

Feeling very miserable and near to tears, I followed my friend's indignant figure back to our cottages. Outside my door she gave me a quick brief kiss, before continuing to her own home and, as I entered my cottage, I knew that it was now utterly beyond me to broach the matter of Daniel Wallace.

The next day's cold wind and rain forced me to remain indoors, so I penned a hurried acknowledgement to William's letter, and was surprised at the ease with which my words flowed. It was only as I penned my farewell that I realised I had not yet acquainted Molly with my new correspondent. I was folding the near paper in preparation for despatch, when my father entered from the stairway. He looked healthier than of late. His cheeks were quite ruddy, and despite the dampness of the weather, his cough had not been in evidence for two days.

"This is your reply my dear?" He smiled, as I gave him my letter. "Good, I will fold it so with mine into a package, and you can give them to Thomas tomorrow. Our friend will have his replies within the next fourteen days, if all Thomas's boasts about our post coaches are to be believed. Now I fear I must leave you, child. Yes, I see the rain, but Mistress Ephraim, the poor bed ridden soul who once did serve as seamstress at the Hall, is sickened, and I did promise Preacher Wyman I would visit. It is a short walk, and I shall soon return."

I watched him go with considerable concern. Contrary to his assertion, Mistress Ephraim lived some distance away on the other side of the village, and the rain had increased. When at last he returned some two hours later, he was drenched and that night I heard him retching heavily. The following morning, very pale and haggard, he pushed his bowl of hot porridge aside.

"I fear I cannot eat at this moment, child, but this good food must not be wasted. Do you ask Bessie to place it safely for my supper, and I would I had more of Mistress Molly's potion, but I did drink it all. Would you, child….."

But I was already hurrying towards the door, calling, "I will go at once, father, I will go at once."

Anxiety made me push Molly's door open without knocking, and after leaving my pattens on the step I hurried into the parlour, but the room was deserted as was the room of physic. Feeling helpless and distraught, I was about to call Molly's name when I heard sounds coming from above. Assuming her to be in her bedchamber, I climbed the narrow staircase to the landing where there were two doors, identical to those in my own home.

The left hand door, which I knew to be Hugh's room was closed, but Molly's door was slightly ajar. From within I could hear sounds of movement and panting and, mystified, I approached and peered around the lintel.

Molly was sprawled naked on the bed, her legs wrapped around Daniel's bare hips as he knelt before her, his buttocks rising and falling in unison to her groans.

CHAPTER 14

October 1657

I stood at the open doorway, trying to comprehend what I was seeing. Then Molly gasped violently and Daniel's movements became swifter. The abruptness of his actions awoke my senses, and I fled downstairs as quietly as I was able. Trembling violently I reached the cottage door from where, on legs that seemed reluctant to obey my wishes, I returned home.

"Molly has been called away," I explained slowly, in answer to my father's enquiring glance. "I will call again."

"Why child, what ails you, you are paler than your collar? Come closer to the fire. As to the potion, it is of no matter. Bessie did tempt me with this warm broth and yon little wench has a way with broth, indeed she has."

I stretched my hands out to the fire, but more than heat was required to warm my blood, and after a short while I excused myself and retired to my chamber. The revulsion and disgust that I had expected to feel were absent. Only bewilderment remained, as I tried to relate Molly's elegant figure with the naked writhing body I had seen on the bed. I stood thus beside my casement, until Bessie called from below, "Mistress, 'tis master, he did send word that he do want ye at church."

I picked up my shawl and descended to the parlour on legs that still seemed dangerously weak. As I emerged from the cottage the sun was shining brightly, and the gentle autumn breeze sent the golden leaves scudding about my feet. Looking determinedly ahead I approached the church as, behind me, I heard the sound of a door opening and heavy spurred footsteps retreating in the opposite direction.

Inside the church I discovered Preacher Wyman standing beside the front pew, staring irritably at my father who, looking strained, explained, "We did think to have the church floor full cleaned, Pleasance. Preacher Wyman does think it highly noxious, and we did think you would like to have charge of this task. I did think the Workmans could be asked, and possibly the Trents, the poor souls who do live beyond the stream. There will be payment fourpence did you not say, Master Wyman?"

"Twopence, Master Fry, twopence, the church has many charges to maintain," the Preacher's lips curled testily.

"Yes of course forgive me sir, so Pleasance, what think you?"

"If Preacher Wyman so wishes," I replied, giving as brief a curtsey as I dared. The minister pursed his lips.

"All is understood then, and as soon as it is possible." He sniffed noisily and with a gesture of his hand in our direction, departed through the open door.

"I had not thought the floor noxious," I murmured, staring down at the inoffensive stone slabs.

My father sighed. "Master Wyman does take the Lord's words most dearly to heart. So, my dear, you have a task afore you. He did especially request that you be involved. I will see the Workmans and the Trents, and I will be by when they come. I would not have you exposed alone, to such as them."

I nodded, and followed him slowly down the aisle. After what I had witnessed that morning his concern for my welfare seemed ludicrous, and a sudden longing to tell him overcame me. I wanted to be reassured that what I had seen had not been true. My eyes and brain had, for a moment, betrayed me. Like the stories Old Mother Burrows had told, of visions that the Devil sent to frighten maidens into chastity. But instead I waited obediently as he locked the church door, and grew very hot when he said, "You will procure from Mistress Molly, a flask of the potion?"

"Yes, father, I will now call."

Slowly, for my father was obviously weary, we returned to our cottage from where I proceeded to Molly's door, and this time my knock received a friendly response. Feeling both nervous and embarrassed, I entered to find my friend kneading bread. She looked up with a smile, and I stared at her in silence, trying to see something of the abandoned woman of some two hours previous. But Molly's dress was as neat as ever, and she returned my look with a steady gaze.

"Pleased I am to see ye Pleasance, for look I have made far more of these pasties than Hugh or I will ever eat. Do ye take six, that ye may have them with your meal."

I could not understand how she could appear so normal, and concern herself with so mundane a matter as food. I tried to speak, but instead began to tremble as I gasped impulsively, "Molly I did see all. I did come for some physic, two hours gone."

I tried to swallow away the tearful lump which threatened to choke me, as Molly continued calmly to knead her bread, her expression and voice unfathomable. "Ye did climb the stairs to my chamber?"

"I did hear sounds, I did believe you to be alone and did come up and the door was ajar."

She scrapped the dough carefully off her arms and hands, and then wiped them on her apron. When she spoke her voice, though calm, was forbidding in a manner I had never heard from her before.

"Pleasance, if aught of what ye saw should reach the ears of those who do not wish me good, then things would go hard for me."

"I will tell no one," the suggestion appalled me.

"Well and good," her voice was now very gentle. "Yer still but an untutored maid who knows little of the ways of the flesh, what ye saw is but natural twixt those who are wed. But how did you enter, for I did lock the cottage door?"

"It was not locked, but Molly you are not wed."

"Just so, 'twas no doubt Hugh who did leave the lock unturned. I did leave him sleeping below, and he was not present when Daniel departed. I'm not wed, but I've the feelings of a woman for a man, and I've them for Daniel. He's a good man, a man of honour, who does respect me as a man should."

I stared in silent amazement as Molly explained away her wantonness. How she could declare that Daniel Wallace was a man of honour was beyond my comprehension. At last, I asked timidly, "Are you to wed?"

She laughed. "Nay lass, 'tis not likely that Mistress Wallace would agree to have me for her beloved son. 'twill end soon enough, I've no doubt."

"But does it not concern you that you should...."

"Behave so for naught," she finished, smiling. "Aye, so it does, but one must take one's pleasure where one can in this world, so did I learn in York."

"You did such in York?" I tried to control the shock in my voice, but Molly did not seem to notice, for she replied calmly, "Aye, 'twas the steward of the Hebrews. He was kind, and did invite me to his rooms, and there it did happen. 'twas the first time Pleasance, and right good too, but not as good as 'tis with Daniel."

I felt myself go scarlet, and she laughed. "There'll come a day Pleasance, when ye'll feel as I do. But for ye 'twill be within the sacrament of wedlock, for so 'tis foretold."

Very ill at ease and deeply embarrassed, I could only mutter, "I know not what you mean."

She smiled at me, her eyes warm with affection. "No matter, time'll show my meaning. Now I'll place this pie within the oven, and we'll have a mug of ale. Is aught still amiss? Do ye not wish my friendship, now ye do know my faults?"

"No, it is not so," I cried out nervously. "But I cannot comprehend, knowing as you do of what your mother and aunt did suffer, how you can let yourself be taken so?"

"Hush dear friend, no man'll leave me as my father did my mother. Come to my room of physic, and I'll allay your fears."

Somewhat reluctantly, I followed her into the other room as she continued, "I'm too wise in knowledge of my body, Pleasance, to be so beguiled. There are ways of doing such as does protect us from the likes of men."

Goodwife Hargreave's old chamber was now devoid of furniture, apart from a stool and a wide deal table on which lay an assortment of pots, jars and flasks, all full of what appeared to be liquid or liniment. Unlike Doctor Percival's gloomy chamber, this room was spotlessly clean and smelled strongly of lavender.

As I stood beside the door, she picked up a small bottle containing a clear yellow liquid.

"This be my secret, Pleasance. This be the potent mixture that does protect all women from the scourge of men."

Still mystified, I stared at the bottle, and she gave a soft laugh. "To be with child, Pleasance, is my meaning. At the first sign that I do not bleed I do take this, and all's once more put to rights. 'tis liquid of the rue plant and does cause the blood to flow. I do have a supply of it with me from the Hebrew's steward. It does have a bitter taste not pleasant to the human palate, and must be used with prudence, for if not so applied there can be madness and lack of balance, for 'tis mighty strong."(32)

"Madness and lack of balance," I repeated, staring at the liquid, almost expecting it to erupt from the bottle.

"Aye, but 'tis so with most physic applied without knowledge. Be not so shocked dear friend. Ye've led a sheltered life, and know not the ways of the gentry. Many ladies of quality do practice acts to avoid the carrying of a child. The juice of thyme and majoram, 'tis said, does have a good effect, but I do consider rue to act to most account. For a woman far gone, say beyond two month, more violent methods are required, but sometimes the mixture applied on a piece of softened wool, wrapped around a thin instrument well washed and applied into the passageway a man does enter, will suffice. But if all else fails only an instrument will accomplish the task."

Appalled, I gasped, "And you have done this?"

"Nay, I have never fallen so, but I have carried out the service for other poor souls left undone by men. 'tis knowledge useful to a maid, I'll teach ye, if ye so wish."

I shook my head. I was beginning to feel trapped in that now oppressive room, and wanted to escape. Then I remembered Molly's visitor. "And you did administer this to Esther Royton, when she came to sew?"

"Yes," Molly replied, with a concerned expression. "The poor little maid did take a tumble, with a lad hired for the harvest, does happen so it does. She did come to me the night yer good father was took so ill, and did beg my help. So I did take her in, but 'twas fearful hard for she were two full month gone. I'll not tell how for 'twere not pleasant, but now all's done, and no more will she tumble, for she's to wed."

The significance of her words horrified me, and I exclaimed, "But Molly, should Esther speak out, should she tell her parents?"

"Bless you she'll not speak. 'tis too fearful she is of what'd happen. No, fear not Pleasance, this secret is as safe as the ground on which we stand. Now, we must partake of our ale, come."

Back in the cosy normality of the other room, I stretched out my hands to the fire's comforting warmth. My friend had revealed a part of herself of which I wished I had remained ignorant. Our innocent walks in the woods and confidences beside the stream had suddenly become meaningless, for Molly was a woman for whom life held no secrets, and compared with her, I was but a child. All my knowledge of languages and books had prepared me for nothing, when faced with life's stark realities.

But what if Esther were to break her silence? The consequences were too terrible to contemplate, for it was a mortal sin to destroy life, no matter the reason. Despite the heat from the blazing wood I shivered, and Molly looked concerned.

"Ye are chilled, do ye drink of this wine, fresh heated with this poker from the fire that 'twill warm yer blood." As I sipped, she continued, "I did receive from William a letter, and he did say he'd writ to you."

"Yes, so he did," I replied dejectedly. William and the idyllic summer seemed years gone. I sighed, but seeing Molly's curious expression tried to hide my feelings, as I told her William had enclosed the verses as promised.

She gave a satisfied smile. "He writes a good letter does Will, and grateful I am to ye Pleasance, that I can now read his letters and answer them in my own hand. Come, do ye eat." She held out a pasty, but I had no appetite and shook my head.

"If you will excuse me, Molly, I have no hunger and should be tending to my father's meal, and the true reason I am here is for his sake. He did request more of the potion, if such is possible."

"Indeed yes, and fie on ye Pleasance, to forget so important an errand but mayhap other matters did make yer mind wander?"

She gave me a sly look, and with a laugh hurried to her inner chamber. I watched her go with distaste. Molly's spotless cottage had lost its charms. It held too many dark secrets, and I was almost reluctant to accept the bottle she now offered, and as she tucked the large flask into my basket I held the wicker firmly against my stomach, thus avoiding the embrace in which she seemed about to enfold me.

Later that night I tossed restlessly, as visions of Molly and Daniel kept running through my mind. Was such behaviour called love? Had my father behaved so with my mother? My flesh burned at the thought. All my dreams of a handsome knight upon his horse had been dispelled. I knew now only the reality of the sins of the flesh, but within marriage and with love, did such an act differ? Molly had not spoken of love, only need. After a while, I put my fingers between my legs, and pressed gently on my private parts. There was no sensation, so I massaged myself but instead of the response I craved, there was only soreness without excitement. Unsatisfied and exhausted, I lay willing sleep to come, but it was nearly dawn before I fell into unconsciousness, only to be awoken almost immediately by Bessie's voice, screaming hysterically from somewhere in the cottage.

Springing from the bed, I flung open my chamber door to see the girl, a steaming jug in her hands, staring wide eyed through the open doorway of my father's room. I ran to the entrance, and stopped. My father lay on his bed, apparently senseless. His pillow and nightshirt collar were stained bright red, and from his nostrils came two thin trickles of blood, which flowed slowly down his chin.

My stomach churning, I gripped the open door for support, and then cried out so loudly I cannot think now but that the entire village must have heard. "Mistress Tyler, do you fetch Mistress Tyler."

Alone beside the door I stood motionless, until my father moaned. Fear stiffening my legs into near immobility I approached the bed, and as I did he opened his eyes and muttered, as he tried unsuccessfully to raise himself, "My dear, what do you here?"

The sound of his voice restored me slightly, and I moved nearer saying, "Do you rest father, I have sent for Molly, she will know what is best."

"Mistress Molly, yes indeed so kind. I fear I must remain a while longer, child, I confess I feel most weak."

His eyes closed slowly and, rigid and cold, I sat down on the wooden stool beside the bed and waited for salvation from the next-door cottage.

CHAPTER 15

The news of my father's illness passed quickly through the village, and those parishioners who had always considered him to be a kind and industrious man, were soon calling with offers of sympathy, and help. Mistress Westley was our first visitor, and she entered carrying an enormous pie dish.

"'tis apple and gooseberry, me own recipe and sweetened too. I did think it might tempt good Verger's appetite. So sorry we are, but I did say only t'other day he looked a mite pale, so I did."

I passed the heavy dish to Bessie, whose eyes bulged at the sight of the appetising pudding, and invited the kind dame to take some refreshment. She shook her head. "Thankee child, I'll not stay. 'tis better ye should rest, for yer looks are much drawn. But if there's aught that ye think I can do, please to send for me at once."

My next visitor was Mistress Machin with a basket of baked pasties, swiftly followed by others including Mistress Royton, carrying a considerable quantity of cream and butter. On her departure, Thomas Whyte entered to offer his mother's services to launder my father's linen.

Reluctant to accept so personal a service, I declined, but as I was ushering him out he hesitated suddenly and then drew a packet from his leather pouch.

"Here mistress, I near forgot two letters. They seem to be in Master Radley's hand, one for Verger and t'other for ye." He gave me a keen look, and I flushed as I thrust the packet addressed to myself into my pocket, whilst placing the other on the table.

I was closing the door after Thomas as Molly entered her arms full of soiled linen. "Bessie," she called loudly, "Do ye take these sheets and see that they're well washed in a steaming tub."

"All of 'em?" My unenthusiastic little maid responded, with a woeful expression.

"Yes, indeed," Molly replied briskly. "The good Verger has been these two days ill, and there is much linen in a room of sickness."

Bessie looked appealingly at me. "The washer woman, I heard Thomas say as she's willing."

Molly looked at me in surprise. "What's this of Mistress Whyte, pray?" I explained and she looked doubtful.

"I did refuse," I added hurriedly. "I did think it wiser for my father's garments to be laundered within our own home."

Molly nodded. "Kind and honest though Mistress Whyte is, the linen might still be seen by prying eyes, which would not be seemly. Now Pleasance, I'll see to the good Verger once more, then ye must eat." I hesitated, but she insisted, "Yer father tells me that ye've remained beside his bed these two nights gone. 'tis foolish for he does sleep the night through, and ye must yer strength regain. For dear heart, strength is important at these times."

I knew without enquiring what those words foretold, and my heart went cold as Molly turned towards Bessie, who was still staring disconsolately at the soiled sheets. "Come now child, when all's soaking and I've tended Master Fry, we'll eat of the tasty offerings so kindly given. As to ye, Mistress Pleasance, ye'll take that rest afore the fire whilst we work."

Lacking the energy to protest I sank into my father's chair beside the fire and soon the warmth, combined with the thick woollen shawl in which Molly had encased me, lulled me into sleep. How long I remained there I had no knowledge, but I awoke to the appetising aroma of an apple pie heating in the oven.

Assuming myself to be alone, I removed the shawl and was about to rise, when I became aware of Hugh sitting at the table watching me with a grim, intent stare. Then, hearing the sound of voices coming from beyond the cottage door, I stood up and pulling it open, discovered Molly and Daniel Wallace outside, apparently arguing. Remembering how I had last seen them together I reddened, but he appeared not to notice as he greeted me with a smile, and expressed his concern at my father's illness.

Before I could thank him, Molly interrupted, exclaiming, "Now do ye leave Master Daniel, for we're to eat and ye should to yer bed, and do ye take care." Her voice took on an admonishing tone. "River water can do a body much harm."

Daniel having departed, she turned to me with a worried look. "He did fall into the Chater, for it did flood a little the night of the heavy rain and he's sustained a mild fever. I've given him a tisane of willow bark to relieve his heat, but I wish greatly he'd rest. He does say he must to Stamford, for to escort his mother home. Mistress Wallace has been residing with her cousin, these three weeks past."

I nodded in reply, trying to hide my distaste. I had no interest in Daniel Wallace's welfare, since to me he represented perfidy of the most iniquitous kind.

Despite my initial reluctance I consumed a hearty meal, and drank quantities of Molly's mulled wine which sent me once more to sleep, to awaken this time as dusk was falling. Rising swiftly, I hurried into my father's chamber and was delighted to find him reading by the light from his bed-side candle.

He gave me a welcoming, but reproving smile. "My child, tonight you must to your bed, for I am much recovered. It is not wise for you to remain awake the full night through. Though I do declare, it does mean much to me that you are by, but you are young child, and must have your rest for you have much to do in my place. Preacher Wyman is aware that you are very able and will prepare the church for service. He has in the past expressed doubts as to your abilities, but I know that you will conduct yourself as always, and carry out the work the Good Lord has given you to do."

Trying hard to quell the pride his words aroused, I replied eagerly, "Yes father, I will do as you so wish, but if I am away from home who will guide Bessie, for she does need instruction?"

"Good Mistress Molly has said she will do all that is required. Fear not child, it will not be long afore I am once again returned to my full strength. Your extra duties will be but momentary. Now, I have received one letter from Master Radley, but Mistress Molly does tell me that Thomas delivered two missives."

I had forgotten that William's letter still remained unopened in my pocket, and replied self-consciously, "Master Radley did send me a letter, but I fear I have not yet read its contents for I did not expect another word so soon. He cannot have yet received my answer to his first missive, but I will read it afore long."

My father frowned, "Why child, indeed you must. It is of no consequence that he should not have first received your reply. Correspondence does not wait upon correspondence. Go you now to your chamber and read your letter, for I will rest afore my supper, I fear I am suddenly a little fatigued." He smiled, and before I had a chance to reply, his eyes closed. As he slept, I extended my fingers and gently stroked the large bony hand, lying so inert upon the coverlet.

Until Molly's arrival he had been my only companion and, to a certain extent, my only friend. His severity of recent years and his lack of communication were now forgotten. He had been my shield against all problems. Even during the war years he had protected me, and while she lived my mother, from the difficulties and privations, by somehow procuring enough food to sustain us all.

I returned slowly to my chamber. The shutters were slightly ajar, and through the opening the early evening moon, which had just begun to materialise from behind a cloud, gleamed coldly. I controlled with difficulty the painful sob which was constricting my throat as I kneeled beside my bed and begged the Good Lord to spare my father's life, but there was no response, and nothing seemed to ease the numbness with which my senses now seemed enveloped.

Years of obedience had taught me never to question the Lord's will, all must be accepted without demur. He, and He alone decided the destiny of all, but passing doubts would persist in entering my thoughts. My father had been a good man all his life; devoting himself to the Church and his fellow men. Why then should he be chosen for such suffering? Were one's rewards, such as they were, truly to be found only in heaven?

Then I remembered my father's unaccustomed praise, and resolved that to accomplish my tasks to the best of my ability, and to give him pleasure in my success was now my only desire. Feeling somewhat calmer, I prayed again. Not this time for the miracle of my father's recovery, but for strength to sustain me in the trial that was to come.

My prayers completed, I drew William's letter from my pocket. The moonlight had now become too dim to read by so I struck the tinder box, and after lighting my candle broke the seal. His second letter was longer than his first. It described a market he had visited at Nottingham, and informed me that he had now hired another apprentice. He also wrote at length of a new book he was reading. 'It is written,' he wrote, 'by one Robert Herrick. Not I fear a man of whom the good Verger would fully approve, for Master Herrick does compare the old order with the new. But I do find his writings to be composed of much joy, for those who would be happy, and fully pious for the heart that does seek more secular ways.'

As if to confirm his views, William had penned one of Master Herrick's verses which, on finishing, caused me to press warm hands against even warmer cheeks, for they read:

'Her eyes the glow worm lend thee,
The shooting stars attend thee;

And the elves also,
Whose little eyes glow,
Like the sparks of fire, befriend thee.'

It was obviously part of a love poem, the remainder of which I did not doubt William would impart as our correspondence increased.

The next day being Saturday, I spent the morning dusting the church, intending to visit Preacher Wyman in the afternoon but he saved me the trouble by entering the building to enquire, in a strangely over-sympathetic voice, "And how does the good Verger, Mistress Fry? Can you convey the happy news that he is much improved?"

"I fear not as yet, sir."

"A pity, indeed a pity. It is now four days, is it not, and four days is indeed a very considerable time, indeed it is, for a Verger to neglect his duties."

"They are not neglected, sir," I replied hurriedly. "For do you see, I have completed the tasks."

"I speak of his OTHER duties," the Preacher interrupted, emphatically. "Consoling the sick, visiting the wayward, tending the bereaved and burying the dead, all duties of importance in a Parish such as ours. He did intimate, Mistress Fry, that you might undertake these tasks, but I fear that is not to be. There are matters such as a maid cannot tend. No, it is more than evident that should the Verger not be in full health by, I think Monday will suffice, then I shall indeed have to consult those in authority who can assist." He drew a small square of white linen from his spotlessly creased cuff, and held it to his nose. "And there is, of course, this noxious floor that task I CAN leave in your hands?"

"Yes, indeed sir, but I do not fully comprehend your meaning, as to consulting others in authority to assist."

"To assist, girl, does mean to ASSIST. I cannot undertake all the duties appertaining to this Parish. Why, it does stretch many miles about. The good Verger cannot in truth expect to receive his stipend for naught. No, I fear if he is not fully able two days hence, matters must be taken further. Good day to you, and do you wait upon me early tomorrow, the Good Lord's day."

With a final agitated nod he swept from the church, leaving me trying to control the tears of anger and fear that were welling up in my eyes. I was not too stunned to fully understand the import of his words and hesitating only to lock the church door, I sped trembling violently to Molly's cottage. Once inside, I collapsed into her arms and sobbed out my conversation with the Preacher.

Immediately, she declared grimly, "This cannot be, to withhold the stipend should yer father not return to his duties by Monday morn. I'll to Sir Oliver Alton, he must know of this."

"Sir Oliver Alton?" I gasped. "Of what concern is it of his? He does have his own minister, and does rarely visit St. Luke's."

"Sir Oliver be the squire hereabouts, and a magistrate and does know the law. If there's aught that can be done, Sir Oliver'll know of it. Now do ye return to yer father, and I'll to Sir Oliver's steward within the hour."

Over-awed by her command of the situation I remained seated, staring unseeingly into the fire. I was still motionless on my stool when she re-entered, dressed in a tall crowned, wide brimmed leather hat, and a dark green fitted overdress. In her hands, she carried a pair of leather gloves with patterned cuffs. The overall effect was one of subdued elegance.

I stared at her in silent admiration, and she laughed. "It does well to meet gentry, as gentry. This over-gown is of a fine wool cloth, and me hat and gloves do suit it well. Will I pass muster think ye, at Sir Oliver's gates?"

"Indeed, yes," I breathed softly, my own problems momentarily forgotten.

Two hours later Sir Oliver's steward, Walter Harris, a short plump man with a complexion like a polished red apple, was standing with me beside my father's bed explaining that, despite his present indisposition and his inability to execute his duties, my father would continue to receive his stipend in the customary manner.

"For Sir Oliver has been told that Mistress Fry will be about to carry out the simpler of your tasks, good sir?"

"Yes, indeed," my father agreed weakly, giving me a slight smile.

"So be it," Master Harris replaced his hat on his head, and bowed slightly. "You will please keep Sir Oliver informed as to Master Fry's progress, will you not ma'am."

"Yes, indeed, sir," I gave a quick curtsey, and then followed him down the stairs. Reaching the parlour, Master Harris turned to me looking grave.

"Sir Oliver did ask that I convey to you his most sincere sympathy, at this most difficult of times, Mistress Fry. Mistress Tyler did tell us that the good Verger's recovery is not anticipated, and that his passing is but a few weeks hence."

"Yes." My voice sounded strangely distant, and not at all like my own.

"And the unhappy news of his future demise is known only to you both?"

I nodded, and Master Harris looked reflective. "It is Sir Oliver's concern that you should not be destitute. Are you acquainted with your father's matters of business?"

"Matters of business, what mean you, sir?" I frowned.

The little man smiled. "Has Master Fry an income, ma'am, apart from the stipend he does receive from the church?"

I looked at him helplessly suddenly aware of how ignorant I was concerning my father's way of life. Every week, since my fourteenth birthday, I had kept an account of our housekeeping for my father to settle, but the only money I had ever seen had been the silver four-pence he had given me to spend in Stamford.

"No matter," Master Harris waved a placating hand. "I did but ask merely for Sir Oliver, and we will deal with such matters when the time does arrive." He bowed slightly. "Now I will to Preacher Wyman, to impart this news. I do bid you farewell, Mistress Fry, and take heart, you have many friends."

"He be a fine one, mistress."

I stared down aghast, as Bessie crawled from beneath the table.

"How long pray, have you been hiding?"

"I was no hiding, I was asleep."

"Asleep, but it is not yet mid-day. What did you hear of our conversation? WHAT did you HEAR?"

"Only that master is to die."

Her words, spoken without feeling, almost overcame me and I cried out hysterically, "It is not TRUE, he is going to recover, he is. HE IS!"

"Bless us, what's to do?" Molly stood in the open doorway, a basket on her arm and a pie dish in her hands.

"Molly, she knows, she heard Master Harris speak of my father's health, and if she knows, so will all the village."

"Not so," Molly declared, and then turning to look at Bessie, she narrowed her eyes and hissed, " For if ye do dare to say one word, missie, of what ye've heard today, I'll turn ye into a TOAD. Do ye hear me, a TOAD."

Bessie's screams, as she grovelled in terror on the floor, were later pronounced to have reached a traveller journeying through the village on his way to Stamford. I put a restraining hand on my friend's arm, but Molly was obviously enjoying herself too much to be diverted. "If not a toad then, but a BEE, a large furry buzzing BEE." Ashen faced and trembling Bessie stared up in terror, and Molly laughed. "Foolish child, go ye now about yer duties. But remember mind, the large furry buzzing bee."

Still shaking, Bessie clambered to her feet and fled into the outshut. I shook my head reprovingly. "Molly, you should not have alarmed her so. It is not wise, for she does tell all she hears to her mother."

"Nay, she'll no speak. So craven a child I have never before seen. Now, to matters of import, Master Harris, what said he?" I explained, and she nodded approvingly. "That be good, I did not see Sir Oliver, for he was preparing to depart for London town. There are rumours that the Lord Protector is indisposed, and many folk of note have been called to the great city. But Master Harris did consult with Sir Oliver, so all's well. Did he speak of aught else?"

"He did ask if my father did have other than his stipend, and I did say I knew not. My father has never spoken of such things with me."

Molly looked at me sharply. "Yer father has ne'er spoken of yer inheritance, when ye should wed?"

I frowned. "Of what do you infer?"

But, instead of replying, she asked, "Yer father was an only son?"

"Yes, and our only kin is my mother's cousin Mistress Frost, in London."

Molly nodded, and appeared lost in thought. I was about to enquire again as to her meaning of my inheritance, when I noted that her complexion was very pale, and she looked somewhat drawn.

"Is aught wrong, Molly, you do appear troubled?"

"'tis Daniel, he's ill Pleasance, truly ill. His fever's progressed right bad. I've writ to Mistress Wallace begging I be allowed to tend him, and I truly hope she'll comply with my request."

At that moment, as though in response to Molly's words, a man's voice was heard calling her name, and immediately she gathered up her shawl and ran from the cottage.

CHAPTER 16

When not tending to my father's needs Molly remained at Daniel's bedside, and those villagers who had initially conveyed their sympathies to me, now directed their goodwill towards Mistress Wallace, leaving me to devote to my father all the time I could spare from church duties.

Having assisted him from childhood, these tasks were far from onerous, but the cleaning of Preacher Wyman's "noxious floor" proved a considerable trial. Never before having been exposed to such coarse language and behaviour, I soon appreciated why my father had expressed his unwillingness to leave me alone with my helpers.

The Workmans and the Trents loathed each other, as only established village dwellers and gypsies can, and on their first day of work stood braced on either side of the aisle like soldiers prior to battle. Endeavouring to deliver my cleaning instructions in clear and confident tones, I was dismayed to hear my voice sound so shrill and nervous.

The sniggers and glances which both families exchanged amongst themselves disconcerted me even more, and it was in a state of near desperation that I at last sought refuge in a pew, having directed the Workmans to work at the back of the church, and the Trents at the front.

At first there was only the occasional muttered oath, but then the youngest Trent son, a youth of eleven, relieved himself at the back of the church. I stared in horrified disbelief at the puddle and exclaimed, "If you please, Ralph, to do such outside the church." The boy turned towards me, still holding his penis from which urine continued to dribble. "Speak ye mistress?"

I heard someone give a loud guffaw and Ralph's younger sister Honor giggled then, to my relief, Mistress Trent cuffed her young son's head. "That be no way to behave to mistress, and her a daughter of church."

"She be no daughter of church, she be daughter of Verger," Ralph retorted, at which Mistress Workman stared angrily at her husband, and declared, "Be you going to let them folk behave so, to Mistress Fry?"

Before I could intervene, Master Workman glared menacingly at Mistress Trent and snarled, "Do ye mind yer son, mistress."

To my consternation Master Trent, a thickset muscular man, some five years younger than Workman, then roared at the other man, "An who be ye, to speak so to me wife?"

There was an answering profanity, and I watched helplessly as the two antagonists leered at each other. Then Workman hit out viciously at Trent, who dodged. Immediately the two families pounced on each other, and became an entangled heaving mound, on the church floor.

I stood motionless for a moment, then something in my brain seemed to snap and with clenched fists and arms thrown wide, I screamed, "Do you STOP, I say, STOP. OR YOU WILL NOT RECEIVE PAYMENT." At the magic word "payment" everyone unravelled themselves, the two fathers stopped fighting, and within seconds everyone was once again on their knees scrubbing the stones.

But my relief was short-lived, for on the remaining two days it took to complete the task both families took every possible opportunity to harass me, either by foul language or behaviour. When at last the task was finished, I felt as exhausted as if I had scrubbed the entire Church myself.

My confidence was somewhat restored later when Preacher Wyman, having examined the pale flagstones with intense thoroughness, admitted grudgingly, "I must give you my thanks, Mistress Fry. It is a task well executed." Then he gave me a strange look and, to my surprise, said, "And you are now what age, Mistress Fry?"

"Seven and ten, so please you, sir," I replied, blushing under his unexpected scrutiny. He gave me another searching glance then, without further comment, departed.

My father listened to the account of my trials, with an amused expression.

"I did fear it would be so child, without me by. But you have achieved much, and I do not now fear your entrance into the world. For though such was not the best way to exert yourself, it has proved you have strength to call upon, when required. Now do you bring me quill and ink, for I would write some letters, and while I am so employed do you take yourself into the fresh air. A quiet walk will be beneficial, for it is a bright, pleasant day."

Subduing my desire to embrace him for the strength and confidence with which his praise imbued me, I attended to his needs and afterwards, donning shawl and pattens, walked towards the Chater stream. I had intended to cross into the woodland beyond, but as I passed the church a sudden desire to absorb the building's peace and tranquillity overcame me, and as I now always carried the key with me, I entered and seated myself in a back pew.

Contemplating my surroundings of sanctity and stone, I thought of the many folk who, like myself, had sought comfort within its walls. The church was very old, and over the years many unhappy souls must have entered to find solace. Then a noise disturbed my reverie, and I looked up almost expecting to see Molly, but it was only a mouse scurrying across the floor towards the open door.

On the eighth day of Daniel's illness I was seated beside my father's bed reading to him from his bible, when we heard the sound of running footsteps. Then the front door was heard crashing open, and Bessie burst into the chamber, gasping, "He be dead, and they say do she killed him and all, and that she be a witch."

We both stared at her in shocked silence, until my father said quietly, "Pleasance child, turn to Psalm one hundred and twenty and read to us what the Good Lord says, that Bessie may learn how to repent of her evil words."

Obediently, I turned to the correct page and began to recite, but when I reached the line, *"Deliver my soul O Lord from lying lips and from a deceitful tongue,"* Bessie exclaimed loudly, "I ain't got no lying lips nor deceitful tongue. 'tis what Mistress Wallace do say, that yon be a witch and she did say she would turn me into a toad, and a furry bee."

"Bessie," I cried, only to be restrained by my father's hand on my arm.

"Child," he looked kindly, at the trembling girl. "Do you come closer and tell me of these wicked lies. Who is so foolish as to speak so, and what of this nonsense of a toad and a bee?"

"They be village folk, sir, and they do all say that Mistress Tyler she did give potions to Master Daniel, and that they did kill him. They did see with they own eyes, so they says. 'twas red with frogs and they did jump out."

"Frogs in a potion?" My father pursed his lips slightly as if to restrain a smile, and I felt myself relax. Whatever Bessie had heard had originated from a source as unreliable as herself.

I glanced at my father, expecting him to look as relieved as I felt, but he was no longer smiling and when he spoke, his voice sounded anxious. "And did this remarkable hearsay come also from the lips of Mistress Wallace, may I ask?"

"No, sir, from...."

"Your mother?"

"No, sir," Bessie sounded aggrieved. "Mistress, she did say I weren't to see my mother, 'twas Mistress Westley who I did hear speak so."

"And what of the toad and the bee, how came by you of these fancies?"

"She did say she would," Bessie's voice rose agitatedly, "and mistress, she were by and heard all."

"I see," my father gave me a contemplative glance. "Thank you Bessie, you may leave us now. I will call you later, when I require more nourishment."

Pouting heavily, Bessie walked slowly from the room, and as soon as she had gone I hurriedly told my father of Molly's foolish threat. He looked grave.

"We know that Mistress Molly spoke in jest, but it was most unwise. Mistress Westley is a kindly soul, but I fear lacks depth of intellect. Amends must be swiftly made to restore confidence in our friend. Firstly, my dear, do you go to Mistress Molly and ask her to come to me, then to Mistress Wallace with our deepest regrets and sympathies. Explain my incapacity, and say that if at any time she should seek succour or guidance, I am here at her disposal. When you have seen her, do you go to Mistress Westley and seek a true account of what she did say, and return immediately to impart her words to me. Go now child, for it is necessary that the truth of this matter is made fact."

To my consternation it was Hugh who opened the door, stuttering that his sister was not at home. Agitatedly, I scribbled a note on Molly's slate and after leaving it in a prominent position, hurried to Mistress Wallace's cottage where a number of villagers were gathered outside, whispering amongst themselves.

As I approached they ceased speaking, and fell back to form a passage way. Their manner, although not impolite seemed cold, and I was aware that the eyes staring at me were not friendly. So it was with some unease that I knocked on Mistress Wallace's door which, at my second attempt, was opened by Mistress Machin. She greeted me politely, but her eyes lacked their usual warmth and as I explained the reason for my visit, she frowned.

"Mistress Wallace does sit with her son. I will tell her you are here, if you will please to wait."

As she moved towards the stairway door heavy footsteps were heard descending to the parlour, and Master Wallace entered. On seeing me, he glowered heavily.

"Mistress Fry my felicitations, and do you come to share with us our grief in my sister's great time of trial?"

His insolence was obvious and I flushed, but remembering I was my father's envoy, I replied firmly, "Indeed I do, sir, and my father does send his very

136

deepest sympathies, and does say that if there is aught he can do, Mistress Wallace has but to ask."

"Ah yes, the good Verger," Master Wallace's voice became harsher. "And he too, so do I hear, has accepted ministrations from the foul woman who has wrought so much misery on this unhappy family. But the Verger I am told, has not yet succumbed, due no doubt to the fact that she is a friend of your house." The violence with which Master Wallace spat out his words was overwhelming, and I swayed backwards.

"Sir, I comprehend not your meaning. Mistress Tyler has administered to my father only."

"Yes, of that I am aware, but WHAT has she GIVEN?"

"A potion that does relieve his cough," I gasped.

"And he is recovering you say? Ah, you shake your head and correct you are, for he never will, and do you be warned to deny access to that vile piece that purports to be a woman. Do you lock your door and bolt your casement else she will find a way to inflict likewise upon you, what she has wrought here. But I do forget. You are a close acquaintance of this strumpet are you not? Speak now, do not try to hide the truth. You blench and cannot reply indeed you cannot."

For some minutes more, the incensed Councillor continued to spit out his invective until a female voice called, "Husband, dear husband."

Unnoticed by either of us his wife had entered from the stairway door, and now laid a restraining hand on the Councillor's arm. Clad entirely in black without any relieving white, and with an expression as dour as that of her husband, she murmured, "My dearest Humphrey, agitated though you are, is it not possible to delay your condemnation of that wicked creature? We must recall that this lady is the daughter of Fretson's most industrious and revered Verger, a hard-working gentleman whose dedication to our Lord has never been questioned."

With obvious difficulty Master Wallace controlled himself, and replied irritably, "I make no accusation whatever of the Verger. I speak not of him I speak only of the friendship between Mistress Fry and that worthless strumpet that this village has taken so trustingly to its heart."

His voice had once again begun to rise, but before he could continue there was a light tapping on the door, which was then pushed open to reveal Mistress Royton, her face creased into a mass of sympathy.

"Ah, me, I'll not intrude. I have but brought some sustenance for the poor lady." She turned, and seeing me cried, "Why, Mistress Fry, I declare 'tis passing strange that you be here."

There was a brief silence, before Mistress Wallace murmured hurriedly, "I am sure my poor sister would be more than happy to see you, ma'am. Do you go up the stairway. Mistress Clay and Mistress Burrows do sit with her now, but you will, I am sure, be very welcome."

As the visitor ascended the stairway Master Wallace continued to glare at me, but before he could renew his vehemence Mistress Wallace enquired as to who was tending my father in my absence. When I explained that he was alone except for Bessie, she declared, "Then you must at once return Mistress Fry, must she not, husband? To leave the good Verger with one such as her is most unwise, and we do all pray for the Verger's swift recovery, do we not Master Wallace?"

The Councillor nodded before saying, in a more controlled voice, "You are young Mistress Fry, and have been sheltered from evil by your watchful and protective sire. Such a life as yours, devoted to your father and the church, has never been exposed to the dangers that life can encompass. Godlessness lurks everywhere, even in the most innocent of places, and an unsullied mind such as yours cannot be aware of the dangers that can be hidden behind a smiling face, or a willing gesture. And for this reason I do advise you, Mistress Fry, to be most wary of your neighbour. Treat with caution any offers of physic, or such like. It is not to your advantage that you maintain your friendship with Mistress Tyler, do you comprehend me?"

Too agitated to reply without losing control, I nodded then bobbed a swift curtsey and stepped outside. The crowd had increased, and as I walked trembling down the path way made for me, I heard mutterings of "witch" and "magic" follow me down the road.

By the time I entered my parlour, I was shaking violently with emotion, and Bessie stared at me with consternation, hissing, "Mistress, she been upstairs with the master."

I tried to concentrate. "Who?"

"Her the witch, be ye ill mistress ye face be all wet?"

"It is nothing. Do you say Mistress Tyler is with my father?"

"No longer mistress, she be here while he slept, but she be gone now. She did leave some bottle and a paper, but I did take it away, and the paper I did burn, lest harm befall the master."

"You BURNED the paper. Merciful heaven and where is the bottle?" I stared frantically, around the parlour.

"Here," Bessie took a large flask from her pocket.

I snatched the precious liquid from the maid's grip and stared helplessly at the flames of the newly backed fire, but my desire to strike Bessie to the ground had to be subdued so, in as controlled a voice as I was able, I said, "Do you prepare a warm drink for me please, and bring it to my father's chamber."

Bessie pouted in protest, but I ignored her and mounted the stairs to my father's room. He was now awake and listened intently to my discourse, before leaning back against his pillows in obvious distress.

"This is indeed a most calamitous occurrence. It would seem that our neighbour has aroused much enmity against herself. I cannot fully comprehend why. Did she not tend poor young Master Wallace, as she has tended all? Wherefore is the source of these tidings? I wish indeed that she had awakened me, for then I could have questioned her. As it is, I fear matters will take a dire turn, if such defamatory rumours are not quickly baulked in their passage. I think it would be advantageous for me to consult with Preacher Wyman as to how this matter could best be resolved, and perhaps, my dear, you would take a note for me to Master Harris. You will kindly write at my dictation, but first I will rest. I fear I have again become exceedingly weary." He closed his eyes, and before I could rise from my stool he had fallen into a deep sleep.

I tiptoed into my own chamber, and opened the shutter. A number of people were standing opposite Molly's cottage, in much the same way as they had stood at the time of the Goodwife's death. Only this time there were no sympathetic expressions, and the crowd consisted not of elderly concerned folk but young boys and girls, who were sniggering and pointing at the front door. Then a stone flew through the air, and I heard the sound of splintering, as it smashed its way through one of Goodwife Hargreave's treasured window-panes. I quickly pulled the shutters too and locked them.

"Mistress?" Bessie stood in the doorway holding out a pewter mug from which a tendril of steam arose. I took it and the warmth felt comforting against my palms, as Bessie continued with a self-righteous air, "And her brother, yon mad Hugh, he did give this paper and he said 'twas of importance, so I did no burn it though 'tis wrong to bring such in this house."

Ignoring her, I quickly read the note. It was unsigned, and brief. *My dearest friend, I have with the Verger left a goodly supply of potion and a recipe in which ye will find the contents. This physic is of greater strength than that which he did have. I think it wise if we do not for some time meet, and I will not visit as I fear I have much trouble at the present time. I have sent word to Old Mother Burrows to assist ye, but as yet have heard naught. Take her if she does come, for the good Verger's nursing will I fear increase rather than wane. I do love you, and God Bless you Pleasance. Take heart, dear one we have right on our side.'*

I tucked it inside my bodice. How typical of Molly to take care not to sign the note, but yet to end so effusively. I smiled to myself, how could anyone wish to harm such a kind, good soul as my Molly, then I stood up as Bessie scampered back into the room.

"Mistress 'tis master, he's shit himself and we don't have no more sheets."

"Go get," I stopped, and for a second had never felt so alone.

"Mistress?" Bessie's voice seemed to be coming from far away, and I stared unseeingly at her, before saying, "We must do the best we can. Here do you take the covers from my bed, and why are there no clean ones pray?"

"He do soil 'em every time he shits and a clean nightshirt, be there one?"

I winced. "Are there none in his chamber?"

"I know not. Mistress Tyler, she did bring 'em with her."

"Brought them with her? But my father does have his own."

"No mistress, he had but two so she did make him more."

I stared helplessly at the girl, but before I could continue, a familiar voice from long ago was heard calling from below, "Be there anybody home?"

With intense relief I ran down the stairway to be met by Old Mother Burrows, her cap awry and her eyes wide. "Lovedy I be here to help, and have ye not heard. Sir Oliver has had yon lass taken, and the Witchfinder be sent for from Oakham."

CHAPTER 17

"Now Mistress Fry, would you be so kind as to repeat for me the words you have just pronounced," Master Oswald the Witch-Finder smiled encouragingly at me. "Come, it cannot be so very arduous to repeat so few words, can it now?" Aware only of the agonising monthly cramp that seemed to have taken possession of my entire body, I could only shake my head. Master Oswald pursed his lips. "I fear Mistress Fry, a nod will not do. We must hear your voice."

Longing to press my hands to my aching stomach I stammered, "I did see Mistress Tyler."

"You did see the Witch, yes Mistress Fry," he interrupted quickly. "You did see the Witch?"

"I did see her walk in the stream," I whispered. Nothing, not even this persistent man would make me call Molly a witch.

"A little louder Mistress Fry, we must hear your words. You did see her walk in the stream more than on the one time?" I nodded again, and Master Oswald frowned. "I fear Mistress Fry as I did say, we must have your spoken word. For how else is poor Master Pryor to inscribe the evidence you do so helpfully provide." He nodded sympathetically at the young clerk sitting at the head of the parlour table, laboriously scratching his quill across a sheet of paper.

Another wave of nauseating pain overcame me as I felt the blood ease its way determinedly between my legs, and I longed to flee as the Witchfinder repeated his question adding, "These walks within the waters of the stream, they did occur did they not prior always to a calamity befalling the village?"

"I know not, sir," I protested, faintly.

Master Oswald nodded, in apparent sympathy. "No matter, all will be revealed with the passage of time." He glanced down at a sheaf of notes which lay on the table before him, and the silence that followed unsettled me more than the questions which had preceded it. Not that the interrogation had so far been frightening, or particularly arduous.

Despite my terror at being told by Master Harris that the Witchfinder would wish to question me, I had been reassured by Master Oswald's outward show of genuine concern on learning of my father's illness. He had also treated me with courtesy, and talked for some time of village life whilst partaking of a mug of ale, and the inquisition had commenced before I realised it had begun.

Perhaps if my woman's time had not descended a week before it was due, and the stomach cramps from which I always suffered had not been so acute, I might have been more aware of what I was saying. But my adversary was a craftsman of his trade, an adept manipulator of nervous witnesses, and in his hands I was but a Corn-Dolly, to be fashioned and twisted in whatever direction he desired.

His appearance had been misleading. Plump and of medium height, he had a full round face that shone with health, as did his ruddy cheeks and abundant copper coloured hair. Combined with his smart brown doublet and breeches, brilliant white shirt, lace collar and cuffs, he reminded me of the country gentlemen at the Hall, and this imbued me with assurance, which no doubt had been his intention.

Prior to his visit I had been occupied with church duties, and although I had longed to see Molly I had abided by her wishes, and allowed myself only an occasional glance at her cottage.

There had also been the task of settling Old Mother Burrows who, to my relief, had been acknowledged by my father with a friendly welcome. Unfortunately Bessie had demonstrated no such amiability towards her new colleague, grumbling ceaselessly because she had extra food to prepare. She was also becoming increasingly slatternly in the performance of her duties, to the extent that I knew an eventual confrontation was unavoidable.

I was trying to decide how to broach the subject the day previous to Master Oswald's visit, when I had returned to the cottage to discover that every floor and wall had been cleansed, and every article of furniture polished. Before I could enquire the reason for this change of mood, I was delighted to hear Bessie agreeing with alacrity to Old Mother Burrows's request for assistance in attending to my father's personal needs.

He had become particularly agitated on learning of the Witchfinder's impending visit, and despite Master Harris's attempts to reassure him that it "was but a small matter" gasped anxiously to me, after the Steward had departed, "The truth my dear, is all God expects of you. What'er is asked speak only what you know, and you must tell Master Oswald that I wish to be addressed. I have much of which I must speak. Please do you make Master

Oswald aware that there are many in this village who do not fully comprehend Mistress Molly's virtues, and Preacher Wyman, I must speak with Preacher Wyman."

As though exhausted by his efforts, he fell back on his pillow and I thought how Preacher Wyman would no doubt refuse such a request, and as I did not wish to give him that pleasure, I decided that although I would obey my father as to his wish to see the Witchfinder, I would pretend to forget his request to see the preacher, but it pained me to deceive this dear man who had for so long been my protector and guide.

And sorely was I in need of such guidance now, to show me how to pierce the mask of Master Oswald's encouraging smile, and discover why he asked repeated questions about our visits to the Chater and the food we had consumed. His interest in such innocent past-times confused me. Surely Molly's herbs, her cat and her tending of the sick had more relevance? But he asked repeatedly, which of us had carried the food, and from where it had originated.

I answered to the best of my memory, thinking how very trivial it all seemed. What could be wrong in eating, sitting, and paddling in a stream? Another spasm of pain engulfed me and I winced, then looked up to see Master Oswald smiling indulgently.

"I am all too aware Mistress Fry, how very tedious must these questions appear to a lady such as yourself, and I do indeed extend my gratitude to you for your fortitude and patience, in this most vexatious of matters. But if you could just once more relate to me the exact times as you do recall them, when the accused did enter Chater stream."

Obediently, I repeated yet again that Molly had on the majority of occasions that we had sat beside the Chater, discarded her stockings and pattens and waded out into the shallow waters.

"And what of her speech when in the stream? For she did speak, or so you did say." The Witchfinder's voice had the purring sound of a replete cat.

I struggled to remember, then replied listlessly, "She did call to me and laugh, and sometimes tease."

"Tease, I do not recall 'tease'," he seemed to leap at the word, like a crouching tiger. "Master Pryor, would you be so good as to peruse your notes. Has the word 'tease' been spoken?"

The clerk glanced hurriedly back through his sheets of paper. "No Master Oswald, the word 'tease' has not before, been spoken."

"So the Witch did tease, and how, Mistress Fry, was this teasing performed?"

"She did splash me."

"Splash you, and pray how was this accomplished?"

For a second I thought he must be making sport of me, and I laughed, exclaiming, "She did bend down and taking water in her hand did throw it at me."

The Witchfinder's eyes narrowed slightly. "She did throw the water with her hand you say, and did any of this water reach your person, did you find aught of it upon your gown?"

"No," I replied, puzzled.

"Not even the merest drop?"

"I believe not."

"But you could not, upon the Good Lord's Book swear to that?"

I blenched, and stuttered, "Upon the Holy Bible no, sir. I could not so swear, for some tiny droplets may have touched me."

"Then they were of a minor nature, most fortuitous. Now upon the day that young Master Whyte did meet with his calamitous mishap. You were, as I do recall you said, walking with the Witch upon the path, having first walked beside the stream? And you did say she pushed you to the ground?"

"Yes, it was to allow the horse to pass."

"And she did remain upon the path?" He interrupted, sharply.

"For a brief moment."

"Just so," Master Oswald carefully folded his piece of paper into a neat square. "You have Mistress Fry, been of the very greatest assistance. We are much indebted to you. Now Master Pryor, I do think we need remain no further. You will have Mistress Fry's evidence prepared by tomorrow forenoon for her to swear to, for we will not desire you to attend the trial as a witness. Your place is here, beside your much respected father."

With the words "trial," "witness," "evidence," and "swear to," repeating themselves in my head, I tried to explain to Master Oswald that my father also wished to see him, but my request was drowned by a sharp banging on the cottage door, and before anyone could move it swung open to reveal Master Wallace, who entered with a grim face and piercing eyes.

"I bid you welcome, sir" Master Oswald declared with obvious enthusiasm. "Master Harris did say you would be so kind as to escort us to your sister, Mistress Wallace. Now Mistress Fry, I do thank you once again for your assistance, and if we do call tomorrow forenoon, that does meet with your pleasure?"

"My father," I gabbled desperately. "He did say he particularly wishes to address you."

"The Verger?" Master Oswald frowned. "We cannot encroach upon him at this time, and would not dream of so doing. His health is paramount, and to disrupt his peace would be most unwise. No, we do have all we need. You have Mistress Fry, as I have but earlier stated, been most helpful and I thank you." Before I could reply, he had bowed politely and followed Master Wallace and the clerk through the doorway.

"Shall I be lighting the candles, Mistress?" Bessie's voice was unusually subdued. Slumping exhaustedly onto the nearest chair I nodded, and then gasped in horror as she murmured, "Will she hang?"

"Merciful Heaven, what makes you speak so?"

"'tis what's said in village."

"I have told you many times Bessie that gossip is against the Lord's teaching. You are most unwise to listen to idle tongues, now do you prepare our supper."

Leaving Bessie still fiddling with the candles, I climbed wearily to my father's chamber where Old Mother Burrows greeted me with her finger on her lips. "He sleeps lovely, best to let him rest. Let's to yon chamber, I would hear what did pass."

She led the way into my room, and I followed sighing, "My father will be much dismayed. Master Oswald would not speak with him, so concerned was he for my father's health."

"I did think they'd no ask him, he being Verger and all, 'tis not fitting that he should speak. A man of God should have no call to be so took up. Did ye speak of the potions he takes?"

"No, they did not ask me."

"Then 'tis best left unsaid. Quiet now, lest wench hear us. What knows she of the potions?"

"Only that Molly did give them to me. But whyfore do we speak so, all the village does know of her healing ointments, and remedies. And many have benefited there from."

"Aye, but less said soon's mended, and what manner of questions did they ask, mention they yon cat?"

"No, they did enquire as to the walks we made through Chater Wood to the stream, where it was our wont to sit beside the water."

"Water, they did ask of water," Old Mother Burrows eyes seemed to cut into mine. "What said ye, child?" The old woman gripped my arm agitatedly, and I winced.

"I did but say that Molly walked in the stream."

"And they did ask if such did occur before a calamity to the village?"

"They did mention Thomas Whyte and Master Daniel Wallace," I replied slowly, in an effort to calm her.

"'tis bad," she exclaimed, looking suddenly pale. "Such does bode no good to yon wench."

"Why?" I demanded, agitatedly. "I understand not your meaning."

"Water, lass," Old Mother Burrows shook her head. "Water and witches, for water is for baptism and witches who do walk in water do defile its purity. 'tis said that if a witch do walk in water afore she is put to swimming, she will sink and rise again cleansed for all to see, despite that she be still a servant of the devil. And water touched by a witch with incantations when thrown on another can carry all manner of wickedness to that poor soul. Did not yon Master Wallace fall ill on emerging from his ducking in the Chater?" I tried to interrupt, but the old woman persisted, "And did they ask aught about splashing upon your person, or mayhap upon the food ye did consume?"

"They did ask if Molly did splash me."

"And yer clothes, did ye say t'was wet upon yer clothes?"

"I said I did not think it was so, but Master Oswald did ask if I could swear to such upon the Holy Bible, and I did then say that mayhap some...."

"Droplets did fall upon yer gown?" The old woman finished, her voice rising.

"Yes," I replied helplessly, trying to succumb the feeling of dread which seemed to be consuming me.

Mother Burrows nodded, her lips tightly clenched. She remained so for a few moments before taking my hand firmly, and in a calmer but serious tone, said, "When they return with that which ye must sign, ye'll not change what ye've said, not by one word. Mind me well lovedy, Witchfinders be wily folk and many a poor creature was misused by Matthew Hopkins. Some as had naught to do with witches did find themselves swinging from a rope, for all they cried their innocence. So ye'll not gainsay a word will ye lovedy, not one word." As the old woman repeated her warning her grip on my hand tightened sharply, and I gasped out my consent. Apparently reassured, she released me.

"'tis well, and now ye must eat. Do ye send me a morsel on a plate, that'll suffice. The potion that the wench did leave it do run down. 'tis only drop by drop as I do use but he needs much sleep. Know ye how to brew more from herbs that we've in cottage?"

"No, Molly did leave the recipe, but it was...."

"Burned by yon interfering scrap of nothing, aye so she did say."

"I do not think she meant harm. She thought it was for the best," I replied, aghast that anyone could be so described.

Old Mother Burrows grunted loudly, "If I'd a golden coin for all folk who meddle so as to 'not mean harm' I'd set meself in a palace. So we have no such recipe, and no such herbs?"

"The herbs can be obtained," I replied, remembering suddenly the vessels in Molly's special room. "Mistress Tyler has them in her room of physic."

"Nay," Mother Burrows shook her head vigorously, "Ye must na' enter yon cottage. What I can brew will suffice. 'tis better if naught is said about potions and such like. I've told yon Bessie that it be but a brew of dandelion leaves, and I did tell her 'twas proper that she did burn the recipe." She patted me gently on the shoulder. "Fret ye not lovely, 'twill all be righted soon as ye can take a breath. Did say where they keep poor wench?"

"No," I replied, in surprise. "Is she not still within her cottage? I have seen neither her or Hugh depart."

"Nay lass, she's no been there for many a day, and they did slay her cow, hens and bees two days back, but the cat it did escape. As to lass, mayhap they keep her in the forge, and Hugh's confined but I know not where."

"Slew her animals?" I exclaimed. "What harm had the poor creatures done? And for why should she be at the forge? Mistress Westley spoke not of this, when she did call yesterday to enquire after my father's health."

"Mayhap they think animals be her familiars, but as to where she be, the forge be only building in village where there be bars."

"What mean you, bars?" I gasped, in horror.

"Master Westley's small barn, behind the cottage," Old Mother Burrows gave me a curious glance. "It does have strong ones, as would keep any felon tight."

"But that building is but a bare wooden structure, and there is no brazier as I recall."

"'tis better still than stocks."

I stood rigid, staring in shocked disbelief as Bessie's voice cried from below that my supper was ready.

"Good," Old Mother Burrows nodded at me. "Do ye eat now lass, for ye'll need all yer strength."

As she ambled slowly out of the room I pushed open the shutters. Master Westley's forge was not visible as the moon was hidden in clouds, but I could hear the faint blow of the farrier's hammer, an unusual sound at that hour. Master Westley had never been known to work beyond dusk, but perhaps a passing traveller had sought help.

I shivered, and hurriedly closed the shutters. Nothing Old Mother Burrows had said about water and Molly's animals made sense. I could have understood if Tannakin had been slaughtered, since cats were always suspect in cases of witchcraft, but a cow? And as for Molly being confined in Master Westley's small barn, I decided that was impossible.

My supper finished, I returned to my father's room where Old Mother Burrows dozed beside the bed. As I tiptoed towards him he opened his eyes, and smiled at me.

"My good nurse sleeps, so we must speak softly. She did tell me Master Oswald did not enquire much of you, but did merely wish to know the length of days that Mistress Molly has been with us. That is good. I am pleased that naught else was asked. It would seem Master Oswald is a fair and just man, with none of the tendencies of his avid predecessor. I do bring to mind one wretched soul who did, in the great witch hunts of some ten years past, confess to Matthew Hopkins of his guilt having travelled some ten or twelve miles so to do. And it was then found after this self same man, a butcher by name of Meggs, had been hanged that he was no witch, but a poor ignorant soul so overcome by events of the time, that he had thought himself guilty of that of which he had no knowledge."

His voice had risen slightly, and the noise awoke Mother Burrows, who started up declaring, "Well bless me, I did fall asleep. I beg yer pardon Verger, 'twill never do for yer nurse to rest while ye are wanting."

"Nay, mistress," he smiled kindly. "You are the most vigilant of attendants, but sleep must come to all, even one so attentive as yourself. Now child do you retire, for I fear I am suddenly quite overcome and must needs rest."

Old Mother Burrows nodded agreement. "Yes, do ye send Bessie to me mistress, and I'll keep her with me for the night, for she may be needed."

Bessie responded almost immediately to my call, and entered carrying a large bowl of hot water. I stood back to let her pass, suddenly gratefully for her presence. The thought of assisting in the cleansing of my father's body appalled me; and I justified my absence by imagining how humiliated he would have been if I had seen his naked flesh.

Returning to my chamber I opened the shutters and looked again towards the forge. The hammering had now stopped, and only the sound of rustling leaves and the occasional cry of an animal in the woods beyond could be heard. But Old Mother Burrows's words about Molly and the forge would not be stilled, and there was only one way to prove her wrong.

Taking up my shawl, I crept quietly down the stairs and out of the back door. Making my way towards Molly's back entrance, I could see in the gloom that the small barn which had contained Goodwife Hargreaves's cow and hens was empty, and that the upturned barrel on which the beehive had stood was lying on its side.

Molly's windows were all shuttered, but there was a faint smell of smoke penetrating the air from above. Relieved, I tapped lightly on the door. There being no response I knocked again, and then jumped as an unfamiliar male voice called out, "Who be there?"

The sound of heavy boots approaching sent me running as silently as possible back into my own home, where I quickly closed the door and leaned against it, breathing agitatedly. Then I heard the sound of Molly's cottage door opening and someone walking about the small yard, cursing angrily.

When at last the footsteps retreated back into the cottage, I sank down onto the nearest chair and tried to control my trembling. Despite this proof, I was still not convinced that Molly had been confined within the forge, but how was this to be determined? Then an idea occurred to me, and taking down a dish of fat from a nearby shelf, I scooped some liberally onto my fingers and massaged the grease into both hinges of the parlour door until, on opening and closing, it made no sound.

I then sat down at the table and waited until Bessie trotted in, her arms full of soiled linen. I stood up, and yawning loudly declared, "I am to my chamber, Bessie. Do you sleep well, I have locked the door."

Without waiting for a reply, I returned upstairs and remained seated on my bed. After a while I heard Bessie and Mother Burrows returning to my father's room, but it was not until I was quite sure that they were deep in sleep that I wrapped myself in my thick winter cloak and crept downstairs. Wearing only the lightest of slippers, since the noise of my pattens would have awakened the neighbourhood, I opened the cottage door and stepped out into darkness so intense, it seemed almost solid.

Silently blessing Mother Burrows for her decision to keep Bessie upstairs, I crept along the road towards the forge. Fortunately Master Westley kept no dogs, so there were no guards to challenge me as I entered the yard and made my way to the back of the small barn. Calling Molly's name was too dangerous, so instead

I scratched my finger-nails against the wooden wall and beat a light tattoo.

At first nothing happened, then I heard a movement, as if someone were scraping an object across the floor and Molly's voice whispering, "Pleasance, oh Pleasance, be that ye?"

"Yes," I whispered in reply. "Why are you here, why are you not at your cottage?"

"Go away," she replied, softly. "I am afeared they'll find ye. Pleasance, I do beg ye to return home."

"I cannot." I moved quietly round to the front of the barn, and lifting the latch, entered.

A small lamp with a single candle was standing on the floor, and beside it lay Molly. Her face was unwashed, her hair tumbled unkempt about her shoulders, and her gown appeared dusty and dishevelled. Overwhelmed, I rushed across and sinking to my knees gathered my friend's cold body into my arms, only to discover that her wrists and ankles were bound with iron manacles.

For a few seconds she lay motionless, before raising her head and whispering agitatedly, "Pleasance ye must go, if yer found here 'tis too fearful to think of, go please for pity's sake."

"But whyfore are you here and not in your cottage, and so bound, and where is Hugh?"

"Pleasance, there be nothing ye can do. No," she gasped, as I tried to massage her wrists. "'tis folly, they'll know someone has been. Pleasance please, I beg of ye to go." Almost distraught, she flung herself as far away from me as her confined arms and legs would allow. I rose slowly to my feet.

"My father," I began, but she shook her head.

"There's naught can be done. Go, return ye to yer cottage and remember," she added with a brief glance of her old happy smile, "I do love ye and always will, and I'll be torn to pieces 'er I do ye harm."

For a moment I stared at her in consternation then I heard the sound of approaching horses. Molly's eyes widened frantically. "Go," she gasped. "And the Good Lord be with ye always."

Hurrying to the door, I hesitated. There was so much I wanted to say and ask but, obedient as always, I slipped out of the barn and crouched down by the wall from where, through the gloom, I could see two horsemen. After dismounting at the gate, they pulled open the barn door and entered. For a few moments there was silence then I heard the sound of a scuffle, followed by Molly's voice giving a muffled cry.

Trembling, I sprang up and ran noiselessly back to my cottage. Inside the parlour I locked the door with shaking hands and then a movement in the shadows made me start, as Old Mother Burrows emerged from the staircase.

"Child ye've no been to see her?"

"Merciful heaven," I began to sob, "she is manacled, and two men have gone into the barn and I heard her cry out."

"Hush lovedy, ye'll wake the house."

I felt the old woman's arms enfold me, and I clung to her helplessly as she whispered agitatedly, "No one must know ye've been, lovedy. 'twill bring down great mischief. But 'tis as well ye know, being so innocent an' all."

"But why have they done this to her? She has done no harm, only good."

"She be taken for a witch lovedy, and there be naught we can do. She's done much that was good, aye that she has. But know ye she's done much as was unwise. Know ye that too?"

"She has done some foolish things," I gasped, trying to control myself. "And perhaps it was unwise of her to administer to Esther Royton."

The glow from the fire highlighted Old Mother Burrow's horrified expression as she hissed, "Know ye of Esther Royton? Lass, ye must know naught. If ye wish not to share yon lass's fate ye know naught. If they do think ye know anything that she's done naught'll save ye, not yer father nor all yer church going. Do ye say yes to aught they ask. That she did splash ye with water and by so doing did bewitch ye into friendship, and that she did bewitch the food ye ate."

"What do you say?" I pulled myself free, and stared at her aghast. "You speak nonsense."

"Mistress, he do spit and bleed," Bessie's agitated voice from above interrupted us, while the raucous sound of my father's cough echoed through the cottage. Old Mother Burrows slowly straightened herself.

"'tis yer life lovedy, do with it as ye will. But do ye let yer good father die his death in peace, for they'll not be a'feared to harm him too, if they be so minded." She sighed before shuffling towards the staircase, leaving me tear-stained and trembling, beside the fire.

CHAPTER 18

The emotional stress of the previous day brought back my stomach cramp, and it was in considerable discomfort that I entered the parlour next morning to be scrutinised sharply by Mother Burrows.

"After yon Master Witchfinder's been ye'd better lie upon yer bed, for ye do look as if ye be about to fall to ground."

I pressed my palms against my back and was about to protest, when everything seemed to move around my head, and I remembered nothing more. On opening my eyes, I discovered I was lying on the floor with my head propped on something hard, and Bessie burning a feather beneath my nose. Beside her stood the Witchfinder, staring down at me in apparent concern, while Mistress Westley and Mistress Machin briskly massaged my hands and wrists.

"Dear me Mistress Fry," Master Oswald's lips parted to form a narrow smile. "Such a sight on which to intrude. I fear you have much over-taxed your strength these past days, for these good ladies do inform me that not only have you performed the good Verger's duties in his stead, but that you have also tended to him when required."

"And 'tis no surprise she be ill, bewitched as she was by that evil wench," Mistress Westley's spittle splattered tiny dots across my gown. "Poor child, and with no mother to guide her ways."

"Lacking a mother in Mistress Fry's situation, while it is indeed to be pitied, has been compensated for by the good Verger's ever present guidance and care." Mistress Machin's controlled, level tones had a calming influence, and Master Oswald nodded.

"Indeed, Mistress Fry has much for which to thank the Good Lord, such a father is not the fortunate lot of many motherless daughters." I noted that his voice, although still courteous, had become slightly impatient as he continued, "Now if you will permit me, Mistress Fry, I will be seated for I fear I am much wearied from my exertions, and when you have recovered sufficiently to conclude our business, I will return to the Hall. Perhaps, Mistress Westley, you would be good enough to summon my clerk from where he awaits outside."

As Mistress Westley bustled from the room, I attempted once more to place my father's request before the Witchfinder, but I had scarcely begun when Mistress Machin interrupted soothingly, "Do not distress yourself Mistress Fry, the good Verger rests above well tended by Mistress Burrows. Have no fear she is a nurse without equal in cases such as this. She did tend," she continued, now addressing Master Oswald, "Thomas Blunt, who had the flux full six weeks and cured him, what is more."

"So I understand," he gave another thin smile. "The reputation of this good woman has preceded her, and without the aid of brews other than those which were wholesome. Alas, I fear such has not been the practice within these walls of late, but now that the evil force has been removed, all will be well. I have been assured that all noxious brews have been poured into the earth. Now I declare, here comes Master Pryor and Master Wallace. How now goes it with you, sir? Most kind indeed of you, to grace us with your presence."

Without replying, the lawyer pushed rudely past Mistress Westley, and took up a menacing and dominating stance before the fire-place.

Breathing heavily, as another spasm of cramp passed through me, I glanced nervously around the room. Wherever I looked a human face seemed to stare back. Even Bessie, who had returned minus her feather, stood in the entrance to the outer room watching with an expression of rapt fascination, while overall stood Master Wallace, a pillar of glowering revenge.

Preoccupied with both my pain and my audience, I was surprised to discover that a long sheet of parchment covered in script now lay before me, together with a copy of the Holy Testament, a quill pen, and a small pot of ink. Somewhat at a loss I commenced to read, but immediately Master Oswald exclaimed, "There is no need at all Mistress Fry, to peruse your words. For all is as you did say, just to sign here is all that is required." He turned abruptly to Master Wallace. "Is it not a fine thing, sir, that Master Fry saw fit to educate his daughter." The lawyer grimaced irritably, but unabashed, the Witchfinder continued with apparent enthusiasm, "And a daughter to be proud of, is she not Mistress Machin?"

But I heard not the reply, for I had now read the paper and was aware of its contents. Horrified, I looked up at Master Oswald, and exclaimed frantically, "Sir, I said not that Molly did push me off the path to make magic for Thomas Whyte to fall from his horse. Indeed, I did not."

"But child ye did so, for I did see ye," Mistress Westley protested, before being interrupted by Master Oswald's raised hand and placating tones.

"Just so, ma'am and I thank you for your observation, but all witnesses must be assured of the evidence they give and such is the case with Mistress Fry. Now Master Pryor, please, your notes."

He leaned in a concerned manner towards his clerk, while Master Wallace snorted angrily, "It is as I said it would be, she'll not sign. There's naught to choose betwixt the two, take both I say, take both."

"Master Wallace, sir, I pray you stay a moment," Master Oswald leaned back, and touched the other man lightly on the arm. "It is merely a matter of words, is it not Mistress Fry? Words can be so flighty, so uncontrollable, now Master Pryor, please to read."

The clerk cleared his throat, and from his own sheet of parchment, recited, "So spake the Witness Mistress Pleasance Fry, in her evidence against the witch one Molly Tyler late of Goodborough in the county of Nottinghamshire, 'I was walking with the Witch upon the path when she did push me to the ground. She did remain upon the path and did so remain to make magic when Master Whyte did meet with his calamitous accident. I did suffer no accident from that said fall.'"

The Witchfinder looked enquiringly at me, "Is that not as you did dictate, Mistress Fry?"

"I do not recall the word 'magic'," I tried to control the nervousness in my voice. "And here you do say," I pointed to the next line, only to be interrupted emphatically by Master Oswald declaring, "No Mistress Fry, YOU did say, not I, all is as you did say. Now, you do wish to question a further matter?"

I drew a deep breath. My stomach cramp was making me perspire, and I was having difficulty in concentrating on the small, closely written script, but knowing I must continue. I indicated some further words, "Here it does say I was bewitched by water from the Chater, and did consume food prepared by the Witch for the purpose of enchantment, and here it is written that she did 'play the devil' with me. Sir, I know not what this means, for no such wrong doing was so indulged in."

"Did I not say," Master Wallace thundered out. "The obdurate wench will not sign. There's naught to chose—"

"Master Wallace I beg of you, BE SILENT or WITHDRAW," Master Oswald's harsh, loud tones made everyone jump, and the Councillor's expression creased into one of sullen outrage.

The Witchfinder, his eyes staring at me with obvious impatience now began tapping a light tattoo on the table top with his left hand, while the index finger on his right pointed downwards, towards the parchment. "Are these not the words clearly writ upon your paper, Master Pryor? Did Mistress Fry not say that the Witch did tease her? Indeed you did, Mistress Fry, you did say that the Witch did 'tease' you. For if such words had not been uttered, they would not have been writ down, now ma'am, am I not correct?"

"Yes," I gasped helplessly, as Master Oswald's persistent voice continued, "And as an educated woman, you do know the inference of this word?"

Almost mesmerized by his malevolent gaze, which seemed to obliterate everyone and everything in the room, I tried to shake my head, but instead heard myself replying, "Yes."

"And you therefore know and understand, that this word does mean all matters that are of a satanic nature. All practices that do imply witchcraft and the demonical and hellish baiting of such poor souls as are innocent of all, but that they have aroused the displeasure of these hellish fiends?"

As though entranced, I nodded. "Indeed, ma'am," the relentless voice continued. "There are other more loathsome and vile practices that this follower of Satan has perpetrated of which you are ignorant. For she did take into her house Esther Royton, an innocent maid and a most dutiful daughter, and from this poor trusting creature drew from her body a Satanic imp for the pleasure of her Familiar. And what of her very greatest crime, the destruction of a gallant officer and beloved son? By such devilry has Mistress Wallace been deprived of that which she prized above all else. And how did this devilish accomplishment succeed? First did the Witch beguile her victim to enjoyment of her putrid flesh, and then by incantations, practise her sorcery on the stream, that it should withdraw the soul of this luckless man for her master, Satan. When her curses failed their evil work she did then, in the guise of a benefactor, befriend the widow and poison her son." Somewhere in the room, I heard Master Wallace utter an oath, but this time the distraction had no effect on the Witchfinder's persistent voice. "And what of your own maid yonder, Bessie Workman? Were you not present when this poor unhappy creature was threatened by that odious follower of the Devil, did she not say that she would transform her to crawl forever on her belly, like a worm? Nay, ma'am, it is a known fact that the creature has weaved her odious magic upon all with whom she did insinuate herself. Even you have not emerged unscathed." He leaned forward, his strangely sweet breath infiltrating my nostrils. "Did she not by evil magic enter your senses and persuade you to be her friend? Did she not bewitch you with spells and incantations to her vile ways? Were you not so roused by this magic that you did strike yon little maid for speaking words of infamy, against this Devil's whore? Only your pious nature, and Godly thoughts have saved you. For how else are we to judge the friendship extended from this house. Have you not been privy to her thoughts? HAVE YOU NOT MISTRESS FRY?"

I recoiled, and then as another spasm of cramp gripped me whispered a barely audible assent. Master Oswald's face creased into a satisfied expression.

"And so has been stated in your evidence. For it was with sorcery she did ensnare you and the good Verger to her evil will. Without such sorcery, and your agreement that such did occur, there would have been no confidences exchanged and no friendships extended. And what of her birth, for she claims no man is her sire? No Christian would thus speak. Nay, you have been tainted, TAINTED, Mistress Fry, by evil spirits. Your eyes have been closed to the truth, for did she not bewitch both you and the good Verger, your so venerated father, with her witch's brews, so that he does rave and bleed and now lies above past all that man can do to save him? Yes, Mistress Fry, all this and more she has committed, and so will be proven at her trial." With his eyes burning like two heated pokers into my face, he drew a deep breath. "You are ready now Mistress Fry, to swear on oath, that all you have said is, in God's name, the truth?"

And so I condemned Molly to her fate as, with my conscience screaming 'no, no,' I placed my perspiring right hand on the Bible and, in a voice scarcely audible, repeated the oath to Master Oswald's dictation. After that there was nothing more to do but sign my name, and from that moment have I lived with shame, at the remembrance of it.

The deed completed, I felt Mistress Machin's arms slide about my shoulders, and heard Mistress Westley give an audible sigh as Master Oswald smiled benevolently, his eyes once more kind and gentle.

Only Master Wallace remained apparently obdurate, muttering beneath his breath as Master Oswald said, "Excellent, Mistress Fry, and so it is done. We are much obliged to you, and now we must away to Oakham for if we tarry more we shall not reach town afore nightfall. Mistress Westley is all prepared, Master Westley has attended to our needs?"

"Indeed so, sir," Mistress Westley bobbed a curtsey. "He has the wagon ready."

"The gold, where has that creature hid the gold?" Master Wallace snarled furiously at the Witchfinder. "Two hundred gold and silver crowns did that

Devil's spawn take from me, and not one coin of it have we found in the cottage. Yon wench must know, I say, for was she not with the accursed creature when it was collected?"

"Master Wallace I pray you, such is no way to speak before ladies," Master Oswald raised his eyebrows, and gently shook his head. "As I did so clearly state, the money is not of consequence at the present time, and as you must surely be aware sir, Mistress Fry's presence on the day of your transaction with the Witch cannot signify if sorcery had been applied, as has so been proved."

"I know not of that," Master Wallace protested heatedly. "I know only that the harpy has somewhere concealed two hundred gold and two hundred silver crowns, that being the number with which I have parted since the Goodwife's death."

Master Oswald looked thoughtful. "It is indeed a goodly sum, and not one that could be easily dispensed with in such a place as this." His head turned suddenly, and I found my eyes once more locked into his gaze. He remained staring at me for a few seconds, before smiling and turning back to the Councillor. "No, I think not, Master Wallace, I fear you will have to seek your bounty elsewhere. I envy not your search, for I fear it will be lengthy. These followers of Satan are oft more wily than their masters. What is to be the fate of the remainder of Mistress Hargreaves's estate?"

"Remainder, what remainder," Master Wallace spat out the words. "Have I not just said—"

"But what of the income from the Stamford properties?" Master Oswald's voice purred soothingly. "Is there not rent due on each quarter day?"

"Oh, aye," Master Wallace, agreed with obvious reluctance. "That amounts to a goodly sum."

"And its fate?"

"There is some villager in Goodborough, a Mistress Slater."

"Goodborough?" The Witchfinder's voice sharpened. "Is that not the village from whence came this Witch and, if I recollect from our conversation of yester forenoon, you did mention a Mistress Slater?"

"Aye, such is the case, but the family of Slater are much respected in that county, and have resided thereabouts nigh on two hundred years. Mistress Slater is a widow of some four and fifty years, whose friendship with the Goodwife did commence in their youth." Master Wallace sighed, as if exhausted by his own anger, "Nay, the good lady is but one more victim of the Witch's snare."

Master Oswald nodded. "Indeed, as have been so many, and it would be

157

unwise to spread ourselves to such a wide extent. We have all the proof required, and so Mistress Fry I do bid you well, and to your father ma'am do I send my wishes for his speedy return to good health. God be with all here, come Master Pryor, to our horses." His voice receded as he walked through the door, and Mistress Machin looked at me with apparent concern.

"I think child you should rest, you are fearfully pale. Are you unwell?" I rose to my feet, but I was shaking so violently I had to sit down again as she called, "Bessie, come at once."

"'tis no use calling of her, ma'am. She's collecting of eggs, and drawing water from well."

Mother Burrows had descended the stairs so quietly she was standing within the room before we were aware of her presence.

"I do think," began Mistress Machin, only to be interrupted by a sharp knock on the cottage door, and Thomas Whyte's voice calling loudly, "Mistress Fry, letters for Mistress Fry."

"There be no one here as needs awaking," Mother Burrows snapped, and I struggled to my feet as she thrust two small packages into my hand. Without studying them, I slipped them both into my pocket. As I did so, Mistress Machin gave them a sharp glance, before murmuring, "If there is aught I can do."

"I thank you, ma'am no," I replied, suddenly wanting her gone.

"But my dear child," she protested. "You have suffered much, and there is yet the Exorcism."

"Exorcism?" I stared in bewilderment.

"To dispel the demons within this place and to cleanse away any witchcraft that may remain. Master Wyman is to visit towards dusk, for then it is that evil spirits are abroad. Did Master Oswald not speak of this? It is of great import my dear, and such must be done. Shall I wait by?"

I stared at her helplessly, and was about to reply when Mother Burrows stumped back into the parlour, carrying a basket of eggs.

"That wench be worthless, broken three she has. Now Mistress Pleasance, be ye to rest for we've to put room right for Preacher. And ye," she twisted her head sharply round to stare at Bessie. "Do ye take bed-warmer to Mistress's bed, and then to yer Master, and bide there till I come. Mistress Machin, will ye return? Preacher did say he would be by at three of the clock."

Mistress Machin frowned slightly, and drawing back replied sharply, "Master Wyman has asked me to be present, as will be my husband and others of this Parish who should attend. There are many who have succumbed to this woman's evil force."

I wanted to protest, but my aching head and body consumed my thoughts, and with difficulty I forced my legs to mount the stairs. Once inside my chamber Mother Burrows fussed about and, having helped me to undress, said, "There lovely, all now'll be well. Dear conscience but I heard all from top of stairway, but yer father did sleep. I did give him yon physic, and he has but just awakened. I did hide flask within his wooden chest with tisane of Lady's Mantle, for 'tis better so. Yon wench, she do think all potions poured away, for so I did tell her. I was afeared to bring ye a draught, lest them folks did ask what 'twas. Ye did right to sign yon paper that ye did. The dear Lord spare us, but these be bad times. There now, do ye lie on yon bed."

Too exhausted to do anything but comply, I climbed between the heated sheets as the old woman held out a small cup, and after she had departed I lay weak and shaking, as I tried to absorb the enormity of what I had done.

That I had caused Molly great harm I knew, but what form that harm would take I can now confess in truth, I had no idea. In my ignorance at the time, I reasoned to myself that, as the Witchfinder knew nothing of Molly's Royalist sympathies and was not aware of her outbursts against Puritanism, these would be to her benefit.

Despite these thoughts and my distraught state, my eyes soon closed only to be opened almost immediately by the sound of my father's voice crying out from his chamber. Springing from the bed, I ran into his room to find him threshing his arms from side to side, in a desperate attempt to avoid them being controlled by Mother Burrows.

"I have sinned, mortally sinned," he screamed, pale pink saliva dribbling down his chin. "In my basest moments I craved the flesh, and did seek that which is forbidden. Not only once, but many times, and the good Lord did see fit to punish us, but it is I and I alone who am to blame. I did use her for myself."

"Mistress, the pillow, pull out the pillow," the old woman gasped, almost bouncing from my father's endeavours to free himself. I dragged the pillow as gently as I was able from beneath my father's head, and tossed it across to her.

"Now there, poor soul, hush thee, hush."

"No, you are smothering him," I screamed as to my horror, Mother Burrows pressed the pillow down on my father's face.

"Nay lass, 'twill no do that, 'twill only quiet him. See he breathes freely. We cannot let him cry his sins so, 'twill bring whole village to see him repent."

"I do not comprehend, of what does my father speak?"

"'tis the past lass, let it lay. A body's life be their own and were he not laid so low with sickness, 'tis not something of which he'd speak. Go ye to yer chamber and rest. See poor soul, he does now sleep."

"I must know of what he speaks," I gasped, but I was too weak to control myself and sank to the floor beside my father's bed, sobbing helplessly. After a few seconds, I felt Mother Burrows helping me to my feet.

"I'll tell all I know, but not now lovedy," she murmured soothingly. "A body can support only so much trouble. Do ye return to yer bed and, may we be preserved in Heaven, what be that?"

At her exclamation, we both hurried towards my casement beyond which screams and shouts could be heard, mingling with the sounds of cart-wheels and horses' hooves. Taking care to remain hidden, we pushed back the shutters and peered down. Below, in the roadway, the two horsemen I had seen the previous evening rode past followed by the Witchfinder and his clerk, and behind them came Master Bailey driving his cart.

Following him was a crowd of screaming children and adults, foremost of whom were the Trents and the Workmans. They were all throwing what appeared to be rubbish and offal at Molly, who lay rolling from side to side on the floor of the cart. She looked no more dishevelled than when she had been lying in the barn, but then I saw, that in addition to the manacles on her wrists and ankles, she now wore an iron collar about her neck.

CHAPTER 19

So distracted was I at the time of the exorcism that I recall only that Master Harris and numerous villagers squeezed themselves into our small parlour, and that I followed Preacher Wyman as he intoned loudly to the Lord.

"Weren't nothing like I've seen, now nor since," Mother Burrows muttered, after everyone had gone except Preacher Wyman, who had remained to pray beside my father's bed. "All that prancing about, man's a numskull so he be, knows naught of exorcising. What do he now?"

"He does pray beside my father's bed for his soul," I protested.

"Pshaw, cock and fiddle," the old woman pulled a face. "I'll say nay more, but there be folks as do say he be nothing. Never goes to those as is sick, nor do he visit Parish folk. That be all yer father's work, good Verger does do work of ten, and so wilt yon addlepate find out and to his cost." Still muttering, she shuffled away into the outer room.

I stretched my hands out towards the fire, and as the flames danced they seemed to reproduce the terrifying sight of Molly manacled in the cart. Despite the heat I shivered. What would become of me when my father died if Molly decided on her release from whatever torment awaited her, to return to Goodborough?

For I was sure she would not wish to have me for a sister, nor would William wish to have me for a wife, when they learned of my perfidy, but there was an alternative. For now, as though I had not enough to concern me, there was yet another distraction to occupy my mind.

The previous evening, after I had sobbed myself dry of tears, I had examined the packets Thomas had delivered and discovered that both were addressed to my father. One was from William, and this I put this to one side, for I sensed the other to be of more importance. And so it proved, for it was from my mother's cousin Edith Frost. A woman of obvious education she wrote kindly, commiserating with my father on his illness, but it was her reference to myself that preoccupied me, for she extended to me an invitation to make my home with her family in London *'should the need so arise.'* Those last five words seemed to resound in my head. That the need would arise there was no doubt, but whether I would accept the invitation was another matter.

Totally absorbed with myself and my problems, I did not even notice Preacher Wyman enter the room until his voice broke agitatedly into my thoughts, "Mistress Fry, I fear the good Verger does need attention. Perhaps your maid," he stood helplessly beside the table, his kerchief held to his nose. To my relief, at that moment Mother Burrows bustled into the room closely followed by Bessie. The old woman eyed the cleric with obvious contempt.

"We'll tend, Preacher, never fear," she snapped. "Ye've mayhap not had much of sickroom, have ye?"

The Preacher blushed. "Illness is," he began, but the two women had already disappeared upstairs, so instead he crossed to the fireplace and held his hands towards the blaze.

I moved slightly away, but he appeared not to notice, and to my surprise seated himself in my father's chair, indicating at the same time that I too should be seated. Angry at his presumption to choose such a place, I sat down expecting a lecture on my friendship with Molly, but after a brief pause he announced, "Mistress Fry, now that this unhappy matter has been laid to rest and all is once more calm, I would speak with you. I am more than aware that I should, were it possible, be addressing myself to your revered father but alas I have sat with him, and seen that it cannot be. So, my dear Mistress Fry, as you have no other relative to whom I can make my intentions plain, I must needs address myself direct to you. I am sure you cannot have been unaware of the high regard in which I hold you. Indeed, I have over the past weeks attempted in my own limited fashion to make that regard plain." I stared utterly aghast, convinced my ears must be deceiving me as he continued, "I am more than aware of the chasm in the stations of life that lie betwixt us, a chasm that can never be bridged, and I fully comprehend that you too are sensible of the disparity in our stations. But I am prepared to disregard that difference, ma'am, for I do know with guidance and teaching, you can learn to live the kind of life that our union will bestow upon you. Guidance and teaching is required in one so young as yourself, and one so easily misled as you have been, but I am prepared to disregard the indiscretions of the past few months. Indeed I have been assured, that such is the high regard in which your revered father is held no blame whatever will besmirch the name of Fry. Sir Oliver has assured me that your reputation, and that of your dear father, is as unblemished as it was prior to that female's presence in our unhappy village."

Desperate to stop the flow of words, and desirous only of escaping from the awful man, I waved my hands agitatedly while crying, "Sir, I do beg of you, please."

But nothing seemed to break his equanimity, and as though to calm my obvious distress he murmured soothingly, "Indeed, I comprehend that you are overwhelmed, and that time for reflection is required to fully absorb the benevolences of my address. But fear not, I assure you I will never reproach you at any time as to the circumstance of your humble past, for no one will be aware of that situation. Sir Oliver has, through his kind offices, secured me a living in the city of Chester. A fine situation, I understand, with a large and commodious house, so superior to the one in which I now reside, and this village has never been to my taste."

"All's to rights mistress," Mother Burrows stumped noisily into the room. "And now we eat, for strength does lie in food, that it do?"

Never before had I been so relieved to hear those uneducated tones, and I almost flung myself into the old woman's arms as she exclaimed, "Why lovedy, what's amiss, ye be trembling like a leaf in wind?"

Before I could reply, Master Wyman placed his lips into what he apparently believed was a smile of benevolence, and murmured, "I fear I have taken already too much of Mistress Fry's time. We have talked, and she is a little overcome. It is the way with maids, at such a time. I will call again tomorrow, ma'am, if such be your will at say, two of the clock?" Without waiting for a reply he continued, "Two of the clock it is then, and I do indeed await the hour with pleasure. Now, with your permission ma'am, I do take my leave."

Both my saviour and I stood as statues, until the sounds of the Preacher's well-heeled boots were heard retreating down the street, whereupon Mother Burrows gave a loud cackle, "Bless us alive!"

I felt my cheeks turn a fiery red. "You heard?"

"Aye, every one word, lass, every one word."

"What am I to do? I cannot see him, I cannot."

"O'course ye'll no see him, man's a fool, and such a saucy knave and all, stations of life, chasms and such, from a man such as him. But 'tis strange, for I declare there be more to yon's impudence than we do know. Not that ye be not comely and all that a man could want," she looked thoughtful. "But 'tis strange that at such a time as this, when all's so bad, that yon silly thick-head should so declare himself. Has yon addle-pate said aught afore?" Her compliment reminded me of Molly's words, that distant day beside the river bank, and I could only shake my head in reply. Mother Burrows looked reflective. "Then this be a strange matter and no mistake, and a house in Chester he's to have? Mayhap yon house must needs have a mistress without which there be no living, and mayhap Sir Oliver has put idea into his mind. I'll enquire as to meaning."

"Oh no please, Mother Burrows," I gasped, horrified at the thought of anyone in the village being made aware of the situation.

She waved a calming hand. "Rest ye lass, I've me ways and nobody'll be aware of aught. Now do ye to the Verger while we prepare meal to eat. I'll call ye when 'tis ready."

Grateful for any distraction, I hurried away to my father's chamber and arrived in time to hear him mumbling to himself.

As the hour passed, his mutterings became louder and more distinct, so I closed the door, and sitting down took his I took his hand in mine, hoping to calm him. Immediately, he turned his head and, with an agitated expression, began to gabble, "I have sinned dearest wife, forgive me I pray, for I fear the good Lord will not. Most beloved of wives I beg you, forsake me not."

Alarmed, I hastened to reassure him that I was his daughter, not his wife, but although for a moment he appeared puzzled, he soon continued in a voice even more deranged than before.

"Listen, for I must needs be shriven 'er I join you dearest Margaret, for there is much that on me weighs. So very early did the Good Lord deem it fit that you should be taken; and I was left with our little daughter. For many years I did care for her, and did give her the love that you would have bestowed, but as the years did pass I did stray. She was a good fine woman, dearest, of grace and stature. I did beg her to become my wife, but she would not, for her estate, it was entailed. Her husband being a generous, but jealous man, had willed it so, and to maintain his benevolence she must needs remain a widow. She did give readily to me, and we did have much company of each other, but our sins were discovered by He who knows all, and she did become with child. Still she refused my hand, and said it was of no consequence and all would come aright. But it was not so, for the child miscarried and she did fall ill of a terrible fever, and when the malady passed she was born down with much affliction of the stomach, and I did condemn myself for her illness, but she would hear none of this, saying that we were friends and that friends we were to remain. And all this I did bring about with selfish passion and now I beg forgiveness, dearest wife."

He drew a deep, painful breath, and began to cough, gasping, "The potion, dearest wife, Miss Molly's potion. For pity's sake, the pain, the pain."

Distressed, and near to tears, I gently released my hand and from his wooden chest took Molly's flask of tisane. Mixing a little of the liquid with some water, I held the cup his lips. He drank deeply, and soon his breathing eased and his eyes became heavy. My mind repeating to itself what I had just heard, I remained seated beside him until a knock on the door preceded Bessie, who told me that our meal was ready.

"I'm to sit with Verger," she muttered, avoiding my glance.

Later, I was to remember that incident, but at the time I was too overwrought to notice anything amiss, and merely nodded before descending to the parlour where Old Mother Burrows placed a steaming dish of broth before me.

"How be he?" She gave my brow a gentle stroke.

"He sleeps, but prior he did speak, and think me to be my mother."

The old woman nodded understandingly. "Aye, so 'tis with the sick. They do see not with their eyes, but with their minds, and do cry out much that should be silent. I'll no speak for papists, and them as hold with such, but 'twas a bad day when we did lose confession. Aye, ye may stare so Missy but 'twas good to go shriven. So ye did learn what I would tell."

"I think, a little, but he must have suffered so."

"Aye, that be the way with men unwed, and more so with them as follows God. Nay, ye must no take on, for 'twill weaken ye and ye do need what strength ye have. Now lass," she began briskly, "there be little wood left for fire. I did ask yon soldier if he would visit the forge and buy us more."

I tried to concentrate, puzzled by her concern. "Whatever is needed Mother Burrows, do you arrange."

"Yeah lovedy, I'll arrange, but 'twill not be for nothing that the soldier will so oblige. He do need paying, as does Master Westley for wood. Them as works earns. Do ye not know where in house is kept the coins?"

Dragged from my thoughts by the practical problems of daily life, I stared at her in consternation as I realised the significance of what she said. During her time with us I had given her nothing, and now realised that the money with which she had provided food and wood must have been her own. As a midwife she was known to earn a comfortable income,(36) but her time in our cottage had been devoted to my father, and no opportunity had arisen for her to serve others.

Ashamed of myself for being so heedless, I muttered almost in tears,

"Please to forgive me Mother Burrows, I have lived off your bounty without thanks or appreciation, and will most certainly recompense you fully. I am ashamed of my lack of understanding."

Immediately the dear soul encased me in a hug. "Now lovedy, take not on so, 'tis of no matter and I've still a little left, but 'tis necessary for us to find more, as I'm no able to work for the time being. Think ye he'd keep it in his chamber?"

I shook my head. I had no idea where my father kept his money, any more than I knew how much he earned. She gave me another hug, and chuckled, "Ah me, 'tis not learning as will heat the house. Let us to his chamber and see what can be found, for if there is money to be had, sure as life 'tis above."

Fifteen minutes later, having dismissed Bessie downstairs, we were still searching the room when Mother Burrows, who had been examining the neat stacks of my father's books, gave a soft chuckle and whispered, "All that learning did have a use, so it did." She bent down, and began to carefully pull one heap of books away from the wall. "See mistress this panel, it be loose," she pushed against the wall. "There be a purse, though by the feel there be little in it."

I emptied the contents onto the floor and counted four pennies and three silver shillings. I looked up at Mother Burrows in relief.

"Here do you take it and do with it what is required."

"Bless ye child, 'tis yours not mine. Do ye give me a silver shilling, and it'll do for all that we do need for next week or so, and put the rest away safe for when 'tis needed later."

The immediate problems of domesticity having been solved, I retired to my chamber to dwell more fully on my father's confession. Our outshut, and the many visits he had made to the Goodwife's cottage, were now explained. But the strictures he had placed on my life I found difficult to condone and yet, despite all, I knew he had loved me, for the strictures had been but to protect me from the outer world. An outer world that had now intruded so violently, that all that had happened to me in the past two days seemed unreal. Even the sight of Molly, chained and filthy, I was convinced was but a nightmare from which I would soon awaken. Only my father's illness was something from which I could not escape. Then I saw William's letter, still lying upon my bed. I hesitated. The contents were not intended for my eyes, but such niceties were of no consequence at the present time, so I broke the seal and began to read.

He commenced with good wishes to my father for a speedy return to strength, and asked him to convey his best regards to me. Then I blushed as I continued reading, for the letter contained a request for my hand in marriage, and it was obvious from the tone of the words that the matter had been previously discussed. The letter was merely the formality that confirmed the arrangement.

Still blushing, I thought of the time I had seen them talking outside the forge, and how disappointed my father had appeared when I had not joined in his praises for the young farrier, and there had been all the walks and meals I had been permitted to attend in Williams's company.

Then I recalled my father's tentative references to his virtues, and William's own delicate and somewhat hesitant manner, together with the long academic conversations in which we had indulged. Had all this been employed to put me at my ease? And had Molly tutored both men in the manner of their behaviour, understanding as she did the shy and lonely girl I truly was?

Molly always Molly, and as I thought of how much I truly owed her, I vowed with all my heart to make amends for my betrayal. But that could only be accomplished after her release, my immediate problem was what to say to William. After considerable thought, I decided that to accept his proposal on my own behalf would be improper. I would explain that my father was so ill the letter had not been opened, and if there was anything William wished to convey to me, he should write accordingly.

I shivered suddenly, but it was not from cold. I was remembering Molly's remarks concerning William's bed, and I spread my left arm out towards the edge of my narrow pallet, and imagined what it would be like to feel the solid contact of someone else's flesh, firm male flesh.

And what of the other, how did it come about? Were there words of invitation? How would William make his wishes known, and how would I respond? There was pain at first that I knew for Old Mother Burrows had once spoken of the pain. Then I thought suddenly of Molly's and Daniel's naked bodies entwined about each other, and imagined myself, and William, in such a way.

Thoughts of Molly reminded me that I must speedily acquaint William of her predicament, in order that he could then go to Oakham and explain that all the terrible things being said of her were untrue, for he knew all her history. I decided to write the following morning, prior to Master Wyman's call. Despite everything, thoughts of the Preacher made me smile, and I thought how entertaining Molly would find the news but, more importantly, how overjoyed she would be to hear my news of William. For I would write to her at the same time, so that they received their letters together.

Now that I was to marry her brother she would not hesitate to return to Goodborough, and how happy we all would be. We would leave as soon as she was free, and in my letter I would beg forgiveness for signing that abusive document. She would understand. I was indeed fortunate to have so kind and generous a friend.

Despite rising early, my letter to William took me longer to compile than I had anticipated, having been interrupted by Old Mother Burrows calling me to my father's bedside. It was near eleven of the clock therefore, with Molly's letter still unwritten, before I delivered my package to Mistress Whyte's cottage where the door was opened by Thomas, who stared at me in surprise.

"Why Mistress, what do ye here? I fear 'tis too late for letters. I did deliver to Stamford this early morn."

I frowned in consternation. "Is it not possible for Master Bailey to take my missive? It is of great importance."

He looked doubtful. "'tis not his custom, Mistress. Who be letter to?" He examined the address, and then looked up sharply. "He be her cousin, be he not?"

"Yes, I have written of Mistress Tyler's great misfortune."

"It be no use Mistress, she be damned," Thomas glanced nervously about, as though he feared being overheard, before continuing, "They have signed papers by witnesses, so 'tis said. It be the rope, so Master Westley do say. Mistress take care, do."

As I swayed against the lintel I felt hands grab me, and Thomas dragged me into the cottage where he helped me to a chair. Summoned by her son's cry, Mistress Whyte hurried into the parlour. Exclaiming loudly, she held a cup of water to my lips. "What said ye Thomas, poor Mistress Fry be a'fainting, so she be."

"I did tell her about yon poor Mistress Molly."

Mistress Whyte's lips tightened, and I saw her give Thomas a warning look.

"'tis not wise to speak of such, as well ye know. Do ye hold yer tongue."

"No, please," I whispered. "I must know everything."

"Well Mistress, as 'tis yerself does ask and as I know ye have poor Mistress Molly's welfare at heart, 'tis only what Thomas did hear this morn in Stamford, that the Witchfinder do have the evidence needed to hang poor lass and 'tis only the trial that is needed to condemn her for Witchcraft."

"This cannot be, it is all lies, she has done nothing."

"Ssh, mistress take care do," Mistress Whyte pressed restraining hands on my shoulders, while Thomas hurriedly closed the cottage door. "Do not speak so. There be much evidence, so 'tis said signed by villagers of this Parish under the good Lord's oath, evidence that cannot be denied."

"You cannot believe this."

Mistress Whyte flushed. "I did say when questioned by yon Witchfinder, that I knew naught. He did try to make me say linen was bewitched, but I answered him as to what fearsome thing did he think linen had wrought upon me, as I was healthy and nothing in my cottage was amiss and he could no gainsay."

"Did he not threaten you?"

"Aye," Mistress Whyte gave a sarcastic laugh. "He did tempt me with dire happenings but I did say I was but poor washerwoman who had suffered much, and that I'd be happy to join me husband but for me son's sake."

"What was his response?"

"He did call me good woman, and then did leave."

I arose unsteadily to my feet. Despite the warmth of the room my hands felt icy cold, and as I glanced about me I saw that the small room which had appeared so destitute on my previous visit, now had in its centre a sturdy table and four chairs, while beside the wall stood a tall oak dresser containing a quantity of pewter crockery.

"Aye, Mistress Fry," Mistress Whyte sighed, "she was good to us was Mistress Molly, and did care about the poor. Yon Witchfinder did say I should cast out all she'd given, lest they be bewitched, but I did say no and that his authority was naught to me, Sir Oliver is master hereabouts."

"But did he not condemn you for such talk?" I was astonished.

"Nay, I'm but small meat, a foolish woman he thought me, who would be more harm than good to him. But he be a dangerous body, Mistress Fry, and do ye take care with yer closeness to Mistress Tyler, an' all."

Still unconvinced that Molly was in any real danger, I protested that I was capable of returning home unaided, but Thomas insisted on accompanying me, a gesture which was much appreciated when I caught sight of Preacher Wyman approaching from the opposite direction. By lengthening my stride, I succeeded in entering some minutes before him, and after warning Mother Burrows, ran quickly upstairs. From the safety of my chamber doorway I heard the Preacher's knock, and then Mother Burrows rough voice telling him that I was not at home.

"Indeed she is, old woman," he expostulated. "I have but just seen her enter the house."

"She be no here," Mother Burrows, replied obdurately. "And I be no old woman to ye, I be Mistress Burrows, so do ye be off."

Whatever the Preacher said in reply was lost in the bang of the front door, and smiling to myself, I was about to descend when Bessie emerged from my father's room.

"Master be awake Mistress, and asking for ye."

Overjoyed, I entered my father's chamber and discovered him fully conscious with no signs of his previous hysteria. He held out a welcoming hand.

"My child, I am indeed pleased to see you. Come, sit beside my bed."

Believing his wild confession to be the delusions of a sick mind, I exclaimed delightedly, "Father you have recovered."

He gave a soft laugh. "I fear not Pleasance, but the good Lord is kind. Today I do feel a little stronger, and have partaken of a morsel of Mistress Burrows's good broth. Now where have you been, child? Mistress Burrows did say you have been writing letters."

Seated beside his bed, his hand in mine, I felt my face become hot, but keeping my voice steady I replied, "Yes Father, I did write to Master Radley a short note thanking him for his missive of some two weeks past, and now we have received a further letter addressed to your good self, from London."

My father frowned slightly. "Yes, such I did expect and would have you read it to me child, but has there been naught for me from Master Radley?"

I arose from my stool, my face averted, as I replied, "No father," before hastening to fetch my cousin's letter.

My poor invalid listened avidly to the news from Mistress Frost, and when I had finished said, "A goodly soul, now child I have two matters I must impart. I did intend so to do earlier, but I fear my illness did incapacitate me, and even now I know I have but little time. You are more than full aware my dear, that I have not long before I join your dear mother. Nay child, do not cry, the good Lord takes us all in our due time, and there are many more fearful ways of dying than will be my lot, and I have lived a full life and been blessed with the company of a most gracious and loving wife, and received the blessing of a dutiful, and ever obedient daughter who has never given me a moment of concern. I did raise you in my ways, and perhaps too harshly, but never did you complain of my strictures, and the hours of study through which I guided you will forever benefit your life. For it is the mind that does divide men, not the benefices that fate heaps upon them. With knowledge, a being can open doors closed to less fortunate folk. But always do you remember, Pleasance, that all men and women are equal in the good Lord's eyes, be they commoner or king, rich or poor, ugly or fine-boned, or whether they follow the teachings of Christ or Abraham, they are all to God one and the same. Now I must hasten, for I fear my voice grows weak. I did write to your mother's cousin Edith Frost, requesting that she might, as your only kin, see fit to take you into her house, and as you see, she has said that she is willing. She is a good woman, if somewhat of the world, and kind. This I know for on occasion we have corresponded, for such was your dear mother's wish. You will be safe and cared for, and I know you will transport yourself with dignity and diligence but now, another matter. Be not abashed child, but Master Radley has asked for your hand. We did discuss the matter afore his departure and it required only his formal letter to seal the pact. I did intend addressing you when the letter was received, but as it would appear he lingers in declaring himself, I must needs speak first. The union has my blessing, and I have been given to believe you are not averse to him. Well child, do you now consider the matter, and as it is not fitting that you should go a maiden alone to Master Radley, you should first reside with Mistress Frost, until such time as Master William visits you and the nuptials take place. And now, dear child, I do beg your pardon," he gasped suddenly, and clutched at his chest. "I fear I must now sleep. Do you remain a while child, your presence gives me much comfort."

I remained beside him until his heavy breathing became regular, then crept back into my own room where my father's letter from William stared reproachfully up at me from the bed.

CHAPTER 20

After my father's last coherent words to me he lapsed into a coma, and from then onwards the only sounds he made were the violent ravings of an unbalanced mind. Concerned that his indiscretions might be betrayed to Bessie, I suggested to Mother Burrows that the maid should be denied the sick room. The old woman gave me a wary look. "She'll no speak lovely, 'tis too feared she be, after what she did." With a sense of foreboding, I asked her meaning. Mother Burrows pursed her lips. "Did ye no hear what Witchfinder said, about yon Molly making little wench crawl on her belly like a worm, and that vile concoctions or some such were brought into this house, and that she bewitched the Verger with her brews. Where think you he did learn such, if not from little wench?"

For a few moments I listened before, overcome with fury, I ran into the outshut and dragged Bessie struggling into the parlour as Old Mother Burrows cried out, "Lass, lass, wait I pray."

But nothing could abate my anger, and towering over the grovelling child as she cowered on the floor I demanded, "Did you speak of Mistress Tyler's foolish threat, to turn you into a toad?" Bessie nodded her eyes wide and staring. "And did you speak also of the food brought into this house by Mistress Tyler?" The girl nodded again, and losing my control I screamed, "AND WHAT DID YOU SAY, WHAT DID YOU SAY?"

Obviously terrified, Bessie gabbled frantically, "That food and suchlike were bewitched for yon man said as 'twould be a beating and the stocks, if I did na' speak out and he said me father 'ud be hanged for he'd taken deer."

As she grovelled, her hands above her head as if for protection, I said with difficulty, "Do you take that which you think your own, and depart this house."

Ignoring Mother Burrows' restraining arm and Bessie's shocked expression, I repeated my words and then stood back to let her pass. For a second her tear stained face looked defiant, before she clambered to her feet and marched noisily into the outshut.

Within seconds, she emerged carrying a small bundle. Approaching the door she eyed me warily. "I be no worse'n ye, for I didna' sign naught," she muttered. "Ye said much that wasna' true, for I heard all. 'twill not be me as'll make her hang."

Her words seemed to cut into my stomach, but I remained motionless while she muttered her way out of the cottage, banging the door too behind her. Mother Burrows shook her head.

"That be foolishness lass, for we did need wench's help. I can no manage alone."

"I will help you," I replied weakly, the impact of Bessie's accusation having drained all my strength. "She could not stay, she is a Judas and cannot remain within this house."

"Aye she did say that as she shouldna', but she be a little bit of a wench, meaning no real harm and them Workman'll be no pleased to see her. They did treat her right bad afore she came here. And she'll pass much round village," the old woman continued. "She'll tell of the words 'tween yerself and yon Witchfinder, and 'twill not be to yer good. For when Mistress Molly's no more, folk'll remember the good she did, the way folk allus do."

"But should Molly go for trial I will be called," I protested, as tears began to well up in my eyes. "And I will deny all. I will say that under great force was I compelled to sign that which was not true."

"Lass, they'll no call ye. Yon poor wench's life's no more, she be good as hanged, so she be. Mistress Wallace she has said much and is to be called, as is Esther Royton. With what they do say and that what is writ by ye," she shrugged. "'twill be all that'll be needed."

"That cannot be," I cried, hysterically. "I shall DEMAND to be heard. I will attend Master Harris, and explain the great force under which I was compelled to sign."

"Lass, 'tis too late to do aught. Master Harris he be in Oakham for the trial, which be today week, so yon soldier did tell me. There's naught ye can do lass, naught I say."

Suddenly overcome with weakness, I collapsed onto the nearest chair only to start again to my feet as a great cry of anguish echoed through the cottage. We rushed up the stairway to find my father tossing about in sheets stained with filth, moaning loudly. The stench was overpowering, and I swallowed heavily in a desperate attempt to stop retching.

Cooing soothingly, Old Mother Burrows gently unbuttoned his nightshirt, and pulled it down over his shoulders. "Do ye bring a clean shirt from yon chest lass, and while I hold Verger up do ye drag sheets from beneath and above him."

Taking care to be as gentle as possible, I pulled the soiled sheets from the bed exposing, as I did so my father's nakedness. Shaken, I averted my eyes and moved backwards towards the door, still pulling the sheets.

Mother Burrows gave a cry, "Lass, take care for pity's sake or all muck'll spread on floor. Now do ye take them below, and I'll tend them. But bring two buckets of water as warm as'll take your elbow, so's I can wash him. There be just two buckets left in barrel, and be quick mind, or he'll chill."

Over an hour later, having heated two buckets of water, lifted and turned my father's body to enable Mother Burrows to cleanse him and dress him, and then sat with the poor delirious man until he fell asleep, I returned wearily to the parlour.

I was hungry, but in Bessie's absence there was no one to prepare the meal or to replenish the water barrel, so I collected the two buckets of dirty water and went out into the yard. Stretched across the ground were the two soiled sheets, before which Mother Burrows was kneeling carefully scraping off the slime of my father's ordure. At the sound of my footsteps, she looked up.

"Do ye throw yon water over sheets, lass. They be ready now and I'll leave them to soak for night." She struggled awkwardly to her feet. "Aye, yon little wench had her uses. I be right weary, will ye make supper?"

As I poured the dirty water carefully across the soiled linen I heard a movement behind me, and turning saw the soldier emerging from Molly's cottage. He smiled, and jerked a thumb towards the well, "Be ye wishing to draw water?"

Remembering our last encounter I would have preferred to refuse, but Mother Burrows accepted his offer in a grateful voice, and proffered him the pails. After filling the buckets, the soldier carried them back into the outshut, and then glanced at me in apparent sympathy.

"Sickness be a hard task for the strongest body, and much water'll be needed. I have more barrels than is decent for a body to have. Do ye mind here, and I'll bring another to ye. 'tis a fresh water barrel, so can be used for aught."

Some time later, our water problem solved and having eaten, I felt considerably better, and still convinced that I would be able to save Molly, I asked Mother Burrows if she knew where my friend was being held.

"She be in Oakham prison lass; awaiting Assizes today week, as I did afore say."

"Think you the soldier will be attending her trial for if so, it is possible he would consider escorting me, for I would fain attend?"

"Lass, do ye listen," Mother Burrows banged her empty mug so violently on the table I jumped. "Yon poor wench'll hang, whether it be right or wrong 'tis no for likes of us to say. But them as do push themselves and try by any ways to cry her not false will themselves be held as friends, and'll hang too." She dropped her voice to a whisper. "Yon Master Wallace did wish to take ye along her, and 'twere only yer father as did save ye, him being a pious man and Verger and all. 'twas Master Harris and Sir Oliver saying as ye being yer father's daughter ye could not stray from path of God that saved ye."

"How can you know all this?" I asked, desperately. "Why was I not told?"

"Wisht lass not so loud, soldier be but a wall away. I've tried to tell ye, oft I've tried, but never have ye listened."

"I cannot believe," I protested vehemently, "that anyone will judge Molly as a witch. She will not hang of that I am convinced. Mayhap some weeks or months confined, but hanged never. And I know from what I have learned of the law, for my father has taught me many aspects of English life, and without a confession and Molly has nothing to confess, there can be no conviction."

"Them as don't speak do, afore long," Mother Burrows replied, looking grim.

"Merciful Heaven, mean you torture?" I gasped.

"Aye lass, so I do."

"But it cannot be," I protested emphatically. "The stocks, or mayhap a ducking may be the sentence. Master Harris and Sir Oliver would never permit such acts."

"Master Harris counts for naught, and Sir Oliver be a Magistrate and sees prisoners AFTER the confession. It be Witchfinder who does make the mischief. Now do ye clear the table and I'll to your father with some broth. 'tis the way of things that he'll need cleaning again afore morrow. I'll wake ye soon as need be."

As she shuffled up the stairway I thought suddenly of William, and wished desperately for his presence and support. But it would be at least five days before he received my letter, giving him little time to reach Oakham for the trial. Then a loud rap on the cottage door made me start.

"Mistress Fry, be ye there?" Thomas Whyte's voice called agitatedly through the keyhole, and I rose quickly and opened the door. The Post Boy looked distraught. "Oh, mistress, 'tis bad news. I do beg pardon for late hour, but 'tis bad news. Yon Master Radley, as I do hear from farrier in Stamford town, he be kicked by a horse and is took to his bed. He be there for least twelve days, so farrier did say."

"Kicked by a horse?" I gasped. "Merciful heaven, what injury has he?"

"A broke leg, but he be not so bad, him being a man of such size. And Mistress," Thomas continued agitatedly "they do say in Stamford as how a nipple has been found on poor Mistress Molly's body, same as devils do use to suckle their familiars."

As he departed, I sat down heavily on the nearest chair. It was Molly's injury he was speaking of, the peculiar protuberance on her left hip over which she had laughed so heartily on that carefree summer's day.

The days preceding Molly's trial passed quickly. Absorbed by duties I had almost forgotten how to accomplish, my hours were occupied by either attending to the cottage, cooking the meals or helping Mother Burrows administer to my father. And there was also the church to dust and brush. I had at first been wary of entering, being nervous that Preacher Wyman might seek me out, but although he was impeccably polite whenever we met, and for him extremely pleasant, he made no attempt to see me alone.

The intervening Sunday prior to Molly's trial was the most difficult day I had ever experienced. Alone in my pew, I was very aware of the numerous glances and nudges in my direction, and noted that amongst my father's immediate acquaintances reactions were varied. The Machins all nodded sadly at me, the Roytons ignored me and the Westleys averted their eyes self-consciously, but Master Workman, followed by his wife and brood including a much cowed Bessie, glared angrily at me making no attempt to hide his obvious fury at the dismissal of his daughter.

Feeling bereft, I tried to concentrate on my *Directory*, then glancing up suddenly, I caught Mistress Whyte's eye as she smiled tentatively at me. Grateful for this kindness I smiled back, and then gave a start as I remembered the last time someone had smiled at me in church. After the service only she approached me, in obvious concern.

"'tis a sad time Mistress Fry, a very sad time."

"I understand not Mistress Whyte why everyone behaves so," I replied with a sigh. "They seem to censure me for my friendship with Mistress Tyler, and yet she did nothing wrong and brought much goodness to the village."

"Hush child," Mistress Whyte looked anxious. "Speak not so for a goodly number of the villagers are summoned to the trial, and I fear 'tis against her for which they go."

With her words resounding relentlessly in my head, I returned home on legs the lifting of which had never felt so heavy. Having reached the cottage, I crept up to my chamber, and sinking to my knees beside the bed wept bitterly. The bright sunlight that had been Molly Tyler was to be forever dimmed, and love, beauty, and happiness extinguished. How long I remained thus I have no idea, I know only that I rose from my knees with a guilt I knew I could never assuage.

The remaining days passed in a mist of work and little leisure, and I remember nothing except the moans and cries which filled the cottage, and my own tormented thoughts. Despite being warned by his mother not to go, Thomas attended Molly's trial at Oakham Castle, and the following evening called to relate to me the dreadful happenings. Even now, so many years later as I pen this chronicle, his words are as vivid as if they had been spoken but yesterday.

Wary of being seen, he concealed himself behind a pillar in the Great Hall with its many horseshoes covering the walls(37)as, from this vantage point, he was able to see the high stall where all prisoners stood, and also watch the curious as they jostled their way enthusiastically into the hall.

Amongst the crowd, standing to the left of the Magistrates' stall were the witnesses from Fretson, exhibiting expressions which, I deduced from Thomas's description, were those of either terror, or disdain. From his hiding place, he had also been able to hear the townsfolk chatter that Molly had not spoken, despite being "questioned vigorously". All manner of "encouragements" had been applied to "assist her" to confess, apparently without success.

As I listened to his discourse, I longed to ask more of Molly, but Thomas was a simple lad, and dwelt overlong on describing the many horseshoes embellishing the walls; how the rumour that the Duke (38) would attend proved false; and how the stench rising from damp garments had almost overcome his senses. But at last he began to describe how a door beside the judge's bench had opened, and a number of men entered, and upon them being seated Molly had been called.

According to Thomas's description, she climbed with obvious difficulty into her stall unaided. There were no visible signs of abuse, he assured me. Her clothes were similar to those she had worn when she first arrived in Fretson, but although she stood with her customary dignity, every now and then her features seemed to wince as if with pain.

To Thomas's dismay, due to the eagerness with which the Fretson witnesses had assisted the Sheriff, the proceedings had not lasted long. He had been particularly shocked when Master Westley took the stand to explain at some length how Molly had caused his bellows to split in two.

I listened to this account in bewilderment. Had I not myself heard William advise the farrier to replace his old bellows with a new improved pair which, William had explained, could be purchased in Stamford?

After the villagers' verbal evidence, Master Oswald was called to the stand. Questioned closely on Molly's ability to bewitch her victims with food and clothing, he had described the plants and potions in her private room and the 'third nipple' on her thigh with which, he claimed, she had suckled her familiar, the cat Tannakin.

But despite all that was said, the Sheriff had still appeared doubtful, stating that as Molly, or the Accused as he had described her, had refused either to confess or speak in her own defence, how could the Witchfinder confirm these findings? I had listened eagerly to this account, for how indeed could a party be proved guilty without the facts being so proved. But Thomas's next words had devastated me, for on being asked whether Molly had any relative or friend to speak in her favour, the Witchfinder had replied that she had no one at all.

Even to this day those words seer me like a knife's edge. Ever caring for those she loved, Molly had been all too aware that one word, one hint of our affection for each other, would have destroyed me. But why had she also denied the only other person who could have saved her? For I knew that William, with the aid of a lawyer, would have proved more than equal to the evidence placed before the Sheriff and his fellow Magistrates. Had she thought that William too would have been in danger, if he had stood in her defence?

I was contemplating this, when I noted that Thomas had dropped his eyes and grown very red. I prompted him, and it was with obvious reluctance that he explained that the Sheriff had still appeared doubtful and had conferred at some length with the Magistrates and clerk. As they were thus occupied, and as though impatient at the delay, the Witchfinder had interrupted them to present his final, and unequivocal evidence.

With a flourish, he had placed my testimony before the bench stating both my name and my father's occupation. He also spent some time explaining that the grievous malady from which my father suffered, had been derived from the potions administered to him by the witch. He had then called upon Mistress

Machin to read my testimony, since that good lady had been present when I swore to the validity of the document. At this point Thomas faltered, and I knew all too well without being told, that but for my damning evidence Molly might have been saved.

There was little more for the Magistrates to do but give the sentence, but first the Sheriff had to explain the reasons for the decision and this, Thomas assured me at the time, he did with vigour.

"His voice mistress, it were so loud it did seem to jump right off the walls. He did say how she were accused of evil and blasphemous crimes of witchcraft, which she did impose by heinous practices, them be his words, heinous practices, upon the trusting villagers of Fretson. He said how us villagers did welcome her and trust her, and how with the aid of the Devil her master she did persuade us to absorb her potions, and suchlike. And he went on and on he did, speaking of Esther Royton and Master Daniel, and how he were but three and twenty, and all the time Mistress Molly stood there, with no look on her face except calmness. It were like she could no hear what he said, like she were no really there."

I visualised the scene. The great hall, with its fetid, ill dressed crowd, and the nervous witnesses ashamed to even glance at their victim; and Molly, as tall and straight as her injuries would allow, strong in the knowledge that no matter what might happen to her, those she loved would be protected by her silence.

Before the sentence could be passed, she had one more chance to speak in her defence, and Thomas's eyes filled with tears as he related how the Magistrate explained that her silence would be taken as proof of guilt, unless she spoke. But Molly had calmly shaken her head without looking in the man's direction, and even when he asked whether she had no care for her immortal soul, he had received the same response. So the sentence of death was passed, accompanied by a subdued cheer from the mob, after which Molly was led away by the soldiers.

As everyone else struggled out into the castle grounds, Thomas had remained beside his pillar. He told me he felt sick, and that his legs were so weak he could barely stand. When at last he felt strong enough to leave the building, he had returned to the stable wherein he had lodged his horse, and falling onto the straw, had sobbed himself into a deep and unrefreshing sleep.

The following morning he had followed Molly, and three other prisoners who were to share her fate, to the place of execution near swooning bridge.(39) The miserable quartet, all of whom were tightly bound, were conveyed in an open cart in which they had swayed helplessly as it rumbled unsteadily along. As is always the case at an execution, people with no other way to occupy themselves threw rotten vegetables and any other muck they could obtain, screaming with laughter when a missile reached its target.

After what seemed to Thomas an interminable journey, the cart reached the platform on which the gibbets had been erected and around which the morbidly curious few had assembled. Scarcely capable of walking, either from fear or from the iniquities she had endured and clad in garments now stained with her own filth, Molly had somehow managed to ascend the platform where she had stood with closed eyes, as the executioner placed the noose around her neck.

Thomas then heard the Oakham Preacher attempt to speak to her, but she appeared not to hear his exhortations so instead he had concentrated on her companions, only to be thoroughly cursed for his efforts. There were those present, Thomas related, who said they heard the witch mutter incantations to the Devil, but he had been near enough to hear only the Lord's Prayer gasped out, as Molly was hauled aloft.

CHAPTER 21

October/November

After Thomas's departure, all I could envisage was Molly swinging helplessly on the gibbet with her head twisted unnaturally to one side. I longed to cry to release my pain, but the tears would not come so I paced the floor, shaking uncontrollably, until I was distracted by the sound of knocking at the back of the cottage. I opened the outshut door to find our neighbour the soldier, carrying bucket of water.

He smiled. "She did swing then, and made a fine sight so did I hear. We now be taking an inventory of her goods. I have another bucket outside mistress, need you more water? You have but to ask."

After he had gone, I wrapped myself in two warm shawls and crouched beside the fire, where I remained until Mother Burrows joined me.

"'tis gone she be child, no use grieving as there were no way she could've been saved. They did for her, damn their eyes." She put her arms around me and we clung together, until she murmured gently, "'tis yer good father ye must think of now. Come, let's to him."

Because he was even more restless than usual that night, we remained sitting each side of his bed, until the sound of a clattering bucket told us our soldier neighbour was commencing his morning ablutions. Mother Burrows pulled herself heavily to her feet. "I'll go see to fire."

I nodded, and then stiffened as I heard the faint sound of horse's hooves approaching the cottage. I sprang to my feet in elation. It was Molly, I knew it was Molly coming home. Thomas must have been mistaken. It must have been someone else that died. I sped into my chamber and thrust open the shutters.

But it was Robert Alton who looked up, and on seeing me pulled in his horse and doffed his cap.

"Good day to you, Mistress Fry. How does the good Verger?"

I pulled the shutters too with a violent crash, and remained shaking beside the wall as Mother Burrows entered looking awed. "Mistress, do ye go down, 'tis the young lord do wish to speak with ye."

I descended slowly to the parlour. Robert stood beside the fire, his left foot resting on the fender.

Something reminded me of my manners and I curtsied, murmuring, "Will you not be seated, sir?"

He looked very uncomfortable, and I realised that this was probably the first time he had ever entered a tenant's cottage. "I did call, that is Mistress Fry my mother did request that I should call, to enquire as to Master Fry's health. It does give us cause for much concern, as I am sure you comprehend."

"I thank you, sir," my voice sounded as if it was coming from far away. "My father continues as before."

"Indeed," Robert smiled, as if in relief. "And there is then an improvement. I am indeed glad to hear it."

"There is no improvement, sir. My father is dying."

The young man flinched, but I did not care. He was intruding on my pain and I wanted him to go and leave me with my grief. As though reading my thoughts he flushed deeply, and stuttered, "Forgive me ma'am, my mother Lady Alton was concerned, and as I was riding past."

As he spoke, his hat, which he had placed on the table, rolled to the floor, and in trying to retrieve it his sword somehow became entangled between his legs, causing him to fall heavily onto the flags, just as Mother Burrows entered the room carrying a quantity of my father's soiled linen.

"Why young, sir, what you be a doing of?"

"Forgive me ladies," Robert struggled to his feet, obviously very discomforted. "A mere mishap I assure you and now, with your permission Mistress Fry, I will take my leave, my very best to the Verger."

He gave me a formal bow, and as Mother Burrows approached to open the cottage door I saw his nostrils quiver. I lowered my eyes knowing only too well what he could smell. Although my companion was a clean woman, and washed her face and hands regularly, there was nothing she could do to rid her garments of the taint of my father's excrement.

As the door closed upon our embarrassed guest, I slumped down onto the nearest chair. Old Mother Burrows still looked impressed.

"'tis a fine thing so 'tis, when the quality do call upon one."

"He did call because I did not acknowledge him," I snapped, suddenly hating Robert Alton, and all that he represented. "I did hear a horse, and upon opening the shutters and seeing it was but him I did close them and he, not having had the recognition he did think his due, did come to show me how grateful I must feel at being so acknowledged. I did touch his vanity, and his vanity must be appeased."

"Nay lass," the old woman protested. "'tis not so. And I declare, never before have I heard ye speak in such a tone. Young Master's presence here does show that them at Berwick House do hold yer father in high esteem, so they do."

"It means what I have already said," I retorted. "They think nothing of us folk at Berwick House. If they did, Molly would be with us now."

My words were drowned by a great sob, which seemed to rise from my very stomach. Mother Burrows looked aghast. "Hush child I beg or yon'll hear."

But I cared nothing for the soldier, and cried out hysterically, "Be silent listen, another horse oh dearest Lord let it be Molly."

"Lass, what do ye say?" The old woman reached out her arms to restrain me, but I had already pulled open the cottage door only to discover that this time the horse belonged to Master Machin. He gave me a kindly glance as he trotted past, but I returned to the parlour without acknowledging him. Ignoring Mother Burrows's concerned expression I re-seated myself beside the fire oblivious to everything except my own pain, until the she returned from the outshut shaking her head.

"'tis bad lass, so 'tis. We've but little of the potion left and he'll have more pain as time do pass. We must give sparingly, so we must. I'll to him now, and do ye drink some of this broth and then do ye lie upon yer bed, for I want not two invalids that I do not."

I tried to concentrate, but my mind seemed in a turmoil preoccupied as it was with the poor sick man above, and my friend who was no more. At last, weariness forced me to retire to my chamber, where I fell asleep almost as soon as I had lain upon the bed.

Two more weary days passed, during which my father's condition worsened and another letter arrived from William, and this time I was the recipient.. He expressed his concern that he was unable to travel to Oakham, but reassured me that he had instructed a lawyer, Master Oates from Nottingham, to defend Molly. As I re-read his words a great surge of life seemed to revive me, as I tried to convince myself, yet again, that Thomas had been mistaken. For a few moments I indulged myself in fancy and then, with sickened stomach, let William's letter flutter to the floor.

When I recall the days that followed, I remember feeling that my body and mind had combined to become a utensil, whose only object in life was to pace ceaselessly from parlour to sick room countless times an hour. During this strange period, during which Autumn turned to Winter, a circumstance of which I was unaware, Mother Burrows told me that Mistress Thomas had called and I was aware that Master Harris had visited twice, but nothing had any meaning any more and the only place where I felt safe was beside my father's bed.

But that sanctuary only lasted for the remaining days that it took him to die. The end was long and painful, and during the last few hours he hovered alternately between delirium and sanity, either screaming loudly in agony and spewing up thick brown blood, or gazing with extreme tenderness at me, and reminiscing at length on either his life with my mother, or his later friendship with Goodwife Hargreaves.

He seemed to have come to terms with his "sin", regretting only the illness he had inadvertently brought on his friend by what he described as his "selfish" desires. Occasionally, mistaking me for my mother, he told me how much he loved me, and I returned his endearments by stroking his hair back from his face, and placing my cheek gently against his forehead. Sometimes I kissed him lightly on the cheek, knowing as I did so that he continued to think it was his wife's embrace, but that was no longer of any consequence. All that mattered was that he knew that he was dying with love.

On one occasion he shocked me by asking for Molly. It was the first time, for many days, that he had mentioned her name."She is well?" He had gasped the words hardly audible.

"Yes father, very well," I had replied glibly. "She is visiting William in Goodborough, but will be returning soon, when she will call and see you."

As his agony increased, we could give him only a mixture of ale and coltsfoot juice to try and induce sleep. But I now know his lungs must have been too lacerated for such a mild remedy, and as the last night progressed his gasps of pain grew louder and he threshed about the bed so violently, it took all of our combined strength to hold him down.

When at last the battle ended and his tainted blood gushed in a short spurt from his open mouth, he fell back against the pillow his eyes glazed and fixed. As the significance of this dawned on me I gave a great scream, and crawling onto the bed wound my arms about his neck and sobbed helplessly on his chest.

Afterwards, Mother Burrows told me, she had summoned Mistress Whyte and they had carried me to my bed where, after considerable quantities of ale, I had been induced into a drunken slumber.

The days prior to my father's burial, slid by without significance. I recall that Mistress Whyte appeared to be living with us, for it was she who now prepared our meals and helped me to dress and wash. Of Mother Burrows I saw little, but learned afterwards that due to my state of mind she had been obliged to carry out the duties which would normally have fallen to my lot. As I recall now, so many years hence, I do not think I fully acknowledged what had happened, both to my father and Molly, until the visit of Master Oates.

A large, robust and noisy man, the lawyer left no one in the village including Sir Oliver, ignorant as to his feelings on discovering his prospective client's decomposing body swinging on the end of a rope. He then moved into Molly's cottage, summarily dismissed the soldier, and demanded the return of all the late owner's belongings from where they were stored at Berwick House.

Mother Burrows told me with considerable glee that everyone had at first been outraged at the stranger's impudence, but as Master Oates's pronouncements on the penalties of perjury were expressed with such conviction, Master Harris let it be known that Sir Oliver was now of the opinion that the Witchfinder may have been too hasty in demanding a trial. We then heard that Mistress Wallace and her brother-in-law had protested that Master Oswald had forced them to give evidence, and that they had wanted a prison sentence for Molly, rather than her execution.

Although Master Oates was too late to achieve anything for my friend, apart from ensuring that she was buried in consecrated ground, he did succeed in obtaining Hugh's release from Oakham prison, where the poor youth had been in chains since his sister's arrest, his existence having been forgotten by all concerned. Unwashed and unshaven, he had deteriorated into an unrecognisable mountain of filth almost skeletal in appearance, since any food offered to him had been thrown violently to the floor.

I never learned how Master Oates calmed him, or persuaded him to wash, change his clothes, and recommence eating. All Mother Burrows was able to discover was that Hugh had returned to live in the next-door cottage with the lawyer, and was apparently now occupied in helping Master Oates pack Molly's belongings.

"And poor lad be going to Master Radley," she told me, dolefully. "He don't know nowt about his sister, and how he'll be when he does I'm afeared to think."

My father's burial was to take place the following day, and I spent the last hours of his presence within our home sitting in his chamber, watching over his pathetic, wasted corpse. The villagers had called with their condolences, but they were like figures on a tapestry I had viewed for many years, and when at last the time came to stand beside his grave, I heard the Preacher's words exhorting all present to remember their Christian duty, as if from afar. They had no meaning, they told me nothing I did not already know, and I looked away tearless towards the cold winter sun and for some reason its pale glow gave me solace. For that sun would continue to rise and set, no matter my pains or joys. If I and those I loved did not exist, there would still be the tides, the seasons would continue, and vegetation would force itself each Spring from the ground.

In our ignorance we believe we have significance, but the earth was created before man, and Adam was but an afterthought; and one which has surely proved to be God's greatest disappointment.

After the burial, I retired into a strange dreamlike state for some hours, until I became aware that Mistress Machin was now living in my cottage, and that of my two previous companions there was no trace. Puzzled, I was about to visit Mistress Whyte's cottage to discover the reason for their absence when Mistress Machin entered the parlour from the outshut, and commenced to fold her cloak neatly across the back of a chair. I tried to comprehend what she was doing in my home. Had she not stood beside me when I signed that terrible paper? With some asperity, I enquired as to the whereabouts of Mother Burrows.

"She did leave," Mistress Machin responded, with a calm smile I found particularly irritating. "Her duties being done, she did leave. Now may I prepare you a little supper?"

"What mean you, her duties being done?" I interrupted, sharply.

"Why child, her duty of caring for your father in his extremities."

"But I did not ask her to depart," I persisted, my voice rising angrily. "She is my friend, she would not desert me."

"Indeed no, but she was here to nurse your poor sick father and now that is no longer required, she has returned to her cottage. And it is not fitting that such as she should be your companion, when such as Preacher Wyman says…. why child where do you go?"

But I had already gathered up my shawl, and opened the door. Outside I was surprised to discover that a thin layer of snow now lay upon the ground, and that the air was bitterly cold. Ignoring the fact that I wore only thin slippers I stepped outside, calling back angrily as I did so, "I am to Mother Burrows's cottage. I did not ask her to leave, and I wish her to remain. And you did speak against Mistress Tyler at the trial. I want you not in my home, please to be gone when I return."

It had been a long time since I had walked any distance, and the snow covered trees and buildings gave the village an ethereal appearance. The thought reminded me of Heaven where now dwelt those I loved, and I gave a great gulping sob as I reached Mother Burrows door, which opened quickly to my timid knock.

"Why lovey, what do ye here? There dunna take on so." She wound her arms about me, and as she drew me into the warmth of her tiny parlour I sobbed out my apologies for her dismissal, and begged her forgiveness.

"Nay, dunna ye fret so, 'tis nothing so 'tis. Yon uppity said I'd to go, but I didna' believe that ye'd no call me back. You canna stay alone in cottage, not yet a while any roads."

"You will come back, and you will sleep within my father's chamber. I know he would wish it so?" I gripped frantically at her sleeve.

"Of course lovey, if so's yer wish. Just let me get me baggage and I'll be with ye, so I will."

As we returned along the now darkened road, I told her of my conversation with Mistress Machin. The old woman chuckled. "'twas not wise lovey, but I wish mightily I could've seen her face, gives herself such airs, and her but a miller's wife. She'll be no there when we return, ye'll see." To my relief Mother Burrows proved correct, and from that day onwards Mistress Machin acknowledged me with only the briefest of nods, a circumstance I found amusing.

But my first Sunday as an orphan in St. Luke's Church, a building I had known so intimately all my life, proved most burdensome. Before entering I visited my father's grave. The stone, which had yet to be engraved, still contained only my mother's name, and since the snow now covered the disturbed earth there was nothing to denote the presence of a second internment.

I stared down, my mind reverting for a moment to my dreamlike state as I tried to convince myself that the agonies of the past weeks had not occurred, and I would soon hear his voice calling me in to prayers. But the only sounds I heard were the movements of the other villagers, as they passed me to assemble in the building.

I followed them slowly, and was puzzled to discover that the walls, pews and stone flags seemed unfamiliar, as if I were seeing them for the first time. Twice

I turned my head expecting to see Molly's smiling face nodding gently, but the two vacant places seemed to stare reproachfully back, empty and disconsolate. After the service I had automatically moved towards my customary place at the back, until I felt Mother Burrows gently pushing me towards the door, and realised that such a service would never be required of me again.

During the days that followed, apart from our visits to the church and the occasions on which Mother Burrows was called to her midwifery duties, we did not leave the cottage. Who was performing my erstwhile holy duties I neither knew, nor cared. They were no longer part of my life.

The only people who intruded upon us during this time were Mistress Whyte, whose presence I found exceptionally comforting, and Master Oates who came to explain that Molly's cottage was now empty, and would remain so until he could find a new tenant.

"As to the boy," he boomed. "Poor youth I cannot tell him his sister is dead. Coward that I am I shall leave such news to Master Radley. A sad matter and I have not as yet seen the written evidence. It was held from me. Infamous man, I am to London to destroy that perfidious wretch even if I have to apply to Cromwell himself. Witchfinder indeed, the man is a devil, a very devil."

At the words 'written evidence,' I felt myself go cold. Master Oates, with his authority and determination would no doubt obtain that "written evidence" and within days William would know all.

That same night there was a violent storm, and unable to sleep I lit my candle and tiptoed down to the parlour. The fire was burning strongly, and wrapped in my thickest shawl I snuggled down in my father's chair. I had been dozing spasmodically for nearly an hour when I heard a heavy footfall cross the flags in the outshut. .

Instinctively I thought of calling Mother Burrows, but something stopped me, and I opened the inner door quietly, in time to see Hugh's tall figure departing through the back door. Terrified, since I assumed he had come to seek retribution for his dead sister and would return, I was looking about me to find something with which to defend myself when I saw a leather object lying beside the milk churn. I recognised the soft green material immediately. It was the purse Molly had collected from Master Wallace's house, on that happy day in Stamford. I picked it up. The weight surprised me as did the soft clinking sound that seemed to fill the tiny room. Returning to the parlour, I opened the purse and discovered a quantity of gold and silver coins, which glittered up at me like the eyes of some weird nocturnal creature.

Astonished, I then remembered Master Wallace's outburst as to the money he could not find. I touched one of the shining circles, and immediately two others, dislodged by the movement, slid with their fellows against my skin, exposing a small piece of folded paper hidden beneath. I withdrew the parchment, and as my eyes settled on the script, Molly's handwriting seemed to jump physically off the page.

'Most dearest of friends, as ye do now know of my love for Daniel and my fear that 'tis his mother's wish that we will never wed, I must tell ye that we will depart this place. Daniel is for Scotland, for he do say that in that country he can find work, and will not be pursued as a soldier. I know not of this, but would follow him to any of the distant lands in the good Verger's book, if such was his desire. Most beloved of friends, it is not my wish to depart from ye, for ye I do truly love above all others, excepting he who has my woman's heart. I have much wealth, for the Goodwife was a woman of much means, and we will be well settled, and he does promise to take goodly care of Hugh. I do leave the good and kind Verger my cottage, for he may sell it and with what he procures do with such as he will. But to ye, dearest Pleasance, I do leave this token of my love. It is little enough for I will miss yer dear presence, but when next we do meet I shall impart more, but meantime I do think it wise for ye to burn this letter. I worry much for ye. There is much sadness in life, and the day does come when ye will be alone. I do know that William cares for ye with all his heart, but should ye not return his love, these coins will help yer life be easier. I will write to ye many letters and God willing one day we shall meet again. Meantime, may the Good Lord spare ye and be with ye always, till we do again speak, Your Molly'.

I remained bowed and weak, until I became aware that the flames were no longer dancing high up the chimney but flirting tentatively with each other in the grate. Shivering violently, I placed two thick logs onto the smouldering wood.

Where had Molly hidden her money? There had been such an intensive search by the soldiers, as well as by Master Wallace. And how had she made Hugh understand what he had to do? But the answers to these questions had died upon the scaffold. A sound upstairs reminded me that Mother Burrows would soon be descending, so I gathered up the purse and Molly's letter and hastened to my chamber, where I placed everything in the chest beneath my bed.

CHAPTER 22

November

I witnessed Master Oates's boisterous departure from Fretson with trepidation. Within a few weeks he would be aware of my part in Molly's death, and I had no doubt the news would be passed to William on the instant. Possibly because I was so pre-occupied, each passing hour seemed but a copy of its fellow, as I filled them either reading my Bible, an occupation from which I gained nothing but eyestrain, or thinking of Molly's purse and where should be its final destination.

Perhaps it was due to my preoccupation with her benevolence that I became persecuted by violent nightmares, the most terrifying of which had been on the night of Master Oates's departure. My father had entered my chamber carrying what appeared to be Molly's head, only it had been more skull than head, with deep holes where the eyes should have been, and he had thrown it with violent force towards my bed.

Deeply troubled, I enquired of Mother Burrows the following morning whether she could interpret the dream. She shook her head. "Nay, lass, I cannot but don't ye fret, 'tis what happens to all bereaved. Time must pass a'fore ye be yerself."

"How long, pray?" I asked, dolefully.

"I know not lovedy, 'tis difficult to judge how folk respond. But ye've much to learn to live with, and 'twill take time." She gave me a concerned look. "Have ye given thought as to yerself where yer to go, for ye canna stay here? They'll be wanting cottage for new Verger, for he'll be coming soon so 'tis said in village." The significance of her words made me fully realise the precarious position in which I was now placed, and I listened with trepidation as she continued, "Ye be welcome to me home lass, but I'd no think it fit for the likes of ye. Was there not a family in London that ye did mention a while back?"

"My father's cousin Mistress Frost has indeed offered me a home, and it was my father's wish that I should accept," I tried to explain, then my problems suddenly overwhelmed me and I started to cry, sobbing, "Oh, Mother Burrows, I am so afeared and feel so alone."

The old woman immediately arose from her chair, and enveloped me in a great hug. "There lass, take ye not on so, 'twill all be put to rights so 'twill. Do ye now write to yon Master Harris and ask him how long ye've here and then, when ye know that, ye can plan?"

Her sensible advice restored me to an element of calm, and a note was despatched, via Thomas, to Berwick House. The response next day was not a politely written reply, but a visit from the Steward himself who explained, in his customarily courteous manner, "Sir Oliver is most beholden to you for your understanding in this matter Mistress Fry, as we did not wish to intrude upon your grief. And for this reason, Sir Oliver has consulted Master Wyman, and from their conversation has gleaned that your future would appear predetermined, after due consideration has been paid to the memory of your late, and most respected father."

With a sense of foreboding, I murmured slowly, "My future, pray sir, to what do you refer?"

The Steward smiled. "Forgive me, I intrude. It is not my place to raise such a delicate matter, and at such a sad time. But I do assure you dear Mistress Fry, that we all have your welfare at heart, and rejoice that your sadness will be replaced so soon with the joy of so fortuitous a union." He gave a slight bow. "With such news to contemplate, and to enable you to prepare for so auspicious an occasion, Sir Oliver has instructed me to donate such funds as will be necessary, both for your daily needs and to enable you to prepare for your future role." He drew a small leather purse from within his jacket and placed it on the table. "I think ye will find all is satisfactory, and now I will withdraw. There is much, I am sure, to which ye must attend but Master Wyman did assure Sir Oliver that two months will suffice for mourning, after which it will not be considered indecorous for the nuptials, but forgive me Mistress Fry, I do intrude and must bid you good day."

He bowed, and as the door closed behind him I stared fixedly before me. No hapless animal trapped in one of Master Workman's traps could have felt more frantic. Then, bracing myself as if for some great endeavour, I hurried upstairs to my chamber where I re-read Mistress Frost's letter, my eyes dwelling particularly on the passage that I would be welcome, whenever I required a home.

I had but to answer for my future to be assured, but how could I leave all that I understood and travel to a life of which I knew nothing amongst people I had never met? But the alternative of marriage to Master Wyman was unthinkable and as, through my actions, I had relinquished any hope of being William's wife, my future was to be the unknown.

Untutored in affection, I understood not that true love never wavers, and an honest heart once won, is won forever. I cannot but pity my younger self, so terrified that I saw no other way but to flee. But I must not digress from this chronicle, for days are passing and of those I have few left.

Having decided to depart, I quelled with difficulty all further apprehension and planned how to proceed. I had no idea how a journey to London could be accomplished, only that for such an undertaking I would require money. Master Harris's gift had been intended only for our daily needs and my supposed nuptials, so once it had served the former, the remainder should be for Mother Burrows to do with as she wished; for it was unlikely Sir Oliver would demand a return of his gift. As to the money I would require for my journey, for this some of Molly's bounty would suffice.

Pulling out my box I lifted out the leather purse and, as the contents poured onto the bed, I experienced a sudden surge of confidence. What had Molly said, 'a widow of great wealth can live as she may please.' Although not a widow, I was now a woman of great wealth, but I knew I must take only what I needed and no more. The remainder would one day be returned to William, its rightful owner.

Then I caught sight of the shirt I had sewn for my father, still lying pathetic and lonely in my box. It had been sewn with such loving care, why had I not given him his gift? Overcome by another wave of sorrow, I remained staring miserably at the shirt until Mother Burrows's voice calling loudly, from below, "There be a good angel called, so there be!"

I struggled quickly to a sitting position, and just managed to gather all the coins into a heap beneath my skirts, as she almost danced into the room holding Master Harris's purse high above her head.

"Look ye lass, a bag of money, and there be two unites so there be, two unites."

"Master Harris did leave them," I replied. "They are for our welfare so do you take what you may need, and you have cared for me these long days good mother, without requesting aught. I owe you much, so do you take the remainder, for Sir Oliver will not expect a return of what we do not use."

The old woman flushed. "Nay lass, 'tis a Christian duty to aid others. Now

I'll use a little of this bounty, but the rest mayhap ye'll be needing a'fore long, if what is said in village be true." She gave me a worried look. "Be it so?"

I smiled gently, and shook my head. "We do both know the paths down which gossip can lead, so it is best for ye to believe only what I do say of my future life, and to discount all others."

"Thankful that I be," she declared. "For I could not believe that ye would consider, heaven help us, what be that?"

A loud knock echoed through the cottage, and I gasped, "If it is Preacher Wyman, I am indisposed."

As soon as she had gone I replaced the coins, and descended to the parlour to discover an irate Mistress Burridge facing an equally angry Mother Burrows who declared, as I entered, "She do want milk. Have ye no cow missus, or be ye hands too fine for women's work?"

In response, Mistress Burridge turned furiously on me, declaring, "It has been the Verger's DUTY to supply to Preacher Wyman, his milk. It has been his DUTY, so I say."

"As my father the Verger is dead," I interrupted sharply. "There is no further duty to fulfil, and until such time as the new Verger can be told that such a duty does form part of his labours, I do recommend you to Royton Farm. They have much milk, and I do not doubt will be pleased to supply your needs."

"Know to whom you speak, miss?"

She glared at me, and with a feeling of triumph I replied, "Indeed I do ma'am, Preacher Wyman's servant. Now if you would be so kind as to withdraw, Mistress Burrows and I have much to do as is customary in a house of bereavement."

For a few seconds the housekeeper appeared to swell, and then with a furious snort she turned and marched out of the cottage.

"'eh,'eh," Mother Burrows rocked back and forth, helplessly. "Her face lass, her face, ye be a deep 'un, ye be."

As I smiled at her mirth, a strange feeling of triumph overcame me. I had made my first conquest, and although I knew there would be many more to face, perhaps it was because of this encounter that I began to plan my future with more courage.

I had grown to love Mother Burrows dearly, but realised she was but human. The sight of only two unites had sent her into transports of delight, so to avoid arousing her curiosity as to how I would defray the expense of a journey to London, I decided to tell her that Mistress Frost had sent sufficient funds for my needs.

As I penned my words of gratitude to my cousin, I decided that, as Preacher Wyman had considered two months a sufficient period for mourning, it was imperative I departed well before that time. I therefore explained to Mistress Frost I had to leave the cottage before the new Verger's arrival, so would be travelling to London in three weeks time. Despite my previous surge of courage, I wrote the address 'Bow Lane'(40) with apprehension, but I overcame the emotion swiftly. I had to concentrate on the present, the future had yet to arrive.

My next important concern was conveyance for the journey. As I had no notion of transport other than that of cart or horse. I tried to imagine how Molly would have advised me to act, but then cast such thoughts from my mind. I was now without the protection of father or friend, but those two people who had loved me more than I deserved had left two great legacies, education and money. The latter to be my protector, and the former my guide.

Then I remembered the private coach I had seen leaving The George on our Stamford day, and how Molly had said that travellers sometimes shared the expense. If such were the case that was my mode of escape, and I decided to consult Thomas, on how to proceed.

These problems having been solved, there remained the contents of the cottage to be dispensed. I decided the furniture could be divided between Mother Burrows and Mistress Whyte, but my father's books were too numerous for me to take, and the thought of leaving them to be handled by strangers and possibly Master Wyman, was abhorrent. The numerous manuals were still stacked neatly beside the wall, and the sight reminded me of how William had studied them, and the memory solved my problem. Thomas could arrange for Master Bailey to convey them to Goodborough in his cart. The only books I would keep, apart from my bible and *Directory*, were my father's map and James Howell's book on foreign travel, for I could not separate myself from all my dreams, and the map had been Molly's favourite.

Nothing now remained but my father's chest. But as I was about to lift the lid, there was a sharp rap from below, and I descended to discover Thomas holding a large dish.

"Look ye Mistress," Mother Burrows declared. "A hot pie from Mistress Whyte, I'll place it by fire and get some plates."

As she disappeared into the back room, I handed Thomas my letter. He looked impressed.

"Be ye knowing folks in London town, Mistress?"

Disturbed by his curiosity, I replied firmly, "I wish no one to know the address of this letter, for they are folk who care not for the company of strangers. I am to visit them," I added casually, as Thomas's eyes widened in surprise. "They do wish to speak of my father, and have requested my presence." My tongue felt suddenly very dry, as if it was objecting to the lies it was being made to utter, but it was now too late for such concerns and I continued, "Mistress Molly once spoke of private carriages that can be shared with other folk who wish to travel to the city. Can one procure such a conveyance?"

"Yes Mistress, it has been done many times by the gentry."

"Then please to put such in hand, and when payment is required I will furnish it at once." Thomas looked even more curious, so I added hurriedly, "And here again I wish not that Fretson folk know, to bid farewell would be too painful for me at this present time. Please to keep your counsel, and should any person ask as to my future plans you will say you know naught."

"As ye wish, mistress," he replied, before adding, "I most forgot, here for yerself a letter from Goodborough."

I glanced down at the all too familiar hand, and as the moment could not have been more opportune I said, "Can I prevail upon you again? There are some books that I would have Master Bailey take for me to Master Radley at Goodborough. Is this within his service?"

Thomas's face brightened immediately. "Indeed yes Mistress, I'll speak with him at once. But as to travel Mistress, all coaches do leave The George right early, afore daybreak, so may be ye'll have to lodge there for a night. Be that in order?"

"Is there no other way?" I asked, shocked at the thought of staying alone in such a place.

"No Mistress, not if yer to take a coach."

"Then arrange such, if you please," I replied resignedly.

As soon as I was alone I returned to my chamber and opened William's letter. I dreaded reading what he had to say about Molly's death, but his references were poignant, but brief. He had been told of her fate by Master Oates, and blamed himself for not being able to travel to her defence. He wrote he intended to investigate the matter fully, to discover why she had been accused and brought to trial. He referred to her as his 'most beloved sister', and said that he had lost his dearest and truest friend. He implied, rather than stated, that he intended to seek redress from those he discovered were responsible for such an unjust act.

But it was not the thought of what William might discover that agitated me it was the official offer of marriage, as promised to my father, that transfixed my eyes to the page. Expressing himself with extreme delicacy and tenderness, he wrote:

'Please to know that these words addressed thus to yourself are not as I had planned. For I did intend myself to call and speak, but unable as I am to bear my own weight upon the ground, I can do no other than write that which is in my heart. But before so addressing you, I would wish you to know that it is not on impulse that I do so write. Your beloved father, had he been spared, would have agreed to my suit for we did speak of it prior to my departure from Fretson. And he did give his blessing to the union, but he did say it was to be only if you, dearest Pleasance, did so wish. And so do I write and offer to you my life and all I possess, but above all I do offer my true and deepest love. I have thought of naught but to see you again. I did wish to approach you prior to leaving Fretson, but did fear that you would find my addresses unseemly. Your youth and innocence did deter me, so I did think to write to you my thoughts in the hope that, in this manner, you would learn more of me. Should you consider such an alliance too swift when seen from the tragedy of both our great losses, but wish to accept my address, and this I do pray for with all my heart, then I indeed comprehend and would counsel that ye reside with one Mistress Slater, a matron of this village, a goodly and respectable widow with a daughter of her own. She was acquainted with dear Molly's late patron, and has a small but commodious cottage, wherein you would have a chamber of your own, and with her you could reside until such time as you did consider seemly our union. Now do I set down that which you must know, for it is necessary for you to be aware of my condition as to property.'

There followed a list of William's possessions, money and prospects. He wrote of his intention of opening another forge, the accomplishments of his two apprentices, and he described his house. Everything of which Molly had spoken was written there for me to see, and the delicacy with which he advised me how, if he received a letter of acceptance, he would arrange to send me the necessary finances for my journey to Goodborough, struck me more forcibly than the loving phrases he had written earlier.

I sat staring at his letter, my mind a turmoil of emotions, until the sound of horses' hooves and heavy wheels followed by footsteps approaching the cottage door, sent me hurrying downstairs. To my astonishment I discovered, standing in the open doorway, Doctor Percival's steward, Edward. He bowed politely, as I watched with even greater surprise the plump figure of the doctor being assisted down from a large, mud splashed, decoratively painted, coach.

"Mistress Fry, ma'am," the steward smiled encouragingly. "It is Doctor Percival's sincere wish that he does not intrude. If the hour be unseemly, he will withdraw."

"No, he does not intrude," I managed to reply. "Please ask him to enter."

Edward gave another bow as, puffing heavily, Doctor Percival arrived at the front step. Swathed in a thick cloak, and with a wide plumed hat pulled down below his ears, he bore a distinct resemblance to an outsize pumpkin. Controlling the first laugh I had experienced for weeks, I held out my hand. Giving me the same exaggerated bow he had exhibited at our previous meeting, he brushed my hand lightly with his lips.

"Most kind, ma'am, I did intend, indeed it was my wish, to pay my respects long since, Edward my cloak."

As the doctor's wine velvet coat, red satin breeches and lace shirt were revealed, Mother Burrows's eyes widened to impossible proportions, for not since before the war when the gentry in their silks and satins had ridden along the road to Stamford, had she seen such a vision.

Apparently unaware of the impression he was making, Doctor Percival continued, "To pay my respects long since, but I have had much travail not unlike your dear self, ma'am." He stopped speaking and to fill the void, I murmured, "Perhaps, Mistress Burrows, the doctor may care for a mug of ale."

She blinked, and hurried into the outshut followed by Edward. Alone with the doctor I tried to think of something to say, but before I could speak he began, "Happy beyond words am I, Mistress Fry, to once more have the pleasure of addressing ye even under such circumstances as these. It was with the very greatest of pleasure that I did entertain you in Stamford, as you may recall."

"I did visit with Mistress Tyler, sir," I replied, irritated that he appeared to have forgotten my friend. "You do know of her sad fate?"

"A sorry business," he shook his head, his lips pursed. "Indeed, ma'am, we have both been visited with great sorrow. Sorrow such as does come upon all peoples I fear, but sorrow can be born, indeed it can, and can be greatly eased by friendship, respect and, dare I utter the word, affection. I did know that my dearest wife suffered, but even I, physician that I am, did not expect so violent a severing of that sweet bond that ties us to those we hold most dear."

Comprehension dawning, I murmured gently, "I was not aware of Mistress Percival's demise. Please to accept my deepest sympathies, and I know that if my father were here he would join me in bestowing our most sincere condolences."

"Indeed yes, most kind, ahhh." Doctor Percival's face contorted suddenly, and he sneezed violently in the direction of the floor. I was disgusted. To deliberately empty one's nostrils in someone else's parlour I considered the height of bad manners, and I tried to control my expression as he continued, "And so I do come, dearest Mistress Fry, with my petition. You are very young, and I fear I am more in years than I care to say. But I am vigorous, ma'am, I am vigorous, and my heart has been yours from that happy day when you first stepped into my house. And it is yours dearest Mistress Fry, all yours, as I did express in my letter."

Utterly astonished, I stared speechless, but at the mention of a letter I recovered enough to interrupt quickly by saying, "Letter, sir, I fear I have not received a letter."

"Not received my letter," he looked aghast. "But it did explain all. Merciful heaven, here's a pretty matter, Edward, please, at once." Immediately, the outshut door opened, but before Edward could speak the Doctor, his face a fiery red blustered, "My letter to Mistress Fry, was it not despatched?"

"Yes, sir, most assuredly," the steward replied, obviously taken aback.

"I thank you," Doctor Percival waved him back into the outshut, and then looked sheepishly at me. "I fear I have unwittingly embarrassed you Mistress Fry, and I do most sincerely apologise. If you are unaware of why I am here then, unseemly as it may be, I must explain. Ah, me, was ever a man so put out." He pursed his lips. "So intense was the malady from which my poor wife did suffer that within two days she had passed from this world. I did then lock myself away and mourn deeply. She had been, for all but one year of our lives together an invalid, but the end though expected, was a bitter blow. Companionship does grow, Mistress Fry, no matter the circumstances and when a dear and understanding face is no more there is an empty void, but this you know, and if I continue in this vein I will bring sorrow where it was my intention to bring joy. As I did say I mourned, but one day I did remember you and your sweetness, and how you did resemble your dear mother, so beautiful a lady with a dignity and grace you have inherited, my dear. I held her in great esteem. I know not if your dear father did tell you?"

"Yes he did," I replied gently, as an idea of how to extricate myself occurred to me. "And although I believe I am aware of what you wish to speak, and am greatly honoured by what you intend, I must explain that I am already promised to another." The doctor's jaw slackened. "To a gentleman in Nottinghamshire, an acquaintance of my father, it was arranged before his death."

Doctor Percival sighed deeply. "A man of youth no doubt?"

"He is I believe three and twenty," I replied.

The plump, unhappy little man gave another sigh. "Ah, youth to youth, I was foolish even to consider, but in my letter I did say that I would accept silence as an invitation to present my suit. I fear I have made a sorry affair of the matter."

He looked so dejected I wanted to reassure him, and leaning forward said gently, "You have done no such thing, sir. I am deeply honoured and will always think of you as a kind, considerate gentleman of whom my father spoke with great affection."

Doctor Pervical's eyes brightened. "Did he so, and such a fine scholar. He could have been a very great man. We did study together at Repton School. Plans were made for his entrance to Cambridge, but I fear Master Fry did not agree. I did try to persuade my friend to withstand his father's ire, but it was not to be. His sense of duty guided him to his parents' ways. Now, dear Mistress Fry, if I may avail myself of your glass of ale, I will then take my leave."

As he lowered himself heavily onto the nearest chair, I realised an opportunity had arisen to learn more of my father's past and asked hesitantly, "Did my father ever speak of disappointment that he had not achieved that which he did aspire to? He spoke not of these things to me, and I know so little of his life."

Doctor Percival smiled. "No, my dear, he did seem always to be happy and never did I hear him complain of aught. As Verger of this place he did lead a life of industry and virtue and that, when we do reach our judgement day, is all the Good Lord requires of us. And" he added, wistfully, "he did have the blessing of a truly happy union, short though it may have been, and enjoyed the fruits of it through your good self."

I dropped my eyes to hide the tears as I thought of how lonely my father had really been, and how he had sought comfort with the Goodwife, only to repent so bitterly afterwards. I wanted to tell the Doctor he was wrong, and that hard work and dedication had not compensated for my father's empty years after my mother's death. But these were matters of which I could not speak, for they were not my secrets to reveal.

When at last the doctor and his entourage had rumbled their way back up the hill to the Stamford Road, I left a still dazed Mother Burrows to clear away the "gentry's" dishes and returned to my chamber, where I pushed open the casement shutters and leaned on the sill to reflect on the extraordinary events of the past few hours.

How Molly would have laughed to learn of my proposals from two such men, and how delighted she would have been to read William's letter. Despite myself, I smiled. Was it not incongruous that I, Pleasance Fry, always considered to be the shy, plain and gawky Verger's daughter, should have received three offers of marriage within two weeks. But my humour soon passed, as my mind wandered inevitably to William, and thoughts of how it would have been if we could have wed.

For I knew now there was nothing in the world I desired more, than to be his wife. My other two offers had only intensified my emotions for this good, kind man, so knowledgeable for his years. I longed to feel his hand in mine, to hear his strong kind voice counselling me, and to listen to his laugh. I imagined us both together in his cottage, with his arms around me. But I had to refuse him, and how to write such words I had no idea. Tears welled again into my eyes. I seemed destined only to cause pain to those I loved. If I had tried to understand my father, I could possibly have eased his loneliness.

But such thoughts were of the past, and difficult though it was I dismissed them to concentrate on the present. The sound of Mother Burrows's movements below reminded me that I had not yet told her of my plans, and I descended to explain. She nodded her head in satisfaction.

"'tis good lass, that ye now know what's to be."

"And if any person should enquire," I added. "You are to say that you know naught, for if Preacher Wyman were to discover my plans he would, I have no doubt, attempt to thwart them."

"That he would, lovedy, so do ye not fear. I'll not speak."

I then explained to her how I would be leaving Fretson, and that Thomas would be making all the arrangements for my journey to London.

"He did say that, of necessity, I will have to lodge at 'The George', for my coach does leave at early dawn."

"Alone in Stamford in an inn," Mother Burrows looked shocked. "Nay, lass, that canna be."

"Then will you accompany me and remain?" I asked, impulsively. "Thomas will escort your return."

To my relief she replied with alacrity, "Aye, so I will. I'd no rest easy were I to think of ye alone in such a place. And when do ye arrive in London town, and who's to meet ye?"

"My father's cousin will send a servant, of that I have no doubt," I replied, with more conviction than I felt.

CHAPTER 23

November/December

Returning to my father's box I discovered, after forty years of an arduous and dedicated life, it contained a few articles of clothing, two prayer books, a small leather box, and some delicate white material. The prayer books were such as I had never before seen. On the flyleaf of one were the words, *'To my* most *beloved Margaret Pleasance, for our nuptials, 23rd June 1639 from your devoted Adam.'* In the second book was written *'For Adam, to whom I do so happily and dutifully plight my troth, on this my marriage day, with the wish that this book shall be passed to our first child, should we be so blessed. Margaret Pleasance Wright.'*

The affection contained within these words seemed to surge through me, for they proved that I had been a child created by deep tenderness, and that love had also conquered duty. For these *Books of Common Prayer*, replaced years previously by *The Puritan Directory*, should have been destroyed but my father, usually so obedient, had been unable to caste away such precious tokens of love. I raised them both to my lips, and kissed the written words.

Then I opened the leather box. Inside was a silver chain from which hung a locket containing a miniature of a young girl's face. I started as I stared at what appeared to be my own broad, white forehead and grey-green eyes, only the light brown hair differed from my auburn tints. And the ease with which the locket opened indicated the picture must have been studied many times over the years.

I examined my mother's face, and saw there was a difference between us. Her expression was one of happiness, and her lips were slightly curved as if to reassure the curious that her smile indicated that her life, though short, had been a happy one. I gently kissed the likeness, then tried to place the chain around my neck, but it was too short, so I placed them both in my pocket

I then removed the piece of delicate cloth, and shaking it gently out discovered the white lawn unfold into a christening robe. I had never before seen so exquisite a garment, and realised that whether or not it was the product of my mother's skilful fingers, the person for whom the garment had been intended had been myself. As this realisation increased, the lowness of spirits to which I had succumbed for so long was replaced slowly by a feeling of confidence, for I had been truly loved, and a child blessed with such an inheritance can face great adversity.

The remnants of my father's life having been examined, I placed the cloak, prayer books and christening robe in my own box, and then joined Mother Burrows who agreed to undertake the task of dispensing with my father's few remaining garments.

I was now left with my most momentous task, the conveying of Molly's coins. After considerable thought I decided to wear them about my person, and for this purpose I would sew a new bodice and skirt, in the hem and pockets of which I would conceal my wealth.

The new dress would also serve another purpose, for I knew now from the little I had seen of the world, town folk dressed differently from country people. Mistress Frost's generous offer could not have been made without the largess to support it, a proof that her family were people of substance, and I did not wish to enter their house clad in a manner that would cause her to regret her generosity.

Having thus planned, I despatched Thomas to Stamford to purchase a quantity of dark grey woollen cloth. A gown made on the style of one I had seen on the ladies of Stamford would suffice, especially when edged with Molly's collar and cuffs. Thus garbed, with my new tall hat and my father's cloak, I felt I would be equal to anything the great city had to offer.

Thomas delivered my cloth with the news that I would be conducted to Stamford by a Master Merryman from Nontwell, and that I would journey to London in the company of a Mistress Carpenter, and her maid.

"'twill be fourteen days hence, Mistress," he explained. "And she be a lady, wife of a merchant gentleman with kin in London. She do travel with her maid Mistress Polly, and Master Wavel be the coachman, and his daughter Ethel be willing to travel as yer maid. She do accompany ladies on long journeys, and second driver be her brother Hal, so ye'll be in good hands and have naught to worry ye as to footpads or highwaymen, for there'll be an outrider as well, and he be armed. Coach'll leave The George at seven of the morning clock, and 'tis two days to Swan, at Holborn, if weather be not bad. If it be bad it do take three."

I listened resignedly. To take a journey that would last two or possibly three days with people of whom I knew nothing was formidable, but the alternative would be disastrous, so I had no choice, even though I had not yet received a reply from Mistress Frost.

Correctly assuming my silence indicated concern, Thomas continued reassuringly, "Master Merryman be a good soul, mistress, and goes about his business without talk. His cart is good too, and his horses be strong beasts as will be needed for a journey through December weather. 'tis one shilling he'll be wanting Mistress, and ye'll please to give me that afore ye leave the cottage. As to The George, ye do have a room and ye do settle for that afore ye leave, and Master Merryman do know ye wish to leave late. He don't think nuthin of that, Mistress, 'cus he thinks women strange beings anyway, begging your pardon."

With this dubious sally my help-mate departed, leaving me to contemplate my uncertain future. But I could not reflect for long as, with my garments to sew, there was little time for brooding especially as I had to sew the coins into my skirt at night, after Mother Burrows had retired.

The bodice however I could sew in her presence, and was so employed three days before my departure when we heard a scuffling sound outside the door. She looked nervously at me. Could it be the dreaded Preacher? He had approached me the previous Sunday with an expansive smile and an outstretched arm, and asked if he might be permitted to call. I had ignored both and curtsied low, murmuring that I felt indisposed and would he be so kind as to postpone his visit for a few days. He had looked annoyed, but with a tight smile had agreed to my request.

The scuffling sound had now become a timid tapping, bearing no resemblance to the Preacher's self-confident knock. Nervously I opened the door, and then recoiled as a blast of strong wind nearly blew me backwards. Gasping at the violence of the storm I glanced about, and saw lying on the ground the half clad figure of Bessie Workman. "I can't walk, Mistress," she gasped. "'tis me leg."

She pointed downwards to where her left leg stretched behind her, twisted and useless. Shocked, I bent down and carried her gently into the parlour. So thin was the skin on her face it was almost transparent, and she shook violently at which her thin hunched shoulders rose like giant quills from their sockets.

"God help us," Mother Burrows exclaimed in horror. "What's amiss, lass, what've they done?"

"Me father," Bessie began with a deep sob, but the child's immediate needs were of more importance than any explanation, and I hurried to my chamber for warm clothing, while Mother Burrows prepared hot broth. As we administered to her, I could not help but remember that other time, when different hands had gently washed and tended her.

When at last she had been fed and ceased shivering, I attempted to discover more of her plight. At first she sobbed convulsively before explaining slowly that, after Molly's trial, she had been sold by her father to a travelling pedlar, from whom she had escaped. A rough, unkind man, he had beaten and starved the girl, "And," Bessie whispered her eyes on the floor, "used me bad."

"Used you bad, what mean you? I do not comprehend."

Mother Burrows sighed. "If ye be London bound, ye need to know summat, lass. She do mean he did take her, like man does take woman."

Angered by my own stupidity I blushed heavily, as Mother Burrows asked Bessie how she had reached our cottage.

"I crawled," she replied, weakly.

"Crawled," I was appalled. "From where, in heavens name?"

"From Stamford, Mistress, I been crawling these three days."

We both stared at her in horror, and I marvelled at the frail creature's tenacity for life. Later, having gently washed her thin wasted body and anointed her cuts and bruises with soothing ointment, Mother Burrows examined her leg. "It be sundered lass," she pronounced dolefully. "And 'twill not mend I fear. Did yon wicked man do this?"

Bessie nodded, but it was to me she implored, "Mistress, please don't turn me out."

Appalled that she considered I could be so callous, I assured her she could remain as Mother Burrows declared, "And she can sleep with me, lass. Now do ye rest awhile Bessie, Mistress and me we have much to do."

Obviously reassured, Bessie snuggled down between the shawls as Mother Burrows beckoned to me to follow her upstairs. Once there, she said warningly, "Ye must no tell her ye be going. She'll no hold her tongue and village'll soon know. She's done it once, she'll do it again."

"But what are we to do?" I asked, helplessly.

"We'll tell her we go to visit Stamford folk, and'll be back next day. Meantime, I'll to Workman tomorrow with some of Master Harris's money and buy her back. Workman need know naught other than she'll be with me, and should he try to get her back I'll tell him I'm to Sir Oliver's steward to tell him all."

The following morning, Mother Burrows having departed to bargain with

Master Workman, and Bessie being safely tucked into my father's bed, I tackled my final task and wrote my letter of refusal to William.

But my rejection took me nearly an hour. Three times I commenced, and three times I threw the parchment into the fire. When at last it was completed and I had read it through, I thought how brief it seemed for so arduous a task. I had thanked him for the honour he wished to bestow upon me, and explained that while I wished it was in my power to return his feelings, I was unable at the present time so to do. I had included the proviso only after a great deal of thought. Even although I could never accept him, I was not yet strong enough to deny him, or myself, hope.

The ending of the letter also caused me great consternation. William had called himself my *"devoted and most loving of servants,"* ending with the words *"until such time as I shall be cheered by the sight of you I do so dearly love."* I could not ignore such overwhelming sentiments so, after more considerable thought, I signed myself his *"most loving and concerned of friends."* I sat staring at my neat copperplate writing until my reverie was interrupted by Mother Burrows, who entered looking extremely satisfied.

"She be mine," she announced. "He were no pleased till he did see the unites, and he be afeared of the law. He be poaching again and I did threaten him with Master Harris, so she be mine and she'll be company, and I've a mite I can leave her when the Good Lord do take me."

The remaining days passed swiftly, and unable to sleep during my last hours in the cottage I lay listening to the familiar sounds of the country night feeling strangely animated by the adventure I was about to experience.

When at last Mother Burrows roused me with the warning that Master Merryman would be with us within the hour, I dressed hurriedly in my new finery and, after one last glance into my father's chamber where Bessie now slept peacefully, descended below.

My apprehension that we would be heard departing was unnecessary since a heavy fall of snow now covered the ground, muffling any sound from the cart's well-oiled wheels. Within moments, I had passed Master Merryman's one shilling to Thomas and been lifted into the wagon beside Mother Burrows, leaving me scarcely time to glance back through the gloom at the small, insignificant building, which had been my sanctuary and where my father had reigned supreme, as king of his small realm.

As the cart lurched on its way, with the wind battering noisily against the canvas walls, we were forced to clutch each other in order to maintain our balance. And when at last we reached The George Inn, I was too shaken and cold to see anything but a blurred impression of my surroundings, as I followed Thomas into the building.

At first the bright candlelight and noise overcame me, and I could only stand helpless in the stone-flagged hallway. Despite the lateness of the hour, the numerous public rooms were full of men either eating and drinking at long wooden tables or wandering about holding mugs and talking loudly. Pressed against the wall I watched, as serving men carrying trays laden with platters of food passed adroitly between the guests, and everywhere there was bustle, noise and movement.

I became aware suddenly that a small group of men were staring at me, and I moved closer to Mother Burrows as Thomas, who had been speaking to a serving man, called out that we were to be conducted to our private room. Apparently accustomed to every kind of traveller, the servant led us upstairs to a small chamber on the first floor. Having now lived in the world and travelled much I know now that, by the standards of The George Inn, our chamber then was one of their more modest oak panelled guest rooms, but to us three villagers from Fretson it was luxurious, with its great ornamental fire place, wide four-poster bed, and carved upholstered chairs.

"Will you be wanting food, ma'am?" The man enquired as he bent down to stoke the fire, but before I could reply Thomas said, "If ye please warm broth and bread and wine for my mistress, and she be joining Master Wavel's coach at seven of the clock tomorrow's morn, to travel with Mistress Carpenter for London."

The man nodded and withdrew, as Mother Burrows collapsed into one of the chairs declaring, as she gazed admiringly around the room, "So this be how gentry live? And Thomas lad did say ye was his mistress, that be rich, that be," she chuckled, as I flushed in embarrassment.

"They will think you to be my servant, Thomas." I protested.

"Nay Mistress Fry, they do know me well here, but 'tis the way the gentry are addressed."

I frowned. "But Thomas, I am not gentry."

He laughed. "'tis better if they do think so. And ye look well Mistress Fry, in yer new gown and tall hat, indeed ye do."

Within a short while we were sitting down to our meal, after which Thomas prepared to take his leave, and as I accompanied him into the hallway I realised, that with Mistress Burrows added departure in a few hours, I would be isolated in an alien world.

As though reading my thoughts Thomas smiled. "All'll be well, Mistress, never ye fear. Master Wavel's Ethel will be with ye early, and yon man'll care for ye right well. He be used to all kind of travellers, and Mistress, do ye give him two shillings for yer board, and add a sixpence for himself. Such is the way with travellers, they do pay for thanks."

"Of course, is there aught else I should know? You have not spoken of the money for the coach," I asked anxiously of the youth, who had suddenly become my guardian and protector.

"Aye, I near forgot. Do ye give Hal a shilling afore ye start, and a shilling on each day, then at The Swan Inn do ye give Master Wavel ten shilling for your fare, two shilling for himself and five shilling for the out-rider. And Master Wavel's Ethel'll need money to pay for yer board and food at the inns, but that she'll tell ye of. She be getting a free ride and all to the great town, but she's known to be willing, so a shillings would be kind if yer so minded. Now farewell Mistress, and may God be with ye."

He blinked suddenly and then moved quickly away, his customary jaunty walk suddenly a stumbling tread, and I closed my eyes tightly to try and control my tears. It was as I returned into the chamber that I realised I had offered him nothing for his pains, and without Mother Burrows noticing I wrapped a gold half sovereign inside a scrap of paper on which I wrote 'For Thomas.'

The night passed slowly. There was too much noise both from the inn yard and the building itself, for either of us to do anything but doze fitfully until the appointed hour, when the serving man brought us food and drink. After I had counted out the coins into his palm, he smiled kindly. "Thank ye ma'am, and I'll be back to escort ye down, just afore the hour."

I was too apprehensive to eat, but Mother Burrows was enjoying a hearty meal, when there was an uproar from below. I ran excitedly to the window in time to see a large vehicle drawn by four horses, and accompanied by a man on horseback, enter the the bustling world of busy stable boys and perspiring horses. In particular, I noticed there were no women to be seen, and I wondered, apprehensively, whether Master Wavel's Ethel had perhaps had a change of mind.

I glanced back at Mother Burrows, now standing by the window her attention held by the activity in the yard below. Thomas would be calling within the hour to conduct her back to Fretson, but before she left the room I had one last duty to perform. In the small purse in which Master Harris had placed his three unites, I now placed two gold sovereigns and Thomas's gold piece.

Just as I had completed this task the old woman turned, and in an unsteady voice said, "'tis near time lass, and 'tis sad I am to see ye leave. And do ye write now, for young Thomas can read letters to me."

I gave her thin shoulders a gentle hug, and as her arms encircled me I slide the small purse into the pocket of her worn old gown. Our embrace was interrupted by a light tap on the door, which opened to reveal a woman of middle years, neatly dressed in customary black and white.

"Mistress, I be Ethel Wavel," she explained, with a curtsey.

My only experience of servants having been Bessie Workman I was uncertain how to proceed, but no such qualms concerned Mother Burrows, who pursed her lips at the stranger and announced, "This be Mistress Fry, and do ye take good care of her for she is to join her fine folks in the great town."

I flushed as Ethel, looking suitably impressed, gave another curtsey just as the serving man appeared.

"The coach awaits ye ma'am, will ye please to follow me."

As he hoisted my box onto his shoulder, I gave my dear old friend a final hug, and after a backward glance of farewell to her sad face swiftly followed the other two down to the inn yard.

The coach seemed to me a vehicle of great size, with its two large wheels at the rear and two smaller ones at the front. As the serving man helped Hal with my box, the out-rider raised his crop in salute, but he was so thickly clad in coat and muffler I could not discern his face. Everywhere people were either entering or leaving the inn, and as I approached the coach door Master Wavel jumped down from the box to assist.

"There be a warm brick for your feet, ma'am, and plenty of rugs to cover yourself, for it'll be a cold drive I fear."

I thanked him, and climbed into the coach to find myself the focus of two pairs of cold, inquisitive eyes, which stared at me from behind black masks. I hurriedly took my seat and gave Hal his shilling, as he fitted the perforated metal shutters on to the window cavities.

With Ethel beside me, and covered in a warm rug which she had spread across my knees, I sat stiff and straight against the upholstery, only to start in fright as a strident sound rent the air and the coach lurched forward, throwing me against the side of the vehicle. Within seconds Master Wavel had urged his horses into a canter, and I gripped the leather hand strap tightly as a sudden decline in the coach nearly sent me falling into the laps of the women opposite. The coach continued to plunge up and down while simultaneously rolling from side to side, and my stomach seemed to climb violently into my chest only to return with equal speed to its customary position.

After an hour, I was feeling both sick and cold, as the brick had cooled. I closed my eyes and tried to sleep, but the motion of the coach denied me rest, and it was with great relief some time later that I heard a double blast echoing through the air, and Hal calling out that we were to stop at the 'Wheatsheaf' at Alconbury Hill, for fresh horses.

Ethel, who had slept continuously since we departed from The George, now sat up and as our companions descended from the coach she withdrew a piece of black material from her pocket, saying, "Ma'am, I do recommend that you enter masked." Before I could reply she had wound the mast deftly about my head, as she explained, "It is the way of gentry, a lady never travels unmasked, and it protects the skin from cold."

Murmured my thanks, I followed her into the inn on legs that seemed so weak I marvelled that they could bear my weight.

Unlike the spruce 'George', this inn was a small, shabby looking building, with a scruffy yard covered in filthy snow and horse manure. A number of dogs were scavenging in a pile of dung beside the inn wall, whilst some children dressed in rags, and obviously hungry, were begging coppers from everyone present.

At that moment, a party of soldiers trotted into the yard. They all looked weary, and their officer, a young man who reminded me of Daniel, had his arm in a sling. Their arrival caused a great bustle, and those stable lads who were not swarming around our coach buckling in the new horses were soon occupied assisting the troopers.

Inside the inn's shabby and un-swept interior, Ethel gave her orders in a calm but professional manner, but she did not invite intimacy, so I ate my meal in silence while she ordered more hot bricks for our feet.

Within a short time we were back in the coach, lunging towards our next destination. Despite the discomforts of the journey, and the lack of communication from my fellow travellers, I was growing accustomed to the feeling of security the coach represented, and at last fell asleep.

The second inn was to be our resting place for the night, and I was pleased to see it was both as large and well-appointed as The George. The accommodation also equalled that inn's standards, but once again we ate our meal in silence. When we had finished, Ethel offered to assist me remove my gown, but the cargo it contained was too precious to be far from my grasp.

"Thank you but no," I said, waving her away. "I will rest beneath the top coverlet, I do not wish to disrobe."

I expected her to protest, but she nodded and retired to the narrow pallet bed at the foot of the four-poster. This ritual was repeated on the second night, and never once did she question my actions, nor did her conversation extend beyond that required by necessity.

It was on the third day, as we were approaching the outskirts of Hampstead Village, that I saw the gibbet. The bad weather had intensified, and the snow turned into a driving blizzard, when Master Wavel pulled in the horses to let Hal acquaint us with the situation. Unable to make us hear because of the wind, he removed the metal shutters for a moment, and as he yelled I glanced past him and saw, beside the road on a higher ground, a gibbet from which swung the decomposing remains of a woman's corpse.

The face had long ago been pecked away by the birds, and the grinning skull and empty eye sockets seemed to be laughing at some secret joke, while the hair, which must once have been luxuriant and black, now stuck out at all angles like the spines of a hedgehog.

I tried to close my eyes, but my eyelids would not move, and my heart began to beat violently as I imagined Molly's face staring beseechingly at me. Then Hal replaced the shutters, and within minutes we were moving away. For a fearful second I thought I was going to faint, as Ethel turned towards me with a concerned expression.

"Ma'am, you look fearful pale, are you not well?"

"The journey," I replied weakly. "I find it very tiring."

"No matter," she replied, soothingly. "Once through the village 'tis downhill, so the horses can pick up speed, and then it be but another hour to the Swan."

Her announcement shocked me into reality. A mere hour was all that separated me from abandonment, and despite the aloofness of Mistress Carpenter and her companion, I had grown accustomed to their silent presence and the protection that the coach afforded me from the rigours of the world. I tried to control the fear that began to fill my stomach as the coach gained speed on the downward run towards Islington Village.

Contrary to Ethel's pronouncement, the icy roads and another sharp blizzard forced Master Wavel to slow his speed yet again, so it was nearly two hours before we drove into the noisy confusion of the Swan Inn Yard.

As soon as the vehicle stopped my fellow passengers struggled past me down the coach steps. Simultaneously, Ethel leaned towards me with the first smile she had exhibited during our acquaintance. I reached into my purse and offered her a shilling. The woman's eyes lit up but to my consternation she immediately jumped down from the coach, and hurried towards the inn. Taken aback, I stared after her as Master Wavel assisted me down. Seeing my surprise he shrugged.

"She be going for her ale, Mistress. My Ethel can't be long without her ale, 'though she'll no drink a drop while working."

"Will she return," I asked nervously, as Hal followed his sister into the inn. Master Wavel shrugged again, as the out-rider heaved my box down from the coach roof.

"Possibly, Mistress, 'tis hard to say. Now if you'd be so kind as to pay me for my trouble I'll be leaving, for I have business in the town."

Hurriedly I dipped into my purse and gave him the required amount, while beside me I saw the horses being taken from the shafts and the coach being pulled to one side. Master Wavel having departed, I stood alone watching helplessly as Mistress Carpenter and her maid were escorted from the yard by a man in livery. Feeling increasingly desperate, I stared first towards the inn which seemed to tower above me like a great maw, and then at the crowds of people who were now either calling to one another, or moving rapidly in different directions about the yards.

Then suddenly a cultured voice said, "Are you being met by friends, Mistress?"

I turned to find the out-rider, now minus his thick scarf, unsaddling his horse.

"I have arranged so, sir, only I did not receive a response to my letter before I left Stamford, and I know not who will be here to greet me."

The man smiled. "Do not trouble yourself, ma'am. I will remain with you until your friends arrive and, should they fail to do so today I will arrange a chamber for you at the inn then, if you will give me their whereabouts in town, I will call on them and tell them you are here."

Overwhelmed with relief, I murmured my thanks and foraged in my purse for five shillings. The man accepted his money with a bow, before picking up my box and escorting me to the side of the yard. For a reason I could not define, I knew he was to be trusted and that I need concern myself no further as to my safety.

We remained beside the wall for some time, during which the life of the inn yard continued before me. I watched as two more coaches arrived, and a thin female was joyously greeted and embraced by an equally thin youth; while a little further away a plump man was escorted by a boy in livery towards a sedan chair The attention they were all receiving made me even more aware of my own isolated state, and a longing for my father's presence made me clench my lips in an effort to control myself.

I was beginning to think I would have to request my protector to seek a room when suddenly I heard my name. I turned quickly, but the out-rider was already waving energetically to a man in livery who hurried towards us. "You are Mistress Fry?" He enquired his hat in his hand.

"Indeed yes, I am Pleasance Fry," I declared.

The man gave a relieved nod. "Pleased will be Mistress Frost, indeed she will. Three times for these past two weeks have I met the Stamford coach. Afeared she has been, Mistress Fry, that you would befall a mischief, not knowing the city. I am Harold Synett, Master Frost's steward. Now if you please, ma'am, I will escort you to my master's house. And do you stay close, Mistress, for t'would be a simple matter to lose a body in such a crowd as this."

As he picked up my box I looked round to thank the out-rider, but he was nowhere to be seen. How he had managed to melt away into the crowd I never knew, for I was never to see him again. And many times over the years I have thought of him, and knowing life as I do now, silently thanked him for his kindness to a young, inexperienced stranger.

But at the time I had no such thoughts as, shaking with weariness, I followed Harold through the mud and slush of the yard, avoiding with difficulty the numerous other passengers and vehicles either just arriving or departing from the inn. When at last we reached the street outside, I found myself in a wide rubbish strewn thoroughfare, which seemed full of people and vehicles, all moving at extreme speed.

The snow had recommenced falling as I was guided towards two plump horses standing between the shafts of a large carriage, on the box of which sat a well-clad driver.

"Here is my master's coach, Mistress Fry. Would you be so good as to enter and yonder is a warm brick for your feet, and a coverlet for your person."

Climbing into the vehicle I collapsed exhausted onto the velvet upholstered interior. Having assured himself that I was comfortable, Harold climbed up onto the box and I heard the driver urge his horses into a bouncing trot. As we progressed I heard, through the covered window aperture, the sound of passing traffic and the cries of what sounded like traders selling their wares. I raised the leather window cover and saw that I was travelling along a wide, busy street lined on either side with tall wooden buildings, all with high peaked roofs and overhanging eaves.

Despite the stench wafting up from filth which seemed to lie everywhere, I continued watching as the coach drove precariously past numerous carriages, barrows and handcarts, either stationary or approaching from the opposite direction. I saw that some of the buildings had open workshops on the ground floor, such as I had seen in Stamford, and everywhere there seemed to be hundreds of people, either pushing hand-carts, riding in carriages or on horseback, or hurrying through the falling snow.

Then the carriage swerved sharply to the left, and entered a narrow street. Here the upper storeys of squalid, dirty buildings overhung the ground floor on either side, giving the area the appearance of a long, dark tunnel. Shocked by the squalor, I covered my nose with my hand as the stench seemed to fill the coach.

To my relief, the vehicle started gaining speed and after traversing a number of further streets, all equally squalid, it made an abrupt turn and I saw that we were now progressing along a road without traders, and where the houses appeared cleaner and better constructed. One or two dwellings even had glass windows, and the shutters and entrance doors appeared substantial, and well kept. Finally, the coach made one more turn into a narrow roadway, before stopping before a tall dark house.

"We be at my master's dwelling, ma'am," Harold announced as he jumped down to open the coach door. "Will you be so good as to alight and enter, and do you take care for the snow is heavy and the ground is thick with ice." He extended his hand to assist me down and, unaware of anything except the wide, high doorway which stood slightly ajar, I hurried up the steps and into the house.

CHAPTER 24

December

"My dearest girl, welcome, I was so afeared that some mishap had befallen you for your letter did not state the day, and so concerned was I that I did send Harold many times to The Swan, and though I did reply to your letter I did fear it would not arrive in time, and so it would appear has proved the case."

Confused by the gloom, and hardly able to discern the short, plump, female figure approaching swiftly across the flagstones, I stammered, "I thank you ma'am," before being interrupted by another flow of words.

"But you are safe, heaven be preserved. Now child, this way to the fire for you do indeed look chilled. Harriet, some warm broth at once for Mistress Fry, and Harold do you take Mistress Fry's box to her room. This way my dear, but one moment, in my concern I have not made myself known to you. I am of course, your cousin Edith Frost."

Ignoring my attempts at a reply, my cousin led me swiftly into a small room, where the high-backed blazing fire and numerous candles illuminated dark panelled walls and carved oak furniture. She motioned me to a chair.

"Do you be seated here my dear, for it is nearest the fire, and now you will tell me of your journey whilst I do continue with my tapestry. Do you work your frame, cousin? I am not acquainted with country ways. Now here does come Harriet with your broth. It has been heating these past hours, for I did intend that you should be made warm as soon as it was possible, for so long a journey in weather so bleak and cold must indeed have been a trial. Do you place the bowl upon this table, Harriet, and take Mistress Fry's cloak and bring my thick red shawl for her shoulders, for it is the very warmest that I have and will suffice, my dear, till such time as you do procure your own."

"I thank you ma'am, you are most kind," I gasped, as swiftly as I could in order to complete the sentence, but my words were lost as Mistress Frost continued, "Nay child, you must address me by my name, for are we not kin?

Cousin Edith will suffice, and how you do resemble your dear mother, though she had not your height. When you are made warm, but drink child, the broth must be drunk while it retains its heat. When you are warm, Harriet will conduct you to your chamber where I do recommend a short respite afore we eat our meal at five of the clock. Not a fashionable hour I fear, but Master Frost does work of an evening, so that hour it must be. You are to bed with Katherine and Frances, our youngest daughters, their chamber being the largest in the house it does accommodate the second bed, now placed within. I know it is the custom to bed three or even four souls a time, but such closeness can breed illness and is not my way. But it is not easy I must confess for this house is not large, and as I have said many times to Master Frost, with four children and servants to board I am truly tried for space." She sighed. "It was not always so cousin, I do assure you. When I came as a bride it was an edifice of massive proportions, or so I did consider, but that was long ago. Now it never does seem vast enough. Always there are bodies everywhere to encounter but I confess so accustomed have I become to such a bustle, I would sorely miss any of the many souls beneath this roof were they to forsake our walls. I do indeed wish I could have given you a chamber of your own, but I fear that cannot be until after Lady Day, two weeks from which our eldest daughter Jane, with whom you are soon to be acquainted, is to be wed. Jane did wish the nuptials postponed but such are the many demands upon Master Frost's time, for he does so often attend meetings of Cordwainer Ward (47) and is much from home, the time arranged could not be altered. Jane does occupy a small but pleasant chamber beneath the eaves of the house, which will serve you well and prove adequate for your needs, ENTER!"

Only the fact that I was too exhausted to react saved my bowl of soup from descending to the floor, as my cousin's strident reaction to a very timid knock, echoed around the room.

Harriet having entered, and under my cousin's close scrutiny encased me in a thickly woven, lavender scented shawl, I re-commenced sipping my delicious soup. Although I had long ceased to concentrate fully on cousin Edith's flow of words, I did observe that her neat figure was clad in an elegant gown of dark red velvet, and a short fur lined, velvet cloak.

My soup consumed, I could feel my eyes begin to itch with sleep, and as the door closed once more on Harriet my observant cousin continued, "I see you are weary, my dear, and it is no wonder considering your journey, but do you now feel the benefits of the broth? You are no longer chilled? Good, then Harriet shall conduct you to your chamber and you will rest. When you require her services you do shake this bell, so. Yes, the sound is fierce, but so it has to be for the servants are below, so a quieter sound would not suffice. There is such a bell in every room. Now, when you are refreshed I am much eager to hear of your life in Freston. Such a fine man was your father, the parishioners must have held him in great esteem and such a loss must have been deeply felt. Harriet, do you now escort Mistress Fry to her chamber, and help her disrobe for her rest, and do you take a candle until such time as Mistress Fry is accustomed to our ways."

Rising with difficulty, I followed Harriet into the hallway. The single candle barely lit our way, but after climbing a wide staircase and groping our way down a dark passage, we finally reached a cold chamber. By the candle's flickering light I could see it was large and contained two four poster beds, the wider of which occupied the centre of the room while the narrower one, at the base of which was placed my box, stood beside the left-hand wall. The hangings on both beds were of thickly embroidered tapestry, such as I imagined might have adorned the beds in Berwick House and there were also some other pieces of furniture, which I could not distinguish in the gloom.

Realising I must divest myself of my gown as swiftly as possible, in order to remove the coins and conceal them within my box, I suggested to Harriet that she might leave me to rest. To my discomfort, she seemed not to hear as she busied herself pouring water into a bowl and lighting two more candles from our single flame. Having completed these tasks, she offered me a piece of white cloth.

"If you please, ma'am, Mistress Frost does wish you now to wash and remove your gown, which she desires I should take to be laundered." She recited her instructions in a voice which seemed to indicate that to detract from one word, would result in dire retribution. I listened to her in consternation before suggesting, with a lack of confidence I hoped was not obvious, that she might leave me. No General ordered to surrender his army could have equalled Harriet's shocked response, as she cried, "No ma'am, I must be by, as Mistress Frost did say, I must."

Realising that it was useless to demur, I rolled up my sleeves and washed, aware as I did so of a pleasant aroma rising from the basin. As I was so occupied Harriet exclaimed suddenly, "Ma'am, Mistress Frost did say to remove your gown."

Feeling far from calm I pretended to search my pocket, before assuming an expression of consternation and declaring, "The key to my box, I must have dropped it."

"I did hear no sound, ma'am," Harried replied, looking puzzled.

"Possibly as I mounted the staircase, I now recall I did hear a slight noise and it is most unfortunate, for without the key the contents of the box cannot be removed as, I believe, is Mistress Frost's wish."

As I had hoped my ruse worked, for Harriet immediately snatched up the single candle and departed, crying that I was to remain until she returned. Quickly pulling off my skirt I opened my box, and with my sewing knife cut out the inside pockets and ripped open the hem. The coins showered down like sparkling leaves falling from a shaken tree, and I thrust them quickly beneath the remaining articles, before removing my other gown, and re-locking the box.

I was standing shivering beside the bed wearing only my shift and Cousin Edith's shawl, when Harriet returned to announce nervously, "I fear I cannot find the key, ma'am. I've searched and searched and 'tis no where."

I assumed an apologetic look and replied as casually as I was able, that it had been residing in another pocket, the existence of which I had forgotten. Obviously confused, Harriet shook her head before pulling back the heavy coverlet and drawing out the warming pan. Easing myself into the embrace of warm lavender scented white linen I lost consciousness almost immediately, and drifted into a deep dreamless sleep. I would have preferred to remain there safe and secure from the world, but my tranquillity was destroyed about an hour later by Harriet, who re-entered the room with four more unlit candles in a holder and Cousin Edith's instructions that I was to join the family for their evening meal.

The room was now ablaze with light, and I was able to discern that, apart from the beds it also contained a substantial fireplace, two large chests and two chairs all of which were ornately carved, and a low table on which rested a square box flanked by two more candlesticks. Like the other parts of the house that I had seen, everything seemed to shine with cleanliness. But despite its luxuries the room was was bitterly cold, and I wondered why, in a house where nothing seemed lacking for comfort, there was no fire in the grate.

As I stood shivering in cousin Edith's shawl, Harriet shook out my unsoiled gown, and as she helped to dress said rapidly, "Your travelling gown was badly torn, ma'am, and much soiled from your journey, and Mistress Frost says I am to clean and mend the tears, and also to empty your box and place your garments and suchlike in the lower two drawers of yonder chest, and for this task I will still require your key. Please ma'am, give me your key."

Her pleading tones and obvious desperation were pitiful, and although I had no intention of complying I did not wish to place her in disfavour with my cousin so, with a comforting smile I said gently, "There are matters within my box that are for Mistress Frost's eyes only, so do not distress yourself. I will explain to her, and after she has seen the contents you may have the key."

Harriet's relief was obvious, and her ministrations having been completed she was preoccupied replacing the coverlet on my bed as I opened the door and stepped into the unlit passage. Behind me I heard her protest that I should wait, but I had a sudden desire to be alone again, so groped my way along the wall.

I was approaching the area beyond which I judged was the staircase, when I heard a sound. Putting out my hand I encountered material, which appeared to be attached to a moving form. Startled, I cried out and staggered back as a young male voice exclaimed in accented English, "My pardon, but I cannot see. You are not harmed? Good, you are to Mistress Frost?" This enquiry was accompanied by the touch of a warm, smooth hand, which grasped my wrist and drew me gently along the corridor. "Come I will guide you. I find the English most strange in their lack of candles. I do think they must have the eyes of cats to traverse a building without lights. There, madam, down this staircase to yonder door."

From beneath a door at the bottom of the stairs a glint of light illuminated my way, and I turned to thank my saviour, but all I could discern was the sound of footsteps retreating along the corridor. Proceeding slowly down the stairs, I became aware of another set of footsteps, this time running along the upper corridor. Thinking it must be Harriet in pursuit I turned, but instead of the servant a small figure bounced down the stairs and yet again my hand was gripped, but this time the fingers were short and thin and the voice that spoke that of a child.

"Cousin Pleasance, is it not? Master James Frost at your service, ma'am. Master Santagel did alert me that you needed guidance. Please to come this way I beg, and please accept my apologies on behalf of this house that you have so inhospitably been left to your own devices."

I stared down at the owner of this adult-like declaration, but it was too dim to discern anything except an abundance of curly fair hair atop of a very short boy, who led me confidently towards what I could now see, were two heavy double doors.

They swung in immediately in response to his knock, and I found myself in surroundings incandescent from the numerous candles situated around the room. As I narrowed my eyes against the glare, James ushered me in as Harold bowed and stepped back to let us enter.

This chamber, like all the rooms I had so far visited, was also panelled with oak throughout but unlike the bed-chamber, had a high-backed fire burning in the expansive and ornate fireplace. There were also paintings hanging on the wall, and brightly polished ornaments on side tables. The room was the most palatial I had ever seen, and as my diminutive cousin pushed me gently towards the wide carved table, I saw that it contained large bowls from which tendrils of steam floated lazily upwards.

Surrounding the same table were seven leather-upholstered chairs, five of which were occupied by cousin Edith, a young woman whom I assumed to be my cousin Jane, two little girls of identical appearance, and an elegantly dressed man of middle years. Everyone smiled as we entered, and the man arose immediately and moved towards me. He was exactly my height, and wore a curved moustache and short, pointed beard. Taking both my hands in his, he kissed me lightly on the left cheek saying, as he did so, "Welcome to our home, cousin Pleasance, I am your cousin Peter and I trust the journey was not too arduous. But all is behind you now, and it is our wish that you will find your life with us as pleasurable as has been your life hitherto."

My new relative had a clipped sharp voice, the antithesis of the warm and considerate manner with which he led me to the vacant chair beside his seat. Having assured himself I was comfortably placed, he then introduced me to the three girls and I nodded shyly, suddenly very aware of how shabby were my clothes compared with the elegance of their attire, especially Jane. But I was surprised to see that her red gown and decorated bodice barely covered her shoulders, and that she wore her hair in long curls which hung either side of her face.

My feelings of inadequacy were not allayed when Harold enquired as to which of the meats I wished to partake. Bewildered by the choice, since he indicated mutton, chicken and neats' tongues from which to choose, I took a little of the chicken, only to be confused again when he offered, salmon or carp.

Concentrating on the different foods, and at the same time trying to answer cousin Peter's questions about my life in Freston, caused me considerable confusion, as did the implement for eating for, instead of a spoon accompanying my knife, there was a shining spiked utensil with which I was expected to spear my meat.

I ate a little because I was indeed hungry, but I was too self-conscious to enjoy the fare, being very much aware that cousin Edith's glance fell on me more than once, even though she appeared absorbed listening to James's animated account of his day. Either because she saw my dilemma, or genuinely wished to consult them, Jane began to distract her parents by discussing a meeting to which the family had been invited the following week.

Despite this relief, the meal still seemed to last forever, especially when I was expected to make another choice, this time between cheese, a tanzy pudding or fruit, all of which were presented by Harold for my inspection. It was not until I was carefully cutting an apple into small pieces that I realised, from my cousins' actions, that it was customary to partake of a little of each rather than select a single item.

When at last the meal was finished, and after prayers conducted by cousin Peter in a hurried expressionless voice were completed, James and his twin sisters took their leave. Unaware of what to do, I glanced at cousin Edith who smiled kindly, and suggested that I might wish to retire.

Grateful for her understanding I arose, and after wishing everyone a shy goodnight, walked out into the darkened hallway where I found Harriet awaiting with an unlit candle. Stepping from the heated room into the cold atmosphere of the public area made me shiver, and I was grateful when I was once again in my warm bed, but this time I could not sleep.

Despite my cousins' evident kindness, I was only too aware of how desolate was my condition. There was no one in this dark forbidding house, who really knew me. They were strangers to my life as I was to theirs, and I now regretted my decision to come. Would it not have been wiser, I reasoned to myself, to have attempted to move to a dwelling in Stamford? Or even to have written a letter of confession to William? At the thought of William, my mind turned to Molly and the body on the gibbet. Immediately I gasped with shock, and then pressing my face into the sheet tried to stifle the violence of my sobs.

"Dear cousin Pleasance, do not weep." At the sound of a young voice calling softly from the other bed, I scrambled to a sitting position. Preoccupied with my woes, I had forgotten my young companions, and I stared into the dark as the same voice whispered, "'tis but Katherine, cousin Pleasance. We did retire afore you. Mother did say you would weep, and it is so. Frances sleeps, but I will join you, and stay until you are better."

There was a rustling sound, followed by a patter of feet upon the bare boards, then my bed curtain parted and two short arms entwined themselves about my neck, as Katherine's warm, soft body snuggled against mine. My tears did not cease immediately, for her action reminded me too much of Molly, but now my sobs seemed to bring relief instead of sorrow and at last, soothed by the feel of life against my heart, I sank into unconsciousness.

CHAPTER 25

"I fear your garments, my dear, though most charming for the country will uffice for the life you will now be living. I will instruct Maria my maid, to summon Master Morton. He is our draper, and you will also require the cobbler, for your boots although stout and well made, are a little heavy for town wear. And we wear slippers within the house and for gatherings which we attend, and to which you will accompany us."

Cousin Edith smiled gently, as if to reassure me I was not at fault, merely innocent in the ways of town life. We had retired to her parlour after she had carried out an examination of my clothes, and I now listened disconcertedly as the gown, cloak and hat, which I had considered so elegant, were summarily dismissed. Guiltily dispelling thoughts of the coins, now safely concealed beneath my father's books, I murmured, "I fear cousin, I have not the means wherewith to purchase garments such as you describe."

She smiled her calm, placatory smile. "Such is of no consequence, my dear. We will care for you, as we would our own, and I have instructed Jane to be by when Master Morton attends. She does make it her business to know much of fashion. As to your own garments, when you are newly attired I would propose they are given to Harriet for despatch. She does know of folk who will, I do not doubt, put them to good use."

After my young cousins had made their noisy morning ablutions and departed, I had longed to remain hidden behind the bed curtains protected from my strange new world, but Harriet had arrived to announce that I was to commence the day with a bathe. At first I had demurred, considering such an luxury to be an indulgence of the nobility or the decadent, but her assertion that "'tis Mistress Frost's wish," left me with no alternative, but to comply.

There was then a considerable clatter, as a tin bath was dragged into the room and filled with water after which, with her eyes averted, Harriet requested that I remove my night chemise and step into the sweet smelling water. Having lowered myself, she drew a modesty sheet up to my chin beneath which she instructed me to wash. Somewhat hesitantly I began lathering myself, but the heat of the water compared with the cold atmosphere of the chamber was so soothing, I had to be reminded of the passing hour by Harriet's agitated cry that Mistress Frost awaited me below.

The remainder of my morning preparations continued with a rush, but another surprise awaited me because, having assisted me to don my now clean and mended travelling gown, Harriet announced that she was to dress my hair..

"But I have always worn a cap," I protested.

"Please ma'am," her eyes had widened appealingly as she lifted the lid of the dressing box to reveal a mirror, so I sat down and watched as she brushed my thick locks into a bevy of plump curls. Never before having witnessed myself in this way, I was engrossed, until I remembered the last time my hair had been tended by another's hand, and for a moment I closed my eyes at the memory.

My entrance into the dining hall where family and servants awaited me, had drawn forth a satisfied nod from cousin Edith and the compliment, "Your hair looks well child, Harriet is indeed nimble with her fingers."

Unused to such praise I had flushed, and then listened askance at the haste with which cousin Peter chanted a few perfunctory words of blessing prior to our meal. A meal as bewildering as that of the previous night, but this time cousin Edith guided me by murmuring kindly, "You are not, I see, accustomed to such choices, cousin. May I suggest perhaps some porridge, and a little buttered bread, and perhaps coffee to break your nightly fast. It is a warm and stimulating beverage, much drunk by city folk."(41)

All her recommendations tasted delicious, especially the coffee of which I drank three cups. Our meal having been completed, and Grace having once more been speedily recited, my cousins had all retired to their respective tasks, leaving me to follow cousin Edith to my chamber. Her verdict on my garments having been pronounced and no reference, as I had feared, having been made to the remaining contents of my box, we had returned to her parlour where she enquired whether I had passed a peaceful night.

Suspecting that she was already aware of my tears, I replied, "After a while yes, and I thank you cousin, for your kindness in taking me in."

"Such expressions are unmerited child, are you not kin? And I trust more restful nights will follow, for all sad memories do heal with time. Now child, why did you not give Harriet your key? She is to serve you, and as such must have access to your box."

The abruptness of her question startled me, and it was with difficulty that I managed to stammer, "My box contains small articles of my father's that he did leave me. And if I may have leave so to do, I would wish to handle them myself. There is but his bible, and two more of his books, nothing of consequence."

My hands were damp with sweat, and I could almost hear my heart throbbing as my cousin gently shook her head. "I suspected it was so, and I have no wish to delve amongst such memories, but Harriet did remark that you wear a locket. Is your dear mother's likeness concealed within?"

Relieved that she seemed satisfied, I quickly untied the ribbon from around my neck and held out the locket for her inspection. Very gently she snapped open the lid and sighed, "How sad that she should have been taken at so young an age, for she had such a sweet temperament, and was indeed a beauty with so elegant a stature. You resemble her closely, cousin, both in deportment and appearance and with two such fine parents, your character cannot but be assured."

I smiled, uncomfortably. I did not deserve her praise, but I had little time to dwell on my iniquities for she continued, "You did leave your village so precipitously, I did suspect a broken heart might be the cause."

Hoping she would attribute my flushed face to the heat from the fire, I replied as light-heartedly as possible, "Indeed no, cousin, I did but leave because the new Verger was to take up residence, and the cottage was no longer mine and," I added unsteadily, "because my father was no more."

"Of course child," she nodded, adding gently. "You did nurse him?"

"Yes, with Mistress Burrows, a woman of the village who had the tending of me as a child. She knew a little of physic..." I broke off as, to my consternation tears seemed to spout from my eyes. Cousin Edith leaned forward with a concerned expression.

"My child, I grieve for you. May your new home and new cousins assist you to live with this great sorrow. And you are now, six and ten years, if my memory does serve me correctly."

"No cousin, I am now seventeen."

"Seventeen, then we must think of a suitable match for you. I must consult Master Frost on the matter. He knows many gentlemen with eligible sons, one of whom would no doubt be suitable. However, eager though we are to provide for all your daily needs, I fear we cannot provide as great a dowry for your marriage, as we would for our own daughters. It is not within our means, though we will ensure that you do not go penniless into your future life."

I acknowledged my cousin's kind words with lowered eyes. Was there no way of avoiding the determination of my elders to embroil me in matrimony? But whatever interest cousin Edith had in my marriageable welfare was quickly dismissed as she continued, "So tumultuous is this house until mid-day, I remain here always alone, but now I have your company and do anticipate some pleasant hours of conversation, but first to matters of family. Jane, as I did afore mention, is betrothed to wed. Her husband will be Sir Simon Perkin's son, Philip, and Frances and Katherine are two months off ten years, while James is but eight years old." She frowned suddenly, and dropped her eyes. "He does not, I fear, enjoy the robust constitution of his sisters, and although not a sickly child cannot, as yet, be exposed to the education Master Frost would have preferred. So he is being tutored within the house, and you will no doubt meet these gentlemen as they traverse the corridors. I know from the few letters we did exchange, that your father believed much in education, and this does give me the opportunity to enquire, not at the moment but when you are rested, whether you would care to guide dear Katherine and Frances in their letters. Nothing so strenuous as languages would be required, only a good hand and reading, and perhaps a knowledge of the past and foreign lands would suffice." Delighted by her suggestion, since it gave me the opportunity to repay her, albeit in a small way, for her kindness, I tried to acquiesce, but the flow continued, "Master Hastings does instruct James in English, Latin and Greek, Master Moore the history of life and the world, and Master Santagel is responsible for James's Hebrew, French and Spanish. I do believe you may have already encountered this "handsome son of Spain" as Master Frost does call him, in the corridor last night?"

"I did indeed encounter a gentleman traversing the corridor, cousin, but it was too dark to see him clearly."

She nodded understandingly. "You no doubt find the lack of candles strange, but I fear in such a house as this it cannot be otherwise. So much oak so many dark corners, I live in fear of flames igniting. It needs but a drop of hot wax, and all would be lost. So it is the rule no candles to be carried lit from room to room, nor on the stairway nor in corridors. And for the same reason I permit no fires in sleeping chambers, but as many warming pans to heat the bed as you desire. Now, I must acquaint you with those members of the house who do serve us. Harold you have already met. A goodly soul who has been steward here since James's birth, he is assisted by David, who also serves at table and has care of all our silver ware. Then there are Charity and Hettie, our house servants, who do daily wash stone flags and polish floors and furniture, Nell our scullion, Alice our cook and Bella our laundress. Mistress Anne Carter is Jane's maid, and Mistress Maria Carlyle does serve for me, and lastly old Matthew, who is now of a great age and almost deaf but who served my husband since his birth, and so lives with us. All these souls do abide within this house, and eat three good meals a day, and at the first sign of illness the physician is summoned. Outside, within a dwelling near the horses, resides Andrew our groom. He has two stalwart sons who tend our beasts, and their mother oft does sew for us. All are cared for with as much diligence as those within the house. Cleanliness too, I insist upon. Regular washing and changing of linen for all within this dwelling is a most important rule. Disease cannot thrive without dirt, and dirt I will not have. There has been no illness in this house for many months. No rats dwell below, and my servants sleep in beds free of lice. And for this care I ask but one thing, obedience to the rules of this house, is that not fair cousin? The slightest spot of grime on hand or cheek or the barest mark on gown or apron, I cannot, and will not allow. And did you not note cousin the cleanliness of the dishes from which we ate? Alice, who does have also the duties of purchasing our food, does preside over a kitchen of which Mistress Cromwell, with her many retainers, would be proud. Now I must to an important matter. David did return last night after the hour that was prescribed, and must be disciplined. I do not use the birch. In this house cousin we do not chastise, we use a greater weapon we use the power of speech, as you will see."

And see, or rather hear, I most certainly did, for David's chastisement last near a full hour, during which cousin Edith in gentle, but strong tones, admonished the hapless recipient for his faults and described the dire consequences that resulted from tardiness. He was then assured of the great advantages that were to be gained in heaven if he would only acknowledge the error of his ways. Finally, as the apparent ultimate punishment he was told, that should be re-offend Master Frost would be acquainted with his misdemeanour. This threat, I discovered, ended all cousin Edith's homilies, for cousin Peter's bland exterior concealed a public image more in keeping with his tone of voice. In addition to being a member of one of the twelve Inquests of Cordwainer Ward,(42) he was also a magistrate who presided regularly at Court Assizes, where he dispensed such punishments as whippings, hangings and confinement in the stocks.

As her voice continued to stream relentlessly around the room, I felt my eyelids begin to quiver as another wave of weariness overtook me. Ever vigilant, my cousin suddenly dismissed the luckless David and murmured, "I think perhaps a rest, child? You are still weary from your journey. Come settle down in this larger chair, and I will tell all to leave you to sleep." I tried to protest, but cousin Edith was already guiding me to her more commodious chair, and before I was aware of what was happening, I fell asleep.

I awoke on this occasion feeling much refreshed, to find James seated opposite. On seeing that I was awake, he declared, "You have slept these past two hours, cousin Pleasance. I did assure mother that I would not wake you, and did creep in most carefully. Mother did say I was not to tax you, but the journey cousin I would know all. I will travel, do you know I have within my…" his flow of words, so reminiscent of his mother, were interrupted by a sharp tapping on the door. "Ah me," my young cousin gave a great sigh, "that will be Harold, he does always call me where ere I be, because it is my habit to forget the hour and my tutors are then kept waiting, and Master Santagel does not care to be kept waiting."

"Master Santagel?" I queried. "The tutor who does teach you Hebrew?"

"The same, but there be so many tutors a man does become bewildered by their number. But today Master Santagel must wait, for first I am to conduct you through this dark but happy house to sister Jane's chamber. I do wager cousin, when we do reach our goal that the lights therein will blind you, for my sister does favour a room full lit, and eschews my mother's preference for gloom."

Jane's small but commodious room had a pleasant atmosphere and was already occupied by Mistresses Maria and Anne, and Master Morton, who immediately rolled out lengths of silks, woollens and broadcloths for my inspection. I had never seen such opulence, but in accordance with the practice of the house I was not required to contribute anything but my person. At first Jane, and then Anne and finally Maria, a thin sallow looking woman with kind dark eyes, held pieces of cloth against my cheeks and hair as I stood, silently turning first this way and that, as instructed.

The materials having been chosen, Master Morton, his short rotund figure bobbing enthusiastically, exclaimed, "And the ruche lace, ma'am, may I suggest the lace. It is the very latest fashion, and worn by Mistress Claypole, no less."

"My Lord Cromwell's daughter does wear such gowns?" I declared, in surprise.

Jane smiled. "It is now the custom in town, cousin Pleasance, for ladies' gowns to be so embellished. Now Master Morton we must to the cloaks, two hooded ones in black for the present, and for next year's warmer weather I think two in light brown, for the colour compliments my cousin's hair."

"And such brightness, ma'am, 'tis rare to see so fine a head," Master Morton gave an expansive bow.

"Indeed," Maria nodded approvingly, while Anne, as plump as her companion was thin, smiled encouragingly. Instead of my customary embarrassment I smiled politely, for I was beginning to learn in this strange new world, that compliments were easy to accept.

My outfits having been decided, I accompanied Jane to her mother's parlour where cousin Edith expression her satisfaction.

"Most excellent my dear Jane, and the first two gowns will be ready for Sir Edward's gathering at the great house? Most gratifying, now I must to Master Santagel, for I would hear James. Jane, do you stay with your cousin. There is heated wine and comfits for you both."

Refreshments having been served, we sat quietly eating and drinking until Jane appeared suddenly to lose her languid air and said, "I would live in the country, were it so possible. To breath the sweet fresh air and walk the fields would indeed be most pleasant."

The vehemence with which she spoke surprised me, and I asked, "Have you never been from London town."

"Yes, but only when we visit Master Perkin's country house. As my mother has no doubt told you, we are to wed next spring. He does study for the law at Oxford, but Master Perkins's town dwelling where we will reside, is but a mile distant from this place."

"And you would prefer to reside in his country dwelling?"

"It would be more to my liking, but the house will remain the property of his father, until his demise." She sighed. "I care not for the town. Did you walk in fields and meadows? Such freedom, to walk as you will." She leaned back in her chair. A pale, slender girl with a heart-shaped face, and thick chestnut hair, her features bore no resemblance to her mother's plump cheeks and determined expression. Her movements also were slow and graceful, not at all like cousin Edith's robust gait, although she shared her mother's lack of inches, the top of her head barely reaching to my shoulder.

"And were there not streams, and trees and birds aplenty?" She asked suddenly.

"Yes, but our cottage had little to recommend it," I explained quickly, not wishing her to think my home was anything other than it had been. "It was but a stone dwelling, with two chambers above and two below, one of which was very small."

But Jane did not seem to hear, because she continued, "It was the freedom that I envy. To walk as you wished whenever it so pleased you."

Unable to explain the source of my 'freedom,' I said nothing, and the silence continued until Jane said, "You did receive much instruction from your father?"

"Yes, he did teach me many things, for he did believe women should be as academic as men, so did give me books to read of our past, and helped me with my languages, Greek and Hebrew."

"Hebrew, you do speak Hebrew?" I flushed. Jane's enthusiasm was embarrassing. "And the Hebrew books," she continued. "With their strange letters, you do read such books?"

"Yes, but you too have seen such books?" I asked, interpreting her interest as knowledge. Immediately, her animation evaporated as swiftly as it had appeared. "No I have but heard of them, that is all. My interest is in chess. Are you acquainted with the game? Mayhap you would care to learn."

Delighted by this offer of friendship, and quelling the feeling that I knew my father would probably not have approved of such frivolity, I nodded and was rewarded with a warm smile.

"'tis little I can do for you cousin, for I have no knowledge such as yours. I fear I can boast but an ill-formed script, and a paltry knowledge of household accounts, but my tapestry would pass muster, or so my dear mother tells me."

"Have you no wish to learn?"

"Once it was so, but now 'tis too late. I see I shock you with my flippancy cousin. Fear not, for my destiny is mayhap along another path, who knows?" She smiled again, but this time in a strange way as if she had a secret she did not wish to divulge.

Within twenty-four hours of Master Morton's visit, two of my new gowns were lying on my bed, and I marvelled that they should have been completed so swiftly, when it had taken me three weeks to sew one travelling dress.

At Harriet's suggestion I donned the russet broadcloth, and then gasped as she laced the stiffly boned bodice. She shook her head. "'tis necessary, ma'am, 'tis the fashion, all ladies do lace, and do you look in yonder mirror, is it not becoming?"

I stared with mixed feelings at the gown which left my neck and shoulders almost bare, and despite an abundance of lace and the addition of a silk shawl, gave a tantalising glimpse of the cleft between my breasts. I blushed, and was shocked to see the flush travel rapidly downwards. I knew my father would not have approved but I knew Molly would have been delighted, and probably have chided me for being too modest.

But the true critic of my appearance had yet to examine me, and it was with some trepidation that I descended to cousin Edith's parlour. But she greeted me with a nod of delighted approval. "My dear, the gown does suit admirably, Harriet has placed the other gown within the cupboard chest? Good, she will take care of your garments, both under and outer wear. And the lotion she gave you for your hands, I see it has improved their looks. Now do you give your nails freedom to grow, and Harriet will cultivate their length. I am to Lady Marchant, and will be from the house till near the evening hour. I did wish that you should accompany me, but Jane does have the headache and I do believe would benefit from your company. I fear she does take the headache often in these times."

Before I could reply she had whirled off into the darkness, a darkness which I had quickly learned not to fear, for despite the lack of candles, the continuous noise obliterated any thoughts of menace. From earliest dawn I awoke to constant sound. Servants trailing up and down, knocks upon the great front door and children's voices echoing down passages, filled the void caused by the lack of light. Not until the latest hour did silence creep like an encroaching flood along the corridors, and tranquillity reign.

I now glanced down at my hands. They certainly no longer bore the scars of domestic chores, but I found so much emphasis placed on the physical well-being of the household puzzling, when so little attention was paid to their spiritual welfare. So lax did seem the Puritan values within the dwelling, that I began to wonder if such behaviour were typical of all London gentry, especially when Jane told me that Mistress Elizabeth Claypole, in addition to favouring gowns of brocaded satin, wore earrings and necklaces made of pearls.

"Surely this cannot be," I protested.

"Indeed it is so," Jane replied confidently. "For it is the custom for ladies of rank to be so clad. I have myself such trinkets which my father did give me upon my betrothal. But they cannot be compared with those of Mistress Claypole, for hers are stones of the highest quality. Mayhap you will soon meet her, 'though I have not seen her overmuch of late. She has been indisposed with a complaint that does leave her much wearied, and the Lord Protector himself has not enjoyed good health for some time past. His is an arduous life, and all such men require the broadest of shoulders on which to bear their burdens."

On my arrival in her chamber she had greeted me with a smile, and for someone suffering from an aching head she was a most animated companion.

She was repeating her preference for a country life when there was a sharp knock on the door, followed by the abrupt entrance of James, who immediately cried, "Cousin Pleasance, I did tell Master Santagel that you knew of the Hebrew and he is most intrigued and would speak with you. So do you come to my school chamber where you may——"

Before he could finish, Jane jumped to her feet and cried, "Silence sir, you intrude. Cousin Pleasance and I were privately engaged."

Immediately, the corners of James's mouth drooped and his eyes filled with sudden tears.

"I beg pardon, sister," he stuttered with a gulp. "And I did mean no harm, but Master Santagel did wish to speak with one who can converse in his tongue."

Obviously struggling to regain her self-control, Jane pursed her lips, "So be it, do not distress yourself. Cousin Pleasance will follow, should she so desire. Now do you return you to your lessons, sir, and do not invade our presence yet awhile."

"No ma'am, I beg pardon," James backed towards the door, his bowed head hiding his still damp eyes, and as the door closed Jane sighed heavily.

"It is wearisome, cousin, to be the eldest of such a family with my years so far from that of my sisters and brother, and it is now a joy to have someone with whom to speak, who is of an age."

I smiled, but said nothing. To be roused to such violence by so trivial an incident was extraordinary, and wishing to leave the fractious girl I murmured, "I think perhaps, cousin, it would be wise for me to withdraw, rest and quiet will ease your head."

"If such is your wish," Jane's voice was barely audible, and I moved quickly to the door and out into the dark corridor. Moving slowly along in the blackness I hesitated, trying to remember where the stairs were, when something touched my hand and I gave a shriek.

"Wisht coz, 'tis only me, James. I did know you would come so I did wait. My sister did use me ill as she is wont to do, though it is not often. Do you now come and I will lead the way, and do you hold tight for there are stairs to climb both up and down."

With James tugging at my hand I groped my way along, until we reached a large airy room with light oak panelled walls, and four candelabra all fully lit. There was also a thick, intricately woven cloth covering on the floor, and a blazing fire before which stood a thin young man of my height, dressed in black outdoor garments.

Somewhat at a loss, I stood inside the door as James rushed up to the stranger. "Do you not see Master Santagel, I did steal cousin Pleasance from my sister. It was a great battle, sir, but I did win."

The young man smiled. "Master James, be calm sir, I beg. Such exuberance is unwise, as well as un-comely, and will you not invite your cousin to enter? It is unmannerly, sir, to leave a lady so."

"Cousin, I do beg your pardon." James ushered me enthusiastically towards a chair, as the stranger made a deep bow. "Is Master Santagel not gallant, cousin," James nodded approvingly. "Such are the ways of Spain."

His tutor laughed. "Not so the ways of England, sir, now present me, please."

James flushed. "Forgive me cousin, I do beg your pardon. May I present Master Isaac Santagel of Spain, as I did afore say. My cousin, Mistress Pleasance Fry, of Fretson, in the county of Rutland."

Isaac bowed again, and I felt myself grow hot as I made a brief curtsey. James nodded approvingly. "Now do you converse in Master Santagel's tongue."

"No sir," I murmured hurriedly. "I speak no Spanish."

"Young sir, you tease too much," Isaac admonished, before explaining. "Master James refers ma'am to my other tongue, that of Hebrew. But I must hasten to enlighten you, that though I was Spanish born I am English bred, and speak daily in the tongue of this country. It is this young jackanapes who does demand that we speak other than the English." He smiled again, this time with his eyes as well as his mouth and, feeling evermore ill at ease, I avoided the proffered chair and moved nearer to the fire. But Isaac Santagel's dark eyes seemed everywhere, and I hoped my companions would attribute my warm face to the heat from the flames. When I could look up again his eyes appeared gentle as he enquired, "And do you like this great city, ma'am?"

"I have thus far seen little," I replied.

He had perched himself on the edge of the table, enabling me to note that his light olive skin, high cheekbones and almond shaped brown eyes resembled some of the faces illustrated in my father's travel book.

"Cousin Pleasance, you do dream, ma'am, I vow you do. Will you not now speak?" James having adopted what I soon learned was his favourite position, legs wide and hands on hips, now stared accusingly at me and I flushed. Lost in my thoughts, I had not realised I was being addressed.

Isaac laughed. "Concern yourself not ma'am, yonder lad does compare well with your tyrant king, both in stance and manner."

"The tyrant king," James nodded eagerly. "Aye our bad monarch Henry, and his daughter Bess, I do declare coz, your height and hair would qualify you for such a role."

"Indeed yes," Isaac replied. "But I cannot believe your late monarch's hair, noble though it may be, can compare to the glory of Mistress Fry's own."

In the brief silence that followed, I sat with fingers tightly enlaced until, directing as steady a gaze as I was able at Isaac, I murmured, "I fear you place me in a higher status than is my right, sir, hair colour and stature do not a monarch make."

"Well said, coz, well said," James nodded approvingly. "But you have yet to accomplish the mission for which you have been invited, some Hebrew, cousin please, some Hebrew."

I hesitated, but Isaac filled the silence quickly, by reciting in that language, "In the beginning God created the heaven and the earth."

"Now the earth was unformed and void, and darkness was upon the face of the deep," I replied, very aware that my accent in no way resembled the accuracy of his tones. But I need not have chided myself for, with eyes full of surprise, he nodded his head while James danced excitedly from one foot to the other.

"Did I not say, Master Santagel, my cousin is indeed a scholar."

Overwhelmed by the obvious admiration in Isaac's eyes, I glanced downwards in confusion, but rescue arrived almost immediately in the personage of Harold, who entered with the news that Master Hastings had arrived. Taking advantage of the interruption, I moved slowly towards the open doorway, but before I could reach it, Isaac turned to me saying, "Mistress Fry, I do trust that we shall again meet, perhaps to consult next time in Greek?"

"Indeed you shall," James exclaimed, and I followed Harold from the room to the sound of my young cousin loudly praising my abilities, but Isaac's reply was lost in the sound of footsteps approaching along another corridor.

CHAPTER 26

December 1657 – March 1658

I was to hear Isaac's voice many times in the intervening weeks. The walls of the tall dark house were thick, but during the day his voice seemed to be everywhere; above me on the staircase, penetrating the wooden door of the schoolroom whenever I passed, and most unsettling of all, echoing persistently inside my mind. On one occasion I even thought I overheard his voice in Jane's chamber, but then rebuked myself for being so foolish.

Despite these obsessive distractions my days were fully occupied, in part listening to Katherine and Frances struggling with their lessons, or accompanying cousin Edith on her many social visits to large, opulently decorated houses. Visits which, my cousin assured me, were an essential part of my introduction into London society. Sometimes, we were accompanied by Jane, but these occasions were rare, as she frequently excused herself, pleading either one of her interminable headaches, or protesting that she was too preoccupied preparing for her wedding.

Although all the people I met appeared to be educated and cultured, I could not comprehend how they could profess to belong to the strict doctrine of Puritanism, especially when they all wore such embellished garments and we women were permitted to expose so much flesh. I was also astonished to discover that at the larger more elaborate dinner gatherings music was played, usually by musicians hired for the occasion, but sometimes by the daughter of the house.

On my first such evening I had sat terrified, convinced that soldiers would at any moment burst into the room to challenge such decadence. But time soon convinced me that my fears were groundless, and that the exquisite sounds emanating from the viol, clavier and lute were for my enjoyment and not censure.

Another revelation had been to learn that a poet called Sir William Davenant had composed a 'singing play,' "The Siege of Rhodes," and that permission had been given for its presentation at both private and public showings.(43)

"And folk are permitted, to attend?" I had asked Jane, incredulously.

"Yes cousin, I remember not a time when music and song have not been permitted. Why it is said that even Master Milton does have an organ within his house upon which he plays, when so inclined."

I listened in subdued amazement, and then marvelled at the rapid changes to which my mind was becoming accustomed. The only part of my new life which bore any resemblance to my past was the Frosts' outward display of Sunday observance, when the sanctity of the Lord's Day in Bow Lane was conformed to with meticulous care. The entire household attended Church for both morning and evening prayers, and after supper everyone gathered in the large parlour where Master Frost would read extensive passages from the Scriptures in an unemotional, toneless voice.

As was my custom, I had at first listened attentively, but as cousin Peter's voice droned relentlessly on and I witnessed the bored reactions of my companions, I realised that outward conformity meant nothing, if it did not include inward conviction.

Another aspect of my London days at which I marvelled, was the remarkable frankness of conversation. No restraint was displayed in discussing the Lord Protector or his politics. His Dutch war of the previous year was argued over heatedly, as was his abandonment of the Major-Generals and his continued interference in Henry Cromwell's governor-ship of Ireland.

At one evening meal, where the subject was being discussed enthusiastically, a large robust looking man sitting opposite me retorted suddenly, "Advice is of no use in such a place. Henry Cromwell has the better brain of the sons, and should be left to shift as he thinks fit."

"I did hear, sir," remarked a lady sitting beside him, "that the Lord Lieutenant did refuse to accept such income as may be had from that land."

"Aye ma'am, so he did," the robust man replied. "A fine, if foolhardy thought, that one should not profit personally from a country poor in resource. But he is a man of much sense, it is a misfortune is it not, that he is the younger and not the elder son."

"Mayhap the father does express concern for reasons not of State." This remark, from my left-hand neighbour, was accompanied by a sarcastic laugh, A thin, weary looking man, he had been presented to me as Lord Clement, and was the only guest present dressed in garments which in any way resembled those that my father had worn. With a dismissive glance at his companions, he continued, "Mayhap his eyes do still raise themselves above such paltry matters, and a calm Ireland would much enhance him should he give thought to the past, and rue his thinking of that time."

The conversation faltered, and everyone seemed to glance uneasily at the speaker. Master Frost was the first to respond, as he said in a mild voice, "It is now near a full twelve month gone since the crown was offered, my Lord. Our good Protector is not a man of procrastination. If he had been so inclined, we would not now so be speaking. No, Cromwell is a man for his people, not for himself."

"As you will," Clement nodded in obvious reluctance. "But think you he would have made such despatch, had his Generals thought otherwise?"

There was another uncomfortable pause, then a lady guest recommenced the conversation by mentioning Henry Vaughan's marriage (44) to his dead wife's sister. Immediately, everyone was involved in criticising the poet's impropriety, but their preoccupation with idle gossip did not last long, and the conversation soon returned to politics. With my eyes on my plate, I pretended to be absorbed in my meal as remarks were made about "the uneasy peace", and significant glances exchanged when someone mentioned "the man in France".

Their allusion to Prince Charles reminded me immediately of Molly's indiscretion, and I thought how unfair it was that people with money and position could express themselves with ease, confident in their security, while less privileged folk on whose labour England depended were punished for the slightest misdemeanour.

Although these meetings with so many sophisticated strangers were at first unsettling, my continued exposure to their manners and self-confidence began to affect my own personality. Consequently, by the time I had my second encounter with Isaac Santagel, I had acquired the ability to converse at ease, and learned to exhibit an outward demeanour of calm, similar to that of my cousins. Inwardly too, I had begun to regard myself as part of the sophisticated life I now led. My memories of my father and Molly had seemed to dim into insubstantial mental shadows which belonged in a world that existed only in my imagination.

It was during the early days of March, while groping my way in the dark from my chamber to cousin Edith's parlour, that I heard footsteps mounting the staircase below. Presuming the stranger to be one of the servants, I called out to warn of my approach.

"Indeed I did hear your footfall, Mistress Fry, light though it be. And if my memory does serve me correctly, is this not how we first did meet?" Isaac's voice seemed to flow into my veins.

"I believe so, sir," I replied in a voice I was gratified to hear bore no resemblance to the turmoil of my mind.

"And are we to have the pleasure of your company in the schoolroom today? Though I do fear your knowledge, which I hear you do impart to your young kin, is far superior to my own poor efforts."

Despite the dark, I realised that Isaac had now reached within a few inches of where I stood, and I pressed myself hard against the wall.

"Come Mistress Fry, do not tease. Will you not enlighten a dreary day with both your presence, and your wit?"

Before I could reply the door beside me opened suddenly, and James's voice seemed to echo through the house, as my effusive young cousin whirled into the corridor. "Master Santagel I did hear you sir, and you are near five minutes off the hour."

"I crave forgiveness young sir," Isaac gave an exaggerated bow. "I was but inviting Mistress Fry to join us, after our studies."

"Indeed yes cousin Pleasance, you MUST come. My sisters do demand too much, I insist you give me some of your time."

With my hand firmly grasped in his, James began to pull me vigorously towards the open door, while Isaac protested sharply, "Nay sir, a lady must be pleaded with, not dragged to one's person like a bale of hay."

Immediately James released my hand, mumbling contritely, "Beg pardon coz, I did mean no harm." He looked so crestfallen I put my arms about him protectively as I turned on Isaac declaring, "Your reprimand sir, was unprovoked."

Isaac bowed, but when he raised his head I was disconcerted to see that his eyes were alight with laughter, although both his expression and voice were solemn. "I do beg my lady's pardon, but I was brought to manhood on the manners of Spain, and my father does assure me it is not the custom to treat a lady so. But to return to my plea, ma'am, are we to anticipate the pleasure of a visit?"

I nodded, convincing myself that it was James's pleading expression that persuaded me, rather than the light in his teacher's dark eyes. Our tryst having been arranged, I continued to cousin Edith's parlour where that lady smiled understandingly, on being told of James's request.

"James is a scamp. I do hold him very dear, but he is a scamp. Any calming influence you can wield will be much to his advantage. His birth was one of great travail," she frowned suddenly. "We did fear at first, but no matter it is now of no consequence, but we do indulge him as you are no doubt aware. So do you influence him in quieter ways, cousin. But gently mind, he has a timid soul that can take little chiding."

With such encouragement, my morning visits to the schoolroom became routine, while my afternoons I devoted to Katherine and Frances.. I tried to persuade myself that it was for James's welfare that I behaved thus, but every morning I awoke with my senses throbbing with excitement, and on consulting my mirror I could see that even my features seemed to glow with anticipation. But I was confused that the sensations aroused by Issac in no way resembled those I had felt for William. Where he had resembled a safe harbour wherein I could have sought shelter, Isaac stimulated a sense of dangerous excitement, and inflamed my senses to such a degree I found difficulty in concentrating on anything that did not immediately relate to him.

Then I awoke one morning to learn that James had been taken unwell, and that the Apothecary had been sent for.

"Master Santagel is with the young master now," Harriet advised me. "Mistress is so distressed, Master James being so delicate."

"I knew not that Master Santagel was an Apothecary."

"No Mistress, not young Master Isaac, it is of his father Master Abraham of whom I speak. He who did nurse Master James through the closed throat." I nodded, while trying desperately to subdue the thought that if James were to die I would never see Isaac again.

For two days Master Santagel remained in James's room, attended by cousin Edith and Maria. On the third day the fever subsided, and the Apothecary pronounced him cured but advised at least a week's rest from endeavour. That same day, alone in my cousin's parlour, I heard the sound of heavy footsteps descending the stairs. Curiosity overcoming my natural caution, I opened the parlour door in time to see a tall back and long flowing cloak being absorbed by the gloom of the corridor.

Consequent on his father's advice, Isaac did not appear but James requested my presence and I attended, ostensibly to read from some edifying tome but in reality he sat engrossed, as I related tales of Fretson village life. Despite this diversion, the days without Isaac seemed endless, and on the morning appointed for his return, I was concerned to learn that Master Santagel had recommended a summer of country air, as being essential to improve James's health.

"To escape the fetid air he does say," cousin Edith exclaimed. "But husband how can that be achieved? We have no country estate, and you are so engaged at this time as to make such a venture."

Cousin Peter smiled mildly. "Mayhap, my dear, when our daughter is wed James may visit and enjoy the beneficial air of Kent?" He glanced enquiringly at Jane who smiled back, but said nothing.

I almost trembled with relief. Life in the tall dark house without Isaac's presence would have been unbearable. I tried to concentrate on being delighted that James had recovered. I had prayed for him assiduously during his sickness, but even then the face of his tutor had seemed to hover in my thoughts, which was probably why I did not hear cousin Peter's question, and with embarrassment had to ask him what he had said. He smiled, kindly. "I merely remarked, cousin Pleasance that we hope you will recommence your visits to the schoolroom, as they proved most beneficial."

Aware that everyone's eyes were on me, I flushed. "I do little, cousin Peter."

"Indeed she does, sir," piped James, only to be hushed by his mother as cousin Peter continued, "Nay Pleasance, be not so modest. Your conversation in the young Master's language does enhance James's studies."

"Master Isaac has affirmed it is so," cousin Edith agreed, enthusiastically. "James listens, and has repeated much to me when reading from his books. His way of speaking the Hebrew has much improved. You must continue your visits cousin Pleasance, but mayhap they are not entirely to your taste. You must speak out, for you help also with Frances and Katherine, and we would not use you to be used thus, if you have other desires."

Trying to control the tremor in my voice, I replied quickly, "I am most content to help James and his sisters, cousin. I care for them all greatly," I finished lamely very aware suddenly of Jane's eyes staring at me, as James gave me an ecstatic smile.

Later that morning, trying hard to appear confident and self-possessed, I entered the schoolroom. Both scholar and tutor rose immediately, and Isaac gave a deep bow. "We are indeed fortunate that you have arrived at such a time. Master James has this moment learned a new tract of the *Book of Isaiah*. Please to take this chair, it is more comfortable?"

I shook my head, choosing instead a seat some distance from the table, while James hurried excitedly up to me, and kissing my cheek declared, with the innocence of his years, "Is it not much pleasanter to be here, though I did enjoy your presence in my chamber?"

"So fortunate is a youth, who may venture where such as I dare not tread."

James having returned to his books, only my ears heard Isaac's softly spoken words and I sat stiff and straight, my eyes staring rigidly ahead. Then James broke the silence by waving a large volume above his head, as he announced importantly "Do you see cousin I am now to learn *Virgil*, is that not oh, who can that be?"

With a mixture of disappointment and relief, I watched the door swing open and David enter to announce that my presence was required in Jane's chamber to discuss wedding clothes. While James made a grimace of disappointment, Isaac murmured, "Tomorrow, Mistress Fry, you will honour us tomorrow?" He had moved to the door and now stood with his hand on the knob, as if barring my way.

"If such is your wish, sir," I had heard this expression used many times by my new female acquaintances, but Isaac's reaction was unlike that of any of the gentlemen I had met. Instead of bowing politely, his eyes gleamed more intrusively than usual. "Indeed it is, ma'am."

Outside the room I pressed my palms against burning cheeks. My words, spoken in innocence, must have some deeper meaning when addressed to a younger man. I wished desperately for someone of whom I could enquire. There were still so many things in my new life I found confusing. I moved slowly along the corridor with Isaac's eyes still filling my senses then stopped, as I heard a muffled sound coming from a room somewhere to my left.

I put out a hand, and opening a door discovered I was in a small chamber wherein sat Jane, sobbing quietly into a kerchief. Shocked, I stammered, "Forgive me cousin, I intrude."

"No matter," she dabbed at her face, "do you enter and bolt the door. Oh cousin, I know not what to do." The last words were spoken in tiny gasps, as the sobbing renewed.

"Dearest Jane," I knelt down and folded the shaking girl in my arms. "What ails you? Nothing can be so dire as to merit this."

"It is my nuptials."

"Your wedding, what of it?"

"It is not maidenly so to speak, but I fear I do not find my betrothed comely."

I had yet to meet Master Philip Perkins, who was not expected in Bow Lane until Holy Week, and knew of him only what cousin Edith had told me on my arrival. Wishing to calm my sobbing cousin and imagining how Molly would have soothed her, I murmured that all young girls had such feelings, and that provided a man was good and kind love would grow.

But my embrace and words seemed to disturb her more, for she eased herself from my arms, saying, "Forgive me cousin, and I thank you for your sympathy but I fear such words have little meaning to me. You see," she murmured hesitantly, "my affections are promised to another."

I stared in surprise. Jane never left the house, unless in the company of either her family, or a servant. Remembering how she had declared her destiny lay elsewhere, I began uncertainly, "Is it not possible, if you did explain."

"Nothing can be done," she looked suddenly determined and patted her curls back into place. "It is of no matter. I will be the mistress of two fine houses with many servants all to do my bidding, but I do fear him." Her voice sounded suddenly desperate as she wrapped her arms tightly about her body covering her breasts, as though to shield herself from an assailant and said, "I know it will be my duty to succumb to his will, but I know nothing of life and what it entails. I know it is indecorous to speak so, but you are of the country, and in the country much is seen." She stared beseechingly at me and I drew back slightly, as I remembered the sight of two bodies heaving in unison on Molly's bed.

"I fear I cannot help cousin, I know nothing," I replied quickly, wanting suddenly to get away from this frightened girl.

At my reaction, Jane's expression changed immediately from panic to cold reserve. "Forgive me cousin, it was wrong of me to encroach upon you so. I have been unwell and when indisposed I am idle, and idle minds are apt to dwell on matters that in full health one considers naught. Come, we will to my chamber where the dressmaker awaits, but I would ask of you one favour," she stared compellingly at me. "Can I trust you cousin, we have not spoken?"

I agreed hurriedly, finding Jane's sudden change of mood unsettling. Some time later, the dressmaker having departed and my presence no longer required, I returned to cousin Edith's parlour to find Isaac Santagel standing before her chair. Surprised and embarrassed to see him again so unexpectedly, I hesitated, but cousin Edith called quickly, "Enter cousin, Master Santagel was regaling me with James's progress, which it would seem is much advanced."

Very aware of the dark eyes following my movements, I seated myself on the other side of the fireplace as cousin Edith smiled benevolently.

"Master Isaac does propose that in clement weather James does make a journey to the Common of Bow where there is much good air to be had beneficial to all, and this would be as your father did instruct, did he not, sir?"

"So he did, ma'am," Isaac's voice replied from somewhere above my head. "Master James would benefit much and so would the ladies, if they can be persuaded to accompany us."

"I see no reason to deny you," cousin Edith nodded approvingly. "With Harold and David as escorts, the party would be complete. When is it your intention this journey should take place?"

"The first fine warm spring day," Isaac replied, in a firm clear voice.

"So be it," my cousin smiled. "Now do you take your leave, sir, for I do know your father will seek your services ere long, good day to you."

Without turning my head I responded softly to Isaac's farewell, and waited tensely for the door to close. As soon as I heard the click of the handle, I felt myself relax and looked up to see cousin Edith watching me. "You do not find Master Isaac's company to your liking?"

I returned my cousin's keen glance with as calm an expression as I could manage. "I know him little, cousin Edith. He does seem a good teacher and speaks well, but I would require greater knowledge of him to form an opinion as to his merits."

Cousin Edith laughed. "Bless you child, I needed but a yes or no." Then her expression sobered. "Yon boy is a goodly lad, and though he is barely nine and ten years, he is the product of more sorrow than we shall see in our entire lifetimes. His father did arrive in London within twelve month's of Master Isaac's birth." She sighed. "His wife, poor lady. met her death most cruelly, for she died of the plague upon the ship transporting them to these shores. The Santagels were of those people spoken of as Marranos, Hebrews who did profess the Papist faith while in secret praying in their own manner. Master Abraham, a physician of note in Spain, did flee with his family to these shores and was given shelter by his fellows until the Lord Protector did permit Hebrews to return. It was a great surprise to see how many folk did turn to Hebrew ways once they were given leave so to do. We did become acquainted with this good and clever man when James did contract closed throat. No doctors could cure him and he was near choked to death, when Master Frost did hear of Master Santagel, and the remedies he favoured. Within minutes of his treatment the child could breath, though I was greatly shocked for he did cut James's throat and insert a tube-like object, but he assured me James felt no pain, for he was first put into a deep sleep. We owe him much, and a kinder, finer gentleman, we have yet to meet."

I listened obediently, my thoughts full of Bow Common and the promised visit. But the weather proved unkind, and Jane's wedding was but a week away before the visit could take place. In the intervening days I met her betrothed, a plump young man of medium height, with a serious, but pleasant face, and receding blond hair. He appeared rather in awe of Jane, and spent a great deal of time standing stiffly beside her chair, despite the Frosts' frequent invitations to him to be seated. I found him polite, but distant.

For some reason he did not seem to approve of my presence, and on two occasions he had, to my embarrassment, remarked, "Country people do arrange these matters young, or so I did believe. Is it not strange Mistress Frost, that Mistress Fry is not wed, nor yet promised?"

Cousin Edith had smiled, as she murmured kindly, "Our dear cousin is not as yet promised, Master Perkins, but it is our sincere wish to see her well settled ere' long. Is that not so, Pleasance?" I nodded nervously, while experiencing intense anger towards this interfering stranger. The question of my betrothal had not been mentioned again since my arrival, and I had hoped Mistress Frost had decided against it.

Master Perkins also objected very strongly, to Jane accompanying us to Bow Common. "Such dalliance is not seemly for one such as Jane, affianced as she is," he stated pompously.

To my surprise cousin Edith glanced at him sharply, and then replied with a bemused expression, "If such be your wish, sir. But Jane has not been hearty of late, and it would indeed be beneficial to her health."

But Philip Perkins was not to be persuaded, so my cousin had no alternative but to comply, which she did with a frigid nod and compressed lips. Secretly delighted, I waited impatiently for the day to arrive when, at last, Master Frost's coach commenced its journey, with Isaac and David riding pillion while Harold sat on the box, and Harriet accompanied us within the coach.

Warmly wrapped in furs and with Katherine and Frances snuggled next to me, I listened to James's animated chatter until, bored by the inactivity inside the coach, he scrambled to the window and dragging the leather cover aside tried to push his head through the aperture.

Immediately, Harriet reached out to pull him back, but avoiding her grasp he exclaimed, "Cousin Pleasance do you look, a party of men so far from town carrying a burial casket. Where do they go pray, I see no church? And see, that is my physician Master Santagel leading the cortege."

I glanced out of the window in time to see a party of some dozen men, all dressed in long black garments, moving slowly along the highway. In their centre, carried on the shoulders of six of them and also covered in black was a large oblong box. Leading this procession was a tall man who, as I leaned forward, turned his head to speak to someone behind. As he did so he glanced up at the coach, and I found myself staring into a long thin bearded face and a pair of piercing dark eyes, which seemed to penetrate the very depths of my skull. Realising that James's strong young voice had been overheard, I pulled him gently back and after hushing him, dropped the window cover.

Still very curious, James asked me in a loud whisper to question Isaac, but I shook my head, murmuring that it was neither the time nor place. Thwarted, my cousin pulled a face, and then subsided into his seat with an audible sigh. As we remained listening to the sound of tramping footsteps, I queried to myself that it was strange Isaac had not accompanied his father on such a dour journey, rather than indulge himself with us.

But I had little time to reflect, for we had reached the Common. An area of open grazing land stretching for some miles to the east of the city, it was famous for the profusions of bluebells and other early spring flowers which grew on its perimeter. In less stringent times many of London's citizens had enjoyed fresh country air on Sundays and Holy Days, but now its only visitors were shepherds and goatherds who came to graze their animals.

After our meal, which was consumed in the carriage, and the ground having been declared too damp to sit on, Isaac insisted on escorting everyone to higher ground where there was a good view of the city and surrounding countryside. I walked slowly, very aware of him following behind with James. The higher ground having been reached and the view admired, Isaac then suggested we all examine some nearby trees and led the way to a small copse. The smell of the fresh grass and the strengthening sunlight reminded me abruptly of Fretson, and suddenly Molly's presence seemed so vivid I gripped James's hand tightly, without realising what I was doing, and he cried out, "Cousin Pleasance are you ill? You do look as if you are to swoon."

Trying hard to retain my balance, I suddenly found my waist held securely by Isaac, only to be released almost immediately as Harriet declared, "Mistress what ails you, you are so pale?"

"It is nothing," I explained hurriedly. "A mere dizziness that is all, and I fear I hurt you James," I added, looking down at my young cousin's anxious face.

"It was nothing coz," he cried. "But you are not ill, are you?"

I shook my head reassuringly, but Harriet looked doubtful and begged me to return to the coach. Very aware of Isaac's concerned stare I agreed, and with Harriet supporting me on one side and James clinging tightly to my other hand, we commenced walking back to the coach. As we progressed I could sense Isaac's eyes still staring at me, and in an effort to divert his attention, I asked quietly, "Master Santagel, your father Master Abraham and the men that we did see with the coffin, where were they going?"

He frowned, and with apparent reluctance explained that the men were carrying one of their number to the new Hebrew burial ground, outside Stepney village. (45) Obviously discomforted by my question, he turned away as if to close the matter, but remembering how I had always supported my father in all things, and deeming it strange that Isaac had not, I asked, "Is it not the custom amongst your people, as it is with us of the Christian faith, for all members of a family to follow a friend in death?"

To my surprise, he flushed before replying, "If mean you women folk, such is not our custom. The women do remain within the home to mourn. It is not the our custom to expose them to the rigours of the burial."

I frowned. He seemed to have deliberately misunderstood me, and I waited for a further explanation but he ignored my look, and appeared absorbed in flicking an imaginary leaf from off his sleeve. He was extremely handsome, and very elegant, but to have deserted his father at such a time, and instead have spent the same hours in frivolous pursuits was not to his credit. Disturbed, I motioned to Harriet that we should continue more swiftly to the coach, and we moved away leaving Isaac to call to the others to follow.

CHAPTER 27

March 1658 – August 1658

Jane's nuptials had been planned with much pomp, the only mundane feature being the civil registration before the magistrate and the swearing before two witnesses.

"So paltry a meeting in so shabby a manner," cousin Edith had exclaimed, in a moment of unexpected confidence. "I remember all too well my own nuptials. We danced and sang 'til dawn's light, and the ceremony was in a church sumptuous with flowers but I must not dwell so, it is the present in which we now live."

But despite being denied these embellishments, my cousin was determined Jane should enter married life with a flourish, and had arranged a meal to which all members of the Frosts' families and acquaintances were to be invited. My cousins own house being too small for such a function, a close acquaintance had lent them a large establishment in The Strand.

The bustle and excitement which increased as the wedding date drew nearer began to infect me, especially when cousin Peter presented me with a row of pearls with which to decorate my blue silk gown. Overwhelmed by such generosity, I acknowledged the gift in the manner I had learned was customary, by brushing my lips gently against his cheek.

I was not too modest to realise that I had become a favourite with him. My academic knowledge seemed to fascinate him, and whenever we were together he encouraged me to elaborate on my knowledge of history and religion, or converse with him in Greek or Hebrew. These instances had become more frequent as the wedding approached, and Jane became too preoccupied to be available for chess which, despite her promise, she had never attempted to teach me.

Perhaps it was for this reason, or so I did persuade myself at the time, that I thought to request Isaac to teach me the game. Having decided on such a course, I first sought cousin Edith's approval which was given with her customary complacency.

"Bless you child learn, if you so wish. Master Frost did at one time wish that I would play, but I fear I am not so inclined. I doubt not that Master Isaac is a fine teacher. Harriet may sit with you or mayhap Maria, if she be free."

Iasaac proved a better teacher than even cousin Edith had anticipated, and he seemed also to enjoy telling me stories of his travels, but despite his loquacity he never spoke of his father, his Hebraic origins or his home life.

After only four lessons, I had learned enough to accept a challenge from cousin Peter and to beat him. He laughed delightedly at my achievement.

"Well my dear, so it seems we do have another exponent of Master Chaucer's favourite pastime. That was a game well played was it not Jane?"

"Indeed, sir, Master Isaac did say cousin Pleasance was an apt pupil."

Mistress Frost looked puzzled. "Why child, I did think you were at Mistress Palmer's and did not return to the house till four of the clock. Master Isaac did leave the house an hour previous."

"Not today, ma'am," Jane's voice sounded strained. "It was yester noon that we spoke. He was traversing the corridor to speak with you, and we did meet."

Cousin Edith nodded. "Indeed yes, he did call upon me to speak of James's Greek."

"My Greek, what of my Greek?" James interrupted, demandingly.

In the conversational melee that followed, I placed the chess pieces back in their box, somewhat perplexed. For Isaac had not been walking the corridors during noon the previous day, neither had Jane. They had met in her chamber from where I had heard their voices speaking in urgent whispers. As previously, I had at first believed I was mistaken but when the door opened Isaac had been illuminated in sunlight. From where I had been standing protected by a buttress, I had watched him give a deep bow and close the door. I had then heard him progress down the corridor towards the area of the school-room.

Believing him to be on an errand for cousin Edith, but still considering it strange that he should be permitted to enter Jane's room unaccompanied, I had continued to the school-room and my chess lesson. To my surprise he had not mentioned Jane, and absorbed by the lesson and the joy of being with him, I had soon forgotten the incident.

But now I realised how foolish I had been to believe that Isaac's gallantry had been intended for me alone. His smiling face and pleasant words were probably the way any Spanish gentleman behaved towards a lady. The knowledge made my head spin, and I longed to be alone to weep out my sorrow, but although I would have to continue my life with his voice and figure within easy reach, I was not forced to endure his presence, and so did I plan.

By explaining that I wished to assist with the sewing of Jane's marriage clothes, I excused myself from further outings to Bow Common. Neither did I visit the school-room or seek further lessons in chess, and whenever I knew Isaac was somewhere in the house, I refrained from traversing the corridors. In this way, I tried to convince myself that the strange pain, which had no physical base, would abate and die.

My efforts at concealment did not meet with James's approval, and he was loud in his expressions of disappointment on being denied my company.

"It is MOST unfair so it is, that on such warm days you are confined, coz. And we do MISS you in the school-room, indeed we do. Master Isaac did but yesterday say that, why cousin what ails you," he frowned. "It is the lack of air, come sister permit me to open the casement."

"James, let be," Jane retorted sharply. "An open casement will permit foul air. We have rose petals, and you should to your studies, go now."

Somewhat mollified by the secret smile I gave him, James retreated leaving behind him an atmosphere of illusionary calm.

Despite endeavours to avoid Isaac, he remained a prominent presence. During the day I heard his voice echoing along the corridors, and he was a persistent intruder into my dreams, and my feelings towards Jane became a bewildering mixture of resentment and envy. I could not understand how she could consent to marry one man, whilst being enamoured of another.

But despite these distractions, I continued to find the excited atmosphere in Bow Lane infectious, as neat heaps of linen articles all considered indispensable to a bride's new home, were laid out on the great monk's chest in Jane's chamber. Cousin Edith's repeated confirmation that I was to inherit Jane's chamber also proved a distraction. I had forgotten how, on my arrival, she had made me this promise when Jane married, and I stared around the elegant room in a daze.

Cousin Edith laughed. "Child it is but your due and you must tell me if there is aught you would change. Are the hangings to your taste for should you so wish, they can be changed? Now I must to James for I fear he has been desultory of late, as to the fittings for his wedding suit."

As soon as she had gone I sat down heavily on the wide four-poster bed. For a few moments vivid memories of that other bedchamber, so tiny and austere, overwhelmed me and I gasped in a dry painful sob. Then I shivered as the faces of Old Mother Burrows, Bessie Workman and Thomas Whyte travelled through my mind. When they threatened to be replaced by those of my father and Molly, I dismissed them by rising and making my way swiftly to cousin Edith's parlour, where James was proudly displaying his wedding outfit.

Being too preoccupied in ensuring that all arrangements were to her satisfaction, cousin Edith had requested me to supervise the dressing of the bride, one of the most important tasks of the day. Flattered at being entrusted with such a duty I arose early, and hurried to Jane's chamber but was disconcerted to discover her still lying in her bed.

"Should you not have arisen, cousin," I smiled encouragingly. "It is near seven of the clock."

She turned her head wearily towards me, her eyes red and swollen. "This day is not of my making, Pleasance. I would fain fall from yonder window than attend my nuptials."

I felt very inadequate and stared at her, nervously. Then I thought of Molly, and how kindly but firmly she would have encouraged Jane to rise and dress. The memory gave me confidence, and I drew back the bedclothes and extended my hands. To my relief Jane responded, and as Anne Carter entered to assist, allowed herself to be led to where warm water awaited in a large iron bath.

As we prepared her, Jane obeyed our requests as though her body was acting independent of her mind, and when finally attired in her cream satin gown she stood motionless in the centre of the room, as though unaware of her surroundings. But I could not but stare at her in admiration and Anne nodded, obviously pleased with her endeavours, but Jane continued to stare blankly at the casement, and when I indicated she should follow me to cousin Edith's parlour, I discovered her hand to be as cold as snow.

The exchange of vows and the signing of a document having been completed, the newly wedded couple led the way to the celebration. Jane still looked pale and uncomprehending, but now she was married and what ever happened in the future would be her husband's responsibility. Besides, there were now many more interesting matters to distract me, such as the opulent surroundings in which I stood.

The marble hallway where the vows had taken place had been impressive, but the high audience chamber with its painted ceiling and wall frescos, was dazzling. Surrounded by guests in their elegant finery, I thought how like a ladder my life had become. Since leaving Freston, each new experience had been like another rung lifting me away from a life that I could almost believe had never existed. Then I thought of Molly, and how she would have revelled in the surroundings and company, and for a moment everything else faded away and I was once more sitting beside her on the river-bank.

The meal following the ceremony was sumptuous, but cousin Edith had one great disappointment. Despite an invitation having been sent with immense ceremony to the Palace at Whitehall, the Lord Protector could not attend, and his absence was almost as potent as his presence would have been.

The bridal pair having departed, life in Bow Lane returned to its customary routine with the exception of my own situation. For not only had I inherited my cousin's chamber but also her place at table, and all the other advantages she had enjoyed, including the carriage, which was placed at my disposal. I also established an even closer relationship with James, who made it quite clear that he was to be my "especial friend," assuring me that whatever I required I had only to ask him, for it to be accomplished.

Considering this event so many years past, I thank the good Lord that I did indeed sustain that friendship, so that it endured and enabled me to learn that my cousin fulfilled his life far beyond the tentative ambitions of his parents, and grew to a manhood blessed with health and strength. For in truth he has proved a valiant friend, and his affection for me has never wavered despite the difference in our stations. He cares not for superficial manners and the divisions of quality, in his enthusiasm for life, all the world is one to him. But again I digress, and must speedily return to the past.

Despite our friendship, I could not speak to my cousin of Molly or mention the coins which still lay buried deep within my box. Occasionally, my conscience tempted me to reveal their whereabouts to cousin Edith, but then thoughts of the consequences of such an action overwhelmed me, and my guilt retreated to remain once more hidden with my spoils. But I did learn more of cousin Peter during those pleasant tranquil days, for the chess board proved our access to communication. An intelligent man with a sharp, swift mind, he soon discovered that I knew nothing of his family's history, and was delighted to enlighten me that the Cordwainers were workers in Cordoba leather and had worked and lived in Bow Lane for centuries.

"Until the hosiers renamed it, when they took residence here," he explained ruefully. "But they too moved on and our neglected little street became Bow Lane, after the church in which we worship."

"But you remained here, sir?" I ventured, and he smiled.

"My great grand sire, and his son and grandson before him have all occupied this house. I fear its bricks would crumble were we to depart. So near is it to my daily work and the workshops wherein my craftsmen ply their skills, it would be a great inconvenience to dwell elsewhere."

He uttered the last sentence with unexpected emphasis, and remembering cousin Edith's words about her dwelling, I suspected he had uttered them many times.

So did my days pass, and so content was I that I had almost convinced myself I had forgotten Isaac and conquered my wayward heart until, one afternoon, there was a light tap on the door. "Enter," I responded, assuming the knock to be that of James or a servant.

"I do beg pardon, Mistress Fry. I did believe Mistress Frost to be within" Isaac gave a slight bow, and then stood waiting in the open doorway.

My heart gave a violent jump, as I tried to speak in my normal voice. "My cousins do attend a meeting in Guildhall, they return not before the evening meal."

The Frosts whereabouts were no business of Isaac's, but nervous surprise made me chatter. He bowed again. I knew it was not my place to dismiss him, but I wished desperately that he would go, or that one of the servants would intervene. Then he said, "Mistress Fry, may I speak with you?" I knew I should deny him, but instead I nodded, and he continued, "Forgive the liberty which I now take, but I fear there may be between us some misjudgement. I have reason to believe that you may think I was enamoured of Mistress Jane. It is not so, I respect her greatly but our friendship was naught else. She was promised to another and I would never have presumed such infamous conduct. I crave pardon for so addressing you, ma'am, but I respect you too highly to give you so wrong an impression. Now with your permission, I will take my leave."

Alone in the now empty room, I sat staring at the closed door for some minutes, before resuming my work. For Isaac to have spoken to me in so open a manner was a liberty which I should have condemned but, instead, I could feel only relief and delight. He had not admired Jane, she had been but a passing friend. My heart seemed to be thudding against my ribs. Was it possible that Isaac had sought me out to proclaim his affection? My mind raced on, prudence and decorum forgotten.

But if his declaration had surprised me, his further behaviour was even more unexpected when, the following evening, I discovered a note beneath my pillow. A verse from Psalm 45, it read:

Thou are fairer than the children of men:
grace is poured into thy lips;
therefore God hath blessed thee forever.

The realisation that he had entered my chamber shocked me deeply, but I was also exhilarated. Despite the fact that the words had been written in praise of a man, I was not so naive as not to understand their implication. But Isaac's behaviour had been exceedingly imprudent, and if either of my cousins were to hear of it he would undoubtedly be dismissed.

Concerned for his welfare, I decided to warn him against any of the same impetuous foolishness, and the following morning I waited in the gloom at the top of the narrow staircase for him to arrive. When at last I heard his knock on the door, I almost shook with nervous palpitations as his footsteps approached me up the stairs, and my voice quavered slightly, despite my efforts to keep it steady, as I uttered his name.

"Why Mistress Fry, what do you here ma'am, in the gloom?" He replied, obviously surprised.

"Please Master Santagel, I do beg of you a word," I interrupted, my voice barely audible.

"I am at your pleasure, ma'am, where shall we speak?" His voice sounded clear and confident, and I drew back as I felt his sleeve brush against me.

"The linen room," I gasped. "I do believe it is not occupied, please to follow me."

Almost unaware of what I was doing, I groped my way along the corridor until I reached the handle of the linen room door. Behind me I could feel Isaac's breath on my bare neck, and as we entered he closed the door gently behind us. In the light from the tiny dormer window his slender body looked unexpectedly large and overwhelming, and I stepped back against the wall.

"The note," I gabbled. "You must send no more, it is unwise."

"But surely you cannot mean this?" He leaned forward slightly, and his breath seemed to caress my cheek. "I do but express my deep admiration for you, ma'am."

"But if they were discovered, and you must not enter my chamber."

"But I do take great care, Mistress Pleasance, and the words are but the expressions of esteem in which I hold you. For paltry though they may seem, they come from a true and devoted heart." Before I could stop him, my two hands were clasped in his, as he continued. "Dearest Pleasance, I have admired you these many months, and yearned to speak out, but always there have been others near, and you have seemed distant. Now I have reason to believe, dearest of women, that you do love me."

While he pleaded I could feel him drawing me closer, and then his arms slid gently about my waist. I stiffened in resistance, but the feel of his hard chest against my breasts and the pressure of his right hand pushing gently on the base of my back overwhelmed me, and I leaned helplessly against him. Immediately he bent his head and lightly stroked his lips cross the side of my neck, making me quiver. Immediately, his lips moved swiftly upwards, pressing light kisses upon my cheeks, eyes and lips. Almost losing consciousness, I clung to him for support as he pressed my abdomen closer against his groin, and I felt a strong pressure against my thigh.

"Mistress Pleasance, are you there, Mistress Frost does request your presence?" Harriet's voice seemed to fill the tiny room, and I struggled to free myself as Isaac murmured, "Hush dearest, no one will find us, when can we again speak alone, as now."

"I know not I must go, please sir, let me pass." My entreaty must have sounded violent, for he immediately opened the door and drew back, allowing me to flee.

For the remainder of the day I was unaware of anything but the pressure of his body against mine own, and I responded to all overtures automatically, without being fully aware of the subject of the conversation. When at last the day was done, I fled to my chamber where I dismissed Harriet and flung myself onto the bed. That I had behaved disgracefully I was too well aware, but what confused me most was the realisation that I did not care. The sensations that I had experienced were all that I could remember. Visions of Molly and Daniel's naked bodies returned with a vividness that made me blush. Was all love violent and passionate? If I had married William, would he have held me as Isaac had done?

Longing to satisfy the urges with which I was now tormented, I drew up my gown and slid my left hand slowly down my belly. The sensitive skin quivered in response, and for a few moments I revelled in the sensations of lust which followed, but when my passion had been sated I was overwhelmed with remorse and distaste, at my own actions. Why had I abused myself when such behaviour was forbidden in the Holy Book, and why did I not feel ashamed at what had taken place with Isaac?

But confused though I was, there was no misunderstanding St. Paul's instruction. Behaviour and thoughts such as mine belonged only within marriage, and I must remove from my presence any temptation to succumb. Fortunately, an excuse presented itself that same day. Cousin Edith had decided that the wall hangings in her chamber should be renewed, and when she enquired of me whether I would care to embroider some panels, I was only too happy to agree.

"Then shall I obtain the materials and the work can commence," she smiled. "I did hesitate to ask, after so many hours spent on Jane's linen, but the work need not commence until the summer wanes. I would not deprive you of your Bow Common visits, for Master Santagel does tell me they are to recommence."

"I do not care to take more visits, cousin," I replied quickly, angry at his impudence in addressing her without first consulting me. "I find the journey disturbing to my stomach, and the pollen from the flowers does make my head ache." I tried to make my lies sound convincing, as cousin Edith stared in surprise.

"Why did you not say, child? I would not force upon you an outing that was not to your taste. You do as you wish in this house."

I flushed. "I did not wish to cause James disappointment, he so enjoys the outings."

"You are James's kinswoman cousin Pleasance, not his servant. If you do not wish to go my dear, then so be it, and selfish woman that I am I anticipate much pleasure from your company, which has been denied me of late through so many outings, and so much chess."

But she was still to be denied my company, for next day she entered the parlour looking harassed. "I fear I must withdraw to Kent. A messenger has arrived from Jane. The staircase having been newly polished, her foot did slip and now I fear there is a broken bone. I will take with me Katherine and Frances and Master Frost will remain. The carriage will I fear be denied both yourself and James, but no matter. He has his studies, and should you yourself require conveyance, then a chair can be called, and Harold can escort you where ere you wish to go."

A considerable bustle followed, until Mistress Frost and the twins were driven away, leaving me to inform cousin Peter, on his return, of the days events. He looked grave.

"A broken bone is a great misfortune, and so soon in her marriage to have such a calamity, but grave though this news is, I fear it is shadowed by an even greater sadness, Mistress Claypole died today. The news did come to us but two hours past. The good Lord Protector is so totally bereft that he knows not day from night. She was but nine and twenty and leaves four children, so very sad. But this happening does mean that I shall be from the house for more hours than is customary. Our good Lord Protector has been so distressed these past weeks, that duties appertaining to the law and civil matters have gone undone and now they must be righted so I shall, of necessity, be gone mayhap a day, or two."

With no pupils to occupy me, and in an attempt to quench the thoughts of Isaac which would occasionally invade my mind, I occupied my time sewing diligently at cousin Edith's panels, and establishing more firmly my friendship with James. At his impulsive request, cousin Peter had agreed that his young son should escort me to the more accessible parts of the city, in order that I might become fully acquainted with England's great capital.

"For cousin Pleasance has seen nothing but the inside of our coach and other peoples' houses which, though elegant, are not our noble city," James had exclaimed, and his father had smiled indulgently and agreed that a conveyance could be hired in order that we may be escorted to the interesting areas of town.

Thus commenced my acquaintance with the London I had known of only through books, as we traversed its many streets, stared in apprehension at the menacing Tower, and sailed the river in a daintily painted barge. But although I was impressed, I also witnessed poverty and squalor such as I had never seen in the country. Even within Westminster, with its magnificent Whitehall Palace, children in rags scurried along the streets and beggars knelt crying out for alms. However, despite these wretched sights, I admit I enjoyed my freedom, but on the ninth of August everything changed.

Preoccupied in my chamber examining my wools, I heard a knock upon the door and assuming the visitor to be James, bid him enter. When I looked up, it was to find Isaac standing before me. "I did but come to enquire as to Mistress Jane. Does she fare well?"

"Sir, please leave," my voice quavered angrily, as he drew back towards the door, his face very pale.

"I beg pardon, I should not have come but I was concerned. You spend much time with Master James, while excluding me. What have I done to displease you, I beg you to explain?"

"There is nothing to explain, please go," I replied, his agitation giving me confidence, but after the door closed behind him I sat down heavily on my bed, very shaken. Not so much by Isaac's sudden appearance, as by the tears that I had seen well up suddenly in his eyes. Was it possible that he really loved me?

But he must be aware that such a love had no future. We were from different worlds, there was no way we could unite as man and wife, and he was foolish to pursue me in such a way. I decided he must be told and, rising, opened the door. The sudden shaft of light encircled him sitting hunched beside the far wall, sobbing quietly. Aghast, I hurried across and, kneeling down, enveloped him in my arms.

Unexpectedly, he pushed me gently away and struggled to his feet. "Forgive me I beg, but I did anger you and I was overcome. I shall withdraw and not again intrude."

Distressed by his demeanour, I exclaimed, "You have not displeased me, I think only that it would be wiser for you to desist, and no longer seek me out?"

"I cannot," his voice was muffled as he added, "you have my heart."

Despite my attempts to subdue the excitement with which his words filled me, I felt exhilarated and replied impulsively, "If you so wish, after James's lesson, we may exchange a few words."

To my surprise, instead of the subdued gratitude I had expected, he looked up eagerly and declared, "When can I come?"

I hesitated, knowing full well that I should return to my chamber without replying and remain there until he quit the house but, instead, I heard my voice inviting him to join me, the following afternoon.

CHAPTER 28

For the following two afternoons, while James was occupied with his other tutors and Harriet plied her needle some distance from me, Isaac asked me questions about my life in Fretson. Despite my attempts to explain, he persisted in assuming that my father had been the Minister of the Parish and that our home had been considerably more substantial than a mere cottage.

"For he did have books so a room for books there must have been and you did have Mistress Burrows and the little maid Bessie. Did they not cook and clean?"

"They did perform such duties," I replied warily. "But they were villagers, such as myself."

"No matter," he stifled a yawn with the back of his hand. "For I fear I must now withdraw. My father does have guests this even and my presence is required, and I much regret to say this is to be my last visit. Master James is to travel to his sister. You are surprised, were you not acquainted with the news? My little charge did but tell me this morning."

As if in response, there was a distant sound of running footsteps and James bounded impetuously into the room announcing excitedly, "I am to Jane, my mother she has sent for me in this note, which did arrive with another for you dearest coz, and which, beg pardon, I did forget to give. On horseback I am to go and you are to follow coz, within a seven day, with David and Harriet in the carriage. And Jane does fare well, it is not a broken bone but a great bruise, am I not the bearer of good news?"

"You are indeed, sir," Isaac replied laughing, before turning to me with a bow. "And now Mistress, with your permission, I take my leave."

Before I could reply he had walked through the open doorway, closely followed by my young cousin exclaiming loudly that Isaac was deserting his post. Bereft, I stared at the closed door. How was I to bear his absence? I glanced down at cousin Edith's note which affirmed all that James had said excepting only that our sojourn in the country was to extend for the remainder of the summer. She ended with her fondest love and a brief note that cousin Peter was to follow if, and when, his duties permitted.

For the next two days I wandered listlessly from room to room, my only diversion the games of chess I could not deny James, but even his happiness was diminished by my anguish, and I was forced to plead a sick headache in order to contemplate my unhappy lot. Without the anticipation of Isaac's visits, and after the departure of James, the house seemed an empty shell and I sobbed myself to sleep. The following morning Harriet examined my heavy eyes in obvious concern.

"Mistress, you are unwell. Do you remain abed awhile and fret you not, with Master James gone there's naught to concern you."

I leaned back against my pillows only too relieved to be cosseted, and let myself drift gently into sleep. When I awoke, Harriet was sitting sewing beside the casement, while on my coverlet lay a folded note. I stared down at the piece of white paper as Harriet explained, "A messenger did bring it. It is no doubt from the Mistress."

I nodded in agreement, while my stomach seemed suddenly to have taken flight. With shaking fingers I split the seal and Isaac's words seemed to spring from the page, with the same energy with which my heart burst into renewed life. *'My father has, like your revered cousin, departed the town. So I too am bereft of company. Can we not meet mayhap for just a few words? I will call today and if permitted, stay for but one hour.'*

I flung back the bedclothes, exclaiming, "My green bodice and skirt and the lace collar, and water I must wash. Come, hasten."

"Gracious sakes, Mistress, what is amiss?" Harriet stared open-mouthed, but I was too busy pulling off my chemise to concern myself.

Isaac called for one hour and stayed two, during which time Harriet once again plied her needle and we played chess, and spoke only of the family in far away Kent. Then he called the next day, and the next, and the pattern passed as previously. On the fourth day, which was very sultry and hot, Harriet enquired if Master Isaac would be calling because, if he were to be absent, the servants had asked if they might be permitted some afternoon hours in which to seek some cooler air. "The mistress has permitted such a liberty before," she explained.

"Most certainly," I agreed eagerly. "Master Isaac will not be visiting today, for he did say that he was required elsewhere."

My lie seemed to satisfy her, and after assuring me that old Matthew would remain in the kitchen as guard and for any needs I might require, she withdrew.

Jubilant that she had chosen the oldest retainer to remain, I waited until after they had all departed, before creeping down the stairs to await Isaac's arrival.

Immediately I heard the familiar sound of his footfall I swung the door wide, and Isaac stared in surprise. "Mistress Fry, you are a lady of unexpected moments," he declared.

Laughing animatedly, I led the way upstairs, very aware of his body close to mine as we groped our way to cousin Edith's parlour. As he closed the door he said, with eyes bright with mirth. "You should not have me here, but perhaps it is most appropriate a place to receive my gift see," he opened his palm to reveal a wide, and heavily jewelled ring, "For you, dearest Pleasance."

Shocked, I shook my head violently. "What can you mean? I cannot accept it."

But he had already taken up my hand, and slipped the ring upon my finger. "See it fits perfectly. You will wear it for me, you promise?"

With his arm about my waist and his breath against my cheek, I had no defence but to murmur my assent but, suddenly, as I stared down at the magnificent jewel an apprehension I could not understand assailed me, and pulling myself gently away I moved to a chair and sat down. For a moment Isaac remained standing, before approaching me to kneel down and lay his head gently in my lap.

As we remained thus in silence, I ran my fingers through his thick black locks until he took my hand and gently pressed his lips into my palm. The sensation made me shiver, and I pressed closer to him as his other hand slipped beneath my skirt and gently caressed my inner thigh. Involuntarily, I began to respond and immediately, with movements far more expert than my own clumsy attempts at self-satisfaction, he roused me swiftly to an engulfing pleasure. The gasping cry I could not subdue he silenced with his lips, before gently releasing me to relax against the chair. After a while, he stood up.

"The servants will return soon and I must away. If perchance they could walk tomorrow, we could perhaps meet again?"

With a burning face I adjusted my skirts, and I muttered that I did not know.

He shrugged. "No matter it was but a thought. Albeit, shall I attend?"

"If it so please you," I replied with difficulty.

He bowed. "It does so please me, ma'am. Indeed it does."

We walked down to the hall in silence, and after he had gone I leaned exhausted against the door, his ring still on my finger. I had permitted a familiarity which would have disgusted all who knew me, except Molly. She would have understood how emotions stronger than discretion or prudence had reduced me to a mixture of humiliation and triumph.

Next day, I suggested to Harriet that perhaps the servants would again care to walk to fresher air. She smiled in obvious delight. "Yes indeed mistress, if you will permit."

As soon as the house was empty, save for Matthew closeted below, I again seated myself upon the bottom stair. This time Isaac greeted me with a searching kiss, his tongue moving dextrously in my mouth and I clung to him excitedly, then pulled away in surprise as he murmured, "Dearest of women, are you not a little selfish to have so much pleasure and I have none."

I stared in bewilderment, and he laughed softly. "So chaste, come let me show you how we can both enjoy and give. For love is for giving dearest one, not for taking alone." His hands pressed harder into my body. "I would hold you thus forever," he murmured, lifting me up in his arms.

Overpowered by my feelings and the sweet smell of his skin, I burrowed my face in his neck as he carried me to my chamber. Once there, he lowered me to the bed before bolting the door, and removing his cloak and breeches. Clad only in his shirt, he pushed my skirt above my waist and then climbed between my legs. Shivering with a mixture of anticipation and fear, I felt his lips move rapidly across my skin until his tongue reached my navel, from where it flicked down towards that secret part known already to his fingers. Overcome with sensations I had never before known, I began responding violently, craving I knew not what.

Immediately, I felt something damp and hard hovering between my thighs. At first it seemed content to quiver in anticipation then, as though charged with a life of its own, it bore insistently into me. The sharpness of its entrance and the sudden burning pain made me flinch and I tried to close my legs, but Isaac's thighs moving relentlessly back and forth barred the way, and I could only gasp as the pain intensified until, stimulated beyond control, I moved in concert with increasing speed until I felt my body quiver again and again with uncontrollable pleasure.

After a few more moments of violent energy he withdrew and collapsed onto me, the demanding penis lying now inert across my thigh. I wanted to remain holding him forever, but after a few moments he pulled away, and climbing off the bed murmured, "The sun has descended beyond yonder tower and the servants will soon return. I must be gone."

As he commenced dressing I sat up and drew the coverlet about me as his penis, now spotted red, swayed lightly against his thighs. Embarrassed, I averted my eyes and was about to climb off the bed when I felt a damp sensation between my legs. Glancing beneath the coverlet I was shocked to see liquid and blood on the inside of my thighs. I drew down my skirt as Isaac swung his cloak around his shoulders, and smiled.

"Farewell dearest, I will try to attend you tomorrow, as it will be our last day. Mayhap the servants will again walk?"

I nodded distractedly. The sight of my blood and the strange white mucus had unnerved me, and I suddenly wanted him gone. But the feeling only lasted until his departure and I had cleansed myself, after which it was replaced by my usual longing for his presence.

The next morning I awoke to see the rain beating against the casement and with profound feelings of relief, heard Harriet's news that there had been heavy thunderstorms over southern England, flooding roads and rendering them impassable. Delighted by the news, since it implied that my departure would be delayed, I was also aware that despite the weather, the servants would be absent during the morning for at least four hours, for it was Sunday and everyone, including Matthew, would be attending church.

I had no difficulty in pleading a sick headache, and ensuring Harriet that it would be in order to leave me. At first she demurred, saying it was not seemly that I should be left alone, but after repeated assurances from me that I would not stir from my room, she agreed.

As soon as the closing of the heavy front door indicated the servants were despatched, I sped excitedly down the stairs to away Isaac's arrival. As I sat behind the door I could hear the rain beating heavily against the wood, and when Isaac at last arrived he entered dripping rainwater profusely onto the polished floorboards.

"Dearest I am saturated. Can I disrobe and have you other garments that I can don?" He dropped his cloak, and I stared in consternation as pools of water spread across the floor.

"Come quickly to my chamber, where you can dry your garments," I declared. "But this water must first be removed, or the servants will discover it."

"Servants," he sounded scathing and his voice rose sharply. "What matters what the servants think, come now, to your chamber."

"I cannot leave such a mess," I insisted. "I must find some cloths."

"No," he leaned forward, and soon his kisses and fondling soon drove all thoughts of the wet floor from my mind.

Our second union was even more exhilarating than previously and afterwards he slept in my arms until the sun indicated the nearing of midday, and the servants return. I shook him gently and he opened his eyes and sighed, "When can we again meet? You are to the country, but the roads may still hinder travelling so I will call early on pretext of Mistress Jane's health, and if the time is not opportune, I will merely take my leave?"

I agreed eagerly, but after he had departed it took me ten minutes of frantic mopping to clear the pool he had left behind, and as I had not the time to find a suitable cloth I was forced to use a sheet from the linen cupboard. Disposing of it without detection was impossible, so I thrust it within my father's chest until I could convey it from the house.

For the next two days, the weather having cancelled my journey, I sat at my tapestry frame with Isaac's ring hidden within my bodice listening for his knock, but our only visitors were cousin Peter who returned looking weary, and a very muddy and dishevelled David who arrived with the Frost's coach.

"'tis bad the roads are, mistress," he announced. "But now the sun does send out heat they will be passable, so mayhap we can depart tomorrow." I could do nothing but agree, despite the voice from my heart crying to be heard.

Due to some of the roads having been heavily rutted by the rain, the journey to Kent took nearly two days, but I was hardly aware of my surroundings, wishing only to return to London and Isaac. Sir Simon Perkin's house, built during the late Queen Elizabeth's reign, lay in substantial grounds some miles from Canterbury town, and after a journey which left me feeling very tired, I was welcomed by cousin Edith with the same effusion she had shown on my first arrival.

"My dear child, how welcome you are. Jane is still abed I fear, but recovering swiftly. I trust James was not unduly taxing he spoke much of his time with you. Now do you tell me of Master Frost, has he yet returned to Bow Lane?"

Despite all my cousins' company, and the novelty of living within a country house with its many social distractions, I could think of nothing but Isaac. Even the riding lessons cousin Edith insisted I should be given failed to absorb me. Instead I could think only of how splendid it would have been to ride with Isaac across the park.

There was also a strange sense of foreboding in the house, which seemed to emanate from Master Perkin. At first I believed he resented my presence, but then realised his manner stemmed from Jane, and not myself. That all was not well between them was plain to see even by me, distracted as I was, but as Jane no longer sought my confidence and cousin Edith seemed determined to ignore the rift, I knew I had to consider it as none of my concern.

But my melancholy was slightly dispelled after a few days by James's continued enthusiasm at my presence. "I have missed you, dearest coz," he announced with a damp kiss. "No one laughs here. Jane is so solemn and Frances and Elizabeth attend always to mother. They do not care to ride, or do anything that I favour."

So I roused myself enough to enjoy the company of my little squire, whose wish to please aided the speed of hours which otherwise would have hung heavily. On the ninth day, cousin Peter arrived unexpectedly, accompanied by Sir Simon. Both men looked very tired, having travelled from London in order that we should have, as swiftly as possible, the sad news that Lord Cromwell had died the previous day.

Cousin Edith went very pale, as I stared in silence thinking suddenly how grieved my father would have been. Then my reverie was disturbed by cousin Peter's solemn voice, "So my dear wife, I trust you will prepare to return to London tomorrow if the weather does hold," he sighed deeply. "Our good Cromwell's internment will no doubt be in five or six days time but the lying-in-state and state funeral have yet to be arranged."

"Forgive my tears, dear husband," Cousin Edith replied with a deep sigh. "He was a good man and now I fear, does follow his daughter to her grave. To love so deeply and to lose the object of that love can I fear, have such consequences."

I nodded abstractedly in agreement, realising only that the following day we would be returning to London and to Isaac. Subduing my excitement was difficult, but I need not have concerned myself for I was lost within the multitude of my companions. Despite cousin Edith's concern that travelling might damage Jane's leg further, Master Perkin insisted that she accompany us, and it was a party of three coaches and two carts which eventually rumbled its way into Bow Lane, from where Jane and a morose Master Perkin left us to travel to their own abode.

With everyone once more ensconced, I found the gloomy atmosphere of the dark house intensely oppressive. I was aware that, from the conversations I had overhead whilst in Kent, Lord Cromwell's death would have immense consequences, but even such momentous events as those seemed trivial to me when compared with Isaac's absence which, after two days, even cousin Edith remarked upon.

"He must have been called away," she murmured. "Or mayhap his father has commissions for him. But it is strange that he has sent no word, for he surely must know that James still requires his services."

On the third day after our return, I was indulging in my greatest pleasure of lying on the bed where I had learned to love, twisting Isaac's ring around my finger, when I heard cousin Edith call my name. Quickly slipping the ring inside my bodice I arose from the bed just as she entered trembling, and with a stricken expression.

Obviously overcome, she sank down on the nearest chair exclaiming, "My dear such very sad news. Our Lord Cromwell's death was a great shock but he was a man of many years, who had used his lifespan to the very best. This death is most tragic. That he should die so young, before accomplishing the greatness that I know would have been his, and his father to be so bereaved, and now to have no one. The messenger awaits below what can I say to him? The poor man hardly knows what he says."

My heart seemed to contract and I breathed deeply to ease the pain. Unable to speak, I listened with a sickened stomach as cousin Edith explained agitatedly how Isaac had apparently returned to his home two weeks previously drenched to the skin, and after contracting a fever had died nine days ago.

"The messenger would have called earlier, but the mourning had to be observed and the eight days are but completed." Cousin Edith shook her head distractedly. "Please my dear, do you accompany me. We must to the messenger with some words for Master Santagel, though what those words can be I cannot at this moment declare."

I still cannot recall how I found the strength to follow my cousin down to the small misshapen man, his red and swollen eyes witness to the tears he had been shedding. Nor do I know how I was able to stand silent, as he broke down again and sobbed heartrendingly into his sleeve. When at last his cries ceased cousin Edith, with gentle words of sympathy, directed him below to the kitchens for some warm reviving refreshment. It was as he was walking unsteadily towards the cellar entrance, that the stone flags suddenly seemed to rush towards my face, and all went black.

I was told by Harriet that I lay for two days in a high fever, but I recalled only Isaac's face hovering above me, while his fingers pressed hard into my back and chest. When at last the fever abated and my senses returned, Harriet welcomed me with a delighted cry, "Mistress you did give us all such a fright. So ill you have been. Mistress Frost she did say it was a country ailment, but Master Santagel he did…"

"Master Santagel," I gasped out the name.

"Yes Mistress, you were so ill he was called. Mistress Frost was loath so to do seeing how he had so much sorrow, but Master Frost did say he was a physician who did not put his own troubles before those of others. He did give you a draught, which did make you cool."

I turned my head into the pillow. So the face I had seen and the hands that had caressed me had been those of the father, not the son. He lay somewhere in the cold earth, lifeless and gone forever. I shivered, and the motion seemed to release from deep within me the tears that had remained dormant for so long. I heard Harriet exclaim in concern, and then felt her arms enclose me as she rocked me gently to and fro until a deep sleep followed, and I awoke a second time to find cousin Edith seated beside my bed.

"My dear so long you have slept, but now you look much recovered, and mayhap tomorrow noon you can rise and join us below, but now my dear may I request even though you are still weak, that James be permitted entry. He has been so distressed, first by the sadness of Master Santagel's death and then by yourself. My poor little son has sat outside your door these past two days, may he enter?"

What could I do but agree, and within minutes my arms were enclosed about my small weeping cousin, who sobbed brokenly into my neck as I tried to comfort him. But not even the important task of sustaining James revived me to full awareness, and although I arose and dressed, ate meals with the family, tutored my two young cousins, and was present as cousin Peter related the solemnity of the Lord Protector's body being interred in Westminster Abbey, nothing seemed to penetrate the anguish which encompassed me.

Our great leader's son Richard had been commanding a shaky, and not very confident reign for two months, when I noted that there were two sets of clean thick linen strips lying within one of my bureau drawers. The cloth was used to absorb my monthly bleeding and instead of the customary ten strips, there were twenty. I frowned, realising as I did so that I had not passed my woman's blood since before my illness. I studied the cloth again, and then drew back my hand as Old Mother Burrows's tales of girls "being taken," and visions of Molly ushering Esther Royton into her back room, poured into my mind.

I sat down heavily on the bed, pressing my fingers deep into the counterpane. I had been ill and had a great shock, and such things were known to disrupt monthly bleeding. Still perturbed, I undid my bodice until I was naked to the waist, and gently stroked my left breast. It felt firm and full, but I had never before touched it in this way so knew not whether it differed from the past.

Subduing a sudden feeling of panic, I drew up my skirt and pressed my palms against my stomach. There seemed to be no swelling, neither did my waist seem enlarged but that was not surprising, since I had lost considerable weight since Isaac's death. Comforted by my own reassurances, I dismissed the matter from my mind and continued with my existence, an existence not eased by James who, although he had reluctantly become accustomed to his change of teacher, repeatedly referred to Isaac whenever in my presence.

It was late one afternoon, some two weeks after I had consoled myself, that a violent dizziness forced me to seek my bed. Cousin Edith being absent and the girls occupied with lessons I had set them, I was able to reach my chamber undetected. Once the dizziness had passed I arose from the bed, and this time, removed all my garments and stared down carefully at my body.

Around my waist was a deep encircling mark where the now too tight ribbons had held up my skirt, and my nipples, which previously had appeared unchanged, seemed now more pronounced. Also my belly had swelled slightly, expanding my navel. Despite the coolness of the room, I flushed violently. Memories of Isaac's body pressed so close to mine flooded into my mind, and I began to tremble. Molly had transgressed with Daniel and suffered nothing, but I knew there was no comparison between myself, an ignorant country girl, and my knowledgeable friend.

I tried to think clearly. Whatever I decided to do had to be accomplished within the coming week, or Harriet would begin to notice the changes in my body. Confiding in cousin Edith was unthinkable, and Lord Cromwell's state funeral was due to take place during late November, by which time my condition would be even more apparent.

To bring such disgrace upon a house where I had received nothing but kindness and goodwill was not to be contemplated. There was only one course open to me, I had to leave. But how was that to be accomplished without friends and guidance? I could not return to Fretson and shame my father's name, but then I remembered Molly's coins; they would take me to Stamford where I could acquire lodgings in the town, and hire a maid.

This course of action seemed a possibility until I remembered Doctor Percival, and realised that if I were to take up residence in the town he would no doubt seek me out. My loneliness engulfed me and, moaning, "Isaac, Isaac," I began to cry. Then I remembered cousin Edith's words of Lord

Cromwell, and how he had died of a broken heart. "It can happen," she had said.

I dried my eyes. I had nothing for which to live. All those I had loved were dead, so why should I not join them? Not by my self-destruction, since that was another mortal sin, but by the gradual forces of nature.

Having made my decision I discovered, from casually enquiring of Harold, the whereabouts of Stepney village, and I knew I would have no difficulty in leaving the house undetected. Due to the unsettled times and the fact that Richard Cromwell had not been attributed the devotion shown to his father, meetings were constantly being arranged between members of the Judiciary and Mayor and Council, which resulted in so many people visiting Bow Lane, the front door seemed constantly ajar.

It was during a lull in one of these visits that I slipped down the main staircase and out into the late afternoon mist. Wearing a concealing veil and mask, and warmly clad in my fur lined cloak, I hurried down the street. Bow Lane was quiet as I turned into Cheapside where, on my many journeys in the coach, I had seen sedan chairs waiting for custom.

At first the carriers refused my fare. "The Hebrew burial ground at Stepney," exclaimed the elder man. "Do you know the distance, mistress? Why, will take all of two hours walk and then we do have to walk back. Nay, do you find some other fools to do your bidding. Though why a lady such as yourself should want such a place is beyond me." He stared at my veiled face in obvious curiosity.

"Please," I begged. "Will you not take me a little of the way? I will pay you well."

The two men looked at each other. "And what do you call 'pay well' mistress?" The younger man leered.

I flinched at his tone, but replied calmly, "Two silver coins."

"Three," he responded loudly, but the older man frowned.

"Nay, we'll take but two. We be not thieves, and such money we would not see in a life's work. Come now mistress, do you seat yourself. We can but take you as far as St. Mary Church Whitechapel, for 'twill be dark by then and we must return."

I climbed gratefully into the chair and leaned back against the headrest. There was a strong smell emanating from the rather greasy upholstery and the floor was very dusty, but I was too thankful to have succeeded to bother about such things.

Before my departure I had written a brief note to cousin Edith, thanking here for her kindness and revealing to her the whereabouts of Molly's money, as

I felt this was the very least I could do to repay her generosity. Now, progressing to my destiny, I tried to extinguish from my mind visions of my cousins' shock on discovering my absence and, especially, James's dejection.

The sounds of activity on the street seemed tremendous, with people crying out their wares and pushing against the chair, which sometimes swayed at an alarming angle. I pulled my cloak more tightly around me as the journey continued until the chair was placed abruptly on the ground, and the door opened.

"'tis here we leave you, mistress. We go no further." The older man held out his hand, and I stared out into the gloom.

"But please, where is this place?" I asked as I gave him his fare. "I see nothing but fields."

"This be St. Mary, and 'tis but two miles to Stepney. Do you follow this roadway as far as you do see it go, then to the right you will see another church. Beyond that lies the burial ground, or so I've heard said. Now do we bid you farewell."

I watched them depart with a sense of panic, and only when the mist had finally absorbed them did I commence walking in the opposite direction. The sensation of Isaac's ring pressing against my breasts seemed to give me courage, and at first I tried moving quickly, but the road was so pitted and uneven I had to take care not to catch my foot in a rut. After what seemed like endless miles, I saw lights which appeared to be coming from some cottages and realised that I must be on the outskirts of Stepney village, but the moon was hidden behind a cloud and I could not distinguish anything beyond the lights.

Now bitterly cold, and with aching limbs and feet I staggered along the village street, my footsteps muffled by the now falling snow. Then somewhere a dog barked and a door slammed, and I realised how defenceless I was, and how easily I could be robbed and killed.

I had walked some distance from the village, when the cloud floated away to reveal what appeared to be an enclosed field some yards ahead. I tried to quicken my step to find an entrance, but exhaustion and cold hampered me and I could see nothing that resembled a tombstone or grave. I slumped to the snowy ground beside the fence, shaken and bewildered.

I could not return to Bow Lane and God, it seemed, had denied me the atonement of dying on Isaac's grave. I drew in a sobbing breath. My sins had been too great, and my bid for penance too small. I pulled my cloak about me and lay motionless on the cold ground as the now heavily falling snow began to cover my body from head to foot.

CHAPTER 29

Warm smoothness seemed to envelope me. Could this be Heaven, or was the Devil jesting with me before casting me down into the violent fires of Hell? I gave a terrified gasp and immediately felt cool fingers stroke my brow, as a man's voice murmured, "Rest child, you have been unwell and must sleep."

The tone of voice was familiar, and I tried to remember where I had heard it before, but the effort was too much so I closed my eyes and let the insistently repeated, "Sleep, sleep," carry me away. The second time I awoke, the pale winter sunshine was filtering through the lattice windows to the left of my bed and I tried to remember where I was. There had been the terrible walk to the burial ground and the fence and the snow, which had been as white as the canopy above my head.

I turned my head slowly towards the heat from the fireplace. A woman with a black face, and a head covered in tight black curls, sat some distance from the bed. She was dressed in a gown of black velvet with white lace trimmings, and appeared to have fallen asleep while reading a book which lay open on her knee.

Very slowly I raised myself to a sitting position. I had visited enough fine houses with my cousins to know that the sheets which covered me were of the finest silk, as was the nightshift in which I was clad, and everything the room contained appeared to be of exceptional quality. Apart from the silken canopy, the bed hangings were a combination of scarlet and white brocade, and the pieces of exquisitely carved furniture shone luxuriantly as did the brassware hanging beside the fireplace. Even the floor's wooden surface where it was not covered with some sort of fine cloth, seemed to shine with a mirror-like quality, far in excess of the polished floors of Bow Lane.

I glanced again at my companion. This was the first black person I had seen and I studied her curiously. She appeared to be young, with a broad forehead and high cheekbones, and her demeanour and dress exuded a dignity which reminded me of Molly. A muted sound from somewhere beyond the closed door jerked the girl awake, and she glanced quickly at me. We stared at each other for a few seconds, before she rose and quietly left the room.

I burrowed nervously back into my bed. There was nothing I could do but wait. Whoever had taken me into their home like the Good Samaritan, would presumably explain what had happened. Then I thought of my child. Was it possible that my illness had caused me to dispel it, and if such be the case could I return to Bow Lane? My cousins would then be forever ignorant of my shamelessness, and I would plead that some trivial matter of which they would not have approved had driven me from their door.

The bedroom door opened and Abraham Santagel entered. I struggled to a sitting position as he approached the bed, followed by the black girl.

"Myon tells me she thinks you are perhaps able to take some nourishment," he said, placing his hand on my brow. "It would appear the fever has abated. I think a little broth Myon, with some dark bread and possibly some fruit. You must build up your strength Mistress Fry, which was so swiftly absorbed by the snow."

"Please," I whispered. "How did I come here and where am I?"

"You are in my home, the house of Abraham Santagel. I did find you beside the fence of the Hebrew burial ground. You must have lain there many hours as you were near dead, but we were able to revive you. There is much of which we must talk, Mistress Fry, but later. You know you are with child?" I flushed a heated red and nodded, as he continued. "It is due a full five or six month hence." He turned abruptly. "I must to my duties. Myon will remain to tend you, she is a goodly nurse."

Too shy to respond, I could do nothing but nod and then sink back onto my pillow. I had gone to Isaac's grave to die with him, but instead had been brought by his father into the family home. Had Master Santagel suspected my child was Issac's, and what of my cousins? Someone would have found my letter by now. Did they know I was safe, and what would be their thoughts of me? I turned my face into the pillow and let the tears flow into the silk.

"Mistress, please no tears," Myon's hand was smooth and gentle. "They take strength. Tomorrow Master will speak, until tomorrow rest."

I closed my eyes. My life would have to take its course like a relentlessly flowing river. I drifted into a fitful doze until dusk, when Myon opened the bedroom door and rang a small hand-bell. In response a tall young man also black entered carrying a narrow bed, which he placed at the foot of the four-poster. He had Myon's tight curls and high cheekbones, and his physique reminded me of William, but his hands and fingers were long and slender like those of his companion.

270

After he departed I lay with half closed lids, as I watched Myon disrobe and then settle down on the narrow bed. The girl's movements exuded a feeling of reassurance and this, combined with the comfort of my own bed, enabled me to enjoy a light sleep from which I awoke relaxed and refreshed.

Obviously pleased with my appearance, Myon suggested I should spend some time sitting in the high-backed chair before the fireplace. This improvement in my health also enabled me to become acquainted with the three remaining members of the household. Pedro, a heavily built man with an enormous paunch who smiled continuously without speaking and renewed the fire and cleaned the room, a gentle middle-aged woman called Juanita who did the cooking, and Carlo the misshapen servant, who was Juanita's husband and assisted Abraham with his work.

Somewhat to my surprise, my host did not visit me again for two more days, and when he did appear I had recovered enough to be seated beside the window from where I could see into the snow covered garden below.

I was contemplating this peaceful scene as he entered, his sombre expression and black garments giving him a formidable appearance and I looked up at him nervously, but when he spoke his voice sounded gentle.

"Myon did say you were now fully recovered. No, do not rise there is no need. I shall sit here in this chair. Now child, first I must speak of your good cousins. They are deeply troubled that you should have fled their home. They knew not the cause and could not imagine a sin so great, you could not stay beneath their roof. I have explained as well as is within my power that you are with child, and that I suspect my son did so abuse you," he hesitated, and I found difficulty in meeting his eyes as he continued, "I find this deeply painful, and would finish as swiftly as is possible. They are deeply shocked, as would be any guardians of youth, but they blame you not. They think themselves to have been amiss, and they want neither your box nor the money therein. Such is yours and will be brought here together with your garments, for I did say that you should, if you be so willing, stay within these walls. You have exhibited to them within your note the shame you feel and that this will not permit you to return to their house with ease. We must consider also James and his sisters. Especially the boy, who carries a deep fondness for you and would not comprehend the need for you to confine yourself away from society, were you to return. So, child, here you must remain. I must now withdraw as I have sick persons to attend, but I will again visit you tomorrow and, God willing, you will soon be well enough to descend to the living quarters below." He stood up, and turned to go.

"Please," I slid inelegantly from the window seat and cried agitatedly, "Please before you withdraw, I must speak. Your son did not abuse me, we did love each other," I forced myself to return Abraham's stern gaze. "I did permit him the house and my chamber, and when I did hear of his death I did not wish to live and did go to die with him." I could say no more as violent sobs shook me, and when I had recovered enough to look up Abraham Santagel was no longer in the room.

A few days later, when Myon had decided that my physical strength had improved enough for me to leave my chamber, I discovered the house to be a substantial, and elegant building. There were wide corridors, high painted ceilings, and consistent warmth and light which poured in through the glass windows. Fires burned ceaselessly in enormous grates, and there were braziers situated all over the public areas of the house emitting heat and a fragrant refreshing smell. I noticed also that on the right hand side of each door-jamb, above eye level and nailed in a slanting position, was the small oblong container within which were the words from Deuteronomy which denoted a Hebrew home. Despite the bitterly cold weather, no shutters obliterated the light and in the evening at the first sign of dusk, every available candleholder held its blazing occupant.

The contrast between the dark forbidding corridors of my cousins' dwelling, and the cheerful aspect of my present abode could not but uplift my feelings and, despite my predicament, as each day progressed I seemed to feel better within myself. The building's decor also appeared to have been chosen deliberately to encourage brilliance. Light blue, yellow and green damasks liberally mixed with white, hung about the walls while covering all the floors were intricately woven light coloured rugs which, Myon explained, had come from a country on the northern coast of Africa.

"Master did bring them back with me and Nyas my brother. We were taken."

"Taken," I exclaimed. "Do you mean against your will?"

"They were destined for the Americas," Abraham voice interrupted, and I turned to find him standing beside an open door. "But I brought them from a slave market in Ceuta(46) and now they enjoy the same freedom to live as you and I. And you do admire my floor coverings, Mistress Fry? They are common enough in other lands, I did but wish to bring with me a little of the warm Spain I had to flee. Your land, though kind to us wanderers is, I fear, not hospitable to the bones of those of us used to a heated clime. Come do you enter the library, where food and drink have been prepared."

Very aware of his tall presence, which seemed to tower above me, I stepped into a panelled chamber, the high walls of which were covered with shelves of books, only to stop abruptly. Hanging over the fireplace and almost dominating the room, was a large painting of a woman, her olive complexion and high cheekbones reminiscent of Isaac's features.

"My wife, Isaac's mother, painted after her death by a Dutchman from this miniature." He removed the golden locket from his neck and held it out for me to examine.

"She was very beautiful."

"So she was," he snapped the locket shut. "Until your good Lord Protector, may God rest his honest soul in peace, permitted us to reveal our true belief the painting remained hidden within the confines of our cellar. The gown she wears is a Hebrew wedding gown, and the ring on her finger is the one, Myon now tells me, you wear beneath your gown."

I stared at him in horrified confusion, and with a trembling hand quickly withdrew the heavy gold band from within my bodice. "I beg your pardon sir, I did not know, please to take it. I was given it by Isaac, but he did not say it was his mother's."

"It is of no consequence now," Abraham replied abruptly. "But I did think you should know from whence it came, and now you do know you can wear it in its rightful place upon your finger, and not conceal it from the world. Please to sit," he motioned to a chair, and then pointed to a tall silver jug. "This is a liquid distilled from the mint herb, and here are pasties and fruit. You have lost much weight and must regain it for a healthy birth, and as you eat I must speak of Master James."

Still disconcerted, and with his wife's ring now sparkling on my finger, I asked Abraham if James were ill.

"Not of the body, but he pines for you. To lose two people he held so dear within so short a time has left him bereft, and so concerned are your good kinsfolk they have permitted him to call, if that be your pleasure?"

"Of course," I replied, stricken at the thought of my little cousin's pain. "He can come whenever he wishes only," I hesitated in embarrassment, "what shall I tell him?"

"The truth," Abraham replied calmly. "There is no reason to speak of the child, but you can say merely that you have been unwell and came to me to recover. Which is the truth, is it not, ma'am? So I will convey to Mistress Frost your agreement, and suggest perhaps tomorrow afternoon after his studies? Good, now please to be seated and eat."

I sat down, discovering as I did so that the thought of James's company seemed to have given me an appetite, and I was commencing my second pasty when Abraham said quietly, "May I speak now of my son? I do not wish to distress you but much to me remains a mystery. I did not know you were acquainted. He spoke not of you, and when I did speak of your presence within the Frost household he denied all knowledge of having met you."

Puzzled, I declared, "But we did meet in James's schoolroom, so that we could converse in Hebrew."

"You understand Hebrew, from whence came this knowledge?"

"My father was a scholar and did teach me," I explained, my gratification at my host's surprised look quickly dispelled by his next remark.

"Indeed, and to what extent does 'teach' imply?"

Stung by his sarcasm, I replied sharply, "The Greek, Hebrew, and a knowledge of the countries known to man, a history of this and other ages, and....."

"Stay mistress," Abraham raised his hand, "I do believe you, but where were you tutored and from which great city did you arrive?"

"My father taught me, sir, and I come form no great city but from a village near to Stamford in Lincolnshire" I replied, still nettled.

"And your father was a scholar in a village? I pray you tell me more, mistress, this seems a story worth the telling."

I looked down into my goblet. To resurrect the past after so long a burial would be harrowing, but this man had saved my life and had a right to know what manner of woman he sheltered beneath his roof. I looked up. Abraham's eyes were gentle and his expression, which had appeared so forbidding, was now encouraging and kind. He smiled. "Come child, I am listening, and would hear your history, if so you wish."

Taking care to avoid all mention of Molly, I told him of my life in Fretson and how, on my father's death, I had been invited by the Frosts to join them in London.

"And your father did instruct you with books of knowledge. He did have a library such as mine?"

"No sir, our cottage was too small for such a room. My father did keep them within his chamber, but they were not of such a number as you possess.

The Squire of our village, he did give them to him when he was but a young boy."

"Ah, a patron, and this Squire did extend his bounty to your father's education?"

"Yes, sir, he did send my father to Stamford School."

"And this was a clerical institute, where he could learn his priestly craft?"

"No, he did learn his church duties from his father."

"And this was the Squire's wish, that your father should apply his academic knowledge in a village church?"

"I believe it was the squire's wish that my father should go to one of the great Universities, but my grandfather did fall ill."

"And the loyal and obedient son returned to his filial duties," Abraham finished, adding with a sad smile, "And what path of learning, if life had been otherwise, would your father have pursued?"

"He did once speak to a friend of the law, sir."

"And your books, do they lie within your wooden chest?"

"No sir, I could not convey them with me, they were too numerous. I gave them to a friend."

"And your father did die of a flux of the chest. He did vomit blood?" I nodded, suddenly too choked to reply but Abraham did not seem to notice my distress for he continued, "But you did say he had such an illness for a full year. Such is not possible, most assuredly not in this clime. The damp, ugh, the ceaseless damp, and your ever persistent rain would kill, no matter how strong the man. How was life prolonged, did he have a physician?"

Unable by now to meet his curious gaze, I glanced into the fire. "Yes sir, a friend from Stamford."

"A friend from Stamford, this country town does indeed contain infinite benefits. And this Stamford friend, he knew much of the art of healing? His name pray, I would consult him on such an art, for it is a rare gift to prolong the life of a man with such a flux."

"He used herbs and has gone to York," I muttered, choosing in my confusion the furthest town I knew of, and hoping this would satisfy my host's curiosity.

But Abraham was relentless and leaning forward, said eagerly, "I have kin in York, a physician like myself. If I may have the name of your friend, I know it would be to both their advantage."

With difficulty I stared back at him, as a terrible idea occurred to me. Was it possible that his kinsman could have been the very physician with whom Molly had been acquainted? If so, fate had struck a vicious blow by despatching me to this house. I passed my tongue lightly across lips which had become very dry.

"Forgive me sir, but I do not remember. So many people did enter our cottage during that time," I looked up nervously, but Abraham was now gazing into the fire, apparently lost in his own thoughts.

Relieved that the questioning had apparently ceased, I stealthily examined my host. His resemblance to Isaac, which at first sight had appeared marked, I now realised was transient. Where Isaac had been thin and slight Abraham was tall and strongly made, and his wide eyes and generous mouth bore no resemblance to Isaac's narrow lips and somewhat Oriental eyes. Abraham's bearing too was one of cultured dignity, and lacked the haughty mien his son had favoured.

Without knowing anything about him, I realised instinctively that he would never have taken advantage of a woman as Isaac had done, and that the shame he was now experiencing for his son's deed was possibly far in excess of mine own. My thoughts overwhelmed me, and in my still weak state I was unable to control the tears that now began to fall.

"No child no tears, it is unwise to cry. It benefits not the child and there have been tears enough in this house."

He leaned forward and held out his hand, but I cried out, "Forgive me, sir, it was indeed my fault your son did die. He came to me in a great storm and was so wet and would not dry his clothes. If I had but insisted."

"No, Mistress Fry," Abraham's expression was suddenly stern. "His death was no cause of yours, but his own foolishness. I did tell him not to venture out but he would go, and when he returned much chilled and shivering he would not bathe away the damp, but would attend a frolic from which he did not return until the morrow."

I stared aghast. "A frolic?"

Abraham shrugged. "It was to his taste, and he did oft attend such gatherings. You find such a revelation disquieting. Forgive me if I give you pain but my son did attend many such revels. Despite the strict regime under which we do live, such dalliance is to be found in many noble houses. You do not care for the dance?"

"I have never danced." My feelings of betrayal made my voice sound unnaturally high.

Abraham gave me an amused glance. "So it would seem it is indeed *'the green-eyed monster which doth mock the meat it feeds on.'* I see by your puzzled glance you are not acquainted with '*Othello*' one of Master Shakespeare's works? Ah, it would appear I have an opportunity to emulate your eminent scholar of Fretson." Rising from his chair, he crossed to one of the shelves of books and took down a thin volume, which he dropped lightly into my lap. '*Much Ado About Nothing*' is a gentle introduction to the Master's great tomes, with which I think you will find favour. It tells of two protagonists who, believing themselves to be the bitterest of foes need only the inducement of friends to discover that they are indeed the most enamoured of lovers. And when you have completed that volume please chose any further of his works, or any of the books written in the English tongue, or indeed the Hebrew or Greek, that you may please to read. The choice is yours, but Shakespeare is a goodly teacher of the human mind. I would I had his breadth and width of vision. To understand so well the deviousness behind the public face is an art indeed." Abraham was now sitting beside the fire, his long legs stretched out towards the blaze. "I know such works are considered scurrilous by many whose minds do contract and not expand, but had a more liberal attitude existed over past years many would have benefited from reading books such as you now hold. I trust you will enjoy it."

"Enjoy," I repeated in surprise. "I have always believed books to be for knowledge sir, not enjoyment."

To my irritation Abraham's mouth twitched slightly. "Is not the achieving of knowledge an enjoyment? My understanding of the word is that it is to experience pleasure from the task one undertakes, and what is more pleasurable than the acquirement of knowledge. To read merely to learn, without drawing from the words the beauty and intention of the writer, is to absorb knowledge without appreciating the enhancement those words convey. No child, knowledge is too precious an attainment not to enjoy it. Do you find pleasure in your book, and forget those who would deny us such harmless distractions. And as to another forbidden pursuit the dance, we did dance much in Spain, my wife and I, at courtly balls and masks. 'tis possible, when the great men of your Parliament have settled matters between themselves, this country will again dance bravely as once she did." He smiled gently. "Look not so puzzled child, I speak of your good Monarch should he return to claim his own."

"But sir," I exclaimed with shock. "We must not speak so. Good Master Richard Cromwell is to remain our Lord Protector's successor, or so did I hear my cousins say."

Abraham shrugged. "He is but a weak and failing limb from a strong trunk, and I do believe that your countrymen now crave a freer, less rigid life." He nodded contemplatively." I do predict we will, in one or two years, see the return of the late Monarch's heir."

My fingers gripped involuntarily on my goblet. He sounded so like Molly I cried, "It is not wise sir, to speak so. What if someone should hear?"

"Why child who listens, apart from we two?" He leaned over and peered beneath his chair. "I see no one, but perhaps beneath the table or above the picture frame?"

Rising quickly, he began prowling around the room. Astonished, I watched for a few seconds then the absurdity of his behaviour overcame me and I began to laugh. Immediately he returned to his chair, and gave me a satisfied nod.

"Good, this house has been bereft of laughter for too long. Now, before you retire I must acquaint you with our ways. As you do know I am a physician, and beneath this dwelling is a stone built room wherein I mix my potions and other healing properties, with which I tend the sick. This work I do for six days of the week but on Friday noon, I cease, and do prepare for the Hebrew Sabbath. This we welcome at dusk with prayer, candles, bread and wine, and on our Sabbath I join in prayer those of my faith gathered nearby. On Sunday, your Lord's day, Carlo will conduct you, if you so wish, to the small church which lies but a short distance from this house. I have spoken with the Minister, and explained that I have residing with me the daughter of a friend who awaits her lying-in. Is this to your liking? Good, and soon will be the celebration of your Saviour's birth. Should you wish for aught in particular on that day, please to tell me and it will be so arranged. Now you have eaten and drank your fill, you should retire to rest for you will need all your strength to withstand the onslaught of Master James's joy."

He stood up to escort me to the door, but before following I asked the question that had been puzzling me since we first conversed. "May I ask, sir," I said hesitantly. "How you did know that Isaac fathered my child?"

"Because you cried his name repeatedly, as you lay sick," he replied quietly as he walked towards the door. "Such is the way with a troubled, loving mind, and I have witnessed such many times amongst the ill I tend."

My disillusionment at Isaac's behaviour in denying my existence did not affect me as much as the fact that, after making so many vows of affection, he had found enjoyment elsewhere in someone else's company. I sat for some time contemplating the matter, before taking up my book and opening the page. Never having before seen a play I sought at first for the beginning, but having soon established that the tale was conveyed by dialogue and intrigued by this unusual fact, I commenced reading murmuring softly to myself as I did so, *'Knowledge is too precious an attainment not to enjoy it.'*

Very quickly I reached Scene II, and would no doubt have continued reading all night had not my candles guttered their protests and left me with no companion but the dark. So I was forced to cease reading just as Hero and Margaret were preparing their machinations to entrap Beatrice and Benedick.

By the time Myon appeared the following morning I had finished the play, and having visited the library had soon selected *'A Midsummer Night's Dream.'* But the complicated emotions of the four lovers were interrupted during the afternoon by the sound of a high pitched young voice demanding my presence, as James burst into my chamber and flung himself into my arms.

"Dearest coz, I missed you so much. Why did you go? Could not Master Santagel have visited our house to tend you? And what has been your illness? So worried have I been." He snuggled down into my lap and I held him close as I explained that, although I had been ill, I was now recovering, and would remain with Master Santagel until I was fully well.

"But you are to visit me as often as you wish," I added hurriedly, before he could protest. "And we can talk, and play chess as we were wont to do."

"Yes," he replied, his voice doubtful. "But I prefer to have you nearer coz, but if 'tis not to be," he shrugged, then added eagerly, "But I must tell you of the happenings since you have left."

Leaning back in my chair and feeling more content that I had for many a day, I listened as he described the ornate procession of Lord Cromwell's state funeral.

"There were six horses each covered with black velvet and each likewise adorned with plumes of feathers," he prattled on. "And there was a canopy of state born by six gentlemen; it was indeed a great and solemn show, but the effigy I did not care for."(47) Without really concentrating, I let his words flow over me until he mentioned Jane. "My mother is much concerned," he explained, "for she is yet again ill. It is her head. Always she has an aching head. Master Santagel did attend her and gave her a potion, so my mother did tell my father, for I did overhear them speak. But nothing it seems does relieve her." His voice dropped to a whisper, "And Master Perkin is displeased for she could not attend the funeral, but this I am not supposed to know."

Intrigued, I was about to enquire discreetly as to his meaning, when a light tap on my door heralded Mynon with food and drink and the moment was lost.

Later, when my young guest had consumed everything in sight and taken his reluctant departure, I once more entered Hermia's and Helena's complicated lives, and Jane's problems were forgotten.

'*The Tempest*' followed next morning, and with this I made a discovery. The lines my father had quoted so long ago were there for me to see, and as I read '*We are such stuff as dreams are made of, and our little life is rounded with a sleep,*' I realised the similarity between Prospero and Miranda and my father and myself, and wondered if he had quoted the verse with the same thought in mind. But Miranda had not strayed and disgraced her father's name as I had, and I put aside the play and read no more, seeking safer waters with '*The Taming of the Shrew*'.

Late next afternoon, after James had departed, I returned to the library for another volume to discover Abraham standing before his bookshelves, with a quizzical expression.

"Master Shakespeare's offerings are much to your taste, Mistress Fry. Four of his plays in so short a time, and Master James. You do indeed enjoy a strong constitution. I do not censure, it is only that I am acquainted with the volumes removed by the dust marks pertaining to each space. My son was not a reader of great diligence and I have, these recent months, had little time for such an indulgence. So I fear the dust has lain undisturbed but no longer, it would seem. I congratulate you, Mistress Fry, to have absorbed so varied a literary diet so swiftly. May I question you on what you have read? I would fain know your thoughts on Puck's negligence and whether Beatrice and Benedick will find true happiness, and Petruchio's wooing of his lusty Kate, and whether you approve of Prospero's revenge?" I stared at him nervously, but to my surprise he began to laugh heartily. "Not this very instant and not, I do assure you, in one burst. First we will eat and then if you are not tired, we will talk. You are of a serious vein, Mistress Fry, and I fear easy bait for those of us who like to tease," he bowed slightly. "I fear my nature is like the restless wind. It sees a stray leaf lying on the ground, and needs must toss it to see it bounce."

I could not help but smile. "I take no offence, sir. I have many times been teased for my lack of frivolity. Why Moll, that is another person did also once say I was of too serious a vein." I felt myself blushing, and Abraham stared curiously at me for a moment before averting his eyes.

His obvious wish to delve my knowledge occupied many hours, during the evenings that followed. At first, confronted with such an erudite mind I was too shy to offer much in return except monosyllables, but encouraged by his interest and gentle humour, I soon became confident enough to express myself and even, on occasions, to disagree. But to no great extent, as our minds were compatible on many subjects, but certain of his views I found irritating, especially in relation to 'Romeo and Juliet'.

"I find that one play tedious," he remarked disparagingly one evening as I laid the book down beside my plate. "Two families who feud so profoundly would never unite after so great a tragedy."

"I cannot agree, sir," I exclaimed. "They did see the error of their ways and the futility of anger."

"Only after having lost all they held most dear?" Isaac had not been dead half a year and I hesitated, but as though annoyed by my silence Abraham frowned. "Please to continue. We must not build a wall around our loss. That way leads to madness. So do speak your thoughts, mistress."

"I think that the tragedy did open their eyes to their own folly. They did see that it was through their own anger that two innocent souls had died. I do not think that such a profound lesson would have failed to penetrate educated minds."

"You do believe that from education does flow tolerance?"

"Such is my belief," I replied, thinking of what my father had taught me.

He sighed. "Would it were so, child, but I have with these eyes seen men educated by the most scholarly of Spanish minds condemn innocent men and women to writhe with agony at the stake."

"The Inquisition?"

"Aye, the Spanish Inquisition is the abomination of which I speak. Independent of the Papacy since Torquemada and de Deza(48), it holds sway over all Spain and will not tolerate anyone who does not share its Catholic faith. Even the Spaniards themselves, devout followers of the Pope though they be, fear it." He frowned heavily, his long fingers twisting the stem of his goblet from left to right. "It was their diabolical tortures that tore out Pedro's tongue and twisted Carlo's body on the rack because they would not betray me. They both knew I was a Catholic by outward appearance only, and that within our home we did follow our true faith but they spoke not, and piteous they were when I was called to collect them from their travail." He closed his eyes for an instant, before continuing in a firmer voice, "No, tolerance does come from the heart not the mind, and yet those very men who did devise such vileness were themselves of Hebrew descent." His voice became harsh and discordant, and he stared fixedly at his goblet before shaking his head and giving me a weak smile. "Forgive me child, I fear my thoughts have wandered. The past is ever with me. I have few friends who remember those days, and to speak of them brings back memories that carry much pain." He shook his head. "I did say to build a wall around one's pain leads to madness, but I fear such bricks are sometimes hard to dismiss."

He looked so despondent I murmured by way of distraction, "When do you leave for your Sabbath, sir. And where do you go?"

He looked up, obviously surprised. "Why, child, to our house of worship in Creechurch Lane(49) where we pray from dusk to dusk, breaking our prayers only for food. Why do you ask?"

"I know little of your faith, sir, and ask only from interest. Forgive me if I pry."

"Indeed, you do not," Abraham's expression became more animated. "If you wish to learn of Judaism I will instruct but did you not say your father told you of our ways?"

"He told me only of the expulsion of 1290 and the fate of the Hebrews of York, and also of the Dutch Rabbi Manasseh ben Israel who did consult with our Lord Protector for the re-admission of your people, but as to your ways of prayer I fear my father was ignorant."

"Mean you our customs? To speak of them would take much time for we have many rituals, some of which you will learn should you give birth to a son for, with your consent, I would have him circumcised(50). But more of that later, enough to explain that on Friday eve we do welcome in our Sabbath with candles, lit by the wife or lady of the house. Then we do drink wine and eat bread dipped in salt, these items being necessary for sustenance. This is the prayer and ceremony that sanctifies the Sabbath and is called Kiddush. It is then our custom to conclude this holy day after sunset with a prayer that divides the Sabbath from all others, by name Havdalah. This is accompanied by wine, special candles and a small silver casket containing spices which do scent the air. And all of this I do partake in the house of my friend, Petrus Joshuah. He, like myself, did come to this country near eighteen years past and practised openly as a Catholic, until the re-admission." He stood up abruptly, and moved towards the door. "With no lady of the house I go where I can be with others of my faith, and I shall be away full eight nights from this Thursday coming, for it is our Festival of Chanukah or Feast of Dedication when we celebrate the miracle of one small jar of oil. You know the tale?"

"Yes, sir, the victory of the Maccabees over King Antiochus, but I knew not that it was called Chankuah."

But, as if he had not heard, Abraham moved towards the door murmuring so softly I could barely hear him, "At times such as these I deeply miss my son, and to be with my own people helps ease my pain."

CHAPTER 30

The eight evenings of Abraham's absence during his Chanukah Festival seemed interminable, especially after the exuberance of the afternoons with James. Without Abraham's acute mind to stimulate my thoughts, my preoccupation with Master Shakespeare's erudition began to wane, until I read *Hamlet* and Polonius's advice to his son *'to thine own self be true.'* The words could have been written for me, but I did not at that time have the courage to answer and as Master Shakespeare was becoming too perceptive for my present state of mind, I glanced about for an alternative and decided to re-read Homer's *Oddysey.*

It was wedged between two thinner volumes and in tugging it out I released the two books on either side, causing both to topple to the floor. On retrieving them I discovered one was written in a language which I remembered from the wording on my father's map to be French, whilst the other was a paper manual, a few pages of which were covered in English script.

The printed manual had the words *'La Premiere Face du Janus francais extraite et colligee des centuries de Michel Nostredame'* embossed in faded gold on the front cover, and inside on the second page were the words *'les heritiers de Pierre Roussin, Lyon, 1594'.* The book was obviously very old, and, from its condition well read.

Annoyed by my inability to translate, I glanced at the text manual. The first page read *'The Centuries of Master Michel de Notre Dame, as composed by Jean Aime de Chavigny and translated by Isaac Santagel of London late of Spain.* I was engrossed. Despite the intimacy we had shared, I realised that I had known nothing of Isaac's true character. Like a whirlwind he had gathered me up, and after wreaking havoc cast me back down to earth. We had rarely conversed, and never in depth, even my chess lessons had been conducted in silence. I had been but a pliable tool in his hands and yet, as I had confessed to Abraham, a tool that had been most willing.

I glanced down at Isaac's spidery ill-formed letters, and compared them with William's clear confident script. There was no comparison. The former was the scribble of an immature youth interested only in his own pleasure, while the latter was that of a man with intelligence and sense, who had treated me with consideration and respect. To distract myself from my thoughts I returned to the text and read:

'Let all who do read these verses judge them naturally,
Let them not be approached by vulgar rabble and fools,
Do all barbarians keep away,
May all who do otherwise be cursed.

These words were followed by a date in the margin of the second page, and what appeared to be a prophesy relating to the Duke of Alba. A further prophesy on the third page related to the death of a young lion over an old, and this was followed by a large ink mark and what appeared to be a drawing of a woman's face.

After this effort Isaac appeared to have become bored with translating, because the next verse was written in French and I stared uncomprehendingly at:

Le Neron jeune dans les trois cheminees
Fera de paiges vifs pour ardoir jetter
Heureux qui loin sera de tels menees
Trois de son sang le feront mort guetter

I was turning the remaining pages only to discover they were blank as Myon entered to tell me that my meal was prepared for me, in the dining hall. Having consumed my solitary repast, I wandered disconsolately back into the library, but books were no longer sufficient. I could not concentrate on the written word, I needed company to escape from my thoughts. Opening the door I listened for human sounds, but nothing seemed to break the tranquil calm until Pedro appeared in the corridor to replenish the brazier. He gave me a bowing nod as I enquired whether he had seen Myon.

Motioning me to follow, he led me towards the rear of the house where he drew back an arras to reveal an open double door, beyond which I could see a wooden staircase. Unlike Doctor Percival's narrow damp steps, these were solid and well lit and led into a spotlessly clean chamber with a stone floor and white walls. There were numerous shelves on which reposed large glass containers full of either liquid or powder, and a tall wooden cabinet containing a number of small drawers stood beside a heated brazier at the far end of the room. In the centre was a long wooden table covered in pots and bottles, and at either side of the table stood Myon and Nyas, apparently working.

Memories of Molly's little room in Goodwife Hargreaves's cottage flooded back into my memory, and I stepped back intending to return upstairs, but a sudden movement from the child within me made me seek a stool as Myon and Nyas welcomed me with smiles and nods. The sensation having passed, I watched with fascination as they weighed out powders on two small sets of brass scales. These powders were then poured through funnels into squat glass jars which were shaken violently first one way and another, before being poured into individual bottles. Absorbed, despite the memories the sight recalled, I was taken unaware when my child yet again stirred and I gasped uncontrollably.

"It is too cold in this chamber, Myon murmured. "Mistress should return upstairs."

Nyas nodded in agreement, and gently taking my hand conducted me back to the parlour, where he left me once more alone with my thoughts. So did I continue until Abraham at last returned a circumstance I was unaware of until I encountered him on the stairway. He smiled in greeting and expressed obvious pleasure that I was continuing in good health.

"And was your service as you would have wished, sir?" I asked.

"Yes indeed," he smiled. "But I have neglected my duties for long enough. I must to my chamber, for Carlo has much to tell me of the sick he has visited in my stead."

Feeling considerably more content, I awaited the evening meal with eagerness, but when I entered the dining hall Myon told me that her master had been called out to attend a patient. So yet again I ate a solitary meal, and afterwards retired despondently to my chamber. My evenings continued thus for two more days, and without James to distract me during the day I fear I would have sunk into a deep misery, but his energy and enthusiasm always dispelled my dejection.

It was during one of these later visits that he astonished me by placing one small hand upon my stomach and murmuring, "Such is my sister, but she takes little pleasure in her state and I fear my mother is much concerned." Although I was all too aware that my waist had thickened, I had hoped that my full gowns and shawls concealed my secret. As though aware of my confusion James continued, "I know I am not supposed to be aware of these matters, coz, but I care only that you will be well and safe, and that is why I will seek to be a physician such as is Master Santagel."

His change of subject enabled me to regain my composure and I replied, "You wish to heal the sick."

"Yes," he replied. "What else does matter but good health. By his skill Master Santagel has many times restored mine, and though I cannot repay him I can, when grown, help others to such a state of well-being."

As I listened to the words of my earnest little cousin, I compared his youthful wisdom with the inconsequential behaviour of his tutor, and blushed at my own naivety. To my relief James did not mention my condition again, but I was concerned that he might have expressed his knowledge to cousin Edith, as the consequences of such a revelation might influence his visits, and decided to consult Abraham.

But it was not until three evenings later that I was given an opportunity to broach the subject when, descending to the library, I encountered him on the staircase. Travel stained, and with thick mud on his boots, I was concerned to see how weary he looked as he leaned heavily against the balustrade saying, "I must extend my apologies, Mistress Fry. I was called from the house to a most complicated lying-in. God be praised we saved the mother, but such was her grief at losing the infant I had to remain until some semblance of calm was restored. Now I too seek only tranquillity, and will join you shortly."

Anticipating some lively conversation I descended enthusiastically to the dining hall, but Abraham seemed so tired our meal passed in comparative silence, until he looked up and asked how I had spent the last few days. Knowing him well enough now not to be evasive, I explained James's revelation and my fear that cousin Edith would curtail his visits.

Abraham gave a low laugh, "It is the foolishness of us grown souls to think that children see only what they are taught. Young Master James has always had an enquiring mind, combined with a discretion remarkable in one so young. I do not think you have anything to fear. Mistress Frost is too pre-occupied with Mistress Perkin who conducts herself with less tranquillity than yourself, and seems to have acquired a despond from which she cannot be roused." He gave me a keen glance. "You did spend much time with Mistress Jane, did you not? Was she of a low humour? I ask not to pry but merely to try and assist, if such is possible. Do you know of aught that may be troubling her." He smiled encouragingly, and I chose my words with care.

"I fear that Jane did not wish for her wedding."

"Such would account for her lack of humour certainly, but it would not answer for her other maladies. When in London she does complain that the noxious air nauseates her, and when in the country she seems to suffer from a continuous dampness of the nose. But how did you deduce that she entered her marriage with reluctance? Her parents have much understanding and care for their children. They would not have forced the girl into an alliance she did not find congenial. May I enquire as to the reason for your statement? Aught you say will remain within these walls."

"She loved another," I muttered.

"Another?" Abraham was silent for a few moments before murmuring, "It would seem my son did find much with which to occupy himself within Bow Lane. Forgive me child, if I am to assist the girl I must know whether there was a union between my son and Mistress Jane?" I shook my head, and he exclaimed, "That at least is a mercy, but it would seem I did rear me a lusty lad."

"What will you do?" I asked, hesitantly.

"Persuade her to apply all her energies towards her child and its welfare. I can do nothing for the other. If she cares not for her husband, that matter lies between themselves. Perhaps with time she may grow towards him, especially after the child's birth. It has been known to happen; now to matters concerning your own well-being. I have noticed that despite the many books you have perused you seem somewhat adrift, as though seeking occupation. I know your time was much taken up in your cousin's house with the instruction of your younger cousins, and although I have no such occupation here there is a task in which you may assist me." Before I had a chance to express my eagerness to help, he continued, "I am sure you know that seven days from now is the day on which your Saviour was born. I am aware that all festivities are barred, but thought perhaps you might wish to be gainfully employed, as I believe is the custom. Good, I thought that such would be the case, and the task is sewing. There are gowns within the house ready cut that do require completing. A neat plain stitch is called for, nothing more. The work has little variety but is needful. They serve as burial gowns for my faith, but should you have objection to such work I fully comprehend if you wish to decline."

Delighted to have an opportunity to replay his kindness, I assured him I would be happy to work the cloth and he smiled, obviously pleased.

"I will ask Myon to bring down the garments and you may commence whenever pleases you. But I do advise, should you feel weary at any time, to lay down your needle until you are once again refreshed."

Next morning I was busily engaged stitching, and the thought that so simple a task gave him pleasure sent my needle flying in and out of the cloth with the speed of silver fish darting animatedly across a floor. But although my fingers were applied to my task, my mind dwelt upon Jane and how I likewise could have been embroiled, had I remained in Fretson. To succumb to a man's passion without love, and to have to permit such intimacies without desiring them, was degrading not only for the woman, but also for the man. Master Perkin was dour and without laughter but he was respectable and, no doubt in his own way, kind, and I pitied him. For if Jane did not warm to him with time, his life would be one of misery.

Re-threading my needle I dropped my thimble, and as I bent down to retrieve it the child moved again within me. I pressed my hands against my stomach, feeling for the first time an enormous joy. This being which grew relentlessly within me was mine to protect and nurture, and I vowed, whatever might be my fate the child would never suffer, no matter what course of action I had to take.

I had sewn two more garments by the time Abraham joined me for our evening meal, and he greeted me with obvious pleasure.

"So many garments completed, in so short a time. If you continue so swiftly there will be no work for your needle on your Saviour's day. But what of your reading during my absence, does Master Shakespeare still reign supreme?"

"I have read more of his works, but looked also upon the other shelves." I hesitated, reluctant to mention Isaac. "There is a book in French, by one Master Michel de Nostredame, which I could not fully comprehend."

"You have discovered Nostradamus, as he is commonly known, a soothsayer of ability."

"Soothsayer," I exclaimed, shocked. "I would not have read it, sir, if I had known it was witchcraft."

"Nay, child, Nostradamus was no witch, though the citizens of Salon did burn him in effigy outside his own dwelling, forcing him to seek refuge at Queen Catherine's court. He was by craft a physician such as myself, and did discover the manner in which plague does travel. It is said he did believe that to cure such illnesses one should introduce into the body the illness itself, thereby quelling the ailment with its own sickness. I know not how this is done, and have been told that he worked such miracles in great secrecy, for such ideas were not accepted by the Church. In those ancient days the faithful did believe the plague to be the Lord's punishment for sin, as do many of the ignorant who profess great knowledge in these times." His voice was suddenly so harsh I looked at him in surprise. "Forgive me, child, my memories flood into my brain and my tongue gives vent to thoughts that should remain silent. Master Notre Dame, yet another of the names by which this man was called, did turn seer in later life and spoke of fate."

"But the Lord Cromwell did say to speak so is pagan," I interrupted hurriedly.

Abraham shook his head. "Fate is but future's decree as to the course our lives will take. No matter what is said now, in centuries past folk believed fate and divine providence to be united as did Nostradamus, who believed that his visions were inspired by God. You appear much disturbed by what I say, but please to remember I speak of near two hundred years ago, when ignorance reigned at even greater strength than now. Though I do confess man has not much advanced, for we do still commit great wrongs in the name of the Lord. As you have seen, Nostradamus wrote down his thoughts and a lengthy volume they do make. Quatrains upon quatrains, they spread across the page. My son, in a moment of great impulse, did attempt a translation but did not pursue the task. I fear it was too burdensome without the lightness of impulse that he preferred, and I fear he did destroy his efforts long ago."

"No sir, he did not," I replied, eagerly. "The volume is here, and if you will excuse me I will get it for you." Within seconds I had retrieved the book from the library and placed it in Abraham's hands. He stared down at it, frowning.

"How can this be, I searched most diligently?"

"It was beside Master Nostradamus's book upon the shelf, though much hidden by *The Oddysey* and very dusty."

"The dust of time is still much in evidence." He brushed his hand across the book like a caress, then opened it and stared down at the writing.

In an attempt to interrupt the prolonged silence, which had begun to seem like a barrier between us, I asked, "Do you speak the French, sir?"

He continued staring down at the book as if he had not heard, and when at last he looked up his expression was puzzled and he said with a frown, "Forgive me, child, you spoke, I heard not."

"The French words sir, on the second page, do you comprehend their meaning?"

"The second page, yes I do see, their meaning in the English tongue I would say are thus:

The Nero new will unto the three chimneys
Cast the young to burn whilst living
Happy be they distant from such a place
Of his blood three will rise to kill him

290

Strange words and I comprehend them not. A conflagration by a 'Nero new,' meaning not the late Emperor who so happily played his fiddle whilst Rome was put to the torch; and children are to burn? I will place the verse within the context of the book, and try to discover the year when such a disaster is to befall." He placed the manual gently on the table. "Thank you for this book, child. It is all I do have written in his hand."

Elated at having given him pleasure I smiled, and for a few moments we sat looking at each other. Afterwards, when we had removed to the library he took down the printed volume of 'Nostradamus' and found the verses.

"You may rest assured, child. It does seem these terrible events will take place many years hence, when you and I are long gone. The calculation is oblique for Nostradamus did count as from the time of Adam, not from Christ, and I would say that this prophesy is a portent for the middle of the third century from now, but exactly which year I cannot say."

"And the 'Nero' so mentioned," I queried. "Who is to be this man, and the casting of the young into the fire, for what reason should such a tragedy occur?"

"I fear you ask me questions of which I have no knowledge. Enough to say a being of monstrous birth will bring havoc to some land, and destroy its young."

"There is no guidance from other of his verses?"

"Yes, I see that now here again we do have the chimneys, and Nero spoken of. A brief translation as near as I am able, would be:

The first of the third will inflict greater than Nero
He will be as valiant in draining as in shedding human blood
Built will be the ovens
Prosperity will die.
He will cause great scandals.'"

I frowned. "He does speak of ovens. What can it mean? In ovens we do bake bread and food, and 'draining' blood as from a body," I shivered suddenly. "I do fear witchcraft, indeed I do."

"I think not, but perhaps some matter even greater in its awfulness. I do believe this may be of interest for dates are mentioned thus:
Many will die afore the Phoenix dies
After six hundred and seventy months is his home
Passing fifteen years, one and twenty, nine and thirty

The first is subject to illness
And the second to danger of his life
And rain of fire is subject to nine and thirty.'

"It would appear then, sir, that in the twentieth century such happenings are to occur in the fifteenth, twenty-first and thirty-ninth year of that century. But to what do the numbers six hundred and seventy months, refer?"

"His age, I believe, when he will die, which would be five and fifty and ten months."

"And this man to cause such havoc will be a man of power?"

"That is the implication."

"But will not good and powerful men oppose him?"

"The good and powerful child, often hide these merits until too late." He tapped out a light tattoo with his fingers on the open page. "You know not the story of my flight from Spain, Isaac mentioned it not? As I feared, he lived only for the present. But if we know not our past our present has little meaning, for our understanding of ourselves is buried within those that have gone before. To comprehend your own life you must know of your parents' world, for they did fashion you from their own experience, but Isaac did not care to hear of such things. Our family was much travelled from the northern shores of Judea to the great continent of Africa, and thence to Toledo where a distant ancestor, one Samuel Halevi, was appointed treasurer to Pedro the First of Castile. Possibly through such an influence we became owners of great ships which plied their trade through the seas of the French and African coasts. Great wealth was amassed which, with diligence and care, grew until we were amongst the richest in the land. Then did come King Ferdinand and his evil spouse and my family, fearful of losing all they had and reluctant to seek sanctuary in lands of which they were ignorant, accepted the decree of Spain and took the Catholic faith. I grew to boyhood before I was aware that I was a Jew. To have betrayed the secret at too young an age, would have exposed my family to great danger from those who would do us harm. But when I did reach my twelfth year, my father took me below to our great cellar, a region forbidden me in my childhood, and there did reveal our sacred Ark wherein lay the Holy Scrolls. He told me of the history of our people, of our wanderings and sufferings, and did explain that I was to learn Hebrew and a new faith, to which I would apply myself in secret only." He stopped abruptly "Forgive me child, I did forget the hour. You must retire and I will tomorrow resume my narrative."

Disappointed I protested I was not weary and pleaded with him to continue, but he insisted, so I had no alternative but to comply, and wait impatiently for the following evening. But as I descended to the dining hall next night, Myon told me that Abraham had been called away on a medical visit. So I passed The Lord's Day alternately praying and sewing in a house which seemed strangely quiet, and it was not until the last day of December that Abraham entered the library. He smiled down at me and gently patted my shoulder, before lowering himself wearily into his chair.

"My apologies Mistress Fry, I fear I have neglected you. There has been much business to concern me, and locked within these walls you have heard little or nothing of the outside world. But great matters are afoot which will embrace us all, and it is important for those of my faith, that all that has been promised to us remains secure. There are those who would expel us again to wander stateless across the world, but they have been confounded for the time being, and all would seem well.(51)But now to matters of more personal import, tell me of your reading and what new revelations may have been revealed by Master James."

Disappointed that he apparently did not intend to continue the account of his life, my frustration overcame me and I declared, "Please continue with your tale, for is it not fitting as I carry your grandchild I should know of the history he is to inherit?"

Obviously surprised, he looked at me as if really seeing me for the first time.

"My apologies, mistress, but what makes you think so strongly that you carry a male child?"

"I know not sir, but it is how I think of him."

He smiled. "It is of no consequence to me, be it boy or girl, so long as you are blessed with a child of health, but a boy would indeed be," he hesitated before continuing with a smile, "I see you wish me to continue with my narrative. Where did I cease? Ah yes, the ceremony of my thirteenth year (52). I was a diligent scholar, but my life became much confused. By day I was a devout Catholic confessing all my sins and praying within the Cathedral, and by night I did denounce that faith and take up the mantle of a Jew."

He frowned, and concerned that he might decide to cease speaking I said encouragingly, "Was it not difficult making so great a change? For so many years you did believe Christ to be the Son of God, how could you renounce so easily that belief?"

"I did not renounce it, not in the manner that the Rabbi would have had me do. I put aside the thought that is all. I realised that it was no longer part of me and that I was a Jew, and a Jew I would remain for the rest of my earthly life. But I did not renounce Christ. How could one deny such a fine and caring prophet, who accomplished only good during his short sojourn on earth? I did not pray to him as in the past, but I honoured him for what he strove to accomplish, and always will. The ultimate end to all journeys of faith is God, and how we wish to travel that road is a matter for our own choice. During my eighteenth year, while studying all forms of medicine, I was presented to the de la Cresques family as a possible suitor for their daughter Isabella; so called in Spain but known as Deborah amongst the Jews. I was accepted, and one year on we were wed. As is our custom we learned little of each other before marriage, but she was very beautiful and did seem to find me comely. Our union was blessed with much happiness for her likes were mine, and her thoughts attuned to mine own. By day we were devout Catholics, continuing the great deception, but by night we entered the world of our true lives, and practised the faith into which we were born. She believed, as did I, that your Saviour was a good man and, like me, did not deny his birth. And in this strange way I continued to practise not one, but two deceptions. To the Priests I was a Catholic who denied the infidel Jew, while to the Rabbis I was a Jew who denounced all but the true faith. But to myself I acknowledged good in both and denied neither. In this way I have lived my life and tried to pray as best I can to He who is Lord of us all. To our joy, our marriage was blessed with a daughter, but within two months she was dead and we grieved deeply. But two years later we were blessed with Isaac. He was a healthy child, but the birth took much toil of my wife and she was confined to bed for many weeks. During that time much trouble came to those of my faith, for many Marranos were betrayed. The name means pig in the English tongue, and was given to those Jews who did pretend to embrace the Catholic faith whilst remaining Hebrew. With those betrayals the Inquisition did enjoy many burnings and hangings, and those of us who wished to remain alive were forced to witness the horror, and cheer. I knew it was but a matter of time before I too was exposed. But the good Lord watched over me, and two more years were to pass before disaster fell upon our house. I had by then become renowned for my physic, and was consulted by both the high and low of Toledo, but there was much jealousy expressed. Then my father with great secrecy purchased many valuable stones and, in this way, much of our wealth was turned to merchandise. But the Inquisition were suspicious of me and, one day, when I was absent from the house, they entered and did take Carlo and Pedro to question them. My wife protested and there was a skirmish, during which she was felled to the ground. If you study her portrait closely you will see a mark upon her forehead. The artist did not wish to include the scar but I insisted. It was a part of her life, and I knew she would have wished it to be shown. When I did return that same night I went at once to the place where my hapless servants were confined and, for six hours, I waited until they were thrown at my feet, bloody writhing masses of pain. As I did tell you, they wrenched out Pedro's tongue and laid hot irons upon Carlo's flesh and racked him. But never once did either of them speak. Within two weeks of that calamity we had fled Toledo on one of our own ships. Prepared as we were, we carried much of the furniture and hangings now in this house. We would have preferred a sunny clime to that of the cold lowlands, but to avoid Catholicism we sailed north, and a long and arduous journey it did prove to be. At last the shores of England came in view, but as we approached I did see the dreaded sores on one man's neck, and knew that we had plague within the ship. So, instead of reaching land as we had hoped, we remained anchored within a secluded cove until the dread disease had had its way. My father, mother and wife all succumbed, as did half the crew and all are buried deep within the waves, but by some miracle of the Lord, Isaac was saved and the sea stayed calm. No one ashore became aware of our plight, and when at last the sickness had run its course, we landed at Falmouth port. I knew nothing of this land or its people, but my father had given me a letter to a Spaniard at the Embassy and, with Isaac and what remained of the servants of my house, I did travel there to seek assistance. All was forthcoming. I was rich and a physician, and such are always welcome. The stones when sold for sustenance far exceeded their value, and they did purchase this house and helped provide my restless spirit with the freedom to travel whenever my will dictated." He smiled suddenly. "Now, child, I have told you all of my life, can I not know a little more of yours?"

Taken aback, I stuttered, "I have told you of my life, sir. I come from Fretson, a village near the town of Stamford."

"I mean not the manner of your living, but the manner of your life. Who were your friends, for all young maidens have friends? Of what did you converse with your father when study was put aside? These are the matters which interest me. And the village folk, of what manner were they?"

"They were rustics and few could read," I replied, hesitantly. "And I had few friends. My father did not wish me to converse with other folk. He desired only that I should learn. But I did help within the church, and there was always much to do."

Abraham leaned back, the long fingers of his left hand drumming lightly on the arm of his chair, and he studied me intently. "And you did also work within the house. You had no servant upon whom to call?"

"There was Bessie, a village girl, but she was with us for a short time only."

"And there was no other maiden of a like mind as yourself?"

"No," I replied, as his eyes seemed to sear into my very brain.

"No neighbours upon whom to call?"

"Our neighbour was an invalid by name Goodwife Hargreaves, but she was a friend of my father's not of myself."

"And this Goodwife, did she not have a daughter or companion with whom you could converse?"

I shook my head, and Abraham pursed his lips. "A lonely life indeed, but from whence did come the wealth that you told your cousins lies within your box?"

"The Goodwife did leave the coins to my father who did bequeath them to me," I replied, my lips uttering the lie as glibly as if it had been the truth.

"I would hear more of this Goodwife, but we have talked too long. You look strained and must rest. I bid you sleep well, child, and have a peaceful night."

I arose slowly from my chair hoping, as I did so, that he would not notice the beads of perspiration that I could feel gathering upon my brow.

CHAPTER 31

1659

So accustomed had I become to the large warm house, I was hardly aware that winter had slid gently into spring as I attained my seventh month of pregnancy. Occasionally, during my infrequent excursions into the outside world or when I was in church, I had overheard murmurs that Parliament had assembled, and during the middle week of April James informed me excitedly that it had once more been dissolved, after a peaceful army coup d'etat.

"Is it not important news, coz?" He declared, standing legs akimbo with his hands upon his hips. "And I did hear David say that afore long we shall once again have a royal lord to rule us."

"Hush sweetheart," I exclaimed. "Let not anyone hear you speak thus, it is not wise."

"Yes I know," he replied, looking secretive. "I would not say such things to anyone other than you dearest coz, but," he added his voice dropping to a loud whisper. "'tis still great news."

Despite this outside eruption, nothing occurred within Abraham's house to disturbed the easy tenor of my life. I had followed his advice as to food and exercise, and when he examined me six weeks before my lying-in he stated that as far as he could judge, all was well but appeared distracted.

"Is aught amiss, sir?"

"No child, but do you know aught of your birth, as to its ease?"

"I believe it was not difficult, or so Old Mother Burrows once told me."

Abraham laughed. "Yet another name from this redoubtable village. Who was she pray, and why 'old mother'?"

Angry with myself for being indiscreet, I replied casually, "I know not why she had that name, but she was a mid-wife and did nurse the village folk when they were ill."

"And when she did first nurse was she not of an age when young mother would have been more fitting? Or was she christened 'old mother' because she was a wrinkled babe of dour countenance, or wed when young an ancient man who endowed her with such a title?"

Despite myself, I laughed. "I think not, sir, her given name was Elizabeth but I did never hear it spoken by anyone. As to marriage, indeed she was once wed but her husband did die many years ago."

"And her healing talents, what of those?"

"She did administer physic when required, and did cure scurvy, Master Barlow's sickly toe and countless fevers of the brain and skin."

"A sickly toe, scurvy, fevers of the brain and skin, so formidable an array of illnesses would satisfy the most industrious of physicians. And your father, she did nurse him?"

Forced to answer, I replied, "She was present, sir, when he died."

"But he was nursed by other hands? The doctor in Stamford, one of so many visitors that his name cannot be recalled? Now I must leave you for my duties, but I would fain know how my healing methods compare with those of the formidable Burrows, both young and old."

Despite his continued attempts at humour I knew he was displeased, but the truth was still too painful to reveal and as he departed I sank back into my chair shaking with reaction, and then glanced down at my swollen belly.

Although the sensations of movement now occurred frequently, I found difficulty in believing that in a few weeks I would be holding a live being in my arms. I stroked the green velvet of my gown gently, as if to reassure both the child and myself that all was well.

"You who lie within," I whispered, "created by two people's folly, help me to remain silent. Be my source of strength." As if in response the child moved, and I stroked my stomach until the sensation ceased.

That evening I entered the dining parlour hesitantly, but Abraham greeted me with a smile saying, "I did call upon your cousins today. I saw only Mistress Frost who is concerned about Mistress Jane who also nears her time. She is I fear still much downcast and this concerns me as it bodes not well for the infant." He gave what sounded like an exasperated sigh. "But this is not of your concern. I mention it only because Mistress Frost enquired as to your welfare, and asked if I would convey a letter. She said she wished to write words of comfort and advice for your lying-in. Here, child, read it at your leisure. I will away to my chamber, and do you not sit overlong, much rest is needed at this time."

Cousin Edith's letter was warm and thoughtful, and included a few words as to Jane's health, and a promise of a visit after my child's birth. Its kindness overwhelmed me and I began to cry.

Almost as if he had been listening outside the door Abraham entered. "Why the tears, child? Mistress Frost did assure me the letter would contain nothing to distress you."

"No, sir, it contains nothing of which I can complain. I weep only because they were so good and I did betray them. I betray all who help me, merciful heaven I am not worthy of this world."

I collapsed into the nearest chair, and through my misery I heard Abraham's gentle soothing voice as he drew me upwards to stand close against his chest.

"Pleasance, child, what means this? Nothing can be so dire and tears are bad for the infant, and that must be your first care." As he spoke I felt his fingers gently stroking my hair, and I leaned heavily against him. For a few moments we stood motionless then, as my sobs subsided, his arms moved away, and he lowered me back into the chair. "Now, child, calm yourself and rest a while. I will to my physic room to bring a draught to ease you and assist sleep."

I closed my eyes. There was no physic that could cure my malady, but I had derived some comfort from his sympathy, and when he returned I drank the liquid in the hope that it would induce oblivion. But my mind was too troubled for a dreamless state, and that night a violent, hideous Molly visited me. Half human, half skeleton, she screamed abuse until I awoke crying out for help. Again it was Abraham who came to my aid, and as he soothed me I heard him murmur softly to Myon, "She is much troubled by some instance of the past. Until I know of its composition I cannot help. Do you share her bed tonight and see if you can sooth her." To my relief, next day apart from asking me if I felt better, he did not refer to my nightmare, and seemed to be more concerned to put me at my ease.

The remainder of my confinement passed slowly. As I became heavier and more cumbersome, the daily walk became a burden rather than a pleasure, and such mundane matters as climbing stairs and rising from a chair required heroic efforts. As my appearance seemed to me almost grotesque, I expressed my surprise to Abraham that cousin Edith still permitted James to visit.

"The boy does insist," he replied with a laugh. "And the good lady can deny him nothing. It does seem that he believes the experience will assist him in his future occupation though methinks he does prepare early for such a life."

It was one morning after I had broken my fast and was preparing for my customary walk that I felt a sharp pain in my lower back. Simultaneously, I realised that liquid appeared to be running down my leg, although I had no desire to pass water. I drew up my skirt and was horrified to see, not only water but blood also and I struggled to the chamber door crying out for Myon.

Within minutes she entered, and calmly helping me back to my chair said, "Mistress, please to sit quietly, or perhaps you may wish to walk about the room?"

I was appalled. "I cannot walk, I am giving birth. Are you not going to call Master Santagel."

She smiled gently. "No, Mistress, much time will pass before the birth."

"How much time?" I asked, with gritted teeth.

"I know not, but come do let me help." She pressed her strong hand against my lower back and began to massage gently. After what seemed to me like many hours, but it could have been but three, Abraham arrived. To my surprise he made no motion of anxiety, remarking only that I disrobe into my night chemise and walk about the room.

"But the child," I expostulated. "My pains are getting stronger and more frequent, when will it come?"

"My dear Mistress Fry, whenever he or she is prepared to emerge into the light of day. There is nothing on the Good Lord's earth that can be done to persuade an unborn child to pacify the impatience of its parent. After so many months secreted away warm without exertion or responsibility, who would want to leave such security to face a world such as ours?" He smiled. "I fear I cannot give you more comfort at this time, but I shall be by and will come to see how you do as the hours pass. Now, will you drink a warm cup, or possibly read as a distraction, and when each pain does come breath deeply in and force down your stomach towards your legs, and as the pain recedes breathe out."

He was so calm, I felt foolish at having created such a fuss. But these feelings soon changed as the pains increased, and I began to find the racking sensations almost more than I could bear. Desperately trying to breath and force my stomach down, as Abraham had directed, I writhed from side to side with each contraction, and then lay perspiring and exhausted as the sensation receded.

After five more hours, Myon slipped away and Nyas took her place, but I had become almost unaware of anything except an overwhelming fear that my body would fail me and that its insistent demands, which were now continual instead of occasional, would culminate in my death.

Some time later, when I truly felt that I could no longer fight the pain, I seemed to slip into a strange dream in which there were no phantoms pleasurable or otherwise, but only a voice deep and insistent, which demanded that I was to obey, and breath as it commanded. Almost at once the pains forgotten, I responded to that voice's demands and sank into unconsciousness.

When next I opened my eyes it was to see Abraham sitting beside the bed, holding in his arms what appeared to be a bundle of cloth. I stared at him as I tried to remember what had happened, and he smiled.

"Here is your son, child. Take him for I have nursed him far too long. I congratulate you upon a great achievement. He is a fine boy, much as Isaac was at birth, except for the colour of his hair in which he favours you. I will leave you to become acquainted, but should you require aught please ring the bell, and Myon will come directly. I shall return later."

Very tenderly he placed the bundle in my arms, and I looked down at the tiny creased face for some moments before fully realising what had taken place. Then the infant opened its eyes and stared up at me and I started, so knowing did his gaze seem, but then he yawned and the sight was so comical I laughed softly.

Although I would have preferred to cradle my son without interruption, Myon soon entered to explain that the time had come to induce my milk. "The babe must be fed," she said. "And the breasts must be gently rubbed until the fluid runs."

She was very gentle, but my breasts were tender and I flinched as she massaged my skin. At last I felt a dampness, and she gave a nod of satisfaction.

"It is done and the child may suck, do you take him to the nipple and let him draw the milk."

Since that day, I have held other much loved infants to my breast, but never have I felt again the wonder and awe that overwhelmed me then, as my first son's tiny mouth drew out his sustenance. At that time the sensation was not entirely pleasant, as my nipple was tender and the child's lips insistent, but I could not help but marvel, that although I was totally ignorant as to the procedure, he seemed all too familiar with the practice, and ceased only when he considered he had completed his fill.

I would have preferred to retain him in my arms and watch him sleep, but Myon took him gently from me and placed him face down on her shoulder.

"For the wind, Mistress," she explained, as tiny hiccupping sounds filled the room. During this procedure, there was a tap in the door and Abraham entered.

"The first meal has been accomplished, that is good. Now you must both sleep and regain your energy. Your birth pangs were longer than I had anticipated, and more extreme. Possibly the walk to the burial ground and the position you did adopt whilst resting there, displaced a muscle. You have no pain now."

"No, a soreness only, and I remember nothing except a voice telling me to obey."

"That is as it should be. I did use a sleeping powder to ease your pain for I had to help the child to birth, and this can cause great discomfort. It is something I did learn from Arab doctors when sojourning in their lands. If you wish to know more I will tell you later, but now you must rest as must the child."

When next I awoke it was to find cousin Edith in a chair beside me. Surprised, I tried to struggle to a sitting position but was quickly restrained by her saying, "No my dear, please do not disturb yourself. Master Santagel tells me you have had great travail, and that you are to remain here for the while. Is this your wish."

"I think so," I murmured, not knowing what else to say, but since she appeared to expect more I added weakly, "do you not think it for the best?"

"My dear, yes, if it is as you would wish. But a welcome in our home awaits you whenever you so desire, and until then I think it wise if communication between yourself and James should be by letter. I will explain that although you are well, you have to rest. As the infant is his grandson Master Santagel will have the raising of the child, and he does seem resigned to such a course. We are now awaiting Jane's lying-in, and have you heard of the serious happenings taking place in this great city?"

I tried to concentrate as I realised, that for all her kindness and outward show there were boundaries across which my cousin would not pass. But I had no right to censure her. I had committed an unforgivable sin within her home and realised that, in her eyes, only the dismissal of my son would illustrate true repentance.

As she continued to chatter, I remembered her obsessive fear of fire and dirt and how, although her benevolence towards all those within her dwelling was almost maternal, I had never seen her extend a loving gesture. A taking of hands or a cool kiss on the cheek, had been the limits of her displays of affection. Even James, who lingered often beside her chair and occasionally flung his arms about her waist, had never received a caress in return. And yet such frigidity had still produced four children.

Considering her, as she stared fixedly at me without ever glancing once towards the cradle, I realised that both of us had demons lying deep within which were best left undisturbed, for their rousing would possibly destroy more than ourselves. When at last she had relieved herself verbally of all she wished me to hear, and waved aside my gratitude, for I did indeed owe her much, she took her leave apparently delighted by the promise I made to return to Bow Lane. A promise I knew would never be fulfilled.

As soon as she had departed Abraham entered, and nodded in apparent satisfaction. "I see the visit did go well, your cousin was eager to see you and would have no nay."

I struggled hurriedly to a sitting position, and exclaimed agitatedly, "She did invite me to return, but without my son."

"I anticipated it would be so, but you know this is your home for as long as you think fit, and you must not condemn Mistress Frost. She has her family to consider."

"Yes, sir, but I now have mine, and it is no fault of his that he is so born."

"So does the lioness protect her cub. Nay, child I lay no fault, but merely wish to explain that you may remain within my protection until such time as you are able to do otherwise, and this infant too is of my blood, so I do feel entitled to impart my protection over him as well. Did Mistress Frost tell you that she wishes communication twixt yourself and James now to be by letter?" He laughed. "I fear she will be disappointed. When last I called on Mistress Jane he was present, and did assert he would soon visit in person. Ah well, we will see who wins the battle. Now, do you remember when we spoke of your child's birth I did then say that if it should be male I would wish him to be circumcised. Good, then I will so arrange matters. It will be but a matter for the religious surgeon, or Mohel as he is known to us, as no prayers can be said for your son is not of the Hebrew faith. But it is the deed that is of importance should he wish when grown, to be a Jew. Why frown you child, know you not of this custom?"

"I have read of God's covenant with Abraham, but why are no prayers to be said? For as Isaac was a Jew, why is not his son?"

"Because we are a matriarchal faith," Abraham explained. "And from the mother comes the child's destiny. Why so solemn Mistress Fry, it matters only that the babe is healthy and thrives? And his name, we have not spoken of his name."

For a moment I resented his manner. The child was mine not his and I answered sharply. "I would like him to be Isaac, sir, but if as you say he is not a Jew then surely he must be christened?"

303

The glow of pleasure that had effused Abraham's face when I spoke his son's name was replaced by a slight frown, but his voice conveyed nothing but concern as he replied, "So be it, I will arrange the ceremony with a friend of mine who administers at a church nearby. And as to name, possibly Adam should be added, which was your father's name as I recall?"

Overcome by the suggestion I immediately regretted my sharpness, but Abraham appeared not to have noticed, for he departed towards the door with a smile saying, "I must now to my duties, and you must rest."

Once more alone, I peered into the cradle at my son with his tightly shut eyes, and minute clenched fists. What was to be the fate of this tiny being, created by the whims of two selfish people? If only I had given thought to the consequences of such an action, how differently I would have behaved. Yet as I watched the sleeping child the protective emotion returned, this time with greater intensity, and I stretched my hand down to the cradle to stroke the downy red head.

The circumcision took place eight days after Isaac's birth. Abraham explained that the operation would last but a few moments, after which he would be returned immediately to me.

"Your presence will not be required," he explained. "It is not our custom for the mother to be a witness as the child does cry, which can be distressful."

On the day prescribed, I surrendered my son apprehensively to Myon and sat listening to the unusual sound of male voices, rising from the floor below. Although aware of what a circumcision involved, I was not really sure what to expect on the child's return, and was shocked to see the red spots emerging through the cloth wound around his loins.

"He bleeds," I exclaimed in horror.

"A little only, mistress," Myon explained soothingly.

"But he does look in pain," I insisted. "See how he weeps and moves his hands and feet."

"All will be forgotten within the passing of a day," Abraham smiled, from where he now stood, in the doorway. "The child is too young to retain aught of the pain but do you feed him, it will calm him, and now I must needs return to my guests."

Only partially reassured, I held Isaac to my breast. At first he continued weeping in tiny gasping sobs, his lips slack and unresponsive, but then the crying ceased and he began to drink. At the same moment the sound of men's voices intensified, and curious to know what manner of people had attended this strange, and somewhat barbaric ritual, I walked with Isaac still feeding to the head of the stairs.

Milling about in the hallway below were a number of men, dressed in the Puritan fashion. The only things that distinguished them from men of my acquaintance were their dark complexions, and the Spanish language in which they now conversed. As I watched, Abraham emerged from the library followed by more men, and everyone raised their glasses to him and cried out "L'Chaim!"(53) Obviously delighted he nodded, and then laughed. The sound travelled easily upwards, and as I watched him respond to the congratulations I realised that I was witnessing an event that would be forever foreign to me. I glanced down at my now sleeping son, and wished vehemently that I had not agreed to his circumcision.

"You are mine," I whispered fiercely. "You are a Christian, not a Jew. You do not belong to those men, you belong to me."

By the end of the second week of Isaac's life I had regained enough strength to leave my room, and return to a more active existence. Abraham expressed his surprise at my rapid recovery.

"It is not customary," he murmured, gently stroking Isaac's hair. "But it would seem you do have the good health that only the young can claim. Do not exert your body in any way, and take care to rest when you feel tired, but should you wish to walk within the gardens I see no harm in such exertion."

I watched his strong fingers until they ceased, and then lifted Isaac somewhat abruptly from his cradle. The child began to whimper, and Abraham frowned."Gently mistress, he is but a babe."

Contrite, I flushed. "I did but mean to hold him as it will be soon time for him to be fed."

Abraham frowned heavily. "Does it concern you that I touch him? I do but caress him as a grandsire might."

Overcome with embarrassment, I could only stammer, "No indeed not, sir. It is but his time to be fed. Please to come whenever you so wish, it is your house."

As the door closed I tried to quench the fear that had been aroused on the day of the circumcision, that there would be a part of Isaac's life that would never belong to me, and I shivered despite the warm May sunshine and the fire burning in the grate.

The following week I felt more composed, for on the Thursday Isaac was christened. Unlike his circumcision, the ceremony was a quiet affair with only myself, Abraham, Myon and Nyas present. Despite their beliefs, the Preacher had agreed at Abraham's suggestion that the brother and sister should be god-parents, and I could not but consider how singular was my small son's admission to the Christian world having, as he did, a grandfather of the Hebrew faith and god-parents who followed the teachings of Rome.

Unlike his previous ordeal, Isaac slept throughout the short service, but pleased as I was to have some part of him that I could claim my own, I wondered how I would answer when, as would be inevitable at some future time, he asked me of his father and where at such a time would we both be?

I had so far refused to consider the future, preferring only to dwell on the present, but I knew it was something I would have to decide within the next few months. We could not remain within Abraham's protection forever, and since cousin Edith's home was barred to Isaac I began to consider the possibility of establishing myself somewhere alone. There were still the coins ensconced within my chest, but were there enough to sustain us both for a lifetime, and if not, how were we to survive when the money was spent?

I glanced at my box. The time had now arrived to act, not to surmise. I placed Isaac on the bed and crossing to the chest, raised the lid. From inside the past surged out with the violence of Pandora's evil hordes, while my father's remaining books seemed to stare up at me reproachfully. It was as if the large panelled chamber with its exquisitely wrought furniture and ornate hangings had been replaced by my father's small, sparsely furnished room. I tried to control the trembling that had overcome me. To use Molly's money would only compound my guilt. How could I live on coins whose owner I had helped to destroy? I wanted to cry, but to indulge in tears seemed pointless. Weeping would not help only calm decisions would be of assistance. Engrossed in thought, I nearly cried out when I turned to see Abraham, standing just inside my chamber.

CHAPTER 32

"Forgive me, I did knock upon the door but you did not hear. I did come to say," his voice rose slightly, "why, child, you are unwell, can I be of help?"

"I did help to kill someone," I cried out, my heart too full to be silent any longer. "Someone I loved. She did live with the Goodwife who was ailing and cared for her, and when the Goodwife died she did leave to Molly all the coins in that chest, and that is why I cannot use them and all is as Shakespeare said."

As my words flowed like a torrent Abraham walked across to the open box, and closing the lid perched himself on the edge. When he spoke his voice was full of compassion.

"And this tale is the source of the nightmares that rack you so violently?" I nodded. "And the Goodwife did bequeath to Molly the contents of this chest?"

"No, the money only," I gulped in reply."

"And the remaining contents?"

"Only some of my father's books which I wished to keep, the remainder I gave away, and one of his garments."

"And Molly did nurse your father?"

I nodded again.

"And she was the body so well acquainted with herbs and medicines?"

"Yes."

"And the folk within your village, they did think her a witch or some such?"

"Yes," I stared up at him in amazement. "But how could you know this?"

He chuckled softly, "I come from a country of superstition and idiocy, where many a poor soul has met her death through such ignorance. Did she burn?"

Still shaking, I struggled to a chair. "No, they hanged her."

"And you were present at this tragedy?"

"No, I was told by a witness."

Abraham laced his fingers together in his lap, and stared reflectively at the floor. "You have travelled a long road in the past few seconds, child, would you care to complete your tale? A broken journey is often difficult to recommence, the distractions are too eagerly grasped."

I closed my eyes. Molly's smiling face, my father's piercing death cries and the Witchfinder's insistent voice sped through my mind in a tangle before I slowly began to relate my tale. When I finished, having omitted only my father's confession and any mention of William, I leaned back against my chair feeling weak, but strangely cleansed.

Abraham looked at me reflectively. "The only part of my late adopted faith of which I did approve, was the Confessional. A few words whispered into a covered grating would release forever the anguish of a lifetime. Many times in extreme youth, before my father's revelation, did I avail myself of its presence. Be they serious or mere trivia it mattered not, through that grating went all manner of misdeeds and the feeling of release I did feel on receiving penance was immense, knowing that with the utterance of mere words I would cleanse myself of guilt. But as I grew in wisdom, I learned that such absolution was in itself not enough. The mind must follow the word. True repentance can be achieved only by acknowledgement of guilt, no matter the path followed to the Lord. But does one know how to recognise that repentance? The relief you feel may prove but momentary. You have shared your secret, but not expunged your pain. I believe, child that you truly regret all that has occurred. You will dismiss I know my assertion that you were frightened and alone, believing that you should have been strong and brave. Would we had such resources within us at all times, but we do not. Our minds are as frail as our bodies, and just as capable of being harmed and influenced by powers stronger than ourselves. There are souls like your Molly, and Pedro and Carlo, who can withstand all duress, but they are few. Judge yourself not so strongly, you are but human like us all, and I have done much in my life that I now regret. But to dwell so upon the past is unwise, for it is dead, only the present lives. You are now not what you were then. Like myself, you have travelled in mind and body to another life, and you have a son. You will not forget Molly. Nor the way she died. But dwell upon the joyous times of shared happiness. To never err is not a virtue, for with our misdeeds we learn to understand ourselves and our fellow men, and without this knowledge we would be as the animals, satisfying only our bodily needs without thought or comprehension. I did once dwell on the past and indulged myself in grief, and that I fear is why my son and I grew distant. I travelled much and left him to a nurse, and when I returned he barely knew me. I know now I should have taken myself another wife, not ached for the return of she who was no more. Such pain can eat within one's mind until all else is dim, and that is why I spoke."

"My father never re-wed," I murmured softly. "I think it is within some men to love but once. I know such men can admire and indulge themselves as men do, but to love comes but the once."

Abraham's eyes widened slightly. "You liken your father to myself."

"Yes, sir, for I did learn much of his nature in the few months before his death. He had in his past that which he did regret, and raised me strictly only that I should not so fall. I think sir, had you met you would have found much upon which to converse." I wanted suddenly to share everything with him, and drawing my locket from my gown, I held it out. "This was my mother, the only likeness I have of her."

Somewhat hesitantly, he opened the locket and murmured softly, "I thank you for such a privilege, and I see a gentle lady and a happy one. Such an expression I did oft see on my own wife's face. A woman who is not only loved, but can love in return, is truly blessed. But why do you not wear the jewel for all to see."

"I found the chain too short," I explained. "My mother was of smaller stature than myself and had a slender neck."

"A small matter easily rectified. Come to my chamber I believe I have a chain that will suffice."

Curious to see a room into which I had not ventured, I followed him down the corridor and through the double doors into a large chamber, where he opened the drawer of a small cabinet.

"My memory did serve me well, even though I have not opened these drawers for many years. All of my wife's jewels I placed within this cabinet and see, child, here is the chain. Take it with my blessing. But I have one final question. You spoke of Master Shakespeare, how does he feature in your tale?"

"My father quoted once some words from *The Tempest*, and on reading the play I first likened us to Prospero and Miranda, for my father did protect me as he did her, but I strayed."

"And that is all?"

I nodded, and he shrugged as he handed me the chain. "So be it, now hopefully all your ghosts are laid to rest, child."

I thanked him and was about to leave, when I caught sight of a small oak table on which stood two large silver candlesticks entwined together by a golden star.

Following my gaze, he said, "The candlesticks are for Sabbath, and I do light them every Friday eve, as did my wife. The star, which was added on Isaac's birth, does denote our closeness, our entwining for life. King David was reputed to wear such a star, and in some lands Jews are made to wear it as a penance but one day, I sincerely pray, we will wear it with pride to show our faith, rather than as a symbol to denote our shame."

As I examined the star an idea occurred to me. Pleading an excuse that I heard Isaac cry, I returned to my chamber where I re-opened my chest, and removed the linen packet containing my father's shirt. Quickly unfolding the cloth I shook out the garment, and as the fine linen quivered into life, laid it carefully across a chair.

It took me some time to draw a six pointed star to my satisfaction, but at last I was able to pin the cut out symbol on a piece of yellow cloth, and by the time Isaac was crying lustily for his next meal, the golden star had been part sewn onto my father's unworn shirt.

Delighted, I carefully refolded the garment and placed it within a drawer of my cabinet. Feeling considerably light-hearted, I decided to enjoy the remainder of the garden's afternoon sun, and having ensured that Isaac slept peacefully, collected my cloak and opened my chamber door.

As I crossed to the stairway, I heard a muffled sound emitting from further down the corridor. Curious, for it sounded like weeping, I walked along quietly until I reached Abraham's chamber door, which was slightly ajar. Concerned, in case he might suddenly be unwell, I looked inside and saw him kneeling beside the bed sobbing "Isaac, my Isaac," into the coverlet. Shaken, I drew back and returned swiftly to my own chamber, where I remained seated by my son's cradle for some time. Had Abraham been weeping for his son or mine, and why had I refrained from telling him how deeply Polonius's advice to Laertes had affected me?

Two days later Harold arrived with William's letter.

CHAPTER 33

The letter remained unopened for two days, and despite being concealed within my trunk the knowledge of its existence seemed to burn into my brain. If Master Oates had at last discovered my treachery, then this missive must be an indictment from William of that fact? If such was the case, I could never return to Stamford as all must now have been revealed, and myself damned forever in the eyes of the honourable and just.

Prevaricating until the evening of the third day, I at last realised that the inevitable must be faced, and with a stomach turned to lead took William's letter from my trunk and slowly broke the seal. The date was three weeks past, and the letter had been written from Fretson. So he had spoken to the villagers and Thomas must have given him my address. I closed my eyes then forced them open to read the first line:

'Most beloved Pleasance, I write this letter with feelings no more changed than those, with which I first begged your hand.' I trembled with disbelief, surely my eyes were playing tricks with me, but no, the letter continued: *'Whatever happened here is past. My poor Molly was betrayed, not by those who loved her but by the stupidity and mischief of the ignorant. You must never hold yourself in any way to blame. Mistress Whyte has told me of your travail. You suffered deeply but your guilt must be held within its proper place, and be allowed to mellow. For you have a life to live, and the Good Lord does expect of you many years yet to fulfil, and those years I again do crave, should be shared with me. My love has grown with the passing months, and the distance has done nothing to diminish your presence in my mind. Of the life you now lead, I know only that you dwell with kinsfolk of your mother, and should you accept this plea, I will to London and beg your hand of them in the accustomed manner. If they know naught of me, acquaint me so and I will write before I travel. I now await your answer with an agitation that I trust, and pray, you will change to joy. Dearest of women, I am yours, if you will have me, Your William. Address all letters to Goodborough, for I will have returned there by the time this reaches you.'*

I have still his letter, and old and faded though the words may be I read it when alone and all the love and care comes back. Many times, during these last months, it has upheld me and given me strength, and when I die they will place it against my heart and bury it with me. For it must accompany me to Heaven to help defend me from the judgement that I fear will still be mine, for it is to our Maker we must finally confess, not to those we love.

But I move too speedily, and must return to the confused and ignorant creature that I once was, for indeed most confused was I, and strangely, in some way angered. If William had berated and condemned me, there would have been no choice to make. But yet again I had to choose, and this choice would be for life. William would not plead his cause a third time, of that I was convinced.

I folded the sheets and placed them in a drawer, the key of which I then removed and put within my gown. It was too soon. I was not yet ready to decide the path my life should take. I know now that it was courage that I lacked. Hidden away in that warm, friendly house, I did not wish to believe that such a life could not last forever.

That evening Abraham seemed pensive, and his grief still vivid in my mind I found conversation difficult. The next day his duties called him from the house, and two days passed before we again conversed. Alone in his library, I was delving through the pages of *The Odyssey*, when the door opened, and he entered.

He appeared weary, and I descended hurriedly from my ladder to proffer wine. He took the goblet, and then after lowering himself into a chair sighed deeply. "It has indeed been an arduous day. I did lose a soul. It should not have been, but he slipped away. It was a foolish accident with a knife, and though I staunched the wound and did sew the skin, too much blood had been lost for him to rally."

"Sewed the skin, I have never heard of such before, and the pain. How can a body bear such pain?"

"Such is the practice with gaping wounds, and I did make him sleep, as did you during Isaac's birth. But sadly, today this ruse saved me nothing."

"I did think my sleeping was the cure," I exclaimed.

Abraham smiled. "Nay, child, it is a trick which, as I said, I learned when travelling in the Arab lands. My tutor was a slant eyed, yellow fellow, who had travelled far and taught me much, the most important of his teachings being, that without pain the mind is at peace and thus does assist the healing. Also the heart is not put to greater need than its strength allows. I do not always succeed in my endeavours, but if I have the trust of the patient then all is well." He laughed. "Indeed child, have you a wish to study my craft?"

"Not at all, sir, for I fear I do not have the capacity for such knowledge. I was but curious, for the sleep was a deep and pleasant one, such as I had never had before."

I had seated myself on a stool before him, my back against the seat of a fireside chair, and his long outstretched legs were but inches from my skirts. He did not respond to my words, merely stared down at me smiling, his eyes almost hidden behind long black lashes. He had looked at me thus many times since Isaac's birth, and remembering now his desperate cries for his son, I believed it to be a glance of censure. Distressed at the thought I returned the gaze, and was surprised to see within his eyes only kindness and affection.

What he deduced from my expression I know not, but it caused him to yawn in an exaggerated manner, and then arise from his chair murmuring that he must cleanse the days' work from his person before we ate. Later that same night, I lay watching the moon glowing through my casement as I listened for the familiar sound of his footsteps mounting the staircase. It was a secure and comforting sound, and I rarely snuggled down to sleep before hearing it, but tonight it was very late. Had he been reading some obscure medical tract? Or had it been the many potions that he used that had occupied his time? I closed my eyes, the problem was too onerous for so late an hour, but on the morrow all such thoughts were chased abruptly from my mind.

I was taking my customary walk carrying Isaac about the gardens, when Abraham emerged from the house. "Do I intrude?" His voice sounded strained, and I replied quickly, "No sir, most assuredly not."

We walked for a few moments in silence before he said, "You did receive some four days past a letter from Bow Lane which, Mistress Frost does tell me, came from a friend within your village?"

Taken unawares I flushed violently. "Yes sir, it was from Molly's brother, but it was so trivial a matter I did not think to concern you."

His mild rebuke could have been my father speaking, and I was near moved to tears as he said, "Letters are never trivial, for they are composed with effort and intent, and such endeavour demands response."

With difficulty I replied that I would respond that very afternoon and, as though satisfied, I heard him mutter: "That is good," before returning to the house.

To have brought his displeasure upon myself disturbed me more than I would have thought possible, and returning swiftly to my chamber I once more unfolded William's letter and commenced an answer. This time I had no difficulty with the opening address, the words 'Dear *William*,' flowed rapidly onto the page, as did the brief confession which he was owed. I thanked him also for his generosity and understanding, but declared that I had sinned and only by acknowledging that fact was I able to live with my guilt.

Having confessed thus, I commenced my reply to his offer, and was surprised at the ease with which the words came to my pen. I thanked him yet again, but this time declared that my feelings although not as yet so fulsome as his own, were of a nature that could grow, and given time, could evolve into the affection which he desired. I told him of my life in London, and of my cousins and the many people I had met, but of the master of the house in which I dwelt, and of my son, I told him nothing.

I wrote as if from Bow Lane, and begged that he be patient and not express himself to my cousins until such time as I gave leave. This leave, I promised, would be forthcoming within two months, and all this I wrote in the knowledge that I intended these promises to come to naught. I had not meant to lie, but a compulsion over which I seemed to lack control guided my mind, and once again I was trapped within my own deception.

The answer written, I returned to my world of security and delusion. Abraham expressed no desire to see William's letter, nor did he display any interest in my reply. He wanted only the knowledge that it had been sent, and having been assured such was the case, gave no further concern to the matter.

During early June I received another letter, this time from cousin Edith concerning cousin James. Surprised, since I had not omitted a single week to pass without corresponding with him, I read my cousin's note with some concern. '*He pines for you,*' she wrote in her firm, round hand. '*Each day he asks when you will return, or when he may again visit you. My dearest cousin, am I requesting too much of you to ask if he could again see you alone, without others. I know I request a great deal, but you know he is so tender, and I would indeed be grateful if you could so comply.*'

I smiled to myself, and glanced down affectionately at the "others" of which James must remain ignorant now lying in my lap. As though aware of my amusement, my son blew a bubble through tiny pink lips and hiccupped loudly. I laughed. Cousin Edith may wish to deny James my son, but I knew my cousin's curiosity would not permit him to remain in ignorance forever.

And so our relationship recommenced, this time never to be sundered. For even after we could no longer meet, we corresponded through his adolescence to manhood, and continued unabated even after all my secrets were revealed to him, for ours was that rare love that crosses all boundaries, be they age or circumstance. I have revelled in his pleasures, and felt keenly all his woes, and to him will be given the custody of this confession.

But again I digress and must return to my sojourn in Abraham's house. As the days passed into yet another summer, the gardens flowered, the bushes bore fruit and my son grew strong and lusty, so lusty that my milk no longer satisfied him, and as I had no wish for a wet-nurse, I weaned him at four months.

"It is early," Abraham observed, "but I have known such before, and does the child no harm."

Indeed, Isaac's new nourishment suited him well, and my nights were no longer disturbed by demanding cries for sustenance. But I missed the joy of holding him as he sucked so, instead, I took every opportunity to hold or caress him, actions which seemed to fill him with delight. In appearance his red curly hair denoted him to be mine, and his sallow skin declared him to be his father's child, but his eyes were his own. At first no one noticed that the pale blue was changing, but one day Myon declared, "Mistress, the babe has tiger's eyes."

I looked down and saw that Isaac's eyes were indeed turning the colour of the autumn leaves, but amongst that shade were tiny flecks of black. Startled, I consulted Abraham who merely laughed.

"Why concern yourself, it is nature acting out her scheme. Your own eyes are as green as verdant grass, my Isaac's were deep brown, so your son has caught both colours to his own design. A strange concept indeed, but not one to alarm."

I flushed. Not for many months had Abraham spoken of his son as the father of my child, and the ease with which he uttered the words surprised me. We were again walking in the garden, for Abraham now spent all the time granted to him from his medical endeavours, with me and Isaac. Daily we would ride abroad in the carriage to take the country air, sometimes with James for company, and despite Abraham's many duties he had begun to escort me to small gatherings in town.

At first I had demurred, apprehensive that I would not be accepted by his acquaintances, but he insisted and so I entered yet another new world, inhabited by men and women who had travelled much, and known great sorrow. Like Abraham, most of them were Hebrews who had concealed their true faith, and travelled to England to avoid the cruelties of their own lands.

I did not delude myself that they considered me their equal in experience, but when they spoke of books or matters of intellect, I could more than hold my own. Never before had I appreciated the depth of my education. To be able to converse with them in their own tongue, and quote the scriptures and other books of learning gave me a self-confidence I was unaware I could ever attain. Many times I would notice Abraham watching me, and it pleased me to know he approved of my demeanour.

And my new friends were generous with their knowledge, for they spoke of their travels, and told me much of the lands through which they had progressed; for most, unlike Abraham, had crossed many countries to reach our shores. From such company I also learned that plans were being made amongst certain great men for Charles Stuart to return, and that a number of Cromwell's erstwhile followers were known to be preparing to leave the country.

Concern for my cousins prompted me to enquire of Abraham whether they would also have to leave, since they had always expressed their strong allegiance to Cromwell.

He smiled reassuringly. "Master Frost's profession was not in any way political. As a magistrate he carried out duties that would not have differed be there king or commoner in power; and the work that sustained his household has been accomplished by his family for generations. You have nothing to concern you as to his safety, but the same cannot be said for those who signed the late King's death warrant. I fear the ultimate penalty will be their lot when Charles Stuart does return."

During those weeks my mind, cosseted by the comradeship and comfort about me, slipped into that deluded state so dangerous to those who would avoid decisions. But like a somnambulist, I was about to be abruptly awakened from my dreams, and like so much of my life so far, it was brought about by my own action. Isaac had now reached six months old, and there was little difference in colour between his eyes and the leaves that had fluttered helplessly to their demise in Abraham's garden.

I was now my host's almost constant companion, and often I visited his Synagogue with Isaac in my arms. The rituals fascinated me, and the room in which prayers were held, although small and without any of the grandeur of St Pauls or Bow Church, had a warmth and openness lacking in my own faith. So taken was I, that one evening I enquired of Abraham how "one became a Hebrew?"

"Why?" The abruptness of his reply surprised me.

"I find the rituals deeply moving," I replied, somewhat at a loss. I could not explain my feelings, but instead of remaining silent I rushed foolishly on, like a lemming to its own destruction. "I feel the warmth and companionship of your faith." The words were trite, the effusion of a mind though educated, untrained in understanding human nature.

"And do you not feel such warm and companionship in your own Church?" Abraham's eyes were directed towards his plate, but his voice displayed an irony I had never heard before.

I flushed. "Yes, that is, it is different," I struggled on, aware only that I wished to banish the sarcasm from his voice. "It is a warmth between myself and The Lord, not between myself and my fellow congregants."

"You have been only to a small gathering of exiles in a foreign land. There are so few of us that our situation forces us to communicate warmly, but out in the world there are vicissitudes in our faith, as there are in your own. Argument and discussion have always taken place in the Hebrew mind, the minute particle you have seen of my faith cannot be considered an example of the whole."

I was annoyed. I had not intended my remark to produce a religious diatribe. For the first time since our acquaintance had commenced, I was disappointed in him. He had failed to understand me, and I pouted irritably into my wine.

Then I started, for he covered my left hand with his own, and with soft and glowing eyes replied, "You are full young, child, to comprehend all you experience. But I did not intend a lecture. There is much in all faiths, as I have before said, to be commended, but I do not think my faith can be judged by the people you have seen, and I would not wish you to be influenced by their ways. To lose one's identity in order to embrace another faith is an adventure not lightly undertaken, for to become a Christian or a Jew, when the reverse was the original, can be likened to removing one skin and donning another. And the pain, although mental, can strike as deep. To deny Christ and the Immaculate Conception in order to accept the will of God as decreed to Abraham, is the greatest step a Christian can take. For you are denying that God's son lived, and such a denial does mean the end of one life and the commencement of another. And the reverse is true, for to believe that Jesus was God's only given Son, is to deny all that the Hebrew scriptures teach of the Messiah."

"But did you not say that you continued to believe that Our Lord did live?" I declared, suddenly aware how cold my hand felt, now that he had removed his own.

"Indeed so, but as a man who loved his fellows and who wished to spread goodness about the earth. Not as the Scion of Almighty God, sent to the earth to redeem us from our sins, as I did so believe until my father told me otherwise.

And it took many months for me to adjust to my true faith. It was a difficult journey, but I was not alone. I had the love of my family to guide and sustain me. Without that love, such a pilgrimage would have been desolate indeed. Most changes of such a nature are taken for love."

His last few words were spoken so softly, I repeated, "Love?"

"Aye, love of man for woman, or the reverse."

The silence that followed was broken by a lump of wood breaking noisily in the grate. Abraham laughed, but his jollity sounded forced, and we completed our meal discussing mundane household matters.

That night, when his footsteps passed my door I could think only of his hand on mine, and how lost I had felt when he removed it. I sat up trembling, and slipping from my bed I crossed to the casement to stare up at the cold disapproving moon. So many times had she gazed down at me like an admonishing parent as I tried to decide the path my life should take, and now she was about to witness the greatest decision of my life so far.

For I knew then, that I could no longer stay within that house. What I had suspected, and had not dared reveal even to myself, was coming true. My feelings for Abraham had far surpassed those of a grateful 'daughter-in-law,' and he with his knowledge and understanding of human nature was only too aware that he reciprocated those emotions.

I took the tinder-box and lit a candle. Then I drew from my father's box his bible, and turned to *Leviticus, Chapter 18 Verse 15*. I read and re-read the words, and shivered despite the fire burning strongly in the grate. All the decisions I had so far made in my young life were nothing, compared to the one that now presented itself. For it was not only myself that was involved, there were two others, my son and the man I loved. For love him I did. Not as I had yearned for Isaac, nor yet as I was intrigued by William's constancy, but with a deep understanding of him and his needs.

Abraham was a man of passion, and that passion once roused would be unremitting and I knew also, remembering his broken sobs, that he had suffered so much he had no will to make the decision himself. Without the words being uttered, I knew the task was mine.

If I stayed, I knew the inevitable would occur. We would become one. Not from fancy or desire, but because we were one. Our minds were tuned to each other, and it would take very little for us to step across that fine line dividing friendship from love. For a while we would ignore the world and its censure, but his servants would know and their respect would slowly decrease, and as time passed so would the opinion of all those who held him in esteem. We would be outcasts, and how would we live with ourselves, knowing we had committed such a sin? He would be totally destroyed, both within himself and with his fellows, and I loved him too much to expose him to that censure.

I spent the remainder of the night staring out of the casement, until dawn's tendrils drove me back to bed to seek solace in a few moments sleep. In the morning Myon declared with concern, "Mistress is not well, so pale and drawn."

"I could not sleep, I had an aching head," I replied with true weariness.

She made noises of concern and recommended a tisane, but I assured her I was quite well, and instead would seek fresh air in the garden. Walking alone beneath the trees, I sensed someone's eyes upon me. Turning quickly, I saw Abraham standing beside his casement. I waved and immediately he returned the salute. For a few seconds we remained motionless, then he turned into the room and I continued my walk.

I breathed deeply, to try and control the agitation I felt. I had been deceiving myself for nearly two years, and I now had to confront that truth, and in some way attempt to regain the honesty, and integrity, which had once been mine. But the first step, which would be to leave the security of Abraham's house, was immense.

I paced the garden from one side to the other, until exhausted from ceaseless walking I sat down on a nearby bench. I had vowed no longer to deceive, but one last deception remained. If I was to carry out my plan, my only refuge would be William. I may never love him as I loved Abraham, but tenderness and caring can create a fondness within even the most enclosed heart. And he was a good kind man who, I knew, would support and care for me with the warmth contained within his letter; but what of my child? There was no way other than to write William the truth and await his decision. If his love was not great enough to countenance a bastard beneath his roof, then I would have to think again, for nothing would separate me from my son.

I must have wandered aimlessly for nearly an hour, before rain forced me to seek shelter. My mind a mass of teeming thoughts, I sought solace in the library, and sat watching the flames rushing up the wide chimney until Myon entered to tell me that Abraham had left the house, but would return in time to eat with me. There was nothing in any way strange about this message. Abraham always asked the servants to so advise me, but this time I fancied I saw, for the first time, a strange expression on Myon's face.

As soon as the door had closed I hastened to it and listened, trying to detect through the wood whether the hall was deserted. When there appeared to be no sound, I opened the door and hurried to my chamber where, quietly, so as not to disturb Isaac, I took paper and pen and wrote to William. I told him that I had again considered his offer, and wished to accept. Then I wrote of my son, explaining that if William could not accept him I would understand, and begged only that he assist me find some dwelling where I could raise Isaac, in respectability and peace.

After sealing it, I opened my father's chest and taking out the coins spread them on the bed. Molly's gift had one more task to perform, before being returned to their true owner. For I knew I must be prepared to leave whatever William's reply might be, so taking needle and thread I commenced once more to sew the coins into the lining of my cloak. Having completed the task, and retained only enough money for my future use, I returned everything into the chest and locked it then, lifting Isaac from his crib took him for his constitutional about the garden.

The rain had left a fresh clean smell in the air, which reminded me of the meadows around Fretson. The memory stirred others, and I could hear Molly's voice and my father's, and then Myon called and my ghosts returned to their abode.

That evening, after Abraham had retired to his medicine chamber below, I entered the library to seek escape amongst its shelves. But nothing seemed to ease my mind and at last, having spent a useless hour taking down and replacing book after book, I mounted the staircase to my room. As I approached the door I became aware that my room was occupied. Tiptoeing to the entrance I peeped inside. Abraham stood beside the crib with Isaac nestled in his arms, and as I watched, he murmured in Hebrew, "My son, my son, I will care for your child. You have left me a jewel beyond compare. He is my life now, all my life. With the aid of his mother, I will guide him along the paths of righteousness."

I hastened back along the corridor, and slid behind a screen spread across the passage to ward off draughts. I remained concealed until Abraham's footsteps descended the stairs, then I returned to my chamber and locked the door.

I sat staring out into the night long after Abraham's footsteps had passed my door. And dawn was breaking when at last I lit a candle and burnt my first letter to William, before seating myself down to write another. With a trembling hand I wrote that I had considered his offer, and that feelings which I had believed dormant were now stronger, and that I wished truly to be his wife. I also explained that I had taken the liberty of advising my cousins of my decision, and that I would leave London as soon as I could obtain a seat within a coach, and would lodge at The George at Stamford from where I would send word. But this time, of my child I told him nothing.

Having completed that letter, I wrote two more. One to cousin Edith, telling her of my decision and thanking her for all her kindness, and another to James, wishing him joy and promising a continuation of our correspondence and a possible meeting after my marriage, should his parents so permit.

William's letter was four days old before I found an opportunity to slip out of the house undetected. Abraham was at a lying-in, Myon was occupied elsewhere, and the other servants were about their business. Acquainted as I now was with the area, I hired a chair and directed the men to the Swan Inn. Returning to a place I had so nervously entered on my first visit, I could not but compare the self-possessed elegantly clad woman I now was, with the callow girl who had trembled with fear that cold winter's day. Masked, I entered the building and enquired of the landlord whether any coaches were to be hired. Having been told a Mistress Matthews had requested a travelling companion to share a coach, I paid out the required sum for a seat on the vehicle for two days hence.

A chair having carried me back a short distance from Abraham's house, I completed the journey on foot and re-entered the building in time to hear Myon calling my name from above. Congratulating myself that no one had detected my absence, I returned to my chamber to find my son sprawled naked on a wide chair, being cleansed. "He soils himself often," Myon declared with a laugh. "A healthy sign so my master does say."

As I looked down at the chubby little boy, with his bright eyes and winning smile, a great pain seemed to engulf me and I turned away to stare out of the casement. Apparently unaware of my distress, Myon re-dressed him and picking him up, held him out to me. As I took him I pressed my face gently against his cheek and he gurgled with pleasure, as he pushed his tiny fists into my hair.

We remained alone thus for some time, he seemed happy in my arms and I could not relinquish him. Then I commenced to whisper in his ear how much I loved him, and always would, and what I was about to do was for his welfare. I begged him not to censure me when he grew old enough to understand, and that he would always have a secret place within my heart, no matter how many children might be mine in the future.

My assurances completed, I replaced him in his cradle and opened my chest. From within I withdrew the white shirt now emblazoned with its golden star, and descended the stairs. For I had one more task to accomplish, before my sojourn in that house could be considered complete.

CHAPTER 34

Abraham was already seated in the library when I entered, and looked up from his book. "Why, child, what have you there?"

"A gift for you, sir, to thank you for your kindness. Please to take it." I held the shirt out as he rose to his feet, and as I pen these words I see now his kind, gentle face, glowing with pleasure.

He did not speak as he took the garment and held it up before him, and I stood back as he stared in obvious wonder at the golden star. "The Star of David, such a gift is beyond words, and the stitching so finely done. You are indeed a craftswoman, my dear, and I feel greatly honoured, that such a gift should be mine. But how did you guess that it would fit?"

"I did make the shirt for my father, he and you are of a size and I did think you would find it pleasing."

"Then I am doubly honoured, and the Star you added, for me?" His expression of pleasure filled me with a warmth that suffused my whole being. I nodded, too full for words.

"Such endeavour, I thank you most wholeheartedly, and I will wear it when we dine at Master Jacobs, for it is too fine for daily wear. So I fear you must be patient before seeing it, until then."

I smiled, while feeling an almost physical pain, for I knew that my patience was never to be put to the test. The next day dawned, leaving me only until that night to enjoy the company of the two most beloved beings of my life. With Isaac in my arms I wandered the house and garden, longing for Abraham's return, and when at last he entered the hallway, I descended the stairs with an outstretched hand in greeting. He raised it to his lips, and together we entered the library.

"You have been engaged today?" He always asked the same question, and I always gave the same reply, "Yes indeed, sir, and has your day gone well?"

"Yes, today I can truly declare has gone very well. Master Brothers, he who had such a sore leg, the liniment has done its work and the abrasion has healed.

Nigh on six weeks he has been ill, but now he can walk again. But I have some dire news as well. Plague has been reported outside the city, near the river." He sipped at the goblet of wine I had given him. "Should I hear of it spreading, we shall have to move until it abates."

"Move?" I frowned, a sudden panic welling up in my chest.

"I have a small dwelling some ten miles south of the city. Have I never spoken of it? No matter, there may be no necessity to move."

So many times over the years have I remembered how we conversed, as if our lives were to continue thus forever. And yet I knew this would be the last time I would hear his voice, or see his face. Perhaps because of this I lingered longer than was usual, and the hands of his clock pointed to near midnight before I at last bid him a good night's sleep.

It had been his usual practice to bend his fine head above mine, and brush his lips lightly in adieu across my forehead, but this evening he took both my hands in his and held them for some moments, before making his customary salute.

Alone in my chamber, I sat waiting until his footsteps climbed the stairs. For the first time he hesitated outside my door, and my heart beat violently as I controlled the longing to call out his name. Then he continued on his way, and I swiftly exchanged my ornate garb for my woollen gown and cloak. For four more hours I waited, and then having placed Isaac's ring upon my son's coverlet, I bent down and kissed the tiny brow. There were no words I could write for him. I was but a shadow in his life, a shadow that would dissolve swiftly once I was gone. For he was a gift, the greatest I could endow, and all I could hope for was that he would be told that once I loved and cherished him.

Others like him have salved the pain and anguish, but they have not removed it. For in severing myself from him to whom I first gave life, I left behind a part of my flesh and body, and never more was I to feel quite whole.

The house seemed strangely silent as I crept down the stairs to the garden entrance. I had with me the key, which I had secreted from the cupboard where it was kept. As I placed it in the lock I marvelled at the ease with which it turned. Then I hurried through the trees to the outer gate. Here again the key slid with ease into the lock and without any effort turned around. Then I realised with a shock, that all the locks had been newly oiled.

Outside I commenced walking along the road. I longed to turn my head, for I sensed that standing astride the upper roof of his house would be a tall dark figure, no doubt enveloped in his cloak, watching me. But I knew if I looked back I would not be able to continue so, instead, I hurried on until I reached the bend in the road, and was gone.

THE AUTHOR'S THANKS

I have been working on this project for so long, that I might inadvertently have omitted one of the many helpful organisations, relatives and friends who have assisted me with their knowledge, for which I apologise. My appreciation and thanks goes firstly to my cousin Joan Wollerton and her late husband Geoffrey, whose help and support made this novel possible; to my Editor Pamela Richardson for her invaluable advice; to Ketton Library, Stamford Library, Stamford Museum, and Oakham Museum for their guidance as to the history of the area at the time of the Commonwealth and to the Guildhall Library for their information on Commonwealth London; to Doctor Esther Rose for her assistance in enabling me to view a copy of The Puritan Directory; to the British Museum for permitting me to view an original copy of The Puritan Directory; to the staff at The George Inn at Stamford who were kind enough to show me the original architecture of the Inn; to Bill MacLaren of the Vergers' Guild for his information on religious matters; to Mary Richardson for all the books and information she so kindly gave and lent me; to Doctor David Hessayon for his information regarding dangerous herbs; to the late Claud and Olwyn Hill for their help on the history of the area; to Doctor Nelly Wilson for advice on the final draft; to Anna Milford for her advice on Commonwealth London; to Marion Sherwood for her support and numerous books on the period; to Maureen Chumas for lending me books on the period; to Jo Carreras for stalwartly proof-reading the final draft; and to the many members of both the London Writer Circle and Society of Women Writers and Journalists for their encouragement and support, especially Jean Bowden, Wendy Hughes, Pamela Payne, Mary Rensten and Pauline Graham and finally to Gloria and Bryce Corp for so generously sharing their computer knowledge and expertise.

NOTES

Chapter 1

Page 1 (1) In the early 1650s church bells were replaced by drums to call people to worship. (GROWING UP IN PURITAN TIMES Amanda Clarke pub. 1980 ISBN 0713433663)

Page 1 (2) In January 1645 the Ordinance for the abolition of the Book of Common Prayer was passed, and in its place was established the new Puritan Directory. Baptisms, weddings and funerals were also disallowed, and replaced with Civil registrations.

Page 3 (3). In 1654 the task of examining candidates for Parish pulpits was assigned to the Commonwealth's Commissioners for the Approbation of Public Teachers. (CHRISTIAN ENGLAND David L. Edwards pub. Collins 1981 ISBN 000627404-8)

Chapter 2

Page 10 (4) A small room added to the rear of the property, to form a kitchen, buttery or milk-chamber.

Page 12 (5) Ladies' Mantle was believed to ease the discomfort of dysmenorrhea. (MEDICINAL PLANTS Hans Fluck: English version pub. 1976 ISBN 057200996-8)

Page 12 (6) INSTRUCTIONS FOR FOREIGN TRAVEL James Howell pub. 1642 see THE EXPANDING WORLD 1492-1762 by Neville Williams pub.1969 ISBN 0091782694

Page 14 (7) Stamford Library, Lincolnshire

Page 15 (8) A radical separatist and later a Leveller. (UNBRIDLED SPIRITS: Women of the English Revolution 1640-1660 Stevie Davies pub. 1998 The Women's Press ISBN 0704344890)

Page 15 (9) A radical political group whose impact lasted from approximately 1647 to 1649. Their programme included extended franchise, religious toleration and the abolition of the House of Lords.

Chapter 3

Page 21 (10) "Molly" was a name sometimes used in a derogatory fashion to denote a woman of loose morals, (possibly a prostitute)

Chapter 4

Page 26 (11) BASUA MAKIN (nee Pell) was born in 1612 the daughter of the Rector of Southwick in Sussex. She was the sister of the renowned scholar John Pell, and was reputed to be conversant with Latin, Greek, Hebrew and French by the age of nine. (THE WEAKER VESSEL Antonia Fraser pub. Methuen 1984 ISBN 0413543609)

Page 29 (12) In 1656 the Council of State accepted the petition from Menasseh ben Israel that the Jewish people should be allowed to re-establish themselves in England.

Page 29 (13) STAMFORD PAST Christopher Davies pub. Phillimore & Co. ISBN 1860772285

Page 29 (14) THE COMPLETE HERBAL by Nicholas Culpepper. The first edition was revised by the author in 1653, and it was published in paperback in 1995 ISBN 1853263451.

Page 30 (15) A gold crown valued at five shillings (25p) in 1657 would have a purchasing power in today's money of £250.

Chapter 5

Pages 33 (16) and 45 (17) see MEDICINAL PLANTS.

Chapter 8

Page 56 (18) Originally called a Groat, the coin originated during the reign of Edward I, and the last hammered groat was produced in 1662 by Charles II.

Chapter 10

Page 64 (19) Anne Bodenham whose key witness for the prosecution was an illiterate maidservant, was accused of witchcraft in 1653 and executed at Salisbury 1653. (RELIGION & THE DECLINE OF MAGIC Keith Thomas pub. 1971 ISBN 014055150)

Page 65 (20) Richard Wolph, a Stamford Alderman and a well-known Royalist, was reputed to have accommodated Charles I at his house in Barn Hill during May 1646, prior to the Kings surrender to the Scots. However, this theory has been disputed and another Stamford Royalist, William Cave, who resided outside the town wall, has since been given credit for accommodating the King. (STAMFORD & THE CIVIL WAR Christopher Davies pub. Paul Watkins ISBN 1871615291)

Page 67 (21) A turned down collar worn instead of a ruff 1540-1670. (THE WRITER'S GUIDE TO EVERYDAY LIFE IN RENNAISSANCE ENGLAND 1485-1649 K.L. Emerson pub. Writers Digest Books USA 1996 ISBN 0898797527)

Page 68 (22) Crowns valued at five shillings (25p) in 1657 were produced in both gold and silver. Molly would have offered a silver crown for her goods which, compared with a maidservant's annual wage of £2 or £3 a year, was an immense sum to pay. SITUATIONS VACANT J. Keith Horsefield.

Page 72 (23) Lady Day = March 25th For most legal purposes, and in according with the Julian Calendar which England observed until 1725, this was also the date on which new year commenced.

Chapter 11

Page 76 (24) Due to an uprising in April 1655, Cromwell authorised the dividing up of the country into districts to be controlled by Major-Generals. In order to finance the system he had to call another Parliament to grant the money. In January 1657 the new Parliament refused to grant him the money and Cromwell had to agree to abandon the Major-Generals, after which Parliament offered to make him King. (THE CROMWELL FAMILY John Cooper & Susan Morris pub Stanley Thornes (Publisher) Ltd ISBN 0859505464)

Page 76 (25) William Harvey 1578-1657 Physician at St. Bartholomew's Hospital, London. He established the function of the heart and the complete circulation of the blood.

Page 85 (26) Battle of Marston Moor 2nd July 1644

Chapter 12

Page 91 (27) John Leland Chaplain to Henry VIII, appointed 'King's Antiquary' in 1533. Thomas Hearne's edition of 'The Itinerary of John Leland the Antiquary' was published in 9 volumes between 1710-1712.

Page 94 (28) Nicholas Copernicus 1415-1543 Polish astronomer who laid the foundation for modern astronomy with his heliocentric theory of planetary motion)

Page 96 (29) Orlando Gibbons 1583-1625 English organist and composer. His compositions included a number of madigrals of which one, composed in 1612, included this verse.

Page 98 (30) Niccolo Machiavelli 1469-1527 Italian political philosopher and statesman. On retiring from politics after being imprisoned and tortured by the Medici family he wrote his most famous work 'The Prince'.

Page 98 (31) Girolamo Savonarola 1452-1498 An Italian Dominican Friar, his strong views on vice and corruption led to his excommunication in 1497 and eventual execution a year later.

Page 99 (32) Levellers, led by John Lilburne argued for the vote, while Diggers, led by Gerrard Winstanley believed that ownership of property by the few should be abolished, and access to farming land granted to everyone.

Page 100 (33) Elizabeth Lilburne 1614-1657 suffered considerable financial and domestic hardship due to her husband's activities.

Page 101 (34) Michelagniolo Buonarroti 1475-1564 Italian sculptor, painter and poet, amongst whose famous works were the David statue and the ceiling of the Sistine Chapel in St. Peter's Rome.

Chapter 13

Page 105 (35) The Sovereign or the Double Ryal was a gold coin with a value in the mid-seventeenth century of twenty shillings (one hundred pence). Being gold it had a purchase value at that time of £50.

Chapter 19

Page 165 (36) A midwife's earnings depended on the social position and wealth of her client, and could range from £300 to as little as one shilling and sixpence (eight pence) if the child did not survive the birth. (WORKING LIFE OF WOMEN IN THE SEVENTEENTH CENTURY Alice Chalk pub. Routledge ISBN0415066689)

Chapter 20

Page 177 (37) The castle is famous for a unique custom dating back centuries, that every peer of the Realm visiting Oakham for the first time must forfeit a horseshoe to the Lord of the Manor. The present total is over two hundred all of which now decorate the walls. (OAKHAM CASTLE pub. Leicestershire Museums ISBN 0850220874)

Page 177 (38) George, Duke of Buckingham who, by marriage to Sir Thomas Fairfax's daughter in 1657, regained the estate. (see OAKHAM CASTLE)

Page 179 (39) Swooning bridge was so called because of the considerable number of people who fainted at the sight of the rotting cadavers left hanging on the gibbet. Rutland County Museum.

Chapter 22

Page 194 (40) Bow Lane was previously known as Cordwainer Street after the shoemakers who lived there, then as Hosier Lane after the hosiers who succeeded them. The present name derives from the church of St. Mary-le Bow and dates from the fifteenth century.

Chapter 25

Page 223 (41) The first London coffee house was established in St. Michael's Alle (off Cornhill) by Pasqua Rosee in 1652.

Page 226 (42) The Cordwainers' Company received ordinances in 1272 and their first Charter in 1439. Master Frost's family having been liverymen of the Company for centuries, he continues to live within the Ward in the family house in Bow Lane , instead of a more select area.

Chapter 26

Page 235 (43) The first full length opera to be performed in England it was composed by Davenant in 1656 and performed the same year.

Page 236 (44) Henry Vaughan 1622-1695 was one of the English metaphysical poets.

Page 245 (45) In 1657 an area known originally as The Soldiers Tenement in Mile End Road, Stepney was granted to the Jews for burials. (THE GROWTH OF STUART LONDON Norman Brett-Jones pub. Unwin Bros., Guildhall Library, London)

Chapter 29

Page 272 (46) Ceuta – a Spanish enclave in Morocco administered as part of Cadiz Province.

Page 279 (47) MAKING THE NEWS – An anthology of the Newsbooks of Revolutionary England 1641-1660 Joad Raymond & Christopher Hill pub. The Windrush Press ISBN 0900075538

Page 281 (48) The Spanish Inquisition independent of the papal Inquisition was established in 1478 by the King to punish converted Muslims and Jews who were insincere. . Headed by Tomas de Torquemada and Diego de Deza, both of whom were of Jewish descent, it was harsher than the medieval Inquisition and the death penalty was the most usual sentence. It was abolished in 1834. (EWISH SPAIN, A GUIDE M. Aguilar & I. Robertson pub.Altalena Editores SA)

Page 282 (49) In December 1656 the Jews of London rented a house in Creechurch Lane from Moses Athias to be adapted as a synagogue. (THE ANNALS OF LONDON John Richardson pub Cassell Paperbacks.)

Page 282 (50) Jewish males are circumcised at birth in accordance with Genesis 17:10 "This is my covenant…. every man child among you shall be circumcised."

Chapter 30

Page 293 (51) Soon after Oliver Cromwell's death, certain London merchants with Richard Baker at their head, presented to Richard Cromwell The Merchants' Humble Petition and Remonstrance in which they solicited the expulsion of the Jews and the confiscation of their property. Nothing came of this, and in 1664 the Jews return was made legal under the reign of Charles II.

Page 293 (52) Bar Mitzvah (meaning 'son of the commandment' or 'man of duty) is a ceremony held in a synagogue in which thirteen year-old Jewish boys reach the status and assume the duties of a man. It is usually held on the Saturday closest to the boy's birthday and was for many years restricted to males, but was extended as a Bat Mitzvah to girls during the twentieth century.